The Book of Here & There

Stuart Nisbet

Praise for The Book of Here and There

'A fascinating story that uncovers an often unacknowledged history, its multiple viewpoints challenging us to question what we think we know about our past.'

Helen Sedgwick, author of *The Burrowhead Mysteries*

'A book about Scotland and Black Slavery, but one with a difference. Not an academic tract, but a compelling story told from the perspective of the enslaved, not the slavers.

The author has researched and published widely on the Scottish connection to slavery and his deep knowledge of the subject lends historical authenticity to this novel. The result is a fascinating book which deserves a wide readership'.

Professor Emeritus, Sir Tom Devine

'We know a great deal about the white Scottish planters, managers, overseers, captains and doctors who sought their fortunes through the exploitation of men, women, and children on Caribbean plantations.

We know too little, as fellow human beings, of the enslaved Africans, from whose labour Scotland thrived and Glasgow flourished. And we think too seldom of the legacies of this history in the Caribbean and for the Windrush generation, and others, in Britain.

For over thirty years Stuart Nisbet has contributed to the uncovering of this history. In *The Book of Here and There* he enters into the world of imagination to add missing and necessary voices to an exploration and reassessment of Scotland's past.'

David Alston, author of *Slaves and Highlanders*

'At last a novel about our Dear Green Place which addresses the darkest of subjects in a simple and illuminating way.

Stuart's debut novel reaches back into history and poses as many questions as it answers. I found it disturbing but uplifting, even though the history was known to me.

Read this novel and it will challenge your view of the past.'

Jideofor Muotune, Creative Director - theafrowegian.org

The Book of Here & There

Stuart Nisbet

Published in 2022 by Broomielaw Books

ISBN Paperback: 978-1-7392074-0-3
Ebook: 978-1-7392074-1-0

A CIP catalogue copy of this book can be found in the British Library.

Published with the help of Indie Authors World
www.indieauthorsworld.com

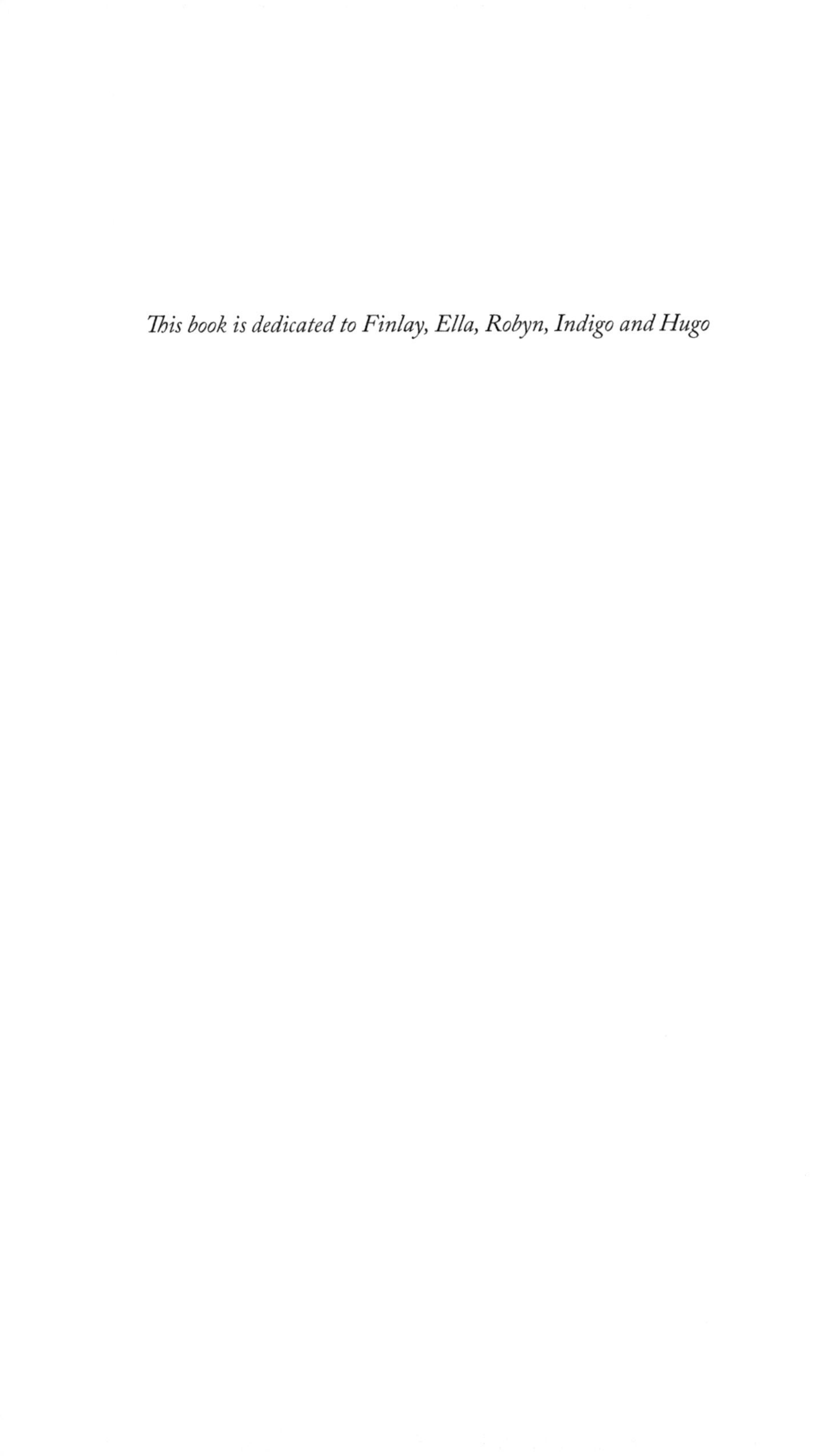

This book is dedicated to Finlay, Ella, Robyn, Indigo and Hugo

None of us is properly to be judged for what happened in the past. It is the city which should be judged, though we, its children, must pay the price.

Lawrence Durrell, The Alexandria Quartet

Contents

Part Four: The Caribbean

Part Five: Back to Britain

Prologue

The Journal of Cato

If I writes down my story, how far back you wan me go? How much blood you wan? How much shit? Restlessness a-ride my soul. I cannot put the most important things in words. Undone, I am undone each day by a word, by a smell, by the shadow of the mountain. But I will not worry you with the tears of my time here. Unable am I to bear the weight of a whole island, only of my own heart.

***

In my eighteenth year, nothin but loneliness inhabits my days & nights. I sit day in, day out at this high desk, copyin letters in the big ledger for Massa Billee. Writin of war with the French & ships & Scalags & hogsheads of sugar.

***

But this day a new day dawns. Lay, I lay aside the letters. Take a razor shell from the beach & slice a blank page from the back of an old, warped ledger. Smooth the sheet flat on my desk & fight back a sneeze from the musty smell. Open the louvre of this office hut, sharpen the nib of my quill & dip it into the ink.

***

This is the day I reappear. Burst through a scratch in the world. Write not only for Massa Billee but for myself. Not only my own story but the story of this island. A simple tale, of a nameless people, told by a young man, on this small island that pokes like a broken tooth from the sea.

Part One
Glasgow and Bristol

Chapter 1

Hamish, Glasgow

My wee man! Haven't seen you since I was twelve!

He peers out at me from the station locker. He's made of wood, wears a three-cornered hat, a long coat, and carries a cane.

I lift him out, and a padded envelope behind, and close the locker door. I push both into the side pocket of my pannier and bump my folding bike down the station steps. Along Gordon Street, the sun glints on my wheel rims, polished silver by the brake blocks. Early commuters force me to one side. These days I'm always going against the flow.

The tyres rumble over new cobbles, rattling my teeth. Along Ingram Street, I glance to the side for the kinky lingerie shop, but it's gone. They've stuck up a big silver pole saying: MERCHANT CITY. As if I don't know where I am. There's something odd about seeing your home city getting on fine without you.

The streets have a strange, squared-off feel. New kerbs, chunky stone benches, even the trees are cropped square. I splash through a puddle and spray a pedestrian, before bumping over an asphalt mound dotted with chewing gum. They still haven't got it right.

High up on a building, I snap a detail with my phone. Each layer of the city's made of a different substance. Stone and brick. Cobble and paving stones. The more I ride, the more I see. Until it morphs into a personal view of the city. A view made up of things I can see and touch. And because it's personal, it's more real.

What am I doing up here? The interview's just an excuse to see Murdo. Anyone can see through the Primark suit and cheap shoes.

An old man passes by in the Glasgow uniform and salutes: crumpled suit, trainers, and a newspaper in his pocket. I slip the *Metro* out of my jacket and chuck it in a bin. It's a narrow gap between work and destitution.

I run my fingers over the peeling paintwork of my bike. Since my Brompton was stolen, I've been making do with this old rust bucket. It's fine for the flat paths and canals. But it kills me climbing hills. The wheels are so wee the panniers brush the ground. They're handy for carrying firewood, but Anne was never impressed by my beach combing. How many folk still collect their fuel from the river?

A dosser with long hair and a beard passes by, his belongings in a Tesco trolley. He smiles down at my bike. He knows a trolley's better. And the Tesco ones are the best. They run smoother and carry more stuff. Next time I pass a store, maybe I'll do a swapsie.

Across the Stockwell, the shops get seedier, the bleached ponytails tied a bit higher. It's one of the invisible barriers in a city. A guy pushing a wheelie bin full of plastic bottles nods as if he knows me. I don't feel out of place here pushing a folding bike, carrying my possessions. Half the folk here are pushing something.

Down Virginia Street, the sky darkens. The weather-girl said the day would be fine, but there's rain in the air. The cold makes me hungry, and I realise I haven't eaten since the overnight train from Bristol. I screech to a halt outside Greggs and rest a foot on the window ledge. A well-dressed woman with a briefcase throws a coin onto my pannier. Recently, the suits have stayed in the wardrobe, but do I look like a beggar? I lock my bike to a lamp post and go in for breakfast. Office workers pass the window, on their way to work. My watch buzzes. A message from my aunt: *Murdo missing?*

I only got the locker key from Murdo yesterday. *Something to check out in our old place*, his note said.

Murdo's gone walkabout? It's not the first time. We'd used the left luggage lockers before, to exchange Christmas presents and models. Why the secrecy now?

From the padded envelope, I tip out a thick Filofax. The brown leather cover reeks of Murdo's pipe smoke. Stencilled in gold letters on the cover is: THE BOOK OF HERE AND THERE.

Murdo often sends me wee models, but this is the first time he's sent one of his precious folders. It's stuffed with typed sheets, interspersed with bookmarks, handwritten notes, train tickets, Post-its, faded pieces of wool, and the tip of a peacock feather.

He types everything on his old Olivetti. Then he clips the sheets into the rings of these wee leather Filofaxes. When they first came out, they were the perfect size to fit the pocket of his army greatcoat. He didn't mind shelling out for the leather folders, which lasted a lifetime, but the paper refills were extortionate. So he built a gadget to combine guillotine and hole punch, and chopped up his own sheets.

I find a pencil and select a blank sheet from the back of the folder. Murdo's wee notes had reached number 90, so I start at 100.

No. 100. Two Cities

My Grandpa's name is James Murdo Hamilton, but everyone knows him by his middle name, Murdo. How early did he take me on his city walks? Way back before I started school in Bristol. Over the floating harbour on the ferry and across Queen Square. Through the arched gateway and up Broad Street to the Exchange. Down the lane and through the market to the old bridge.

And after I'd spent some time in school, the whole family moved back to Glasgow. And we continued our walks there. Down Jamaica Street and round past the Custom House. Over the suspension bridge and along Carlton Place. Across Glasgow Bridge and up the Saltmarket.

And the two cities were so alike that through my young eyes one merged into the other.

The Book of Here and There

***

I stuff everything back into the pannier and head off again. Up on the ledges of an older building, the buddleia are in leaf. First sign the owner's stopped maintaining it. Within five years it'll be knocked down. A shiny new office block built in its place.

I've worked with so many old buildings, it's like I've got X-ray eyes. I can see right through them. Bricks and roof tiles. Rafters and joists. The frame that holds them together. Way down to the foundations. It's the curse of being a structural engineer. At least I used to be.

Once, when I was out walking with Anne, I showed her a favourite old building. 'Obsessed with your Grandpa's hobbies,' she said. She didn't have much time for Murdo's interests. Gradually she had less and less time for me. She was right. It was pathetic. Twenty-nine years old and still copying my grandpa.

The drizzle changes to big drops of rain. Pedestrians fumble with umbrellas or head for shelter. Under an arch, I reach up and touch the soffit of the stone. I close my eyes, hoping for a transformation, but nothing comes. I need this, a portal to something earlier. Arches seem a good bet, they go back to the Romans. They also give good protection against the drizzle.

As the rain gets heavier, I back into the shelter of the lane, and I run my fingers down the edge of a doorway. Grit rubs between my fingers and water trickles down the corner, before growing to a flow. A miniature river, carrying away tiny pieces of the building. Worn off the surface by the wind and the pelting rain. I draw further into the shelter of the doorway, slip out the wee notebook and find a pencil.

No. 101. Nothing Lasts for Ever

Buildings are the memory of the city. Wee grains of sand, cemented together by pressure.

But over the years the rain washes them away. Smoothes out the details.

Nothing lasts for ever, not even stone.

How long does it take to dissolve a brick, a building, a whole city?

The Book of Here and There

***

Pedestrians splash by. Along the lane, through an arch, stands Glasgow's only surviving merchant villa. How much better would the city be if it still had its rows of Georgian houses? Not the six-storey Victorian warehouses which replaced them. If it had the quirky wynds and hills of other port cities. Not the flat, regular grid of a North American city. Too easy to raze and rebuild.

The rain stops and the buildings are bathed in sunlight. I've still got most of the morning to kill before the interview.

I mount the bike and pedal through the Merchant City, then turn left up High Street. At the top of the hill, I freewheel into the Cathedral grounds. I brake, take off my yellow jacket, and stuff it into my pannier. Then I reach out and run a hand over a protruding stone: angel or gargoyle? Maybe if I rub hard, it'll wear away to nothing.

Across the Bridge of Sighs, I struggle up the winding path to the summit of the Necropolis. I dump the bike and jump up onto a pedestal. Pigeons scatter, then settle on the shoulder of John Knox. I admire the view of the city.

I slip out the wee folder and turn to Murdo's old story.

No. 40. The Power and the Wealth

Old Glasgow was an ecclesiastical town. And the ministers looked down from their manses on the hill and mocked the merchants. But, little by little, the power and the wealth slipped down the High Street to the flatlands by the river.

And it was on this floodplain, formerly rigs and cothouses, that the merchants built their city.

***

My knees press against the stone parapet. If I lean forward, it's too low to stop me tumbling down the hill. It's a while since I've thought of jumping.

My watch buzzes. Aunt Mary again: *Murdo gone.*

I always seem to get important texts in high places. Like I'm an antenna for bad news. I try Murdo's number, but it goes to voicemail. I don't expect an answer. His mates say he keeps his phone in the fruit bowl. I can't believe he's gone.

Way down in the Tennent's brewery, barrels clang off a lorry. The pigeons rise again and settle on another monument. As I capture the panorama with my phone, another dark cloud draws across the sky, like a curtain. Is this another of his silly games, or something more serious? I need to check out his haunts before I go back home.

I put away the wee leather folder, mount my bike and fly back down to the city centre.

No. 102. Hamish Hamilton

Riding through the city, I'm here and there. My body in Glasgow but my head in Bristol.

I should be working, but I'm not.

I'm thinking of a girl, but she's gone.

I've come to see my grandpa, but he's missing.

I'm Hamish Hamilton, an engineer, riding a folding bike with dodgy brakes.

***

I cut down Jamaica Street. I'd forgotten how much the street names mirror the city's distant connections. Round by the river, the oldest building I can see is the Custom House. But it's Victorian, a replacement of an earlier one. All the original buildings are gone. Now Murdo's gone too. But where?

I've already checked the locker. What about his other hiding places? It might be childish, but it's the way he works.

Along Clyde Street, red footprints lead towards the edge of the quay. I follow the steps onto the cobbles, where the tea clipper *Carrick* used to berth. The footprints stop at the edge. An invitation to step over? But why jump a couple of metres into cold water? It needs to be much higher to do the job properly.

I cruise across the suspension bridge. The tide's low and the banks reek of salt and mud. I imagine myself here, aged ten, with Murdo. Murdo knows everything about the river, its history, its flow. He's the only person in the city who still runs his life by the tide.

I hide the bike in a bush and cross to the edge of the bank. Down in the mud is a dark shape. Can he have fallen?

Back among the trees is a cast-iron hatch in the grass: BO-NESS IRON Co. I grab my screwdriver from the side of my pannier, wedge open the lid, and climb down the iron rungs. At the bottom, I duck out through the circle of light and brush down my suit. Over on the muddy shore, I kick the shape. An old coat.

Out on a wooden pile, a cormorant stretches its wings like a pterodactyl. I'm back in familiar territory. A linear strip through the city, fringed with trees and quays and tunnels. Way back to my childhood walks. It's the same in Bristol: I always end up at the river.

A few weeks ago, I'd gone for a long walk with Anne. We reached a collapsed wall by the Avon.

'My favourite spot,' I said. 'Goes right back to the start of the city.'

She didn't answer, just looked at her dirty, ruined shoes.

'Ach, it's only mud,' I said.

It was the beginning of the end.

My phone buzzes again. Aunt Aggie: *When did you last see Murdo?*

Why does everyone think I know his movements? Is he in trouble?

I duck under the suspension bridge and push my hand into the gap in the stone wall, where Murdo used to leave clues. There's nothing inside but the dry twigs of a bird's nest.

Out in the river, a big tree trunk drifts past. In between the traffic, I can hear rushing water. Away under the arches of Victoria Bridge, white water tumbles over the tidal weir. What is it Murdo says? *The tide flows up, but the river comes down. A special place where the two meet. Where the merchants built a city.*

Over towards the cormorant are a few ripples in the water. As the tide turns, the ripples become the ribs of Murdo's boat, poking out of the water. Still there after all these years. Like the best secrets, plainly in view yet rarely noticed. A clue. A paradox. A path to the past. In any other city, the archaeologists would have dug it up and put it in a museum.

I pick up a stone and chuck it into the water. The cormorant flaps off.

Now I throw out bigger stones and bricks, until I've started a wee causeway. I step out into the shallows, then onto a rock. The water hardly covers the soles of my shoes. But then the stepping stones peter out. I turn around, but stumble from stone to mud. My left leg sinks. I stand still to avoid being sucked deeper. Cars race along Clyde Street, oblivious to my peril. If I fall to the side, I might drown. If I go forwards, I'll be trapped in the mud.

My left leg sinks another centimetre. I need to move fast. With a big effort, I pull one leg out, then the other, in big squelching steps, back to solid ground. I sit on a big rock. My muddy trousers stick to my legs and my feet are soaked. At least I'll have time to dry out before getting the Bristol train this evening.

Water pours from an old fireclay pipe onto the beach. I cup some in my hands and sniff. Not sewage. I clean my muddy trousers as best I can, wring out my socks and shiver as I roll them back on. Where the pipe pokes from the bank, a section of old wall has collapsed. Worn sandstone blocks, some tumbled onto the shore, expose a vertical face of earth. I squelch over and peer at the bank. Halfway up, I run my finger along a dark layer and pick out a wee piece of tile with my nail. I turn to something Murdo wrote:

The surface of the land, before the city came.

The fields pegged out by the surveyor for the merchants' houses.

Lost in time, but preserved in this slice.

Way back at the beginning, where it all came from.

My trousers are filthy. I call and cancel the interview. Ach, it was a long shot anyway.

I make a mental list of what I need to resolve:

My career (find a job)

My love life (in limbo)

My accommodation (find a new flat)

The three things are always the same. It's just their order that changes.

***

Back along the beach, I pick up a squared piece of sandstone, then a smooth bit of driftwood. Up at my bike, I put them in my pannier and find a dry pair of socks. I unlock the bike and head off. In the middle of the bridge, I stop and pull out the piece of driftwood and chuck it into the river. A shout echoes above the sound of traffic. A figure in a bright yellow jacket paddles out under the bridge, in a blue kayak.

The yellow figure shakes a fist, then paddles on. Is this all that can navigate the Clyde these days? This shallow, muddy river. Such a fragile link to the ocean. Tamed and deepened to let Glasgow's imagination leap around the globe. They set off in wee ships. Returned, if they were lucky, with a hold full of stuff and a bunch of ideas to make their fortune. Turned the old town into a city.

I carry on to the end of the bridge, then lay the bike against the parapet. Ach, sometimes I feel twice my age. As if I'm dragging around a pile of invisible chains like Jacob Marley. What the hell's my problem? Losing my flat? Anne walking out? The way the job centre grinds me down? Now even Murdo's gone and left me.

I fight to control myself. A girl in a grey anorak with a ponytail and a camera asks if I'm OK. I'm only a stone's throw from Murdo's flat. Aunt Mary still stays below, in the old family flat. If Mary hasn't seen him, he's not up in his den. But I need to check.

I pull myself together and ride up the Stockwell. I lock the bike to a drainpipe and climb the five storeys to the old family flat. The storm doors are firmly shut.

I lay down my pannier and sit on the worn oak bench on the landing. The warm air holds familiar childhood smells. Until I was ten, this landing was the edge of my free world. I'd sit on the floor, legs dangling between the cast-iron railings, and peer down the stairs. Gran wouldn't allow me down the five flights on my own. She was feart of the characters in the city centre. It took me way back to the day we found the secret den and how Murdo wrote it up.

No. 25. The Secret Den

Once upon a time, up in the big family flat, everyone else was out but myself and the boy. I took him by the hand and led him out into the lobby.

'Aye, it sounds like a cat,' I said.

The sun poured through the brightly coloured stained glass. I shut the right-hand leaf of the storm door and we stood listening. I tapped the wall behind, making a hollow sound.

'It's coming from inside,' I said.

I fetched my wooden toolbox and prised open the tall cupboard. So long disused, its hinges had been painted over. I switched on my torch, took the boy's hand, and we climbed a narrow stair to the attic.

'We must be inside the walls.'

At the top was a wee landing and three doors. The top half of the biggest door was panelled with coloured glass and bore a faded sign which said: CARETAKER. *Inside was a great circular room, hidden inside a dome in the roof, dimly lit by four windows. I crossed to the west window and tugged at the cord. The old roller blind sprung up and disintegrated in a cloudy orange haze.*

The late-afternoon sun poured through the glass, picking out dust motes in the air. Over by the south window was a big wooden desk, covered in dead wasps. To the side were three folding chairs and a Belfast sink with a single tap. In the sink was the skeleton of a pigeon.

'Yuk,' said the boy.

Everything was covered in dust. In the centre was a spiral stair, painted dark green. As we climbed the stair to the centre of the dome, my feet clanged on the iron steps. I put a shoulder to a narrow door and burst out onto a wee circular platform. Our hands and knees were filthy from the dirt and dust. I went back down and brought up two folding chairs. We sat on the wee balcony and listened to the noises of the city.

My arm moved round in a panorama. As the sky darkened, I picked out the silhouettes of all the old towers. Up above, the sky swarmed with stars, and seemed to multiply. I picked out the Pole Star. I told the boy how this was a special place, right at the heart of the city.

And it seemed that our eyrie was at the very centre of the world, and everything else moved around it for our benefit.

***

I rest my hand on the wee folder. All my childhood memories are here. The stories which make sense of my life.

I'm brought back to the present by footsteps shuffling up the stone stairs. I hope they'll stop on the floor below, but they continue up. Mary?

A voice echoes in the close. 'You'll be wantin' these.'

A tall man with white hair in a ponytail comes into view. He's wearing a dark suit, black shirt and red braces. From his mouth hangs an unlit fag. He holds a bunch of keys. I smile.

'Archie!'

Archie's tall, thin and narrow-jawed. His pale blue eyes sparkle behind silver-rimmed spectacles.

I grab my pannier and take the keys. I select the biggest key and unlock the storm doors. Then, instead of opening the main door to the old family flat, we step into the lobby and close the storm doors behind us. Then we turn to face the secret door in the side wall. I select a smaller key and put it in the lock. Out in the close, a door bangs and we hear footsteps.

'Quick,' says Archie.

I turn the key and open the narrow door. Archie follows, switches on the stair light and closes the door. He raises a finger to his mouth.

'Shh!'

We wait in the darkness, but the footsteps recede. Archie snibs the door and leads the way up the narrow wooden stair. On the small landing at the top, light spills through the mottled glass door onto a brass sphinx on the wee hall table. I run my finger along the old sign in the middle of the door: CARETAKER.

I hesitate, but there's no sign of Murdo. The room's dim and the curtains are closed. Archie's panting from the effort of climbing the stairs.

'Need a fag to get my breath back.'

We stumble through the gloom to the spiral stair in the centre of the room. I lead the way up to the roof light in the big dome, with Archie shuffling behind. Our feet clang on the iron steps. As we reach the mezzanine level, I glance at Murdo's big bed, half expecting him to be lying there. Archie sits down for a rest on the edge of the bed.

At the top of the stair, I slide the bolt and turn the handle. The wee door opens with a loud crack. Pigeons flap noisily from the parapet. The circular platform's hardly big enough to swing a cat. I turn and give Archie a hand. He straightens up and shades his eyes.

'Best view in Glasgow,' he wheezes.

'Just a minute.' I climb back down and fetch two folding chairs. Side by side, we look out at the roofs and towers of the Merchant City. It takes Archie a few minutes to get his breath back.

'He loved it up here,' I say.

'Where he got all his daft ideas,' Archie says, through a cloud of smoke.

'Where can he be?'

Archie turns to face me. 'Sent you anything recently?'

'Like what?'

'Roll of papers or anything.'

I shrug.

'Turned up something dodgy about the city,' Archie says.

'He's always chasing new stuff.'

'Some things are better left buried.' Archie stands up and waves his fag hand in the air, scattering ash. 'Some of us are tasked with protecting the city's image.' He looks like Gandalf, dispensing wisdom from the top of his tower. He grips my shoulder with a bony hand. 'If you find out what was bugging him, come to me first.'

It's not a suggestion. It's an order. Archie's involved in some of the city's oldest clubs and societies. Remnants of trade associations and gentleman's clubs. Powerful groups, with fingers in many pies. Some say they still run the city. Murdo takes all their charity dinners and shenanigans with a pinch of salt, and always winds up Archie about it. Sometimes he goes too far and they don't speak for ages.

We sit in silence, looking out over the roofscape. After several more fags, Archie says, 'It's makin' me dizzy. Just remember, come to me first.'

He gets up, ducks through the wee door, and leaves me with Murdo's view all to myself. I rub my shoulder where Archie grabbed it. Then I go downstairs and snib the narrow door. It's hard to see Archie as an enemy, but I don't want him sneaking up on me. He's a hero from my childhood.

When Murdo took me on his walks, Archie was always there in the background.

No. 39. Let Glasgow Flourish

> *Once upon a time, the boy had a day's holiday from primary school. It was a sunny May morning. Archie joined us, carrying his drawing kit. He tore out a big piece of paper from his sketch pad and took a thick pencil from his top pocket. He bent down and held the paper over a green cast-iron electricity box in St Vincent Street.*
>
> *Archie showed the boy how to rub the pencil over the raised logo and bring out the pattern. The banner curving across the middle of the coat of arms said:* LET GLASGOW FLOURISH BY THE PREACHING OF THE WORD.

***

I gather my things and pick up my pannier. Archie's gone off with the keys, so I take a spare set from the hook behind the door. I lock up, look at my watch, and cycle up to Central Station.

Chapter 2

Hamish, Bristol

At ten the next morning, the overnight train pulls into Temple Meads. I didn't get much sleep. We were held up several times, and the buffet car was closed at breakfast. I drag my bike off the train, unfold it, and head for my flat.

As I reach my street, I hear a voice.

'Hamish?'

'Jenny!'

'Aunt Aggie told me you were in Bristol,' she says.

'Couldn't get a job in Glasgow. How about you?'

'Finished my degree. Work part-time for the museums.'

She looks like she's going to a festival: brightly coloured backpack, long boots, yellow tights, short red skirt. She's my cousin, sort of. Last time we met, she was a gawky teenager. She touches the handlebar of my bike.

'Down on your luck?'

'Do I look that bad?'

'Ha ha. Only kidding!' She crouches down and pulls Murdo's wee folder from the side pocket of my pannier. 'Writing?'

I grab it back. 'Ach, just notes. Buildings and stuff.'

'If you need any help, I can get things through the museum.' She fumbles in her bag. 'Came round to give you this.' She hands me a parcel.

'For me?'

I tear it open. It's a wee model of a Georgian house. I sniff it. 'Where did you get it?'

'Aggie asked me to give you it.'

'Cool!'

'Still following your Grandpa's interests?' she says.

'Murdo?'

'Mum never had much time for him,' she says.

I shrug.

'You were always the golden boy,' she says.

'Let's not fall out again.'

'Water under the bridge.'

'Ever see Murdo?' I say.

'Asked me once, out of the blue, to unravel a dodgy old document.'

'Sounds like Murdo!'

'Heard he's dead?' When she sees the look on my face, she says, 'Sorry. Probably just gone away for a bit.'

'Wouldn't be the first time.'

'My old neighbour used to go walkabout,' she says. 'Found her miles from home.' She opens her shoulder bag and loads of papers slide out. She shoves them back and pulls a card from a bunch held together with a rubber band. 'Might be of interest?' she says. 'Trying to set up on my own.' On her thumb are a bunch of coloured rings. Her email and mobile number are at the bottom of the wee card. 'Give me your number,' she says.

I take out my phone, but she hands me a marker pen and holds out her wrist. Her hand's small and warm. I scrawl my number on her wrist, beside a wee rose tattoo, and get a whiff of her scent. Lemon sorbet? I hold on a moment too long. She frowns, pulls away, and looks at her phone.

'Got to go.'

With a wave, she turns and crosses the road. I get another hint of perfume from her card. It's an invitation to a street tour, tomorrow. I take out the wee Filofax and slip her card into one of the pockets in the leather cover.

***

Back at the flat, I padlock the bike to the lamp post and drag my panniers up the front stair. I unlock the door, put my phone on charge, and slip out the stone from the Clyde, from the day before. Up on the shelves is my collection, gathered from demolition sites and old buildings. I lift down a bottle of correction fluid and smear a wee white band on the new stone. Once it dries, I'll label where it came from.

I lift a pile of Murdo's most recent letters and scan them for clues. It's mostly city stuff. We might be close, but Murdo's not the sort to share his personal problems.

After supper, I sit at my desk by the window. The curtains are open and the sky's a deep blue. Across the roofs, the red light flashes on top of the Cabot Tower: a faint reminder of the city's maritime past. The same light I watched as a boy from Murdo's flat. I seem always to have lived in top floor flats. Anywhere lower would be claustrophobic.

Later, as I lie awake, a door bangs somewhere deep in the building and gives me a fright. I jump again as my phone buzzes. A message from Jenny: *See you tomoro at 2 x.*

I screenshot her message. Then I enlarge her wee kiss with my fingertips into big, blurred pixels, like my grains of sandstone. Ach, it's just a girly thing. A wee cross. It means nothing. But with the power to save my stupid life.

***

Next day, after lunch, I head round to meet Jenny.

'Sorry!' we say in unison. We've bumped into each other at the corner. She stretches up and pecks me on each cheek. A rumble shakes the ground beneath our feet.

'Hope that's not thunder,' she says.

'City needs rain.'

'Thanks for coming. It's the first time I've done this tour, so it's a bit experimental.'

No one else has turned up. Maybe they've all got jobs to go to? We turn up All Saints Lane. I crouch and touch the rough limestone at the base of the wall.

'What you doing?' she says.

Anne always mocked me for it, but Jenny crouches beside me. Her fingers caress the brownish-yellow stone. Our hands touch.

'Sorry,' I say.

'Don't keep apologising!'

We stumble from the gloom into Corn Street and shade our eyes from the sun. She raises both arms to the Exchange and her silhouette stands out against the lightness of the stone. She lays her palm on the surface of a quoin.

'Finest building in the city,' she says.

In the distance the sky's dark grey. As she turns down towards the medieval gate, I glance up at a big hotel with a deep cornice. It's more like St Vincent Street, Buchanan Street. Canyons of tall Victorian buildings, twice the size of this lone survivor.

'Glasgow in miniature,' I say.

'Want to run the tour?'

'Sorry.'

Then she raises her arms to a Georgian facade.

'How old's that one?' I say.

'You're the architect.'

'Engineer.'

Well, I used to be. We pass a job centre, and I turn the other way. We turn under the arch of the old town gate, cross the road, and climb Christmas Steps, then round past the Red Lodge.

'Now for the highlight,' she says.

'Clifton!'

Her wee card says: Bristol's Georgian Gems. But she waves an arm and turns the other way. 'Clifton's for pussies,' she says.

I glance at her reflection in a window: ear piercings and dark eyeshadow; yellow jacket, long pink dress, green tights; an odd mix of Goth and bright colours. I'm in my usual shorts, trainers and T-shirt.

'You're far too smart for a tour guide,' I say.

'You're digging a deep hole for yourself.'

We carry on down Orchard Street and I brace myself for the old cliches. As we pass the end of the street, I glance along at Blackbeard's pub. She closes one eye.

'Oooh arrrr me luvver...'

I frown.

'Fuck the pirates,' she says. 'Prefer the grots.' She points up at the wee grotesque faces protruding from the lintels of a Georgian terrace. 'Dad brought Sally and me here when we were small. Scared the shit out of us.'

Jenny might be crazy, but I love her wee details. The way she stands on her tiptoes when she points up. The hem of her long skirt, which rises to reveal the wee symbol visible on her ankle through her tights.

She carries on, then stops at a gap in the terrace.

'That's the problem with Glasgow,' I say. 'Hardly a Georgian building left.'

'Thought it was superior?'

'Got too big. Old merchants' houses didn't stand a chance against Victorian warehouses. Knocked them all down.'

'So small is beautiful,' she says.

A gust of wind blows her hair to the side, revealing another tattoo on the side of her neck.

The traffic roars away from the lights and she's off again. I've got her all to myself, doing her performance. When she reaches a favourite building, she does a wee twirl. As we approach the timber-framed Llandoger Trow, I cut in.

'Pub where Defoe wrote *Robinson*—'

'Who's doing this tour?' she says.

'Sorry.'

'Defoe bollocks,' she says. 'Hate the popular stuff. Haunts of famous writers. Antique desks preserved for all to see. Does it help us understand them? It's all crap.'

She perches on a low wall and I join her.

'Worst form of history,' she says, 'making a house important 'cause someone famous stopped there.'

'Aye, jeelie piece.'

'Jelly peace?' she says.

'Glasgow jam sandwich.'

I take off my backpack, slip out Murdo's wee folder and find the right bit.

No. 37. The Jeelie Piece

Once upon a time, I delved into the story of an old National Trust property. Spent months chasing it. Then I wrote it all up, and took my findings to share with the local Friends group.

But the posh chairwoman said, 'Oh no, we're not into facts and figures, just wee stories. We like to sit round an open fire on winter evenings and reminisce about our childhoods. Like how we crept up to the back door of the mansion and the benevolent housekeeper made us jeelie pieces.'

***

'Murdo doesn't like cliches?' she says.

'Isn't a fan of the old tales.'

'Who writes your little notes?'

'Me, Murdo, the tooth fairy. They're corny.'

'Wish I had someone to write me stories.'

A well-dressed woman pushes past, holding a red umbrella aloft, leading a rival tour.

'Posh bitch,' Jenny says.

Jenny might be a bright spark, but her language is worse than my workmates. Ex-workmates.

She taps my wee folder. 'Why Here and There?'

I turn back to Murdo's first page and hold it out.

No. 1. Here and There

Once upon a time, there is a town on a tidal river. Romans pass through; a saint builds a church; Vikings navigate the shallow river; folk dabble in trade. Old traditions, familiar tales.

Then, one day, something magic happens: the town becomes a city. A special event. Something which happens to few towns.

So, how do wee towns grow into great cities?

Here, they grow thanks to riches brought from There.

Here and There.

But why do the city's stories only tell of Here?

***

She closes the folder and hands it back. 'Here and there,' she says.

'Murdo's favourite phrase.'

'Glasgow or Bristol?'

'Depends where you're standing.'

She leads on down a lane, but it's blocked by red and white tape.

'No!' I say.

A big yellow digger sits, abandoned, on top of a pile of rubble.

'One of my favourite buildings!' I say.

For years it's been an empty shell, waiting for restoration. Now nothing's left but rubble. I check nobody's about and force my way through a gap in the fence. Jenny isn't dressed for it, but she follows. We clamber over the debris, then down to the stumps of the walls.

Among the rubble is a dark opening in the basement wall. I clear some rubble from the window ledge and we both sit down and swing our legs into the cold darkness. Slowly I slip over the edge and land among a scatter of bricks on the floor. I turn and hold up my arms and help Jenny down.

We're in a sort of pantry. Our phone torches hardly penetrate the gloom. The shelves are stacked with empty bottles and rusty tin cans. A doorway leads through into a big room. At the far end, the timber ceiling's collapsed with the weight of rubble. I kick a few bricks into a corner, then tip one over with my toe.

'Into bricks too?' she says.

'Murdo started with bricks. Switched to stones as he moved back in time. But bricks are easier to date.' I push across the one I've selected: CATTYBROOK BRICK CO. LTD., BRISTOL.

'Cool.'

The timbers above our heads give a loud groan.

'It could all come down on us!' she says.

In one wall, a stair curves up to nothing. On the far side is a massive stone fireplace.

'Kitchen?' I say.

Further on, light comes through another opening, where the floor slopes down to a wall of earth. Down at the bottom, the vertical face is made of fine silty mud. Halfway up, it changes to ash and pieces of brick.

The house foundation presses down onto the dark layer in between. I rub my finger along it.

'Start of the city,' I say.

'It's only earth.'

With my nail, I pick out a rusty coin. In the corner is another window opening. Light pours through onto an old wooden table, covered in dust. I slip off my backpack and take out the Jiffy bag. 'Just came from Murdo.'

I tip it up and the wee man clatters onto the table. Jenny stands him upright. I take out Murdo's leather folder, find the page I want, and turn it to face her. She moves it into the ray of light.

No. 9. The Wee Man

Once upon a time, I took the boy's hand and led him east along the Trongate into London Road. I lifted a piece of mesh, and we climbed through a gap in the fence, behind some advertising hoardings. We struggled down a steep slope into a building-sized hole in the ground.

'Tenement used to stand here,' I said. 'We're in its basement.'

The edges of the site were held up by thick sandstone walls. We crossed to where part of the wall had collapsed, exposing a vertical face of earth. Near the bottom was a dark layer. Above the layer, the earth changed from yellow clay to ash and rubble. I pointed at the vertical face of soil.

'River used to flood right up to here, before they raised the ground and built the Merchant City.'

I picked out a piece of broken slate. Then I ran a finger along the dark layer. The boy copied me.

'A boundary?' said the boy.

'A special layer.'

'Like when the dinosaurs died out?'

I laughed. 'Aye, but not so dramatic. Just when the old town turned into a city.'

The boy peered closer at the layer and picked out wee bits of blue glazed pottery. 'Treasure?'

I smiled, pulled out my hanky, and collected the pieces. Then I laid them out, like a jigsaw. They formed the bones of a wee porcelain figure wearing a three-cornered hat. I wrapped the bits and put them in my pocket.

Back home, we cleaned up the pieces, dried them on the window ledge, then tried to glue them together with china cement. But too many bits were missing.

A few days later, I handed the boy a cardboard box. Inside, wrapped in tissue paper, was a wooden figure.

'A replica of the wee man!' said the boy.

***

Jenny closes the folder. 'You're the boy in the stories?'

I stand the wee man on top, in the beam of light.

'Maybe Murdo wants you to write his biography?' she says.

'Aye, right.'

'This part of your layer obsession?'

'Obsession?'

'Bit big to be following Grandpa's hobby?'

I manage a smile.

Another crack comes from the floor above. I grab the wee man and my folder and stuff them back in my bag. We hurry to the window where we entered, and scramble out into the daylight. On the way out, I retrieve my brick. As we head for the fence, a loud rumble shakes the ground and a cloud of dust pours from the window opening.

'That was close,' says Jenny.

I pick the squarest bit of rubble I can find and slip it into my backpack. The brick's too heavy to carry around, so I plank it in a gap in the wall. 'Collect it later on my bike.'

We carry on down the lane and come out into a narrow street.

'Recognise where we are,' I say.

'Know a lot about the old city for a Scot.'

'Goes back to Murdo and his walks when I was wee.'

The lane's noisy with pedestrians. She turns and leads me back round through Prince Street.

'Look out!'

She pulls me from the path of a cyclist. Her fingers leave a warm imprint on my wrist. A column of buses stands pulsing in a traffic jam. The lights change, and we join the surge across the street.

'I'm saying too much,' she says.

'Sorry?'

'You're not listening.'

'The buildings speak for themselves.'

Jenny slips out her phone and flicks through details taken from high up on buildings. Animals, cherubs and mythical beasts.

'They're brilliant.'

We head on, driven by distant thunder.

'It's my first attempt at this route,' she says. 'Don't think it's going to work.'

Does she only mean the tour? 'It's fine,' I say.

'Just fine?'

'It's great, honest. As long as we miss out the basement bit.'

'Ha ha.'

I take a side glance at her. The wee scar below her right eye: what's the story behind that? The creases in her brow and the corners of her mouth when she frowns. Her slightly turned-up nose. The waving of her arms to emphasise a point. The glimpses of tattoos.

She halts outside a charity shop. Without a word, she disappears inside. I sit on the window ledge.

Ten minutes later she reappears with an armful of brightly coloured clothes. 'Sorry, can't resist a bargain.'

Across the road, we find a bench by the harbour. I help her squeeze her purchases into her backpack. Strands of dark curly hair blow across her cheek. She touches my elbow to point out a seabird, and I savour the imprint. Then big warm drops of rain begin to fall, breaking the spell. I pull a light rain jacket from my bag and she joins me under it.

'Coffee?'

Round the corner, we climb the five stories to my flat. I put the kettle on.

'Sorry, it's a mess,' I say.

'You should see mine.'

Half my stuff's already packed in boxes, though I've nowhere to go. On the radiator in the corner hangs a bra and pair of tights. I throw them into a bag, my cheeks reddening. 'An old friend,' I say.

Jenny smiles. 'Thought you liked dressing up.'

My cheeks get redder. I take the wee man from my pocket, stand him on the coffee table and go through to the kitchen. I come back with a tray of coffee and biscuits.

'Like the bricks,' she says.

Around the window, the wall's lined with a layer of bricks, each a slightly different shade of reddish brown, bearing a different manufacturer's logo. Jenny goes over and tries to slide one out, but her phone rings.

'Not going to answer it?' I say.

She shrugs. 'Museum's a dead-end job. Hired me for my qualifications but uses me to teach kids. Gertrude's been promoted above me.'

'Better qualified?'

'Did some research, got it published.'

'What's stopping you?'

'Suppose that's my ambition. To find something special, write it up, make a name for myself.' Then Jenny grabs the wee figure from the table and holds him up in the air. 'He's like one of the little figures,' she says, 'a Lewis Chessman!'

'Aye, but with a cane instead of a sword.'

'He's very light. Does he come apart?'

'His hat used to come off, but don't break him!'

Jenny twists it. With a crack, it comes off in her hand. 'He's hollow!' she says. She pokes a long purple nail inside and teases out a wee roll of paper. It's typed like Murdo's sheets, but even smaller.

No. 91. The Start of the City

Dear Hamish,

I've spent my life chasing my city story. Buildings and stones and layers. Further and further back. Back to when it all started.

Now it's time to write it up. I've decided to do it through a story. The life of one man. The founder of the city?

But it's too big a task, and my time is running out.

I would be honoured if you could pull it together and publish it. You're the only one in our warped family who's ever cared about my interests. I can think of no better candidate to complete it.

Murdo.

***

'I need to find out what's happened to him,' I say.

'Maybe if we follow his quest, we'll find him?' She stands the wee wooden man up on the table. 'Who are you?' she says.

'Must be a merchant,' I say, fiddling to put the wee hat back on his head. 'They're Murdo's obsession.'

She holds out the piece of paper. On the back is a sketch of the wee man. Underneath is a name: Billy.

I hold him up. 'Meet Billy!'

Jenny grabs the wee figure and studies the detail. 'Must be really old.'

'You think?'

'He's got a little patch of woodworm in his left leg.'

'Ha ha!'

She taps the wee Filofax. 'Maybe there's clues here too?'

'Don't care much for documents,' I say. 'Prefer bricks and stuff.'

Her phone pings again. 'Got to go,' she says.

Outside, the rain's gone off. I walk her back to her flat, then head home again.

Maybe we can be friends? These days I could do with a friend.

Her presence lingers all the way back to my flat like a ray of sunshine, lifting me above the rainswept city like a kite.

***

Later, Archie calls. 'Sorry about last time,' he says. 'I was worried about Murdo, I mean, still am.'

'You think something's happened to him?'

'Thing is,' Archie says, 'I've got the funding together to publish his Great Work, but he's found something new. Any idea what he's up to?'

'Haven't seen him since I was last up.'

'I know he's been sending you stuff,' Archie says.

'Murdo's been writing to me since my teens.'

'Aye, but history stuff,' he says.

'What else does he write about?'

'I don't care what you're hiding. The one thing I won't tolerate is trashing the city.'

'City?'

Archie cuts off the call.

Two minutes later, the phone rings again: Jenny. 'Tell me more about Barry-boy,' she says.

'Billy. I'll try to write a summary.'

***

Sitting on the big sofa, I pick up my tablet and download an old history of the city for free. I search for Billy's name, but the text is too small. I turn it ninety degrees, and the keyboard takes up most of the screen. I throw the device onto the sofa.

On one wall of shelves, I still have a row of Murdo's old Glasgow books. He spent years building his own collection in Glasgow, from second-hand bookshops and charity shops. When he found a better copy, he gave me the old one. But I've only got a fraction of his collection. When did I last look at a history book? These days I read the odd e-book on holiday, but that's it.

I lift one down and get a musty waft of old paper, mixed with a hint of tobacco. I sneeze and knock over wee Billy. 'Excuse me,' I say, but he doesn't bat an eye. I prop him back up on the table, in front of the bookshelves.

It would be easier if you told me your story, I think. But wee Billy just squints back with his cockeyed stare. I study the spines of the books. They're arranged in chronological order, from McUre in the top left to Devine in the bottom right. I lift down the oldest one and open it. The frontispiece is dedicated to Billy's grandson, Provost of Glasgow. Both his son and grandson are Members of Parliament for the city.

I check the indexes at the back of a few more. Billy's mentioned in every one.

Jenny's right. I need to check them all. But I need to do it systematically. I place a pile of Post-its in front of the wee man and begin a search of the indexes at the back of each book. Each time Billy's mentioned, I copy the text into my folder, and mark the place in the book with a wee yellow Post-it. Then I replace the book, back to front, with the yellow tongue poking out. By lunchtime, I'm a third of the way along the shelf.

Jenny calls. 'What you found?'

'Tell you when I'm finished.'

Much later, with wee Billy propped up in front of me, I work my way through the last few tomes. Despite my dislike of books, Billy's mentioned in most of them. I pat the wee man's hat.

Finally, by the early hours, I reach the final book. I lift down the orange paperback about the Tobacco Lords. I flick through the index and the list of merchants near the end, but for once Billy isn't listed.

I put away my pad of yellow Post-its, sit back and look up at the books with their wee markers sticking out. I take a photo, caption it *Billy's tinged the wall yellow*, and send it to Jenny.

***

Next morning, after breakfast, Jenny comes back with a wee smiley.

I cut and paste the highlights into a draft and choose the best curly font, to give it a historical feel. Then I go over to the shelf and spot the blue cover of Murdo's first book, *Glasgow Abridged*. I use its style and phrases to cobble together a summary of Billy's story.

No. 103. Founder of the City

This is the tale of a humble lad and his rise to untold success. How, with his long family descent and social prestige, he held the regard of everyone as he stepped with his gold-headed cane along the causeway. With a house in the town, and land in the country, he set up direct trade with Virginia and founded the city's biggest merchant house. With his wealth of experience, he dragged the old town up by its bootstraps.

With mansions and estates and ships on the seas, Billy was the most notable figure in town, the founder of the city.

***

I take a screen grab of the text and send it to Jenny.

A few minutes later she calls back. 'Founder bollocks.'

'It's Murdo's lifelong aim,' I say, 'to get back to the city's origins.'

'Way back to saints and legends?'

'Just when it changed from a town.'

'It's exactly the same as your layer stuff!'

I'm too tired to be evasive. 'Guess Murdo and I aren't so different,' I say.

'You mean all your ideas came from him?'

Maybe that's not such a bad thing.

***

I put the wee wooden man in my trouser pocket. Then I change my mind and elevate him to the top pocket of my shirt. But before I go to bed, I take out my folder, find a pencil, and stand wee Billy in front of me.

No. 104. Come in

You've come creeping to me from the Glasgow soil. Whispering in my ear from the old books. Poking from the beginnings of a city, dusty with sand scraped from old stones.

My wee wooden man.

I didn't know your name back then, but I carried you around in my pocket. Brought you out and played with you. You were always there in the background. When Dad walked out, you kept me sane. When Mum died, you kept me company. Now Anne's gone, you're the only friend I've got left.

I turn you around in my fingers, weigh you in the palm of my hand. Look closer at the patina of the wood, remember your expression. The wee flaw that half-shuts your left eye. The wee dent where I dropped you from the top deck of a No. 38 bus.

I know your name. You were important. I look you in your squinty eye.

'Come in,' I say, and you shuffle along, tapping your cane, to tell me the story of your life.

Chapter 3

Jenny, Bristol

Her Favourite Archive

Ogo-Pogo Eyes!

Jenny spotted them in the window of the old-fashioned sweetie shop on the way to her favourite archive. She hadn't tasted them in years.

She climbed the stairs and checked in. She had a couple of hours before her afternoon shift at the museum. Her favourite desk had a distant view of the harbour. But this morning it was taken by the tall man in the tweed suit. Jenny kicked the leg of his desk as she passed, making him jump. 'Sorry,' she whispered.

Jenny found another desk, in the corner. Tweed Suit got up and brushed past Jenny's desk. His clothes were so old-fashioned, he could be anything between thirty and fifty. Most of the men and women sitting at the desks were plain and reserved.

He was well known around the archives circuit. He'd published stuff in history journals. His articles said more about the hallowed halls than about what he'd found. It was a thing with the most boring history: describe the wallpaper, not the contents. But the history thing had got to her.

Years ago she'd caught the bug, seen the chance to get to the bottom of things. There was always a new story out there, once you knew where to look. She found gaps in the big picture, did the research, became a sort of expert.

Bollocks, she thought. I might share Tweed Suit's hobby, but I don't need to look like a nerd.

Mary, Queen of Scots

For three years now, Jenny had worked at the museum. It was boring, but it helped her chase stories from the past.

What kept her going? The belief that, one day, she'd stumble on something important. Something that would fix her up for life.

It was the Mary Queen of Scots syndrome. Find an unknown letter by a famous person, and it could make your career. Like celebrity syndrome, but with history, if that wasn't a contradiction. History, exciting? It could be.

Once, waiting on the bus to work, she'd crossed the road and jumped on a bus going the wrong way. Like a kid playing truant, she spent the day in the library.

'You risked your job for this stuff?' Kelly said.

'Hard to explain, but it gets you, the excitement of the detective trail.'

'Can't you just search it on your laptop?'

'If it's on the Web, someone's put it there. New stuff's different, needs donkey work.'

Closest

When Jenny got home, she dug out a letter she'd received from Murdo a while ago. He knew about Jenny's degree and he'd asked her to transcribe some old deeds written in lawyer's *secretary hand.* Afterwards he'd expressed his gratitude politely, but not enough to make her feel welcome.

She'd only met him once or twice, when he'd stayed at Aggie's. It was her Mum who'd fallen out with him, not Jenny. Mum and her sisters had little time for their dad's quirky hobbies. It was Hamish who'd always been closest to Murdo.

Jenny took out the little house model from its box. She hadn't told Hamish the full story. The parcel had come direct from Murdo, not via

Aunt Aggie. And it contained something else. Inside the box was a cardboard tube. He'd even paid extra for recorded delivery.

She picked up the heavy tube. Through the Sellotape at the ends, she could see a thick roll of papers. She pinged off the elastic band and released an A4 sheet wrapped around the outside. Four words were written in the centre in big letters, in Murdo's handwriting: THE JOURNAL OF CATO.

On the back of the sheet was a note, typed on a little Filofax sheet, like the ones in Hamish's folder.

The Skeleton and the Trunk

A week or two ago, Archie and I were up in the den playing at whist when we heard sirens. From the north window, we saw flashing blue lights. We put on our coats and hurried down to a red-and-white taped barrier in Garth Street. Bright spotlights illuminated the shape of a ribcage at the bottom of a sewer trench. A police officer wearing a light blue boiler suit was talking to a woman in green overalls.

'Male, aged sixty or more,' said the woman.

She handed him a small polythene bag containing two copper coins, stained green. 'Seventeen forty something,' she said.

But after dark, I fetched my rucksack and a big torch and went back. When I got there, the foundations of an octagonal building had been exposed. Some kind of summer house? The stones surrounded a blue tarpaulin, which covered the skeleton.

Nobody was about, so I climbed down. At the bottom, I steered clear of the bones and knelt to examine the stones. Then the torchlight picked out something glowing a dull yellow. I scraped off the clay with the trowel, and tapped the lid of a brass trunk. I dug around the sides till it came out of the clay with a sucking sound. I struggled up the ladder, wrapped the trunk in my jacket, and carried it home.

Up in the den, I put the trunk on the draining board beside the sink, cleaned it up and dried it. Over at the desk, I got out my toolbox and picked at the rusty lock. Inside was a big glass jar, padded with layers of cloth, which had rotted away to fragments.

Slowly I prised the lead seal from the jar and tipped out a roll of papers.

'Jesus,' I whispered. 'The Dead Sea scrolls.'

***

Jenny twirled the roll in her hand. Murdo's scrolls?

She found a craft knife in the drawer, slit open one end of the tube and tipped it up. The roll of old papers slid out onto her desk, along with dust and fragments of paper. The documents were originals, not copies. They were so old and tightly rolled that they would take an expert to unravel. From what she could see on the outside, the writing was faded and too small to read. What on earth could they be?

Dan

Next morning, Jenny rolled Murdo's papers inside her yoga mat and smuggled them into work. At lunchtime she took them down to the basement. She showed the roll to Dan the conservationist in his den. Dan was in his fifties, balding, and wore a white lab coat. They called him Bug, because the flip-up lenses of his thick-rimmed glasses stuck up like insect eyes. It was an affectionate term. Bug was one of the good guys. Always willing to wind up Gertrude.

Bug laid out Jenny's roll on the white table and unwrapped it. 'Help me,' he said.

He stood on one side, and Jenny on the other. Slowly they unrolled the bundle and placed heavy brass paperweights on the corners.

'Somebody's been at them already, separated the first few sheets,' Dan said. He flipped down his lenses and peered at the flattened roll. He brought out his toolbox, selected a scalpel, and parted the top sheet from the roll. Carefully, he laid it on a board and carried it to the big scanner in the corner. The machine scanned both sides at the highest resolution. Then he slipped the sheet into a clear archive-quality pocket. 'Come back at home time,' he said. 'If nothing else comes up, I should have time to scan and file all the sheets.'

At five, Bug handed Jenny a memory stick and a box containing the bundle of pages from the roll, all neatly filed inside a thick folder. Despite being held in clear sleeves, the pages were trying to curl back into their roll.

'If they fall apart or fade away, you've got a spare,' he said.

'I owe you,' Jenny said. She handed him a multipack of Fry's Chocolate Creams.

'Bribery will get you anywhere,' he said.

The Scrolls

When Jenny got home, she made several copies of the file on old memory sticks and hid them around her flat. She put the box of originals in a drawer.

As she sat down at her desk, the last rays of sun lit up the bookshelves along the wall. Carefully, she lifted the original sheets out of the box. She pulled on a pair of white cotton gloves from work and slipped the first sheet out of its sleeve. A gust of wind rattled the venetian blinds, making a long whining noise. She barely touched the paper, in case it crumbled to dust.

She switched on the big green desk lamp she'd got from a charity shop. The writing was so small, and the ink so faded, that it initially seemed illegible. She slotted Bug's memory stick into her laptop and opened the first page. She used an old transcriber's trick and changed it to black and white, then tweaked the contrast. Now it was much clearer. The ink was dark and the paper pure white.

Jenny slipped the original away and took a fresh sheet of lined paper. She enlarged the page on the screen, licked the tip of her pencil, and began to write.

Slowly, she deciphered the first line. Then the second. If a word was too hard to read, she skipped it, and returned to it later once the cramped writing became more familiar. As the first faint traces of daylight appeared through the curtains, the meaning began to take shape.

The Journal of Cato

THE CITY

Tis many years since I was brought by Massa Billee to this city. This jumped-up rainy town on the edge of the world. Narrow are the streets & wet is the rain upon my head. Cold, I thought the west wind was cold until I felt the wind from the north. The breeze off the river is like a slap in the face. Sometimes the sun gets sick & does not come out of the east till noon.

CLOSE TO THE END

Sit, I sit here at my high desk, finishin copyin Billee's letters. I dab the ink with the blotter & push the big ledger to the side. From under the desk I slide my ledger containin my own tale. I run my fingers over the rough paper. All is written here & in the others hidden in the trunk under the floor of the summer-house. I write my life story on unwanted paper, surplus like myself.

Close, I am close to the end: the end of a story & of a life. Under the orange light of the oil-lamp, I open my final ledger at a blank page. I trim the nib of my quill, dip it in the ink & start to write.

MY LIMP & QUILL

After a while I stand up. My legs are stiff. I wrap my bundle of ledgers in cloth & slip them inside my coat. Like my own life, only a few blank pages remain. I descend the stair to the library. The fire has reduced to a dull glow in the grate. I shiver & throw on a few more coals. I cross to the window. In the distance, the Tolbooth clock strikes five. Close, I close the curtains, shuttin out the winter gloom. I hobble across to the mahogany table with a quill in my right hand. My limp imprints me in the household: My limp & my quill. Otherwise I might slip through unnoticed.

MY NAME IS CATO

Tis a given name, not my birth name, a name given when I was sixteen years old. Explain, I have explained it all here, in my story.

I look through the library window at the long snow-covered garden. Cold, the day is cold & white. Now & then a blackbird crosses the deep blue sky. Inside the garden tis quiet, but over the high stone wall rises smoke & the bustle of the town. Some say it will soon be a city, all on the back of Massa's trade. I shuffle from the side gate of the garden, through a pend, up the Trongate.

Fortunate am I to be here. Fortunate to have escaped the canefields. Worn, I am worn out, but not from hard labour. Rarely am I beaten. I have other pain. The pain of havin time to think. Of my family who I lost long ago.

PUT THE NEGRO AWAY

Cross, I cross the corridor into the Blue Room. I look out over the front wall, topped by the sculptures & stone sphinxes, straight down the Stockwell. In the distance, the risin moon reflects off the river. Every few seconds, the moon is obscured by a cloud of steam from a tall chimney on the west side of the street – the steam from Billee's sugar-house.

A fog of his makin, but the makin of his fortune.

I stand in the hall waitin for Massa Billee to come downstairs. The hall fire is unlit. Tis only the second week in October but cold as Christmas. I see myself in the tall mirror. In blue livery with epaulettes & shiny brass buttons. I hear Massa Billee climbin slowly down the stairs, yellow-eyed & stoopin. I am no more active myself – the mistress says the Massa only keeps me because a younger man would make him look poorly. Only last night I overheard her again: 'Put the Negro away.'

MEMENTOES FROM A TROPICAL ISLE

Stand, I stand back in the library. I cross to the shelves with the plantation accounts & letter-books. I pull out the very oldest. How poor was my writin in those days. The fire has caught again & the wind puffs wisps of smoke into the room. Other than the desk there is little in the way of furniture. A small portrait of the King. A table with a decanter & glasses. A porcelain chamber-pot by the fireplace. A picture of a tropical isle. The source of my Massa's fortunes, this city's fortunes.

Outside, the Tolbooth clock chimes six.

Already a book has been published in the city which boasts of Massa's greatness. My story is another story. No doubt Billee's epitaphs will attest to his sainthood.

Whether they are correct is for you, dear Reader, to decide.

ESSENCE

Further on down the Stockwell is Massa Billee's confectionery shop, on the corner of his great sugar-work. In his shop, Massa has his sugar cut into small pokes & sold for large prices. Every four weeks, I sit in the back office, on a high stool, holdin my quill, tallyin the books. Through a crack in the door, I spy on the customers. Wealthy ladies, dresses rustlin on the stone floor, hair piled high, too much rouge on their cheeks, repeatin their wee ritual.

McKean, the shop-keeper, in his white apron, lifts a lump of sugar from a dish with his silver tongs. Closes, the lady closes her eyes & offers her tongue, droolin in anticipation of a favour, of a sacrament, of fellatio. As she sucks the sugar & swallows its essence, she shrieks with delight. Among her squeals, the grindin of her white teeth, I hear the crushin of bones, the death of a friend.

The hidden curse of sugar, buried so long in this city. The only consolation that the sweetness will rot the ladies' white teeth. Yet their minds remain ignorant of the cost of bringin it to their wet tongues.

CEMENTED WITH BLOOD

At the foot of the Stockwell, by the lime-kiln, a man mixes mortar in a pit & adds a pint of blood for good measure. To the side lies the carcass of a pig. In a doorway, a dark-skinned man begs, one ankle chained, his wounds bound with cloths, his blood mixin with the animals'.

In Bristol they say, 'A city of stone, but cemented with the blood of Negroes.'

But say, I say, tis not the same in Glasgow?

MASSA & SERVANT

'Bring more water,' says the nurse to the maid.

Now Billee is asleep in the main bedroom of his country house. His bones raise sharp points in the cotton sheet. He grips the bed with long pale fingers, draws air over his tongue through his open mouth. Wisps of white hair scatter over his wrinkled brow. His life recedin, like one of his sugar ships passin over the horizon.

His wife is in Edinburgh. For a few minutes, the servants leave the room, leavin two old men.

Massa & servant.

Owner & chattel.

White & black.

***

As Jenny finished the first jotter, at the bottom of the page, without thinking, she'd scribbled in pencil: *Massa Billee.*

Billee.

Billy.

Hamish's Billy?

Hamish bollocks, she thought. Cato's story could be just what I need.

Chapter 4

Hamish, Bristol

The following day, at lunchtime, I put wee Billy in my pocket and go round to the museum. I hope it's one of Jenny's work days. I find a bench between the staff entrance and the sandwich shop. After a few minutes, she appears. I can't miss her in her bright green dress and red boots. As she crosses the grass, she sees me.

'Lunch?' I say.

In the cafe, she takes a wee package from her handbag and pushes it across the table. 'A present,' she says.

Inside is a wee wooden model of a sandwich. 'A jeelie piece!' I say.

'Jam topper. The Bristol version.'

'Where did you get it?'

'Pal Jamie at the market. Carves anything in five minutes.'

I pick at the thick red band inside. 'It's carved from a single piece of wood!'

'You were going to lend me a book,' she says.

'What about work?'

'Nightmare. Only wanted me half the day again.'

***

Back at my flat, among the clutter, Jenny spots a row of wee curios. 'More Murdo models?' she says.

'Came in a box this morning.'

'He's back?'

'I called Mary, but she still hasn't seen him.'

'Where's he hiding?' Jenny puts on her glasses and lifts the models, one at a time. 'You can tell they're by Murdo,' she says. She moves them back and forth, in and out of focus. 'At arm's length they look perfect,' she says, 'but up close, they're a bit ragged.'

'"If I made them perfect," Murdo told me, "they'd just be models. But to be real, you need to let the rasp slip now and then. There's no points for neatness. Real life is tough."' I stand them in a row. 'Clues about Billy?'

'You want his story?' she says. From the mantelpiece she fetches Murdo's wee house from our initial meeting. 'Well, this is his townhouse in Glasgow,' she says. Then, with her other hand, she picks up the one shaped like a wee circular tower. 'And this one's his castle in the country.' Then she pushes the ship's hull across the table. 'And this is his ship, which sailed the seas and made his fortune.'

I join in, placing the barrel on the hull. 'And this is the tobacco he traded on his ships.' Then I take a wee building with a big chimney. 'And this is his factory.'

Jenny picks up the wee sword. It fits into Billy's right hand. 'A merchant with a sword?'

'Some books say he was a soldier before he was a merchant,' I say.

'Took a lifetime's experience to be a top merchant.'

'What about the last one.'

'Looks like a pyramid, but its sides aren't perfect?'

I take wee Billy and stand him in the middle of the objects, with the wee house and tower on one side and the ship and barrel on the other.

'It's a 3D model of Barry's coat of arms!' she says.

'Well, that's his story sorted.'

'Didn't take long.'

'Something else to show you.'

Jenny picks up wee Billy from the table and follows me through into the spare room. Her heels echo on the wooden floor. We reach a low door in the corner of the room.

'Ladies first,' I say.

She ducks through into the big attic space. I switch on a row of bright spotlights. Dirty dust sheets cover most of the floored loft.

'Give me a hand,' I say.

Together, we drag off the covers. Hundreds of wee buildings line a network of streets.

'A miniature town!' she says.

'The Glasgow Grid.'

I fetch Jenny a stool and find the right page in the wee notebook. She puts on her glasses and reads aloud.

No. 27. The Glasgow Grid

Once upon a time, on our daily walks, I spotted four big wooden boards behind a tenement in Rottenrow. I went into a phone box and called Archie. We dragged the boards back to the close and carried them upstairs. When we laid them together, they took up half the floor. Then I took a pencil and a big steel rule, and began drawing out the criss-cross streets of the Merchant City over the boards.

'The Glasgow Grid,' I said.

It took weeks, because we kept going down to the streets to pace out lengths of streets and wynds.

And when the grid was all drawn up, I opened a box of poster paints, and we painted the streets grey. And when the paint was dry, the boy drove his toy cars and buses around the grey streets of the Merchant City. And each time he came up, we painted more detail. The outline of brown buildings, lanes and pends, blue burns and the river.

Then I read stories about the old merchants and their walled gardens. And we painted the grass green and stuck on Lego trees for orchards.

Then, one day we were out walking, I said, 'Choose a favourite building.'

And even if the building was long gone, we would go round and stand and stare up at its replacement. And in the Merchant City, where many of the old buildings were converted into flats, this was a problem. For folk weren't too keen on an old man with long white hair, wearing an army coat, staring up at their windows.

***

Jenny stops at the bottom of the first page and says, 'He was a carpenter?'

'Sort of.'

'A historian?'

'Did his history PhD when he was fifty, but it's just a hobby. His real job was an aviation engineer.'

'A rocket scientist!'

'There's more.' She turns the page and continues.

Every time we went out on our walks, I wore a big rucksack and collected pieces of timber from skips and office renovations.

'More timber in the city centre than flotsam on a beach,' I said. 'Boardroom furniture, balusters, exotic woods from every part of the empire.'

And in the evenings, smoking my pipe, I ran my finger over the grain and told stories of where the wood came from. Wood so fine that, once I'd fashioned it into a wee building, I grudged burning the offcuts in the stove. And my collection of hardwoods spilled out into the big attic.

'Ach, you might be a quiet man,' said my mate Eck, 'but that's how you express your love – by making things.'

And every time we went out on our walks, I asked the boy to choose a favourite building. And the next time he came up, I had modelled its shape in hardwood and put it in its place in the Glasgow Grid. And we found a more convincing story with our feet than in the old books. And it had a ring of truth, because it was backed up by what we could see and touch. And by filling the gaps in the model, we were seeking truth just as much as filling the lines on a page.

Even Archie was impressed. We would sit in a haze of smoke, Archie with a fag in his mouth, me clutching my pipe. One day I looked down on the finished model and said, 'Wouldn't it be a fine thing, to be outlived by something worked with your own hands. Something folk handled and admired.'

'Maybe an even better memorial than writing a book,' Archie said.

I ignored him.

'Imagine,' I said, 'making a toy which your grandchildren handle and love. Something which will make them smile. Nothing but a few scraps of wood cut and glued, but a connection stronger than DNA.'

'Aye,' Archie said, gazing out the north window, over the wet roofs. 'If only life could be reduced to a model, a puzzle, some kind of parable.'

***

Jenny hands back the wee notebook, hitches up her skirt and kneels beside the model. 'It's a masterpiece, a child's fantasy, but the real thing.' She leans over, takes wee Billy and places him at the centre of Glasgow Cross. 'Where's his house?'

'Not sure,' I say, then, 'Wait a minute!' I go back, fetch the wee house model and hand it to Jenny.

'It's more detailed than the rest,' she says, 'but where does it go?' She peers closer. Where Argyle Street meets the top of the Stockwell, a wee empty dowel pokes up from the board. She stretches over and pops the house onto the dowel. It fits perfectly. 'It's right at the centre of the city. Maybe he's important after all?'

'Bit of a coincidence that you found it in Aggie's house.'

She holds up her hands. 'OK, I lied. Murdo sent it.'

'Thought you hardly knew him!'

She lifts a green and yellow double-decker Corporation bus from a box in the corner. 'Brrrmmm!' She drives it up King Street, then west into the Trongate, and stops in front of Billy's mansion. 'Kind of recognise the street grid, but the buildings are all different.' She crouches down and peers along Glassford Street. She abandons her bus, and with two fingers walks up Queen Street. 'Never seen anything like it.'

'City Council used to have one, for planning new buildings. Architects had to build a wee scale model to judge how it looked. Stuck it in the museum store. Use a digital model now.'

'Can't beat a wooden model,' she says.

'Trying to tell you that since we met!'

***

Jenny spends ages exploring the city model, but the attic's warm and stuffy and she asks for a drink of water. Before she leaves, she takes lots of photos of the model. She hands me the wee man and we go back through to the living room. On the way out, she clocks a taller and younger model in an alcove in the corner. Unlike the others, it's a Victorian tenement rather than a Georgian villa. She turns it around. The back's open, giving a full view of the interior.

'Family flat in Glasgow,' I say. 'My sister used it as her doll's house.'

Jenny crouches down and peers inside. The first five floors are conventional tenement flats, with living rooms and bedrooms and kitchens. But the top storey's one big circular room, hidden inside a dome on the roof. Up on the summit of the dome is a wee eyrie.

'Murdo's den,' I say.

'A secret den, with its own tower!'

'Need to go back up again, look for clues about Murdo,' I say.

She heads for the door. 'Walk?'

I pop the wee house model in my pocket and fetch my jacket.

***

When we reach Broad Quay, I say, 'Murdo used to tell me that ships came right up here.'

Back in tour mode, Jenny taps an iron grating with her red boot. 'Best stuff's beneath our feet.'

'Aye right.'

She takes my arm. 'There's another way down...'

On the way, she stops at a pound shop, picks up two head torches and a pack of AA batteries, then waits for me to pay. We turn down Leonard Lane. She looks up and down the curving alley, hitches up her skirts and crouches. To the side are two thick timber hatches, like the entrance to a beer cellar.

'Help me,' she says. She pulls at an iron ring. I tug at the other, and we heave open the hatches. Steep stone steps descend below. She nods down the hole. Is she crazy? I don't want to admit I'm scared.

We don our head torches, climb down, and close the hatches above our heads. We're in a stone tunnel. We descend a gradual slope, with water dripping around us. The air's cold and damp and we can see our breath. To the side of the passage, a bucket hangs over a deep well. I shine my torch at a dark layer in the wall, but she beats me to it.

'Start of the city?' she says.

'You're a quick learner.'

'Start bollocks.' She runs her finger lower down. 'Georgian… medieval.' Then, lower still, 'Roman.'

I shine my torch deeper, but I can't see the bottom. Jenny reaches over and picks at the dark band with a long pink nail. She pulls out the bowl of a clay pipe, with a wee face on the front,

'Shit, you're right,' she says. 'It's full of treasure. Need to bring you along as part of my tours.'

'Do them much?'

'Try to find different ones. Test out my findings on the public. Make a bit on the side.'

'Bring folk down here?'

'Too dangerous.'

'But not for me?'

'You're dispensable.'

I put the wee treasure in my pocket and carry on down the tunnel. The floor's slippery, condensation drips on my hair, and cobwebs brush my face.

'Stop!' Her voice echoes in the stone vault. I shrink back. Something like a snake writhes across the path ahead of me. Then I realise it's not a solid surface but dark, slow-moving water. Every so often, white flotsam floats by. Paper cups, empty plastic bottles, pieces of polystyrene. I nearly walked into an underground river.

'Forsooth,' she says, 'many things lie undiscovered beneath the old wynds.'

'Wow!'

'Bollocks, it's just the Frome. Ships used to come right up here until they covered it over. Half an hour ago we were up top.' She points at a thin shaft of light coming down a drain. Then she turns along a narrow ledge, like a towpath, running beside the water. Every so often, light streams down from gratings in the street. There's a constant rumble of traffic. In the damp air is a hint of sewage. Something scuttles away beyond the reach of our torches.

I struggle for breath. We could drown down here. Or suffocate. Further down, light pours through a bigger opening, but it's blocked by an iron grille. 'Need to get out,' I say.

'Don't panic.' She takes my hand and pulls me away from the water, back up a narrower sloping tunnel. But it stops at a dead end, so low the damp roof brushes my hair.

'Can't breathe!' I say.

She points up. 'Push.'

I raise both hands and press at a cold metal surface. It opens. My torch shines up into the dark basement of a building. I drag myself out, gulping big breaths of air. Then I reach back down and help Jenny up. She heads for a low door which opens into a brightly lit corridor. It takes a while for our eyes to cope with the bright light.

Jenny pushes me back against the wall, lifts a finger, and wipes a streak of muck from my cheek. To the side is a disabled toilet. She tilts her head and we both go in and take turns to clean up. Back in the corridor, we open another door and enter a busy cafe, then out into the bright street. The sun beats down on us, but in the distance the sky's still black.

On the way back round by Broad Quay, we pass Edward Colston's plinth, empty since demonstrators chucked him in the harbour.

'Used to pass him every day on my way to work,' I say. 'Always reminded me of the Glasgow merchants, strutting the planestanes.'

'Colston?'

'It's what Glasgow needs,' I say, 'a father figure—'

'Where you been the past few years?'

Someone's defaced the stump with paint. Jenny unfolds a sheet of paper from her bag, takes a pencil and does a rubbing of the text on the plaque.

'Can I keep it?' I say.

She hands it to me. I fold it and slip it inside my notebook. 'He's just like Billy,' I say. 'A city father.'

She grabs my arm. 'Time for a diversion.' She leads me across the road and up Corn Street. Workers on flexitime are starting to head home. We pass the Exchange, turn down a lane, and she pushes open the side door of an old church. Our footsteps echo along the aisle between the pews. We reach a reclining white marble statue, with an epitaph etched above.

'Colston again?'

Jenny ignores my question, but I spot his name on the wall. The old church is some sort of community centre. Jenny looks back to check the attendant isn't visible, and crosses to a children's activity table. She picks up a big white sheet of sugar paper, and a thick red wax crayon from an enamel coffee mug. She leans across the reclining statue and places the paper against the cold white marble at the bottom of the epitaph.

'Hold it up,' she whispers. She rubs the surface hard with the wax crayon.

No. 105. Edward Colston

He was one of the Most
Virtuous and Wise
sons of the City
What He did in Secret
is believed to be not inferior
to what He did in Publick

***

'They might have chucked him in the harbour,' I say, 'but nobody's perfect. Cities need heroes. Glasgow's never really had one, not an early one, a father figure.'

The crayon breaks in two and a big chunk rattles down behind the plinth. Footsteps approach. Jenny finishes the rubbing using the stump.

'But Colston's probably the most controversial man in the —'

'Can I help?' A posh-looking lady steps round the corner.

'Just admiring the sculpture,' Jenny says. She lays the piece of crayon back on the table, folds the paper roughly, and passes it to me. We turn and head back down the aisle, leaving the caretaker staring at our backs.

***

I leave Jenny at her flat. Later, I sit at my desk at the window. The floor vibrates as the neighbour's washing machine finishes its spin cycle. I hear a wee clonk inside the desk drawer and slide it open. The wee man's lying on his side. I open my folder at the next blank page and write.

No. 106. A Gash Bit of Hardwood

You've come rattling at me from your drawer. Pestering me to dig down to your layer.

I dust you off and prop you up on my desk. I suppose even a wooden man needs fresh air every now and then. I take you through, place you in front of your mansion, in the middle of the city model.

It's not that easy to take a gash bit of hardwood from a skip and turn it into a model. But Murdo modelled his way through the city. Through all the villas, churches and warehouses fronting the streets.

Now you're back, nagging at me from a drawer. I've got someone who never sleeps, wanting me to uncover the story of his life. A famous merchant. A city father. Glasgow's Colston? But you'd better be careful. Your story needs to be sound. I don't want to have to dredge you from the bottom of the harbour.

Chapter 5

Jenny, Bristol

Jenny's Family Album

How could Murdo have known Jenny would take the bait? Her dad got remarried, to Murdo's youngest daughter, when Jenny was four. Was there such a thing as a step-grandpa?

Stuck to the pinboard in her dad's study was his adopted 'family album'. Dozens of postcards and sketches of family members, mixed with city worthies. In the centre was a black-and-white picture of her grandparents, her earliest surviving family photo. Posed in a studio, with a frilly pot plant in the corner. Underneath was a faded colour photo of Jenny, aged eleven, dwarfed by the statue of Bristol seafarer John Cabot.

'The ultimate outsider,' her dad had said.

Jenny might not admit it, but most of her interest in the past came from her dad. Her first classroom was a pram with a lining of pink flowers, her father gently rocking it, telling his Bristol tales.

The special thing about Jenny's dad's city tales was that they went right back to the original explorers and venturers. He called them 'kinsmen'. It meant their family story started at the same point as their city.

It was a bit of a jump in time, not to mention historical veracity, but her dad wasn't daft. He was aware of the pitfalls, but it opened up a new world. And, as he was into people, that was all that mattered. He believed all people left an equal imprint in time. Not just the rich and famous, whose names she read on statues and in tourist tales.

Discovery of America

John Cabot was the earliest city figure Jenny's dad adopted into the wider family. It made a good opening line at parties: My kinsman discovered North America.

OK, it was far-fetched, but the city did the same thing: Bristol's most famous son? The accolades rarely mentioned that Cabot was born in Italy and didn't speak English. If Cabot could be famous, what about all the other Bristol folk who came from far away?

Dave

After meeting Hamish, Jenny went back to her flat and dropped her bag at the door. She followed the trail of clothes through the hall to Sally's bedroom. Since her dad had died two years ago, Jenny had shared the old family flat with her sister Sally. Now Sally had left to work abroad for a few months.

In the living room Jenny put on some music, drew the curtains and filled the kettle. She heated a microwave meal and brewed a pot of tea. She hadn't got used to living alone since her boyfriend, Dave, had moved out. Dave wanted Jenny to join him in his new flat near Glasgow, but absence hadn't made any of her grow fonder. She'd more or less decided to ditch him. But there was a complication. Her best friend, Kelly, was also moving back to Glasgow, giving Jenny two reasons to visit.

But distance wasn't the issue with Dave. She was just fed up with his demands.

Home

Jenny walked the length of the hall.

Her ambition was to own a mansion, a house big enough to take a walk around, but the most she could do was go through the hall into the kitchen, then into the box room, where the ceiling was sloping. In the corner was a narrow door into the roof space. If she scrambled along the eaves, she came to a little mock turret in the corner of the roof. It had three narrow slit windows, where she could have peered out over the city.

If only the windows had opened to let her clean off a century of grime. Then she could crawl back along behind the lath and plaster wall and emerge in her bedroom cupboard. She'd only done it once, and she'd nearly got stuck. It would have been a perfect circular route, if she was only three feet tall.

Luck

Jenny's interest overlapped with her hobby. Before she worked at the museum, she'd spent four years at university translating medieval documents. For a while she'd chased things in the archives for her guided walks. She preferred to avoid Wikipedia and the old clichés and check things out for herself. Her friend Kelly told her most big breaks came about through luck.

But you only get the luck if you're already looking, thought Jenny. There were always new stories out there. Gaps in the big picture. She did the research, became a sort of expert. A hobby, a dedication, holidays spent travelling to archives in the capital. Searching for that obscure paper, even having to pay for it, as she wasn't an academic.

Show Me the World

Jenny had started using her hobby to dig deeper.

To find things in archives, most folk searched the catalogue. But her dad had taught her that, to find something really juicy, something nobody had ever seen before, you had to use more subtle methods.

Jenny's favourite place was the dead-end corner in the remote east wing, where few others went. The old double oak doors were like the entrance to a wardrobe: her personal portal to Narnia. Down a dark corridor was a long-forgotten room. The shelves were packed with old tomes and indexes to lawyers' collections which had never been scanned or catalogued. The colours of the spines were faded into muddy reds and greens and browns, like autumn on a shelf. It was Jenny's favourite place at the end of the day, when she had half an hour left before closing.

There might be a book here that could show me the world, she thought.

Talking, Rustling, Drinking

Jenny fetched her coat and went round to the private archive. She smiled. Her favourite desk was free. She sat down and opened her yellow laptop, adorned with flower stickers. Under the SILENCE sign, she hit the keys hard, raising a few bushy eyebrows. She pulled a packet of sweets from her pocket, rustled the wrapper and popped a mint in her mouth. An elderly lady caught her eye and raised a finger towards the sign on the wall: NO EATING.

Jenny smiled at the woman. Her throat was as dry as the musty papers. She needed a coffee, but the place didn't sell any. Some imbecile might bring it into the reading room and spill it on the old papers.

The health of the musty documents came before that of the humans at the desks.

Talking, rustling, drinking, even breathing too loud: they were all taboo. Eating was most dangerous. It took so long to order out documents that it was a risk to go out for lunch. You might come back and find all your papers had been put away again and you were back to square one.

Boiled Sweets

When Jenny spent a full day in the archive, she was worn out and dehydrated. Her teeth were sensitive from chain-sucking boiled sweets, and she craved something savoury. One day last week, she had slipped out a packet of crisps under the desk. She managed to get past the noisy opening stage and halfway through the contents before she was told off. It wasn't so much the noise as the greasy fingers on the old papers.

Jenny might be an alien in her bright clothes and sparky manner. But she'd caught the bug. Research? She preferred to call it her Detective Trail. She was determined to find something important, without surrendering her free spirit.

In Person

The man in the brown coat pushed over a trolley of books and papers. He selected the document Jenny had ordered and laid it in front of her. His badge said his name was John. He did a little bow as he laid the papers down. Jenny smiled at John.

The first document she'd been working on was tied with a faded pink ribbon. On the outside it bore the remnants of a red wax seal. It was for the purchase of a piece of land in Bristol. The owner was from Cork.

She took the second document, untied its ribbon and opened it. The edges of the sheets crumbled and made her fingers dirty. It was an indenture for a teenager in 1710. A Bristol apprenticeship for a boy from Portugal, whose father imported wine. What fascinated her was the name at the bottom. There was nothing like finding an original signature. She checked nobody was looking, and ran her finger over the faded ink.

After spending weeks chasing someone, it was like meeting them in person.

The Nice Ones

There were two grades of staff in most archives. John was in the bottom grade. He took your order and retrieved the documents from the bowels of the building. It was important to keep in with the Johns. Like most hierarchies, the lowest on the scale did most of the work. And, because they knew the secret of where things were kept, they took their time doing it.

Jenny preferred to avoid the bosses at the front desk and befriend the Johns. When she went to a new archive for the first time, she made a point of wearing her strangest, most colourful clothes. Most of the staff eyed her with suspicion, but one or two gave her a smile. It was a subtle way of picking out the nice ones.

There were lots of other rules and regulations. If your document was bigger than normal, you had to sit at a special desk. If it was valuable, you had to take a front desk, in case you stuffed it up your jumper. One of the first times Jenny was there, she was so tired after a full day without a break that she fell asleep on one of the soft white pillows. Nobody had told her they were for supporting fragile tomes, not her curls.

Scream

Jenny had read that ninety-five per cent of records never saw the light of day. So it shouldn't be hard to find something special. Something to make a name for herself. It was only a matter of time. The other day, she'd heard the sound of someone making a big discovery: a contented sigh, like a satisfying orgasm.

Sigh? When she had her big Mary Queen of Scots moment, she thought, she'd raise her long skirts and jump onto the desk in her red high-heeled boots. Then she'd scream.

A Secret

That evening Jenny started again on her Cato transcripts.

Hamish called. 'What you doing?'

'Just work stuff,' she said. She wasn't sure why, but for now she'd decided to keep Cato a secret.

The Journal of Cato

THE FINAL TIME

Hear me now. My time has come to write down my story for the final time. My Massa's presence in this city is part of a great disruption, a change in the course of its story. My own presence here is another kind of change. A man from a distant country, come to live in a new city. Writin a different story from the tales in the thick city tomes.

MASSA BILLEE

I sit here at my high desk, finishin copyin Billee's letters. Today on the back stair, Bella the kitchen maid spoke with anger in her voice, her pale cheeks turnin red. 'You give us Billee's instructions,' Bella said, 'you are no better than Massa Billee.'

So, I ask you, dear reader, which story do I tell? My own or Massa Billee's? What was it my friend Hermit said? 'Spend, you spend much of your time in Billee's shadow, so your story is not your own but the story of Massa Billee.' Tis true. Live, I live in Billee's shadow, thus even though I write my own tale, Billee's story is my story.

Thus, if you will forgive me, perhaps I will also tell a wee bit of Massa Billee's story too.

MY STORY

So, I commence my story, lookin back from the end of my life in Glasgow.

Listen to me now. Tell, first I will tell of my childhood. How I was carried to the islands. How I came to work for Massa Billee. How he rose through the canefields. How I returned with him to Glasgow.

When I first arrived on the islands, my Engly was poor, I had no time to write. Store, I stored my stories in my head. When I started workin for Massa Billee, I wrote them down on some blank sheets, torn from the back of an old tome. Hid, I hid them in a tin box under the floor. In 1699 the hurycane carried away most of my papers & I rewrote it all. In 1706 the French came & burnt everythin on the island & I started once more.

Twas not difficult. The words were imprinted in my head.

CURIOS

Hurry, my story hurries me on. The warm light from the library grate flickers off the timber panels. Massa Billee's ornaments peer from narrow shelves surroundin his bed, tellin the story of a life. Trinkets so familiar they are ignored. The framed sketch of his first plantation, faded brown from years of tropical sun. The purchase deed for his first sugar plantation, with a red wax seal, inside a glass frame. The little oil-lamp brought back to Glasgow by his first wife, just before she died of the smallpox. The cylindrical brass gudgeon from his cane mill, re-invented to hold down a pile of papers. The model of his first sugar ship, trapped forever inside a dusty bottle. The hardwood sextant inlaid with ivory, left by his late brother, Captain David.

His grandfather's worn copy of *The History of the Caribees*, the book which started everythin.

A CLOCK CHIMES

Somewhere deep in the house a clock chimes. I draw my fingers along the backs of a row of sea-shells, rough & spiny to the touch. I lift down the big conch, its insides echoin the island surf. I rattle it in my hand with the skeleton of somethin trapped inside. The shell which Billee's young son feared puttin to his ear lest some parasite crawl into his skull & scoop out his brain.

Other mementoes have meanins hidden to all but myself & Massa Billee. Easin the lid off a coloured glass jar releases a faint fragrance, a silver brooch in a bed of dry rose petals, returned by an old lover. The little music box with the inlaid lid, a gift from Madam Mead after they first lay together. Releasin its lid spills out the faint notes of a popular waltz. Slidin open the little wooden drawer in its base reveals a lock of dark hair of yet another lover.

AN INNOCENT STAFF

Stretchin up to the top shelf, I lift down the stubby ebony staff from his early years on the sugar plantation. The handle worn smooth by years of use. Pierced at the end for a leather thong, stained brown with sweat from his hand. Here in Scotland no more than an innocent staff. Elsewhere, much darker memories. Yet a club which rarely cracked a skull in anger.

'Yet who is worse,' said my friend Hermit, 'the man who kills with his own hand, or the coward who does it through his lackeys?'

LET HIM LIVE

I shiver as the fire struggles to overcome the night chill. Massa Billee lies now on his left side, his right arm trailin over the edge of the bed. By his side stands Peggy, his good-tempered dark-skinned maid who shares his hooked nose. Peggy is only fifteen but work, she works sixteen hours a day. How many other servants here are his bastard childs?

End, I could end his life here & now by graspin his throat. I ask myself again why have I not done it before. How can I mourn the plight of my brothers & sisters when I let him live? Questions I have never answered.

Suddenly, he stirs under the sheet, startlin me.

'Are you awake, Massa?' I whisper.

His eyes open slightly. They look straight through me as if I am not here. But I am here in the shadows, always here. Hearin everythin but sayin nothin.

Earlier, I overheard the doctor: 'I give him a day or two.'

MY HOME

In the end, my favourite place in the city lies down the Stockwell. Beside the river, my gate-way to the world. I lean against the parapet of the bridge. The cold breeze from the water clears my head. When I was younger I would climb down below, to the ford. Dip my fingers in the Clyde, taste the salt at high tide. The same water that laps the island shore, the shores of Africa, my home.

Great is my fear that each winter will be my last. Or Massa Billee's last, then his lady will sell me or throw me into the street.

Only last week she said again, 'Put the Negro away, he is old & useless.'

'Leave him be,' said Billee. 'He has been my scribe ever since I landed on the islands.'

EVER TOO LATE

Perhaps I am too old, but is it ever too late? When I was fifteen & forced to work the canefields, I doubted I would last a month. Now I am near five times that age. Despite everythin I have been fortunate. Sometimes I feel that I will last forever. Not in this frail shell but in some other medium, in my thoughts, through these humble words.

Jenny's Family Album

Jenny began a list, starting with a note she'd found on the edge of one of the scrolls:

Cato, 17, scribe, £35.

Bella, kitchen maid.

Peggy, 15, house servant, Scotland.

Part Two
Glasgow

Chapter 6

Hamish, Glasgow

The next morning, the postman brings another of Murdo's wee parcels. Where have they come from?

What do they mean?

I start to open the parcel, but when I see what's inside, I wrap it up again and put it in my bag. When I meet Jenny later in the cafe, I slide it across the table.

'A present,' I say.

She unwraps a wee wooden desk, with drawers the size of match-boxes. 'A jewellery box!' she says. Then she sniffs it and wrinkles her nose. 'One of Murdo's?' She takes off two of her thumb rings, slides open the top drawer and pops them inside. 'It's brilliant!' she says.

'It's more than brilliant,' I say, 'it's a clue.'

Her face falls. 'Want to keep it?'

'No, honestly, you can have it. It's a replica of Murdo's chest of drawers in his attic den. Came this morning.'

'He's alive?' she says.

'Maybe. It's telling me I need to go back to Glasgow to chase Billy.'

'Going north too,' she says. 'To stay with Kelly.'

'Meet there for a walk?'

'Trying to convert me?'

'There's always hope.'

As we part, she pecks me on the cheek and says, 'Thanks for the model.' She disappears round the corner.

Maybe we can just keep doing this, walking the streets and exchanging models. These days, I'm easy to please.

***

Two days later, another wee parcel comes from Murdo. I put it in my pocket, heave on my backpack and cycle down to the station to catch the overnight train north. I always enjoy the journey from Bristol to Glasgow. There's something special about travelling that gives a sense of purpose. I might not be going anywhere special, but at least I'm out and moving. And if I'm also writing, fellow travellers might think I'm working. Recently, my sanity has depended on being part of what's going on around me. Even if I'm only pretending.

As I wait in the dark for my connection at Preston, I call Jenny.

'Hi,' she says.

'Am I too late?'

'No, it's OK.'

'Wanted to catch you before you went to bed.'

'You have – just.'

'What you doing?'

'Looking at the news on my phone.'

'Rain gone off?'

'Nice sunset,' she says.

'Raining here.'

'It's a long way from Preston to Bristol. Just arrived at Kelly's in Glasgow,' she says.

'Meet up tomorrow?'

'Queen Street station at two?'

'Cool.'

***

Next morning, I yawn, unfold my bike and bump it down the side steps of Central Station. Along Union Street, the Greek Thomson building's still shrouded in scaffolding. The city hasn't learned from its mistakes.

Now they've torn down all the Georgian buildings, they've moved on to the Victorian ones – and they've started with the best.

Along Gordon Street, the cropped trees are already in light green leaf. I pass the big museum building. Used to be a merchant's house. If I look closely at the pillars and pediments, most of the stones are old and grey and worn. But a few are white and brand new. What's it called? Indented. Slotted into the old fabric to replace ones which have worn away to nothing. Tourists come towards me and force me to one side.

Still going against the flow.

I ride round to Queen Street to meet Jenny. I'm ten minutes late, but her train's late too.

We kiss lightly on both cheeks. 'I'm hungry,' she says.

For once, I've put on jeans instead of shorts. Somewhere beneath the odd clothes and the swearing, Jenny has a touch of elegance, so I avoid Greggs and McDonald's. I lock my bike outside an old-fashioned tea shop in Royal Exchange Square. All waxed flower-print tablecloths and fairy cakes on tiered stands, smelling of vanilla and chocolate. It matches Jenny, in her pink jacket, hair ribbon and Laura Ashley dress. She looks the part, apart from the nose ring, fishnets and red lace-up boots.

We have tea and buttered scones with home-made jam. When we finish, she says, 'Can I see Murdo's flat?'

'Mary would have said if he's back.'

'Just a quick look.'

I lead her round to the Stockwell. The building's built of red sandstone, but Jenny reaches up and touches a big block of blonde sandstone built into the entrance.

'Murdo said it was from the merchant's house which predated it,' I say. It's stained with age, but the lighter stone's coarser to the touch than the red.

'Older and rougher: I like that,' she says. She pokes her finger into wee cup marks worn into the wall.

'Not from ancient civilisations,' I say. 'From my childhood. If we twisted a ten pence piece long enough against the stone, it dug a wee round divot.'

Jenny's phone rings and she moves away to take a call. I pull a pen from my pocket, lean my notebook on my knee and write.

No. 107. Stone

That's the best thing about stone. How you can scratch it and scrape it. And way in the future, long after you're gone, an imprint of you will remain. And someone who knows how to read it might even revive a memory of you. And the more time you spend engraving your story in stone, the greater the chance a wee bit of you will persist.

Which, of course, is nonsense, as buildings are demolished all the time. Especially in Glasgow. Nothing's safe. No matter how important.

***

When Jenny comes back, I say, 'What if he's lying up there?'

'Come on,' she says, pulling my arm.

'Someone in the family might see me.'

'You need to get over your family hang-ups.'

Maybe you're one too, but a good one, I think.

We cross to the cafe on the other side of the street. I park my bike outside and we sit right at the window so I can keep an eye on my stuff. I point across the street and way up high.

'Whole family lived for years in the top floor flat.'

'The one he modelled!' she says.

Across the road, a slim middle-aged lady emerges from the close and turns up the street. I shrink back behind a fake rubber plant.

'Aunt Mary,' she says. 'Haven't seen her for years.'

'Now's our chance.'

We wait for a minute, then go out and cross the street. The close door's ajar. I take off my bag, fold my bike and lock it to a downpipe through the back of the close. We climb the stairs to the top landing. I lead her into Mary's lobby, shut one leaf of the storm door and face the narrow door in the wall behind it.

'Think I remember visiting here when I was small,' she says, 'but Mary's flat, not any higher up.'

I slip my key into the lock.

'The secret door!' Jenny says.

I click the light switch, reach back and snib the door behind us. The stair's only wide enough for one, so Jenny leads the way. I struggle behind with my pannier. When I reach the small landing, I run a finger along the faded sign: CARETAKER. The big circular room smells of attics: dry, dusty and warm, with a hint of tobacco.

Jenny takes off her boots and does a twirl in the middle of the floor. I'm glad she's with me. I half expect Murdo to be sitting at the big desk. The curtains are open on the four windows, facing the compass points. Someone's been up since I was last here. Murdo? Jenny moves lightly round the room in her stocking soles, peering out each window in turn. 'It's amazing,' she says. 'And nobody knew about it?'

She pokes into shelves and alcoves, at books and models, and draws her fingers round the curving wall.

'What's up there?' Jenny says, pointing up the green spiral stair.

I lead the way. Our feet clang on the iron steps. Half way up is Murdo's big bed, neatly made up.

'He sleeps up here?' she says.

I open my wee notebook and hand it to Jenny.

No. 75. My Favourite View

At first I used the attic den for my books and writing. But, after Gran died, I moved up into the big circular room and made it my own. And I added a mezzanine in the centre, for my bed, and a shower room off the landing.

And the four windows of my den looked out to the compass points, over the roofs and towers of the Merchant City. And my favourite view was to the south, to the sailing ship on top of the Merchant's Steeple. And across the river, to the pointy minaret. And I loved the reflection of the dome of the mosque in the evening sun. And I said, 'Cities always have connections with distant places, some clear and some forgotten. And long ago, the merchants used to climb their tower and watch for their boats coming up from Port Glasgow.'

And the boy stood beside me, and we looked away down the river towards the distant sea.

***

At the top of the stair, I bend down, slide the bolt and turn the handle. I put a shoulder to the door and it opens with a loud crack, scattering starlings outside. I stumble out onto the wee circular platform. Then I turn and give Jenny a hand. She straightens up and shades her eyes with a slim hand.

'It's like a fairy-tale castle. The way you found it. The dome. All the different levels. How did it stay hidden for so long?'

'Started out as the building caretaker's office. Murdo reckons it was sealed off before the family bought the flat below, and nobody remembered it.'

We look out over the parapet at the roofs and towers of the Merchant City.

'Murdo's favourite place,' I say.

'He's not daft.'

We stand in silence for a few minutes, taking in the panorama.

Then Jenny says, 'Don't you ever wish you could escape this crappy world, shrink down to the size of your little man, walk the streets of the model, go inside the buildings, climb the stairs...'

'Every night in bed.'

As she turns, the wee man jabs us both on the hip. I pull him out of my pocket. 'Hope Barry's not going to come between us,' she says.

We climb back downstairs, and Jenny starts browsing the bookshelves.

'You need to check them,' she says.

'Take weeks to do them all.'

She stops at the big noticeboard. I watch her peruse the family photos and their captions. Three of the photos are of Jenny in her youth. I go over to the coffee machine by the sink and poke in drawers for some beans. I find a packet and make real coffee. Jenny admires the shiny chrome pipes on the big old machine.

'Murdo found it in a lane behind a cafe and repaired it,' I say.

After we've had coffee, I leave my bag in the flat and walk Jenny to the stop, to catch the bus back to Kelly's.

As we part, she says, 'Maybe if we chase Barry, we'll find Murdo?'

I've given up correcting Billy's name. I head back to the flat, savouring the word *we*.

I take the wee wooden man, one of the folding chairs, and climb back up to the eyrie. The sun's setting down the river. The sky's extra clear, but the wind's cold.

Is it safe to crash here?

Will Mary find me?

Where's Murdo gone?

I can't face sleeping in Murdo's bed. I go back down and fetch my old sleeping bag from a cupboard. Up top, I lay down a plastic sheet, unroll the bag and climb inside. The city's settling down for the night. As I lie there, the cold wind and most of the street noise is cut off by the parapet. The sky's clear. I find the Plough, and just as I reach the Pole Star, a shooting star whizzes across the sky.

I grasp the wee man. 'Bet you arranged that,' I say.

I doze off, then wake with drizzle on my face. I gather my things and go back downstairs. I find some covers and lie down on the big sofa and soon fall asleep.

***

At breakfast time, through the north window, I see a woman hanging out washing on the balcony of the modern flats across the lane. I can make her out through a narrow gap in the chimneys. She's too far away to see clearly, but I imagine she's my age and very pretty. I call her Jessica, from a song I'm listening to on my earphones. She only appears for thirty seconds, but it cheers me up. These days it doesn't take much to keep me sane.

I put the kettle on and do a few laps in my bare feet to wake up. Across the big room, the morning sun falls on the desk, turning the bookshelves along the curved wall a dull orange. At the sink, I stand wee Billy on the draining board and wash my recent collection of treasures from the layers. Pieces of coloured glass, glazed pottery, a coin. Evidence from Billy's time. Right back to the start.

It's windy outside and I'm spooked by wee creaks and groans in the roof. I half-expect Murdo to appear. Around the big room, wee wooden models stand in every nook and cranny. I pick out ones from shelves and cupboards that I played with in my childhood. I form a wee street on the table, like a miniature version of Murdo's Glasgow Grid. Then I take the wee wooden figure and walk him between them.

Up on the wall is Murdo's faded engraving of a man with a thin face, wearing a wig and cocked hat. I've always assumed he's Murdo's hero, Daniel Defoe. Or could he be Billy? He has a strong resemblance to the wee man. How long's Murdo been chasing him?

I tip out all the wee models from Murdo. These are my biggest clues, not a bunch of old books.

Then I take out the latest parcel that came in the post from Murdo. I turn it upside down, tap it gently on the table, and four wee wooden numbers slip out. I stand them up: a one, two sixes and an eight. I try them in different orders. What are they, a code or a date? I don't even know what period Billy lived in.

Murdo's wall of books has ten times more than my feeble row in Bristol. I can't remember which books I've already looked at in my flat, so I start with the thickest ones. Again, I copy out the entries for Billy.

By teatime I've found an obituary:

He was the most popular man in Glasgow during the 1740s. Jovial and carefree, he was the darling of the city who did much to shape its social and human qualities…

He died in 1749. Assuming he lived a reasonably long life, he must have been born in the late 1600s. That doesn't mean a lot, but it does seem early. I write *1749* on the first blank sheet inside my folder.

I'm about to send Billy's epitaph to Jenny, but change my mind. It's a bit over the top to modern eyes, but it does confirm that Billy's special.

***

Early next morning, I'm woken by a siren echoing somewhere below. Bells chime nearby in a clock tower. Streaks of light cross my vision. Another clock strikes five times. Pinpricks of light dot the dome of the ceiling, like a personal planetarium, reflected from car headlights way down in the street below.

A shape down at the door spooks me, but it's only Murdo's old army coat hanging from a hook by the door. I lie listening to the patter of rain on the slates and the water streaming along a gutter. I say a silent thank you to Murdo for this roof over my head.

But where are you? I think.

At breakfast time, Jessica's there again through the chimneys. Her washing's all the one colour. I'm learning to use it to forecast the weather, like the wee figures that pop out of a Swiss clock. The rain's gone off. This morning her washing's red, and the sun's shining.

I need to check out more about Billy. But I also need to work up the courage to go down and speak to Aunt Mary. I pack away my stuff, creep down the narrow stair and lay my pannier out in the close. I come back in and ring her doorbell. Mary appears, hair bedraggled, in a dressing gown. I step forward to give her a hug, but she's a bit surprised, and we fumble and bang noses. Her social skills are on a par with my own.

'Sorry,' we say in unison.

She looks out at my bag on the landing. 'What you doing up here?'

'Just visiting.'

'Not got a job to go to?'

'A few offers.'

'Still chasing your grandpa's nonsense?'

'No. Well. I…'

'He still got a hold of you from the grave?'

'Think he's gone?'

'Jesus, Hamish, you're not clinging to a hope that Murdo's alive?'

'Last time I was up, he was a bit confused, but he said nothing in his letters.'

'Had good and bad days. Tried to keep it quiet.'

'But he can't have just disappeared.'

'Something upset him. He was on one of his fads again. Had to rescue him from a few places. Last month, he said he was going on one of his archive jaunts to Edinburgh. But we found him at his old seaside haunt of North Berwick. Then Eck had to fetch him from Carlisle.'

'Carlisle?'

'He was heading down to see you but got off too early.'

'Oh shit.'

'You weren't to know. Most likely he's lying in a ditch somewhere.'

Tears come to my eyes. 'Think he topped himself?'

'You know better than most of us what he's like. Who knows what he'd do if he was desperate?'

'Wish I'd known.'

'Probably set it up that way. Keep us all in suspense.' She turns and glances at an open suitcase in her hall. 'I'd invite you in for a cuppa, but I've got a train to catch.'

Of all Murdo's daughters, Mary's the least hospitable. Murdo quips that it's because she's the one born in Edinburgh.

'Holiday?' I say.

'A few days with Aggie in Bristol.' She looks at her watch.

'I'll go,' I say.

She squints at me, then puts a hand on my shoulder. 'Take care of yourself.'

I pick up my panniers and descend one flight of stairs. I hear her shut the front door, give her a minute, then tiptoe back up. I half-close her left-hand storm door, fetch my bag and creep back up the narrow stair.

If Mary's going away, I can stay up here for a bit. She's never approved of Murdo's den, any more than his hobbies. It's unlikely she'll come up before she leaves. But I creep around in my stocking soles and don't flush the toilet, paranoid that she'll hear me down below. I open the cupboards quietly. I find some oatcakes in a tin, which taste OK. There's a few other tins. Beans, soup and macaroni. The teabags I've been using are only a week out of date, but I need to have the tea without milk. Once Mary's gone, I'll go down and get some fresh food. If it gets cold, I've got the old wood-burning stove in the corner.

From the dining table, through the north window, I can see a glimpse of river. The tide's low. I fetch Murdo's big ex-army binoculars. The wee boat! I can just make out the prow. I sit at the big table with the wee man in front of me. I lean forward and look him in his squinty eye. Who are you?

Out on the landing, I open the smallest door. It leads into the cavernous roof space of the tenement: a forest of rafters, like the upturned hull of a ship. One corner's floored for Murdo's workshop. On the other side is a huge stack of timber offcuts, enough to fuel the stove for a few Glasgow winters. Might come in handy someday.

Murdo can never throw away a piece of wood.

It makes me think of my own life. What do I know?

I know how to use a fretsaw to cut shapes from wood.

I know how to design a steel beam and a concrete foundation.

I know a wee bit of French.

I know how to bake bread.

Yet it seems I know nothing of value.

I do what I always do when I'm down. I fetch my cycle helmet, creep downstairs, unlock my bike and head up the riverside path.

No. 108. My CV

Name: Hamish Murdo Hamilton

Age: 30

Occupation: Conservation engineer

Current employment: Between jobs

Hobbies: Cycling, collecting stones and wooden models

Chapter 7

Jenny, Glasgow

The Earliest in the World

The next day, Jenny tapped into Kelly's Wi-Fi. If Billy was famous, maybe she could find something new about him. Something Hamish had missed?

She typed his name and pressed Enter, but she got two million hits. Then she typed *Cato*. She was looking for a Cato who had lived three hundred years ago. But most of the results went much further back: to ancient Rome.

But there was a connection, sort of. The Roman Cato had also been a scribe. *The earliest historian in the world.* There was even an image of him. If her dad was still around he'd have adopted Cato into the wider family.

Jenny copied the picture of Cato into a new folder, named *Family Album*.

To Dump Him

Ever since Jenny had first seen the destination boards in Temple Meads as a child, she'd been fascinated by Scottish places. Her dad told her they were the furthest you could travel in any direction.

Now Dave had moved to Glasgow, Jenny wished it *was* the end of the world.

After meeting Hamish, she tried to work up the courage to cross the city to Mount Florida and find Dave's flat. When she was lonely and bored in Bristol, she'd thought she needed him, but she'd already made up her mind to dump him.

Just a Friend

Later, Jenny appeared back at Kelly's in Byres Road, in tears. Half of Kelly's stuff was still in boxes. But, unlike Hamish, Kelly was moving in, not out.

'Couldn't face Dave,' Jenny said.

Kelly gave her a hug and made a cup of tea. 'Where you been?'

'Met Hamish in town.'

'Dave replacement?'

'Need to tell you something.'

Jenny poured out her story: Cato's jotters. How they were found. How she was hooked on transcribing them.

'You've swallowed Murdo's bait?' Kelly said. 'Thought you hardly knew him?'

'It's odd. He's got photos of me up on his wall.'

'Not as many as of Hamish?'

'They've been best buddies all their lives, through stories and history stuff. But they're not the type to get emotional.'

'Jealous?'

'I'm different,' Jenny said. 'I need hugs.'

'Told Hamish about Cato yet?' Kelly said.

Jenny didn't answer.

'You've hidden the scrolls from him!'

'I'm not spoon-feeding him. He needs to find Billy's story for himself.'

'Isn't it a different version from what he's turning up?'

'I'm a selfish bitch. Hogging it for my career.'

'You're a stubborn pair of bastards, and you're heading for a showdown.' There was another silence, then Kelly said, 'You fancy him!'

'Yes. No. Maybe I'll have decided when I work up the enthusiasm to tell him about Cato.'

'You've never been shy about telling boys how you feel.'

'This one's different.'

'The biggie?'

'He's my cousin, but not a blood relation.'

'What you waiting for?'

'Dad married his aunt when I was four.'

'It's his grandpa's quest. Friend or boyfriend, if you don't tell him soon, you'll lose him.'

Jenny fumbled with the lid of the jam. 'It's not just about my career, it's about Bristol and Glasgow too.'

'Aye, Glasgow first,' said Kelly, exaggerating her accent.

'See what I mean?'

'Shit, Jen, what's more important: city rivalry, or finding a new friend?'

'He might be sweet, but right now I need another boyfriend like a hole in the head.'

Silly Games

Before supper, Jenny called Hamish. 'Am I too late?' she said.

'Still up.'

'Can't you contact Murdo, instead of playing silly games?'

'Where?'

'His mobile?'

'Line's dead.'

'Must be around if he's sending you stuff.'

'But where's he staying?'

They talked about Kelly's new flat and the weather, then she ended the call. She hadn't worked up the courage to mention Cato.

She needed to transcribe a bit more, find out where it was going. It could be her big break, just what she was looking for. If only Cato had settled in Bristol, not Glasgow.

A Mortal Sin

Next day, Jenny caught an early train to Edinburgh. It was packed with commuters. She climbed the steep steps and crossed Princess Street to the big archive. There must be something there about Cato.

It took her most of the morning to register and get a photo and a reader's ticket. She found a locker for her bag, took out her notebook and fumbled for a pencil. But she could only find a gel pen. Shit, she thought, I'm going to have to commit a mortal sin.

The problem was, you didn't know how fussy each archive was until you experienced it, so you were wide open to bossy clerks. Clarissa at the front desk, with her name badge and glasses on a silver chain, spotted Jenny's pen right away. It was hard to hide, with its purple and yellow stripes. Clarissa confiscated the pen and gave Jenny a pencil from a tub on her desk. It was like being told off by your infant teacher.

When she got back to her seat, Jenny stuck out her tongue in Clarissa's direction, just as Clarissa raised her head. Jenny turned away.

Had the clerk seen her?

Did Jenny care?

Pens or pencils? Jenny hadn't even ordered any documents yet. She was still at the indexes. She could have done it at home on the Web, without the hassle of coming here. But it was familiar territory. Quiet and soothing, in an old-fashioned sort of way. Maybe, just by being here, some of the magic might rub off.

Magic bollocks, she thought. What keeps me going? The excitement of finding something important.

Up Her Sleeve

Jenny searched for Cato without success. But she had other tricks up her sleeve. She slipped out her phone and opened a file, with the names of some of her favourite Bristol characters. She started checking them in the catalogue. When she reached Pedro Dias, a Portuguese wine merchant, she found a whole wad of papers. He'd imported Madeira wine to Bristol, but he'd also had an agent here, in Leith. Maybe Pedro was related to Bartholomeu Dias, the original explorer?

Way back before John Cabot was born, it was the Portuguese who made all the important finds. Ventured further and further down the African coast. Each time they sighted a bigger mountain, they measured and mapped it, decided it was the tallest in the world.

Their first high mountain was Teide.

Jenny had climbed Teide on a winter sun holiday on Tenerife when she was twelve. She'd been sick twice in the bus on the winding roads on the ascent. Sister Sally had a panic attack on the cable car. When they finally reached the summit, she could hardly breathe in the thin air.

Tallest in the world? The Portuguese reckoned it was, until they got halfway down the African coast and sighted Mongo-Ma-Loba. It so happened that Teide and Mongo were erupting when they were first spotted, which may have swayed the Portuguese a bit.

In 1488, before Cabot or Columbus reached the Americas, Jenny's hero Dias was the first to round the Cape of Good Hope and head for India. But Dias hadn't found any mountains higher than Mongo-Ma-Loba.

She searched Google Earth for its location.

Cato was born in Cameroon.

The Journal of Cato

MONGO-MA-LOBA

Write, shortly I will write of the origins of this island. Howsoever, first I write of my own origins. Three continents I lived upon. Two islands. One city.

Squirm, I squirm from my mother's belly as Mongo-Ma-Loba roars. Tallest in Africa, the sailors say. Hot at its roots, but sparklin white at its top.

Member, the first thing I remember is the mists & rainbows. The creeks & shores which skirt the high slopes. Grow, my father grows sweetcorn & plantains. Dependin on the season, he hunts antelope in the high grass plains. Once a year the men of the village travel a great distance, dig great pits which they cover with branches. Trap elephants.

MY FATHER

My father teaches me many things.

To make fire.

To plant tubers.

To tether & milk a goat.

To catch small game in a noose.

To swim the big river.

MY CHILDHOOD PLACES

The slopes in sight of the coast are my childhood places, the damp creeks where rushes grow. The corner of the meadow favoured by antelopes. The great ferns which rise above my head. The summit of Mongo, high up against the sky, coloured dark blue. The old baobab limb which hangs over the track, where I watch my father drivin his goats home at dusk.

See, I can still see them passin under me in the pink haze. As I close my eyes, the sound of their hooves in the dirt grows fainter, vanishin beneath the chirpin of insects.

MIST & DRIZZLE

Member, I remember the sounds & colours of my home. The warm air. The crack of thunder. The red-brown earth. Blue & yellow butterflies which tickle my face. The great river flowin west to the distant ocean. The patter of the rain on the leaves which swathes the slopes in mist & drizzle for many months of the year.

The tree roots provide giant steps up the slopes. On each side of the path are deep forest dells & ravines. Slippery rocks show up through the ground in every direction, patches of satin-leaved flowers & clumps of tree-ferns. Above all hangs the mist, tumblin down from the mountain towards me: creepin, twinin round & streamin through the moss-covered tree columns. Wrappin me round in a chill embrace.

ELEPHANTS WITH WINGS

When I was a boy I liked to draw pictures with a stick in the dirt. I invented imaginary animals. Elephants with wings. Snakes with legs. Write, we did not write in the Buckra fashion, but I made up stories & dreams in my head. The only things I did not draw were those I was afraid of. Lions & the great mountain.

ESCAPE

Life, my life passes in seasons like the mountain. Fourteen years till the great mountain roars again. The summer that Father goes to the coast with the other menfolk to fish. Once he has left, we are no longer safe. If only he had been there the day the slavers came.

Hear, we hear a great commotion outside. Tear, I tear at the bark wall of our home until my fingers bleed. Burst, I burst through the back wall. From that moment, I break through into a new world.

Slide, I slide down a dusty slope into the ravine. Slide & roll, slide & roll. Swallowed by the mist. Earth fills my mouth. Reach, I reach the bottom. Tis a mercy my fall is broken by water, not rock. Tiredness fills me, spreads from my legs to my chest with deep breaths. I am covered in dirt. Fear comes upon me. I hear noises all around, magnified by the echo of the rocks, confused by the rush of water. I wade out to a small island & lie there. I swear I hear my sister Nala cry in the distance, but save, I cannot save her.

Far above I hear more screams, the faint smell of burnin flesh. Spirits cross the ravine, over & up, wisps in the mist.

I MUST RETURN

I lie till mornin, cold & wet. Alone, I have never been so alone in the dark forest. Wake, by the time the sun returns, I awake. A bird flies overhead. The mist has gone. I am exposed on my rocky isle. I wade back through the water to the shelter of a bush. Hide like an animal. Should I go higher, or follow the water down to the coast? I stick to the rocks & gullies. My way is blocked by a deeper ravine. I cross from one side to another, upon a tree bridge. Balanced high above the river, which rushes beneath it over a boulder-strewn bed. Tired, I am tired. My legs shake under me after the trials of the previous day. My feet slip. I reach a wall of rock. I can carry on no further. I must return the way I came.

I crawl from the sound of the river, up the bank to the jungle, familiar sounds & scents give me comfort. Gather, I gather fruit. I spend another night in the bush. Lie, I lie fearful of wild animals, yet more fearful of men.

LOOK THE OTHER WAY

Mistake, tis my greatest mistake to return to the village. Bein fifteen I have one foot in manhood but another in childhood. See, I see the hole in the wall from my escape. The door, broke in from the outside. The burnt roof. The red cloth torn from Nala's back.

I want to go to my mother, to touch her, turn her over, see her one last time. But I see enough from afar. My mother's face is not her own. Her limbs are twisted with the fallin. Thrown aside like a rag doll. Turn, I turn away from her nakedness. The spirit has left her body. Why kill if they can be sold for gold on the coast?

They only exchange gold for the young, my father said.

Which is worse, to be dead or a chattel?

I hide in the edge of the bush. The mist descends again. I watch a whorl of air move its way towards me, spin & rise up. They come back with dogs. I cannot hide from the dogs. I know, suddenly, that Nala is also gone. As they drag me away, I pass her shell. Look, I look the other way.

I will not say what they did to my sister.

MY FATHER'S FACE

Member, I remember my mother standin at the door. My sister by her side. Try, I try to recall my father's hands. The colour of my mother's hair. I hold the shape of my father against the light. Unlike my mother, whose beauty I still recall, my greatest regret is that I can no longer see my father's face.

If I had remained in the bush that night, my life would be so different. Warned, I had been warned many times about the slavers. Spirits, more dangerous than lions, comin over the hill to carry you away forever. Told so often that they became fables.

In my journal I must write of some people as if I bid them goodbye. The dead are all around. My mother is with me. She has halted to say goodbye. My father beckons her from afar.

If I cannot rise with them, let me sink into the water.

Jenny's Family Album

Jenny opened the cover of her notebook and added a name to her list:

Nala, sister, Cameroon.

Chapter 8

Hamish, Glasgow

Is Murdo really gone?

Can he be gone if he's sending me clues?

I go out for some fresh air and find a bench in George Square. I prop the wee man on a litter bin and take out Murdo's wooden numbers. Most of the dates on the statues in the square are Victorian. I fiddle with the numbers in various orders.

1866. Too late for Billy?

A big seagull lands close by and peers at the wee man. I look the bird in his squinty eye.

I want to see the city in the wee man's time. The buildings Murdo modelled. I don't want to lose him again.

I head off and follow Billy's route along the Trongate to his townhouse, then down King Street to the Green. If I'm going to write Murdo's whole book on foot, I'm going to get through a lot of pairs of shoes.

My tidal app tells me the level of the river. It's low, so I head down. The day's grey and the sun's obscured by a plume of smoke from the distillery chimney. Murdo used to bring me down here to the tidal weir. Where the fresh waters from the Clyde pour into the salt water from the ocean. We'd dip our fingers in the water, and he'd tell me we were in touch with all parts of the globe. When I pulled my fingers out, they were cold and tasted of salt. When I told Mum about my discovery, she took me to the sink and scrubbed my hands.

'Dalmarnock Sewage Works is just around the bend. My stupid father will have you poisoned with typhoid or something.'

She banned me from going near the river. After that, I kept my Murdo adventures to myself.

Across the bridge, I climb the fence, then down the manhole to the shingle beach. The skeleton of the wee boat sits way out in the flow. I throw out more big stones, adding to the length of the causeway. Another few years and I'll reach Murdo's boat.

Back up top, I'm naked without my bike, but I've got nothing to carry. I head for Ingram Street into the Ramshorn Kirkyard. The sun's still shining on the merchants' memorials: 1795, 1783. I grip the wee wooden man in my pocket. Am I getting warmer?

On the way back, an old man with white hair, in a long coat, disappears round a corner. At the end, I look both ways, but all I can see is a girl pushing a buggy. Then I realise where I am. The lane's hemmed in by wooden hoardings, daubed in graffiti and faded posters. Further along, I peer through holes in the boards. Someone's forced two panels apart. I squeeze through.

Among the rubble, the cracks in the old cobbles have turned green again. A lone silver birch pokes out of a mound of old bricks. Then I spot it: the stone arch. A fragment of old Glasgow.

I clamber across the rubble and run my fingers along the soffit of the arch. Years ago, Murdo brought me here. Back then, it was inside a wee pend, surrounded by old buildings. Now it's the only thing left. The sun illuminates the arch, poking up through the rubble like a fragment of Troy. A last remnant of the original Merchant City. The cut of the stone hints at a building of quality – the undercroft of a merchant villa? The first building to stand on this street when it drove across the old rig and furrow.

After a quick sandwich, I go round to meet Jenny. Usually, she's bright and sparky, but for once she looks like she hasn't slept for days. She's carrying a big rucksack, which I take from her, and we continue in silence until we get up to the flat. I've started to think of Murdo's den as home, to forget about going back to Bristol, especially when Jenny's here.

'What's up?' I say.

'Fell out.'

'Kelly?'

She avoids my gaze. 'I lied,' she says. 'Wanted to patch things up with my boyfriend. But we've split. For good.' She looks up with her big brown eyes and dissolves into my arms. 'Kelly's mum's come to stay. Unless I catch the overnight train back to Bristol, I need to find a hotel in Glasgow.'

'You can stay here,' I say, too quickly.

She glances up at the big bed.

'I'll sleep in the box room,' I say.

Jenny goes out to the toilet to dry her tears, then I hear her make a call to her work. She comes back through. 'I'll stay for a few days.'

Across the room, I lift a catch in the wall. One of the bookshelves swings open, revealing a big cupboard in the eaves. Its white-painted walls are lit by a wee skylight in the coombed ceiling. The room's half full of junk, but there's a mattress made up as a bed on the floor. 'Used to be my bedroom.'

'I'll sleep here, if you get rid of the spiders.'

'What about work?'

'Gertrude's messing me around again. Only uses me when she has the schools in.'

I dump her bag in the wee room. Jenny boils the kettle and finds a teapot in a cupboard. She heats the pot with a wee splash of hot water, takes a tea strainer from the shelf and makes real tea. I watch as she moves lightly around the room in her stocking soles. She's attractive, but her quirky dress is a distraction. I like it that I've made a discovery. That I've got her up here, all to myself.

'Maybe I don't need to worry how to write up Billy's story,' I say. 'Just do a Murdo and publish my notes.'

'He's published before?'

I find a dog-eared copy of Murdo's first book, *Glasgow Abridged*, and hand it to Jenny. She turns to the reviews on the back cover and reads them out.

A new perspective on the roots of a global city, Local History Review.

Fills a gap which the city novels haven't reached, Glasgow Literary Bulletin.

A lively scrapbook of new ideas, Archaeology Today.

A convincing mix of new research, old ideas and mischief, Press & Journal.

'Gathered the info for years,' I say, 'but he had the same problem as me. Not what to write about, but *how* to write it. Spent years on drafts but never solved it. It nearly killed him. Lost his job, had some kind of breakdown. Finally he just published this scrapbook of random extracts. Claimed he'd left the reader to join the dots. The critics thought it was inspired, rather than luck.'

No. 45. Writing

I'm the last of the chancers and storytellers. All the others have vanished. Some are in the grave, some are in the asylum, and the rest are academic historians.

Depending on the weather, I write in cafes, parks, stations, the library. If I have writers' block, I ride the Subway. It's like white noise, great for clearing the brain.

Once I'm on a quest, I can't rest until it's written down in order, at least in what I think is a logical order. Archie says I'm the Samuel Pepys of Glasgow. I don't have the guts to point out that he's three hundred years too late.

After I graduated in aeronautics, I worked for Rolls Royce and moved to Bristol. What frustrates me most is my writing style. It's fine for work reports, but it's my personal handicap to have trained as an engineer. It's the scientist's curse – an incurable addiction to fact. 'Quite unusual for a historian,' Archie says.

Writing is all about finding a pattern, then hoping one day it will morph into something special: science into art, history into novel.

As if it's all so easy.

***

'Ach,' I say, 'where do I go next?'

'Check primary sources.'

'Prefer stones n' stuff. Suppose it's all original evidence, though.'

'One day I'll convert you.' Jenny leafs through the folders and papers on the higher shelves, above the books. 'Some of this stuff should be in an archive,' she says.

'Wouldn't believe what he turned up over the years.'

'Maybe he's popped his clogs and someone else is sending clues.'

I turn away. Jenny comes over and puts a hand on my shoulder.

'I'm sure he's fine,' she says. 'He's just playing games. We need to find him.'

***

Next morning at breakfast, Jessica keeps me company through the chimneys. Her washing's light blue and matches the sky. Jenny appears from her wee room and runs her hand over the dark wood of the dining chairs.

'They're all the same design, but made of different coloured woods,' she says.

'Door chairs. Murdo made lots of them from old hardwood doors, to his own design.'

She tips up the chair and reads out a thick pencil scrawl under the seat. 'Seventeen Candleriggs?' she says.

'Address the old door came from.'

'Door chairs! I love it.'

'Eked out the timber in each big old door to make a single chair. "Can't get wood like this any more," he'd say. "A joy to work."'

Jenny circles the room, picking up models from nooks and crannies, asking what they represent. She crosses to the dining table and picks up the wee circular castle tower which came from Murdo. For a door it has an arched entrance. She searches images on her phone. 'Not a castle,' she says. 'It's a windmill, for crushing sugar.'

'Obsessed with Bristol stuff?'

She takes her coat and bag and goes out.

***

Next day Jenny says, 'Still haven't given me a personal tour of Billy's haunts.'

'Maybe I can get you back for your Bristol tour.'

I'm ready to dodge a push, but she pecks me on the cheek. 'Give you marks out of ten,' she says.

Downstairs, we head along to Buchanan Street. It's just past midday and the sun shines straight up the street. The side lighting's perfect. Jenny takes the lead, picking out details high up on Glasgow's Victorian buildings with her long lens. She's always looking up, at statues, sculptures and faces carved in stone. Every so often she stops to leaf through a green book she found on Murdo's shelves about Glasgow sculpture. Although it's thick and heavy, she carries it around in her bag, leafing through it like a copy of the Bible.

'Think I agree with you,' she says. 'Bristol's Glasgow in miniature.'

'Sold out your home city already?'

She sticks out her tongue and takes my arm. We turn right along Argyle Street, fighting against throngs of shoppers, then through St Enoch Square and back along the Broomielaw. A shuffling figure asks for a bus fare. I fumble in my pocket and give her a pound coin. Out in the river, a lone cormorant stretches its wings on top of a wooden pile. Jenny turns up her collar against the wind.

'If this was Bristol, there'd be tour boats, riverside cafes, people.'

'Murdo always says Glasgow's turned its back on its river.'

We stop at a black marble cube. The whole quayside's been given a makeover: coloured granite paving, regular beds of shrubs and cropped trees. Despite all the improvements, it's deserted. Even the seagulls look bored.

Up the river walkway, beyond a casino, we pass under a low bridge. The tide's nearly at its lowest. The tips of the ribs of the boat stick out of the water, making trails in the current.

I lead on. 'Building at the end used to be a merchant's mansion.'

'Used to be?'

We turn along Wilson Street and up Glassford Street. '1790s. Maybe one of the Adams,' I say.

She touches the pale sandstone with her fingertips. 'Too smooth. Refaced?'

I point along Ingram Street. 'Gallery of Modern Art. Former merchant's house.'

'Former?'

Her camera picks out the inscription on a tower.

'First hospital in the city,' I say.

'Rebuilt in 1803.'

Further along the street, I say, 'Ramshorn Kirk—'

'Churches don't count,' she says. 'Always last longer. Where's all the merchants' houses?'

'Suppose Glasgow got too big. Merchants moved out to the country.'

'What about their businesses?'

'Gone too.'

She points up at the street sign: BUCHANAN STREET. 'Beyond some street names, your Merchant City's merchantless,' she sighs. 'So, if the buildings are gone, and the river's deserted, how can you convince me Barry's Glasgow was as important as Bristol?'

'Been through a lot of changes,' I say.

'How come Murdo likes the city so much, if there's nothing left?'

'That's why he went to Bristol, to see the real thing.'

'Feeble excuse.'

I lead her along Argyle Street, past the end of Virginia Street. Jenny stops and takes a photo of the street sign.

'Tobacco trade,' I say.

'Too late for Billy.'

'Expert on Glasgow now?'

'When did he die?'

'1749.'

'Quite a bit before tobacco.'

I don't know enough to contradict her, so I say nothing. But I'll need to check it out. If he isn't a tobacco lord, what's his story?

We stop beside Marks & Spencer. I take out the wee model of Billy's house and hold it up.

'You brought it with you!' she says.

'Original mansion stood here, in the middle of the road.'

The lights change, and a convoy of buses crashes through Billy's virtual parlour. Across the street, the east wing's now a derelict Gothic bank. The plaque on the wall says: THE BONNIE PRINCE SLEPT HERE,

Beyond the West Port of the town are corn-fields, where the merchants build their houses, surrounded by kitchen and flower gardens, and beautiful orchyards, abounding with fruits of all sorts, which send forth a pleasant and odoriferous smell. M'Ure, who wrote his grotesque History of the City in 1736, speaks of 'the great and stately Lodging, Orchyard, and Gardens, belonging to Billy, on the North side of the Trongate.'

When Charles Edward Stuart visited Glasgow in 1745, he took up his quarters in Billy's house, as the principal lodging in the city.

Nay, tis not long since old Bessie passed away, aged upwards of a hundred, who was a servant in Billy's house at the time. She herself 'baked cakes for Chairlie', and knew him well.

***

'Murdo used to shake his fist at the plaque every time we passed. "Biggest jeelie piece in Glasgow," he'd say.'

'Still, he must have been important if a prince slept in his house,' she says.

Is she mocking me? I'm never quite sure.

Across George Square, we head back through Royal Exchange Square. She continues picking out details high up on the buildings. Then she stops, lets out a big sigh and holds her hands wide. 'It's fine,' she says, 'but I don't want the stuffy tourist trail. I want the spiky spanking striptease tour.'

I blush and turn away.

'Time you stood up for your city,' she says. 'The original Georgian buildings, the river, the old stones. The real bits underneath.'

I make a decision. 'Come on,' I say.

We cut through Old Wynd, along Osborne Street and across Clyde Street. On the quayside, we dodge two more vagrants and approach the riverside fence. I look her up and down. She's wearing a long yellow pinafore dress, her red boots and a red top. 'Don't mind me,' she says. 'I'm game for anything.'

I cup my hands together and she rests one foot on my palms. She holds up her dress to stop it snagging on the fence, but misjudges the drop on the other side and disappears into a thicket of tall weeds.

I hear giggling, so I pull myself up and jump over. I follow her trail of tramped-down grass to the edge of the river. She's sitting on top of the old riverside retaining wall like Little Miss Muffet, banging her heels. Just below her feet, the river flows past. She rubs the top of the sandstone cope. 'If only these stones could tell us who came up this river,' she says.

'Which story would you like?'

'Got more than one?'

'I've got saints, Vikings and Irish navvies.'

'Saints sound good.'

'You can have wee boats, longships or steamships.'

'I'll take the saint in the wee boat, please.'

'Good choice.'

I lead the way through the long grass, back to the railings. Then we follow a rough path upriver until we reach a bit where the stone facing's peeled off the wall. I crouch down until I find my dark layer. 'Start of the city?' she says.

'Layer Billy walked on.'

She kneels down and runs her finger along the damp soil.

'Feel the print of his boots.'

Below the dark strip is silty mud, but above it, it's ash and bits of brownish-red pottery. 'So everything above here is man-made, filled up, built on,' she says.

I shrug.

'Same as Bristol,' she says. 'Filled in the Marsh, built their Georgian houses.'

I fumble in my backpack for my notebook, find the right page and pass it to her.

No. 74. Dig and Toil

Everything starts with the digging. A great city rises from the labour of many forgotten men and women. For centuries they drain and plough and plant the bogland. Then one day it changes. They labour and dig, but for a new purpose. Carry soil down to the flatlands. Tip it onto the Low Green. Raise the level of the floodplain. Dig and toil, day in, day out, until they are bone-weary.

Beneath it all lies an earlier, invisible landscape. Everything that moves in the sunlight is driven by the imprint of hard work sealed beneath: the old fields, the buried ditches and burns.

Like the pull of the moon, the balance of the city walker is disturbed by the corrugations and shadows of buried rig and furrow. Riven long ago by folk ploughing and turning the earth.

***

She points back at the layer. 'Serious about this?'

'Maybe. I mean, it's what his life was about. Always going further and further back. Back before the cliched stories, to some sort of beginning. The only real stuff left is under our feet. And Billy goes right back to that time.'

'So, to find the start of the city, we need to dig a tunnel,' she says.

I point further upstream, under the arches of the big red sandstone railway bridge. 'Already done. The naughty tour starts there, with Mungo's tunnel.'

I'd forgotten how much my mood improves when she smiles. We get up and fight our way through tall grass beneath the railway bridge. Torn blankets are scattered around, and the remains of a fire.

We reach a big sandstone tunnel in the riverbank, big enough to drive an old Mini through. It's blocked by a wrought-iron portcullis.

'In the year 596, Mungo jumped out of his coracle at this spot and followed the Molendinar all the way up the hill, to where he built his wee church,' I say. 'Is that too cliched?'

'No, love the Mungo stuff,' she says. 'It's like Greek mythology. Great story, even if it's utter crap.' She touches the ground. 'Where's all the water?'

A stone-paved channel drops the short distance from the tunnel mouth to the river, but it's bone dry. I kneel and fumble about in the long grass at the bottom of the grille. Then I lie down and slide under the portcullis. I stand up inside and rattle the bars. 'Let me out!'

Jenny takes a photo of me in my prison. 'What's the smell?' she says.

'Come on. Need to get you back for your Bristol tunnel.'

'I don't mind spanking and strippers, but I draw the line at corpses.'

I slip my hand into a recess in the stone by the gate. 'One of the places Murdo used to leave clues.' There's nothing there.

'Took you inside as a kid?' she says. 'No wonder your mum was worried.'

I slide back under the grille, and we climb up onto the Saltmarket and start to trace the route of the Molendinar on the surface. Up Shipbank Lane, behind the High Court, past the mortuary, across the Saltmarket. Up Turnbull Street and across the Gallowgate. We stop across the road from the Barras.

'How do you know the way?' Jenny says.

I point up at the street sign: MOLENDINAR STREET.

'Ha ha.' She crouches down at a drain. 'Can you hear it?' she says. 'Rushing water. Same as the Frome in Bristol. Once it was a big part of people's lives. Now it's buried, like some kind of secret.'

'You've only been here two days and you've sussed it,' I say.

'Got a good guide. What now?' she says.

'Time for coffee.'

'Thought you'd never ask.'

At the corner of the Saltmarket and the Briggait is an old-fashioned pub. I hold the door for Jenny and she finds a wooden table in a corner while I get the coffees. Everyone else in the pub's drinking pints and haufs. When I come back, she's admiring the decor.

'Odd place to come for a coffee,' she says.

I push across my folder. 'Found it in Murdo's notes. Site of Billy's bank. His son finished it just after he died. We're inside the pub that replaced it.'

'You and your secrets!'

The whole pub looks over. I hold up my palms.

Once we finish our coffees, we go back out and cross the Saltmarket. Jenny follows my gaze up, towards the roof of the tenement above the pub. She reads out the big letters which curve around the parapet: Old Ship Bank Building. She changes to a telephoto lens. 'Nice building,' she says.

'First in two cities that we've agreed on.'

'Quite a thing, though, to start a whole bank,' she says.

'Must have been worth a few bob.'

We turn into Bell Street. I stop to point up at the pediment of Babbity Bowsters, but she's looking the other way. Further down, she catches the fenestrations of the City Halls.

'Same old story,' she says. 'Everything's a rebuild, a second phase. All the original stuff's lost, demolished, replaced.'

I trail in her wake, trying to keep up. Then I tug at her sleeve. 'Best survivors are down the bottom,' I say, pointing along the street.

Down at the foot of Candleriggs, a big bright gap looms at the junction with Argyle Street. As we approach, a giant yellow excavator growls like a dinosaur on top of a pile of rubble, its jaws crumping the last fragments into dust. I sigh.

'What's up?' she says.

'Don't believe it. Last surviving eighteenth-century tenements in the city. They've knocked them down.'

'Come here,' she says, and puts a hand on my shoulder. 'You take this stuff seriously.'

We stand together, arm in arm. Up on the gable of the tenement next door, a slice of the missing building is still preserved. Fireplaces, cupboards, wallpaper, even a framed picture, hang suspended in space. As we watch, a gust of wind blows a cloud of pink willowherb petals across the rubble, like the spirits of the inhabitants on their final flitting. Up on the invisible floors, suspended in space, I imagine the faint outline of folk passing back and forth, still going about their daily lives. And the longer they inhabited the space, the stronger their presence.

Then the moment passes. I bend down and select a piece of sandstone from the edge of the rubble. I unzip my backpack and drop it inside. Do I hear a muffled cry as I squash the wee man?

I lead the way to the Cross and up the hill. Rain greets us at the top of High Street. We cross the busy road and run down the path to the cathedral. Inside, we pass dozens of gleaming brass plaques, fixed to the walls.

'Same as Bristol Cathedral,' she says. 'Spoiled by the epitaphs of Victorian merchants – what did they think they were doing?'

In the choir, we speak to a guide whose badge says his name's Gordon.

'If you're into merchants,' Gordon says, 'you need to see the heads.'

'Aye right.'

'Across the road, behind the oldest house in the city.'

Back outside, the rain's stopped. We cross High Street at the lights. In the back garden of the old tenement, a row of larger-than-life sandstone heads are mounted on a wall.

'Wow!' Jenny says. 'Giant grots!'

I read the wee sign. 'TONTINE HEADS. USED TO BE MOUNTED ON THE TOWN HALL.' Some are likenesses of men, maybe merchants. But every second one's contorted in a tortured grimace.

Jenny's in her element, snapping the big stone heads from all angles.

I stop in front of one with a thin face and sour grimace. A shiver runs down my spine. I pull out the wee man. He bears a striking resemblance to the stone carving. I reach up and touch the big grot's nose.

Jenny clocks it too. 'Barry?' she says. Then she moves to the scowling face on the left. 'His alter ego?' she says.

The wee man twitches in my hand. I grab him tight and push him into the side pocket of my backpack.

Jenny reaches up and touches the contorted face. 'I wonder what the merchants did to become devils?'

***

Later, in bed, I take out my notebook, prop up the wee man, find a blank page and write.

No. 109. It's All Too Late

You've come wandering the streets. Scraping the cobbles with your boots.

Now I'm following your footsteps. Seeking out your haunts. Chasing your shadow.

If I hadn't found Jenny, I wouldn't have got further than the old city tales. Wouldn't have pursued you down the years, tried to get under your skin. There wouldn't have been you and me. Two people separated by 300 years of earth and time, covering your tracks and mine.

I've gone back to basics. Down to the layer you walked on. Up the Molendinar, in the footsteps of Mungo. Inside your bank. Seen your ugly mug. Put up with Jenny's awkward questions.

But it's all too late. The dates are wrong. The buildings are gone. I'm left with a row of stone faces. They're better than the old books. I can take a picture of them, touch them. Survivors from your time.

If only they could tell me your story.

Chapter 9

Jenny, Glasgow

The City's Story

The next morning, Hamish was sitting in front of a pile of Murdo's tomes. 'The books are fine,' he said, 'but it's the same few facts, repeated over and over until the original story's lost. Regurgitated for the tourists, transformed into legend.'

Jenny wasn't into books either. They might be OK for general background, but she preferred archives, where the book stuff comes from. 'Didn't they teach you the city's story in school?' she said.

'Had to cobble together our own version: St Mungo, Vikings, Bonnie Prince Charlie, Tobacco Lords, shipbuilding, and something about culture.'

'Same in Bristol,' she said. 'Vikings, Cabot, sugar, the Middle Passage, and stuff about building Concorde.'

It was kind of Hamish to let her stay for a bit. Murdo's den was a cosy refuge in the heart of the city. To keep her occupied, she'd got a few hours a week in a charity shop chain she'd worked for in Bristol.

Sugar, Not Tobacco

At lunchtime Jenny met Kelly, near her work.

'How's the quest going?' Kelly said.

'Hamish is too hung up on the old cliches,' Jenny said.

'Tobacco Lords?'

Jenny held out her phone. 'Found this line in an old book: "*Glasgow's first fortunes were made in sugar.*"'

'Sugar, not tobacco?' Kelly said. 'It's Hamish you need to convince, not me.'

Published

Jenny was impressed that Murdo had published before, and she decided to search his name in the big library. She found lots of his local history articles in obscure journals. They were well-written and she enjoyed them. But she'd avoided doing the same with her own research. History journals rarely got beyond a few specialists. Even Hamish hadn't mentioned Murdo's articles.

Personally, Jenny preferred to air her findings in her street tours.

Later, on a very old map, she managed to find the location of Billy's sugar house, that Cato had mentioned. She also checked out where the scrolls had been dug up.

Cato had been dug up inside what had been Billy's garden.

A Stranger

The morning after, Jenny went out early for a jog along the river. On her way back, she passed a little man coming down the stairs. He was clean-shaven and dressed in a denim jacket and jeans. Round his neck was a pink and blue checked scarf. Jenny described the stranger to Hamish.

'Sounds like Murdo's wee mate Eck,' he said. 'Lives in the trendy flats on the edge of the Green with his boyfriend.'

'Murdo OK with that?'

'Murdo's cool with anything, but Archie's old-school. Still winces if he meets an Asian or a Catholic. Even someone from England.'

'What about me?'

'Makes an exception for the pretty ones.'

Eck

The next time Jenny came back from a run, she met the wee man at the entrance to the close. She blocked his path. 'Eck?'

'Jenny?' he said.

'Trying to deceive us?'

He took her arm. 'Please,' he said, 'don't tell Hamish. Murdo's left me instructions.'

'He's been in touch?'

'Not since he disappeared.'

'You're leading us on a wild goose chase.'

A Bird in the West End

Eck pointed across to the Val D'Oro restaurant, where Murdo and his mates met every week. Inside, he fetched her a coffee and sat down. He took Jenny's hands and peered at her through metal-rimmed specs.

'You must be worried sick about Murdo,' Eck said.

'Hamish is, not me. When did you last see him?' Jenny said.

'Day before he disappeared. He'd been acting strange, even by Murdo standards. And he's getting more forgetful.'

'Where do you think he's gone?'

'There's been rumours of a bird in the West End.'

'At his age?'

'Ach, we're nay deid yet.'

'A girlfriend?

'Keeps his cards close to his chest, even to his mates. Met her up at the university last year. Mature student named Anna. Archie spotted them in a cafe in Byres Road.'

'Could Murdo be staying with her?'

Eck shook his head. 'She's from abroad. Read one of Murdo's articles. Found some common ground.'

'Could he have topped himself?' Jenny said.

'Murdo? No way!'

'Can't he finish his book himself?' she said. 'His history stuff's good.'

'He's been going downhill. Sometimes he's fine, then he has funny turns. Left me instructions in case he went away. But I don't know where he's gone.'

'Doesn't explain all the subterfuge,' she said.

'The scrolls triggered it all. Until then, he thought he had his book sorted.'

She jumped to her feet. 'You sent them!'

He held up his hands. 'Murdo thinks you're the best bet to unravel them.'

'But he barely knows me!'

Eck shook his head. 'Thought a lot of you.'

'Bollocks,' she said, 'he's playing us off against each other! Me, Hamish, even you.'

'Said two minds would get four times the answer.'

'And you're dropping the clues!' she said.

'Wee bit of encouragement.'

'Hell of a roundabout way of doing it,' she said.

'What does Hamish think about Cato?'

She fiddled with her spoon and saucer.

'You haven't told him!' he said.

'Was Murdo able to make much of the scrolls?'

'Enough to get the gist,' he said. 'You got any extracts?'

Jenny opened the file on her phone and chose an entry at random:

'Think, I think often of myself. A man from another continent, another world. Come to live in a growin town. Carryin the weight of a great secret. How a city is bein built on the shoulders of others.

As the sun sets, I walk around the side of Massa Billee's mansion. Touch, I touch the cold stone of the gable. Everythin here is bought with Massa's sugar money, from the labour of my brothers & sisters on the islands. In the low sun, as tears blur my sight, I pick out their faces in the whorls & cuts of the sandstone.'

'You'd better watch out,' Eck said. 'Archie's determined to get rid of them.' They sat watching the traffic outside, then he said, 'Any chance of a copy?'

Jenny thought about it. 'Long as you don't tell Hamish.' She reached out and shook his hand. 'Thanks for the coffee,' she said.

They swapped email addresses.

Jenny stood up, gave Eck a hug, and he headed off down the street.

The Journal of Cato

MARIA

Morn, this morn the mill gudgeon breaks & McConnelly tries to fashion a new one from the heart-wood of a Diddle-doo tree. I ride up with Maria on one of the janky carts carryin empty molasses firkins. We reach the horse mill & watch Scalags feedin cane through the mill roll. I help Maria count the carts of cane trash headin to fuel the sugar-boilin coppers. She recalls the time Colhoun's cart overturned & crushed two Scalags.

Maria tells many stories & I stand with ears a-listenin. 'Aye, & maybe half of them's true,' Irish says.

Later we see a ship arrive from the south & we go down to the quay to collect four bales of Negro smocks from Colhoun's agent in Scotland.

THE STORY OF THIS PLACE

Most nights, after dark, I go down to the midden behind the kitchen. Great is my fear that I will be caught after the curfew. I give two taps on Maria's window & climb inside. Many times I ask Maria about the story of this place. 'The story of this island is the story of my people,' says Maria.

One night, she closes her eyes & sits still for a long time.

Then slow, slow she starts to tell.

MARIA'S STORY

'They say the first sound of my people is heard far away to the south. With a splash of paddles, they move north. Up the chain of small islands from South America. Tarry at each for a while, grow a few crops.

'When they reach this island, a woman walks up the beach, out of the surf. A mountain pokes above the forest, circled by a ring of white cloud. The woman's skin is dark, perhaps reflectin her origin, perhaps from the sun. She is the very first to land on this island. Her people leave signs, carved into rocks.

'Many generations pass. My great grandfather peers from the forest, watches Cristoforo Colombo sail by. They say he discovered these islands. Claimed them for Espania. Claimed many things. Claimed my people was cannibals.

'Sixty-two years old am I, daughter of a Carib. Five brothers & three sisters have I. None of them's eaten nobody yet, far as I know.'

SPANISH FOR SNOW

One mornin I ask Maria the name of this place. She points up at the ring of white cloud around the peak of the mountain. 'Colombo looked up, named this island Nieves, Spanish for snows. Never been snow here, but Buckra don't know any better.'

Many times she repeats her tales. Store, I store them in my head.

PATHS & SIGNS

Lead, Maria leads me up the high paths in the forest. Shows me the old signs & markers. The narrow gap between two rocks. The big Calabash tree, too stubborn to cut down, markin the boundary between two plantations. The hot water risin from deep in the earth near Bath Springs.

One day Maria leads me up, past the faces carved in the rocks at Stone Fort. I run my fingers over the notches in the sacred stone. Tally the generations since her ancestors first walked up the beach. Countless people came & went. Climb, we climb higher to the cave full of sea-shells & stone tools. A thousand feet above the ocean.

Tell, she tells me the names of the islands. We look south to St Eustatius. On a fine day we can see as far to the east as Antigua.

FAMOUS MARINERS

Bring, Maria brings many books from the library in the big house, shows me how to pick out the letters & words, teaches me how to read n write better. Maria reads to me slow-slow, so that I feel the shape of each word.

One day I find some scraps of paper, write down notes, begin to capture what she says, hide my pages under the floor-boards of my office hut.

Many are the tales & large is the print, in Maria's books. Her favourite is *The Life of Raleigh*. Maria tells of the famous mariner, how he sailed to our island.

Howsoever, instead, I favour the story of Raleigh's African green monkey. Two monkeys, in fact. The breedin pair which escape from his ship in 1618, when he anchors off the island for two weeks to partake of its fresh fruit & water & write home to his lady.

More ships arrive. Trees are the crop hereabouts for a time. The monkeys are joined by men. Many ships arrive, cut down Lignum Vitae & other hardwoods, carry them away. Soon after, Raleigh loses his head in the Tower of London.

Lest I accord too much fame to the green monkey, there is a humble island saying here which perhaps Sir Walter should have heeded: The higher monkey climb, the more he show his bottompart.

THE FIRST SETTLERS

Walk, a man walks up the beach in the story. 'Tis one of Raleigh's party,' Maria says. His name is Warner. The green monkeys are joined by a band of settlers, who carve farmland out of the steep, tree-covered sides of the volcano. As the settlers burn & clear the forest, the monkeys are driven further up the mountain. Look, they look down from a great height at the newly enclosed fields.

Maria's book tells how the islands were given to a friend of the king, Sir James Hay of Kingask. Though he was a Scot, Sir James is better known as the Earl of Carlisle. Like my monkeys, Scots have been invisible in the early part of my tale. Nevertheless, many are the Scots on this island.

'What is Scot?' I say.

'Scots is like Engly,' Maria says, 'but tougher.'

After several big battles, hundreds of captured Scots are shipped here. After workin for a few years, most are set free & given land. If they survive the heat & the mosquitoes.

THE MEANEST OVERSEERS

Tell, Maria tells many tales about her people. 'But for the story of the Buckra,' she says, 'you must speak with my man, Colhoun.'

Next mornin, we draw alongside Colhoun topside, watchin six Scalags bailin cane trash. Colhoun raises his walkin stick & I lift my arm to ward off the blow, but he's just pointin.

'Aye, they say Scots is the meanest overseers,' says Maria, 'but they won't all beat you for pickin your nose.'

COLHOUN'S STORY

As Maria goes to fetch water, Colhoun speaks with loudness in his voice. 'Maria?' he says. 'Her words chatter like the pods of a Woman-tongue tree in the wind.'

Colhoun tells his stories to boast, but Maria is different. She holds the words in the air, tastes their meanin. Howsoever, there is nothin he likes better than to tell a good tale. He raises his voice & waves his stick in the air. His pet monkey rattles its fine chain, jumps from the edge of the porch onto his lap & startles us.

'Spanish wouldn't tolerate no settlers, but ships from many nations stopped. Old McDade dug up a clay pipe engraved WR in his high field. Says it belonged to Raleigh. Used it to smoke his best Virginia.'

'Father arrived as a cabin boy with Warner in twenty-four, after a ten-week crossing. Jungle came right down to the sea. Back-breaking work cutting down the trees, even harder grubbing up their roots & burning them. Father got a wee bit land. They call this parish Figtree, 'cause that's what Maria's people grew here. Good soil. Plenty sun. Plenty rain, most times. Grew divers root & bush plants, too many to mention.' Colhoun strokes the fur of his monkey on his lap. 'As the settlers burnt & cleared the forest, the monkeys were driven further up the mountain slopes.'

'Aye, aye,' Maria says, comin back into the room, 'but the biggest danger was the men with measurin sticks & string. Saw the land as something to be divided & owned. Laid out long narrow fields, stretchin down to the sea. Grew many crops. Changed the island forever. My people hid further up the slopes. Some was captured, some worked in the fields. Some settlers laid with our women. Fortunate was I. Met a kind settler.' She looks at Colhoun. 'Took me as his housemaid, then as his woman.'

'Monkeys?' says Colhoun, strokin his pet. 'Ach, anybody's accepted here, long as they work hard, they're not Spanish & their skin's not too dark. French, Irish, even us Scots. Married Maria in sixty-five, taught her English. Love of my life. Watered & fed me. Grew a wee bit Indian corn & cassava root, favoured by her family, made a fine bread. British wiped out Maria's ancestors at Bloody Point in 1626. More worth in Maria's stories than all the rules coming out of London. Always talked of taking her back with me to the old country. Doubt she could stand the cold.'

A gust of wind disturbs Colhoun's papers on the verandah table.

'Aye, the god of the wind respects no man. Returns every few years, reminds us of his power. Blows away everything cept the stone cellars. Other times, the earth god comes & shakes the buildings to pieces. Sank the first capital beneath the sea, so they say. This year, across on Montserrat, the fire mountain's ruined half the plantations.'

'Aye,' said Maria. 'No matter how loud they talk, the Buckra are not the most powerful hereabouts.'

Look, Colhoun looks at me. 'How long you been on this island, boy?'

'Five month.'

'How you avoid labouring in the canefields?'

'I read a wee bit Engly.'

'A Scalag knowing English?'

I open my mouth to explain, but Maria says, 'Leave him be. Dangerous thing for a boy to wag his tongue. Anythin out the ordinary draws a good whippin. Boy just wants to know the story of this place. Wants to write it down.'

'A Scalag speaking & writing English?' says Colhoun. 'Now I've seen everything!'

SUGAR CANE

Later, Maria continues.

'After a few decades, the fruits & berries favoured by the monkeys begin to disappear. As they watch from the trees, the whole island turns the same shade of green: sugar cane. Planted everywhere. In the fields, the sides of the ghuts, so much so that, lest we gorge on sugar cane, ships must bring in every morsel we consume.'

ARRIVALS & DEPARTURES

Sit, I sit on the porch & read from Colhoun's latest letters. Arrivals & departures, hogsheads of sugar, flagons of rum. He gives me a wee bit bread if I write replies on his behalf.

Try, he tries to persuade the sons of his friends to come out. 'Lots of Scots have come here to make their fortune,' he says. 'Indentured for a few years, then got a wee bit of land like myself. Turned into good farmers. My friend McIntyre was brought a prisoner from the battle at Dunbar. Made a good farmer too, after he'd worked his time. But times are changing. Now most of us small farmers are being bought out by the big planters.'

'As the sugar work becomes too hard for the white servants, my monkeys are not the only creatures captured & brought here across the ocean. The planters find that the sugar cultivation is too heavy for free indentured labour. The Royal African Company sets up their fort here. This island has the pick of the best Scalags. Many Scots are brought as overseers. Good news for the Scots, but less so for those in their charge.'

'Another young man walks up the beach out of the surf,' says Maria. 'His skin is dark, so dark it could be called black. He walks with difficulty, as his ankles are held by a heavy chain. One of many dark-skinned men & women brought to these islands against their will. One of millions.'

Nevis

As Jenny finished Cato's next jotter, she doodled at the bottom of the last page:

Nieves.
Neves.
Nevis.
Island in the Caribbean?

Chapter 10

Hamish, Galloway

Next morning at breakfast, Jessica's washing is black. I'm not sure about the weather, but it matches my mood. I dip into more of Murdo's books, but they tell me nothing new. Over the centuries, they repeat the same few facts. The more modern the book, the more the story's diluted.

Murdo seemed to have reached the same conclusion.

No. 79. The City Books

One way or another, the city's story comes from books. Things feel safe when they're written down. You know where you are with them. But the world of the city's writers is tightly enclosed. For centuries, their pen has been held by those who seek to promote their own image, not the truth. Their story, the story of the rich and famous, is hypocrisy.

Each successive history feeds on the previous one, in an incestuous cycle, until the original story is so watered down it is lost. The city has reached that curious sense of distorted reality, where its myths matter more than the truth.

The world's images of Glasgow are the creation of vivid imagination, supported by selective interpretation. And though it's much too young to be a classical city, it's already a mythological one.

To its historians it's like Jerusalem in the school Bible. The city lies at the centre of their world.

Maybe it's time they went for a long walk and looked back.

***

I stand in front of Murdo's shelves, pick a hefty old city history at random and weigh it in my hand. Then I drop it on the floor, with a satisfying thump. I pick another and do the same. Lucky Mary's not downstairs.

After a few minutes the top shelf is empty. Dust swirls in the air in the rays of sunlight streaming through the window. I stand in the middle of the floor, knee-deep in books, fighting for breath.

Ach, they're thicker than bricks. A foostie brown barrier to common sense.

Jenny appears back from the shops. 'What've you done?' She picks up a book, its spine broken. 'Even the first editions!'

'Remember on your tour,' I say, 'you asked me if the city stories were true?'

'So?'

'Ach, they're all mince.'

'But you found Barry in most of them?'

'I've been wondering,' I say, 'if you're not good with names, or if you call him Barry to wind me up.'

She isn't listening. She stumbles through the pile of books, picking out the valuable ones.

'Like I said before, it's the same two or three facts repeated over and over.' I pick up wee Billy. 'And another thing. They only cover the end of Billy's life. I can't write his story without the start and middle.'

She gives up and sits down in the middle of the pile of books. 'We've been doing it all in reverse,' she says. 'It's always the same with the rich and famous – we start with their success and epitaphs. But we need to go right back to the start.'

'Back to his birth?'

Jenny sneezes, blows her nose and climbs over the books to the noticeboard. She pins up a big piece of paper and picks up a thick felt pen. She writes up the bones of a family tree, with the spaces left blank. 'Birth, parents, grandparents.'

I go over to the fireplace, pick a block of stone. 'Prefer something solid.'

'Need to squeeze a rock pretty hard to eke out its story.' She waves her arm at the rows of files and papers above the books. 'There must be something here.'

'Take forever to check.'

'You can't be bothered?' she says. 'What about his desk?' She wades through the books to the big bureau and plomps down in Murdo's captain's chair. She runs her hands along the armrests. 'He build this too?'

'Four oak beams we found in Narrow Wynd. Sliced them up with his bench saw and carved them into the chair.'

She taps the desk. 'Looks like the wee model you gave me.'

Three solid drawers make up the lower parts. When she lifts the lid, there's a faint aroma of hardwood, inks and pencil shavings. At the back is a myriad of pigeonholes, nooks and crannies, fretted and carved. Wee drawers hold sticks of sealing wax, staples and paper clips. I lift the heavy manual typewriter to the side, fetch a door chair and sit beside her. Then I reach under the folding leaf, turn a boss disguised as a floral decoration and slide open a long drawer beneath the fold-down lid.

'A secret drawer!' she says.

'Part of the ritual when I came up as a boy. He always had something inside. A comic, sweets, a toy.'

On top are some old black-and-white glossy magazines, 1960s vintage. Jenny lifts them out. Half-naked women pose in lacy girdles and suspenders. 'Porn!' she says.

I grab one and flick through. 'Milder than today's tabloids.'

'You a connoisseur?'

My cheeks redden. 'Maybe Murdo put them on top to distract nosy relatives.'

'That's what they all say.'

I reach underneath and feel for another catch. It releases a false bottom in the drawer. I lift out a cardboard box. On the lid is a pencil drawing of a wee figure in a cocked hat. 'Should have checked this earlier!'

Inside are some old notebooks and papers. Jenny picks one up. Billy's name is on the cover, in childish script. 'Diaries?' she says.

I pick up another and open it carefully. 'Just what I need to write up his childhood!'

Underneath the wee books is a pile of old papers. 'Letters?' she says.

I study the top one. 'Signed by Billy!'

'Bit too convenient?'

'A set-up?'

'Whole quest's a set-up,' she says. 'The wee models, the Filofax. Why couldn't Murdo write it up himself?'

'Has a problem finishing things.'

'He's unwell?'

'Ach, he's always been crazy. Now he's confused.'

I put the letters in a big envelope and open one of Billy's diaries. It's so fragile the cover comes off in my hands. It's more like a notebook than a modern diary. The date and month are handwritten at the top, and I can't find a year. Jenny opens another. 'They're easier to read!'

'Easier than what?' I say.

Inside the front cover is a sort of summary of Billy's youth, in his own words. I fetch the wee Filofax and take a green cardboard divider from a pocket in the back. I clip it in near the front and write: BILLY'S DIARIES in big letters. Then I start copying the first page of the diary onto a blank sheet.

No. 110. My Father's Library

I was born in the cattle lands of Galloway, of a good family. Being the fifth son of the house, and not bred to any trade, my head began to be filled very early with rambling thoughts.

Today I overheard Mother in the pantry tell Cook that I am a boy of few words. Nevertheless, though my older brothers attend school in Glasgow and Edinburgh, and are groomed for the estate, the Church and the law, Father sends me to the local parish school. Perhaps tis because, as a heritor, he seeks to recoup his support for the school. Perhaps tis because of my fascination with measuring things. Sailing toy boats down the burn, laying out wee markers along the banks, measuring their rate of progress after different amounts of rain.

And when I started school, I could read and count to a hundred, thanks to my elder sister Mary, who taught me, and to my interest in my father's library at Garthland.

***

'He was born in Galloway,' I say.

'Ireland!'

'Galloway, not Galway.'

'Let's go.'

I check my phone. 'Weather's meant to be fine tomorrow. Catch the early train?'

She picks up the wee man. 'How long's Murdo been chasing him?'

'The city stuff, or Billy?'

She taps Billy's wee hat.

'Not long.'

'Thought he carved him years ago?'

***

Jenny goes round the charity shops to find some cycling gear. At dusk, she's working on her laptop, then she goes to bed early.

She's right. I need to keep working on Billy's story. Anything to keep her on my wavelength. The quest thing's fine, but it's got too many ups and downs to keep me sane.

I don't know what I'll do if she leaves.

I open her laptop, curious to see what she's spending so much time on, but I don't know her password. What's her date of birth? I'm not even sure.

Up in the wee eyrie, I listen to the night sounds of the city. There's something secure about being hidden up a tower in the city centre. Maybe I can hide up here with Jenny for the rest of my life?

Back downstairs, I lie on Murdo's bed. Although I'm tired, I can't sleep. It's the right time to open the cabinet and pour a half of whisky: I'm Scottish, after all. Instead, I go to the fridge and fetch a can of Irn-Bru. I could try to explain why I don't drink, but that would be pandering to one of the reasons why I don't: that I should need an excuse for *not* doing something.

***

Next morning I'm up too early for Jessica. Jenny claims she hasn't ridden a bike for years, but she's dressed in Lycra shorts and a colourful top. She looks ready for the Tour de France. Down in the close, I unlock my folding bike and push it alongside. One of the advantages of living in the centre is seeing it when it's deserted. Litter blows across our path like tumbleweed in a Western, and a van drops a bundle of newspapers in a doorway.

The early Stranraer train's a rickety old diesel. We might be early, but behind us, four big Irishmen are already into the bevvy, talking at the tops of their voices. I follow Jenny through to the quiet carriage. It's almost empty, apart from another Irish voice shouting eight-figure numbers into a phone. We pop in our earphones and turn up the volume. The train follows the coast to Girvan, then cuts inland through forest. On my map, I plot a circular route, taking in Billy's childhood haunts.

When we arrive in Stranraer, we find a bike shop which has just opened. I hire Jenny a bike and helmet for the day for £20, plus a deposit, on my card. We have breakfast beside the railway, facing the pier. Jenny looks around the deserted cafe,

'Bit of a dead-end town?' she says.

'Ferry used to leave here for Ireland until they moved it up the coast, away from the railway station.'

'Sounds sensible. How far are we cycling?' she says.

'Just a few miles.' I unfold the map and stand the wee man on top of Stranraer.

'This is where he started out?' Jenny says.

'Not far from here.'

We collect our bikes and head uphill. The wind's against us, and Jenny spends a lot of time pushing. 'The gears,' she says, 'they keep skipping.'

We swap bikes and head north, up deserted back roads. Jenny gets on much better with the wind behind her. After an hour, we reach a headland overlooking Loch Ryan. Over on the far side of the loch, the Larne ferry departs from Cairnryan. It heads north up the middle of the loch, then turns into big waves in the open sea. I slip out Billy's diary,

No. 111. Ships from the Indies

Today, Father took us east to the Bay of Fleet, so-called because part of the Spanish fleet was wrecked there. In the inn at Gatehouse, an old

man told us how, as a child, the masts of many great sailing ships could be seen poking from the bay.

In stormy weather I like to ride north to Loch Ryan with my brother David, to where vessels from the West Indies, bound for Clyde, take refuge from the storm.

***

'Brought me all the way just for that line?' she says.

'Giving you a sense of place.'

'Sore bum and sorer legs.'

'You should have got a bike with a lassie's saddle.'

We stand together, Lycra-clad hips touching, looking out over the loch. Then the moment passes. We put on our cycling gloves and head south. After another hour, we reach a farm with grand gateposts and a tree-lined avenue. Jenny reads out the name: 'Garthland.'

'Billy's home,' I say.

Up the driveway is a farmhouse, bigger than average but nothing special. Facing the gates, across the main road, is a mound. We climb the gate and eat our picnic lunch on the grass, watched by black-and-white cattle. I dig at the ground with my heels, kicking out stones.

'What you doing?' she says.

I lift out a square piece of sandstone, edged with moulding. 'Old castle stood here.'

'This why we came here, to fetch a bit of old stone?'

'And to get you some exercise.'

She wrestles with me for the stone. 'It's OK really,' she says. 'I mean, it's mad, and I'm knackered and my hair's ruined, but I enjoy an adventure. How much further?'

'Only a mile or two.'

'I've heard they have cars out here in the sticks.'

'Can't beat a bike for seeing the lie of the land.' I haven't admitted I've never learned to drive.

Five minutes down the road, we turn left up a farm track and stop at a circular mound of stones on the edge of a field. 'Another castle?'

There's a faded signboard at the side, with a sketch. 'Wait a minute!' I unzip my bag and pull out the wee circular tower. 'Another windmill.'

'Aye, but for grinding oats, not sugar.'

No. 112. Three Things

Three things fascinate me on the road to school. The first is Culgroat Windmill. This day, I watched the miller trim the sails and carry sacks of grain out to his cart. Father told me how, across the ocean, his friend Colhoun employs a windmill to crush the juice from his sugar crop.

In the side of my windmill I have a secret slot for my precious things: a brass ruler, a pebble, and a shell from a tropical island. I know every stone and opening in the wall of the mill.

On windy days, I come to sit and read and watch the turning of the vanes.

***

Over the fence, I fetch another piece of stone, then put it away and pick a smaller piece. I zip it into the pannier of Jenny's folding bike.

'Expect me to carry your rubble?' she says.

'Old cycling rule. One with the best bike's the donkey.'

'Want to swap?'

A bit further along the road are a few cottages. The sign says: STONEYKIRK.

'Where Billy went to school,' I say.

We stop outside the church.

No. 113. The Coat of Arms of Glasgow

The second thing which fascinates me is in the tower of Stoneykirk Kirk. On my return from school today, I met the parish minister. He recognised that I am a curious boy and led me up the narrow turnpike stair to the tower. In the garret hung the great bell, cast with a wee picture of a tree, a bell and a fish on the side.

'The coat of arms of the town of Glasgow,' said the minister. 'Cast by a Dutchman thirty years ago but shipwrecked in Luce Bay.'

This is the tree that never grew,
This is the bird that never flew,

This is the fish that never swam,
This is the bell that never rang.

***

'Bit of a coincidence,' she says, 'that Glasgow's greatest merchant grew up beside the church which pinched the city's bell?'

On the way back to Stranraer, we loop around higher ground and stop to look across rolling fields, where Galloway cattle graze.

'His father owned all of this?' Jenny says.

'And Billy mapped it all.'

No. 114. A Plan to Survey the Lands

The third thing which fascinates me is the burn which runs through the estate. On the way to school we build wee boats and sail them down the burn. I note how, after heavy rain, the water flows faster. Today we cut toy boats from sticks, and I name my boat Speedwell, and it beat David's all the way from the standing stone at Cuddy's acre down to Munro's field.

One day, we follow the burn all the way down to the sea at Luce Bay.

In my fifteenth year, I have an idea to make my mark on the land. I order five hundred of the straightest willow poles on the Cumbria boat that comes via Whitehaven. With the help of two boys from the estate, I lay out a straight line all the way across Calf Park, each pole separated by a distance of two chains. And I continue my straight line east and west to the bounds of my father's lands.

And when I am finished, I lay shorter offsets, perpendicular to my great line. And in this manner, I measure the whole of Father's estate. And in the Factor's office I pin out a large piece of vellum on the big table and draw a pencil map from my measurements. Then I take a box of water-colours and paint the pasture light green, the arable land yellow and the bogs brown. I colour the hedges dark green, the roads grey and the burns blue.

And when I am finished, Father comes to view my map. And he stands back, removes his hat and scratches his head. Tis the first time Father has seen his lands split and quantified.

'But more than half my lands are brown bog?' he says.

I point to a tabulation in the corner, where I have listed the area of each tenants' lands in acres, roods and falls, broken down into arable, pasture and moss. 'Aye, Father. But I have a plan to straighten the burn and drain the high moss,' I say.

And Father almost believes me.

***

'Last lap,' I say.

We climb back onto our bikes and head back to Stranraer. We take Jenny's bike back to the shop, and catch the next train back to Glasgow. Jenny falls asleep beside me and is soon breathing deeply, leaning against my shoulder. I lay a hand on her arm, lots of Billy thoughts going through my head. But right now I'm just happy to have a new friend.

***

Shortly after we get back to the flat, the doorbell rings.

'Mary?' I say. It's late. I tiptoe down the stairs in my stocking soles and peer through the spyhole.

Archie! He's got his own key, but the door's bolted from the inside, so he knows I'm here.

The letterbox flips open. I press my back into the corner and hold my breath until the flap shuts and the footsteps recede.

***

Next morning, my legs ache from our cycling trip. Jessica's there at breakfast, through the chimneys. Today, for once, her colours are mixed. So is the weather.

'What's the plan,' Jenny says, 'once you lose the Bristol flat?'

'Murdo always said he'd leave me this attic den. Sent me legal papers about it.' I've been trying to avoid thinking about Bristol and jobs.

'You're special to him.'

'He's not one for affection.'

'You've got a place to stay in Glasgow?'

'Mary would dispute that.'

'Can't we invite her up?'

'It's Archie we need to meet.'

'I'd like that.'

'He's a pest.'

'Maybe he can tell us more about Murdo?'

***

Archie's flat's in Parnie Street, behind the Tron Theatre, above second-hand sci-fi bookshops and tattoo artists. He meets us at the door, running his fingers through his long white hair. When he sees Jenny, he takes a step back.

Round the table, in the bay window, are four chairs, all the same design but different shades of wood.

'Door chairs!' Jenny says, her fingertips caressing the polished grain.

Archie nods. 'Aye, Anchor Lane, Havannah Street, Bell Street and Monteith Row. The old door from Anchor Lane nearly killed us carrying it up the stairs. Three-inch-thick ebony from the Congo.'

We make small talk about Murdo. Jenny's presence keeps it civil.

Then Archie says, 'Murdo leave you anything?'

'Told you before he didn't.'

Archie stands up. 'The old trunk from the hole in the ground. You seen it?'

'Trunk?'

'Cool it, you two,' says Jenny.

'Inside was a roll of old papers,' Archie says. 'Murdo tried to read them, but I don't think he got far. Problem is, I've got the money together to publish his *Great Work*. But I won't tolerate him trashing the city.'

'Think he found something dodgy?' I say.

Archie sits back. 'Ach, he was cracking up.' He gets up and pours more coffee, but only for Jenny. 'Made some kind of discovery, spent his last few weeks up in his den, poring over old papers. But he wasn't fit for it.'

'Papers?' says Jenny.

'He always had the writing bug, but this time it was an obsession. One day I met him in our usual haunt. He was worn out,' says Archie.

'Wasn't it easier,' Jenny says, 'now he's chasing one man?'

Archie turns on me. 'A man?'

I shake my head at Jenny, but Archie sees me. 'Mentioned a merchant,' I say.

'Merchants are his mates,' Archie says. 'Even if they're dead and buried centuries ago. He's on a mission, but he's lost the plot. Talked of giving it all up. You know better than anyone how history's his life. Then he went downhill.'

'Wish I'd known,' I say.

'Next time I met him, he says, "I'm setting sail for a tropical island."'

Jenny catches my eye.

'"Caribbean," Murdo said. So I says to him, "Is this another of your Crusoe things?" "Crusoe?" Murdo says. "It's the answer to the city's origins. The whole malarkey." "You're going to sail there?" I says. "Aye, replicate the voyage of the original sojourners," Murdo says. "I'm going to book a cruise full of old codgers, then I'll jump ship."'

The wee man twitches in my pocket.

'"Jump ship?" I says. "Murdo, you're eighty effing years old."'

We sit in silence. Then Jenny changes the subject, and admires the colourful paintings on the wall.

Archie seems to have warmed to her. 'Into art?' he says.

'Dabbled a bit in acrylics.'

'Know the Glasgow Boys?'

She looks puzzled.

'You need to see the Art Gallery. How about lunch tomorrow?'

'It's a date.'

On our way back to the flat, I say, 'You shouldn't get too close to Archie. He's dangerous.'

'Think I want to jump him? That was Dave's problem. Wanted to control me.'

***

Jenny goes off to do an afternoon shift in the charity shop. When she comes home, she's quiet. For the first time, she isn't carrying a bag of clothes.

'What's up?'

'New girl started today. Asked me where I came from,' she says.

'Hope you said Bristol.'

'Yep, but then she said, "Where did your parents come from?"' Jenny goes over to the sink to make a cup of tea, then turns to me. 'Maybe you're only chasing this colonial stuff 'cause I'm black?'

'Shit, you've rumbled me!'

She takes a square parcel from her bag, wrapped in brightly coloured paper. She bends down and pecks me on the forehead. 'Happy birthday.'

'How did you know?'

'Some tips for your writing.'

It's a thick book titled *Sugar and Empire*. It looks expensive and new, but she's forgotten to remove the 99p sticker. The spiel on the back cover calls it an 'epic': '*Those who chose to gallantly undertake the fearsome Atlantic crossing in search of a brave new world were generally tough – or else dangerously foolish.*'

Next time she leaves the room, I bury it under a pile of magazines. Maybe I'm looking for something more down to earth?

***

Next morning, Jenny goes to meet Archie. I take a ride up the Clyde walkway. On the way back, crossing the Green, I meet Eck.

'On my way to stick this in your letterbox,' Eck says. 'Came a couple of days ago. Postmark's too blurred to read.'

Eck hands me the card, with a picture of palm trees and a sandy beach. The message side's blank.

'Tropical island?' Eck says.

'Archie said Murdo might have gone off on a cruise?'

'Murdo never told Archie the truth.'

'You think he's got worse?'

'It's like his first book all over again. He'd gathered all the jigsaw pieces but couldn't fit them together.'

'Should have noticed.'

‘Didn’t trust anyone else with what he’d found. Except you.’

‘Gives me a bit of responsibility.’

Eck waves a hand and heads off.

***

When Jenny comes back, I’m sitting by the south window. I hand Jenny Eck’s postcard. ‘One of the books said Billy spent time on a tropical island, met his wife there.’

‘More secrets?’ she says.

‘Thought you’d say it was far-fetched.’

‘You mean too far away from Glasgow to be important?’

While she makes supper, I pick up another book she’s brought back from work. It’s a thick hardback with a purple cover: *The Glasgow Novel.*

Later, I take it and climb up to the wee eyrie. The sky’s turned grey, but it’s still dry. If I can sort Billy’s story, how should I write it? I’ve got no experience beyond dry engineering reports. Jenny’s purple book tells of Guy McCrone, Alasdair Gray, Archie Hind. They wrote about Arthur Moorhouse, Duncan Thaw and Mat Craig. An interesting bunch of characters, but none of them go back as far as Billy.

Maybe I should write up Billy’s story as a novel, not boring history.

No. 115. The Bones of Your Puzzle

You’ve come slipping into my head with your childhood tales. Pestering me to visit your boyhood haunts.

I’ve gathered more bits of your jigsaw. One of the corner pieces. Where you were born. A few of the early bits: your childhood, your family, your ambitions. I’ve stood at the gates of your father’s house. Walked the land you measured. Touched your favourite things: windmills and bells and burns.

But that’s only the bones of your puzzle. What about the other clues of the pieces? The tropical island where you met your wife. The time spent in the army. You need to come clean with me.

Chapter 11

Jenny, Glasgow

Protect the City

Archie took Jenny to the big red sandstone museum in the West End. Jenny was bowled over. It had paintings by most of the Impressionists. They only had time to cover a small part. Archie had to leave early, but first he took Jenny to the cafe. He only seemed to know about Hamish's part in the quest.

'Murdo wanted to tarnish the city,' Archie said.

'Isn't it big enough to stand up for itself?'

'Know anything about scrolls?' Archie said.

Jenny shrugged and looked out the window.

'Buried for centuries in the ground?'

'Doubt if paper would survive long if it was buried.'

'Murdo had them. I need them.'

'Into research?' Jenny said.

'Need to bury them again.'

'Suppress evidence?'

'Some of us are born to protect the city's image.'

Jenny was about to laugh, but she saw the look in Archie's eye and left it.

A Secret Knowledge

Once Archie had gone, Jenny carried on exploring the museum by herself.

Glasgow was a huge port, much bigger than Bristol. Must have had African connections. But all she could find were tribal masks in a big glass case. From Sierra Leone, the Republic of Congo and Benin. The theme of the display was 'Masks Which Share a Secret Knowledge'. Jenny knew these countries were a main source of slave labour.

Were Glasgow's connections with Africa still a secret?

Level With Hamish

Jenny hadn't slept properly for several nights. Apart from the hard mattress, several things were tormenting her.

I need to get home to my work. But what will I do with Cato's story? Is Murdo controlling me? Should I tell Hamish? I like him, maybe more than like, but he's too trad Scottish to show his feelings. Maybe I need that, how he accepts me as a friend, takes everything slow. Right now, slow's good.

Slow bollocks. We're heading for a showdown.

The Journal of Cato

HARVEST

Morn, this morn, Maria drives the janky cart up the rutted track, whippin the mule with her supple-jack. Wavin her jippi-jappa hat to drive a flock of hoppin-dicks from the track. Sugar juice leaks into the stone bowl cradlin the copper, with a great hissin of steam from the trash fire in the vault below.

'Worst time for a break,' she says, 'just at harvest.'

Many carts of freshly cut cane line the road to the works. Cane which will spoil by sundown if not crushed & boyl'd. Make, I make notes in the book as Maria tallies the carts. As each one passes, she reaches over & picks a stalk, breaks it, tastes the juice. With a lick o' the whip, the mule draws the cart to the front of the queue.

SECRETS

On the way back, we take the old track topside, along the edge of the forest. I help Maria down from the cart. Tell, Maria tells many stories, handed down by her ancestors. Secrets from before the Buckra came.

Young, when she was young, Maria was cook, but most is now done by Pedro. Maria's skin is brown, darker than a Buckra, lighter than a Scalag. In the quiet times she teaches me better Engly. Brings me scraps from the kitchen. Tells me names of birds: the Chicken Hawk, the Frigate-bird. Names of bushes: the Cush-cush, Silk-banana & Cattle-tongue.

Above the windmill, two Scalags work, cuttin the forest edge, grubbin up roots. Maria tells me the names of trees with fruit & leaves which heal: the Belly-ache bush, Wild Coffee & Knuckle-Seed. Said this island was once covered in forest, too thick to enter. But soon the canefields will reach topside the mountain.

KINDNESS

Maria turns across the garden to join her man Colhoun on the verandah. Old, she is too old to look after their plot & keeps the great house when the owner sails to the other islands.

'Wait there,' she says & turns into the shade. Return, she returns with somethin wrapped in a small cloth. She looks both ways & slips it to me. Where the path passes in the shadow of a Jack-fruit tree, I unwrap Maria's bundle & take a bite from yesterday's bread. There is nothin worth more to a Scalag than a wee bit food.

Where would I be on this island without Maria's kindness?

PROUD

Ask, I ask Maria what possessed the Buckra to endure the long & perilous voyage to this tiny island.

She reads from a big book. 'The early settlers describe *"brilliant sunlight & a palette of splashy colours: startlingly green vegetation, fruits & flowers in flaming reds & yellows, mountains in shimmering blues & greens shading to deep purple, the moon & stars radiant & sparkling at night, & the encircling sea a spectrum of jewelled colours, from cobalt to silver."* Perhaps there were some advantages,' she says.

How early did the first settlers drive the monkeys uphill? Colhoun says this island is the first colony in the fledgling British Empire.

That soon it will become the richest. Richer than the whole of North America.

The monkeys should be proud.

I LOOK AWAY

Stand, I stand on the shore. The sun is already bright. The view is fine, down the slopes & out to sea. In the distance, a ship heads for St Eustatius.

But look, sometimes I must look away. This mornin Niven beat & bucked young Nancy, age fifteen, by the side of the road & threw her in the ditch. Just now, down the trash path, I hear the cries of a young boy as Campbell the overseer cuts him with the lash. Topside McDonald's piece, two dark figures swing in the trade wind from a Hookie-tree.

BANNED

Sit, I often sit on the porch with Colhoun, read to him from his latest letters. Arrivals & departures, hogsheads of sugar, flagons of rum.

'Sold his wee farm ten years ago to Stapleton,' says Maria.

'Aye, most of the small farmers been bought out by the big planters,' says Colhoun.

'Captain Gibson, just arrived from the Clyde on the Mary,' says Maria. 'Word at home is that Scots is banned from here. English Navigation Acts.'

'The more we're banned the less trouble I get, so long may the rumour last,' says Colhoun. 'My sugar goes on the Nelly to Gravesend, but I sent a hogshead or two on the Adventure for New Port Glasgow, on the Clyde. They say tis a good port & that Glasgow may even exceed Bristol in a few years.'

I STORE TALES IN MY HEAD

Store, I store Colhoun's tales in my head, write them down each day at day cut. Pass, we pass back down the track to the great house. I tarry a while. Colhoun sits on the verandah. I crouch below, behind a bull hoof bush. Bring, Maria brings me a glass of water.

'But now a new day's dawning,' says Colhoun. 'Scots is rising up the ladder. Make them young gentlemen,' he says. 'Beat the Bristol dandys any day.'

Recent months, Colhoun's had me writin to an old friend in Scotland. Has an opening on Colonel Smith's plantation next door, for a trainee overseer. Colhoun's tryin to persuade his friend's son to come out.

'Rise to the highest heights,' Colhoun says, 'become a manager. Maybe even a planter. Great is the opportunity here for a young man with ambition.'

Chapter 12

Hamish, Port Glasgow

Next morning at breakfast, Jessica hangs out lots of grey towels. I'm not sure why: the sky's overcast. I should be going back down to Bristol to clear the flat, but it's easy to avoid. Jenny's decided to stay a bit longer, to help chase Billy. I have a recurring dream where Murdo comes back in the middle of the night and catches me in his bed. I'm glad Jenny's here. I love it up here in the den, but I wouldn't last long on my own. Murdo's presence hangs in every corner.

After breakfast, we head outside. Jenny takes my arm and leads me a few blocks up the street. 'Did more checking,' she says. 'South Sugar House stood here.'

'Thought it was Glasgow tobacco, Bristol sugar?'

'You think it was so clear-cut?'

Sugar? I've still got a few things to sort out.

Later, I stand the wee man on the window ledge, crouch down and face him. 'I need your help,' I tell him. 'What about the claim that your fortune came from your marriage?'

I find the right page in my notes. One of the old books claims Billy's spouse was a 'plantation heiress'. Sugar plantation?

I google the phrase and scroll through images of dark-skinned workers toiling in the sun.

When I was a child, Mum taught me to put my problems and fears in an old mahogany chest at the end of my bed. She called it 'Pandora's box'. Over the years, it worked well. Now, instead of a chest, I take a sticky label, write *Pandora* on it in thick felt pen, and stick it over the zipped compartment in the back leaf of my leather folder. I start a list of dodgy words. Then I fold it in half, slip it into my Pandora section and zip it shut.

Maybe Archie's right. There's some things I can't write about. Not for myself, not for Murdo, not even for my city feud with Jenny.

At the big desk, I lay aside the diaries, and bring out the wee man. I slip out the envelope with Billy's letters, and start copying out the first one.

No. 116. Measure, Measure, Measure

Dear James,

I have engaged Watt the surveyor, at my expense, to measure all seventeen wynds of the town. I am in hope that the Council will now see fit to commission Watt fully, to prepare a plan to further the improvements. The laying out of King Street is now well advanced and Prince Street should follow. However, I have again petitioned the town clerk to discourage the erection of unauthorised timber buildings, lest we see a recurrence of the great fire.

Measure, measure, why measure? My friends say tis my greatest obsession. But measuring is the first stage of improvement. Foolish is the man who does not measure, for he knows not what he owns.

***

I show it to Jenny.

'Might have been born more than three hundred years ago,' I say, 'but his language is quite modern.'

'Aye, no "wee braw lassies".'

'Sir Walter Scott has a lot to answer for.'

She picks up her sandwich and cup of tea. 'Need to see the view again.'

I lead the way up the spiral stair. We sit, side by side, and eat our lunch, looking way down the river. Jenny's curly hair blows across her face. Over the back court and across Bridge Street, the sun picks out the shadow of the old steeple. I bring up a model of the same tower.

'Merchants Steeple,' I say. But each level's distorted and twisted, like a reflection in a rippling pond.

Jenny runs her pinky along the twisted sides. 'How'd it get so warped?'

'It's the way he made it. Said it gave as true a likeness as the city's histories.'

'Ha ha.'

'One of the few buildings Billy would have known,' I say.

'Looks like something in Amsterdam.'

Right now, it's partly shrouded in scaffolding. 'It's one of Murdo's favourites,' I say, 'but he never got a piece of stone.'

'Serious about the stone stuff?' Jenny takes her cup downstairs to the sink and starts to put on her coat. 'Let's go,' she shouts.

'Wait a minute.' I go and change my shorts for long trousers, and put on a shirt and tie. I expect a sarky comment, but she looks me up and down and nods.

'Hope you're taking me somewhere nice.'

I grab my jacket and follow her downstairs, through the back lane and across Bridge Street. Outside the steeple are two Portakabin offices, stacked one on top of the other. The side door to the tower's open.

'No,' I say and turn away.

'Come on.'

Inside, yellow vests and hard hats hang from a row of hooks. Footsteps come round the corner, and a man appears in a boiler suit, carrying a hammer and mason's chisel.

'Suits are up top,' he says, and walks on.

We don yellow vests and yellow hard hats and adjust the size. Then I change my mind, hand Jenny a white hat, and swap mine for white too.

'White's for bosses,' I say. 'If anyone challenges us, we're from the council. Come to take photos from the top.'

We start climbing the stairs. After a bit, we step through an opening, out onto the scaffold. Someone's been repairing one of the big louvres over the windows. Pieces of old stained timber lie scattered on the deck. I choose a big piece, but footsteps descend from above. Jenny shakes her head and I lay it back down. We move round to the far side of the scaffold, pressing our backs to the wall. The voices continue past us. We wait, then I turn to climb back down. But Jenny says, 'This is our big chance!'

I turn and follow her up to the next level, then the next, higher and higher, getting hotter and hotter in my tight yellow vest.

Finally, we reach the top of the scaffold, gripping the rail. With my other hand, I hold the wee wooden man in my pocket, trying not to look down. On top of the spire is a golden ship. From street level it's tiny, but up here it's huge. The sky's blue, with white clouds. We're high above Murdo's wee eyrie, just across the car park. I touch the stone at the top of the steeple.

No. 117. The Merchants Steeple

Dear Brother,

My ship Mary, commanded by John Murdoch, is late. I requested a message, by express, from the New Port, advising me of its safe arrival. This morn I climbed the Merchants Steeple and was relieved, with the aid of a ship's glass, to see a string of lighters with Murdoch at the prow, approaching the Broomielaw with the rising tide.

I have no time for the man and his excuses. I go down and dismiss him on his arrival.

***

We both take photos in every direction. Someone's been repairing the lightning conductor. Three hundred and fifty years of weathering have left the stone around the top in poor shape. The softest parts are being replaced with new pale-coloured stone. I select a piece of the old dark stone from a heap on a wooden pallet on the scaffold.

'Murdo would give his eye teeth to get his hands on the lot,' I say. 'He could build a scale model of the tower, not just in wood but in original stone!'

Then we turn back down and I pick up my piece of timber on the way. We pass two workmen and a woman at the bottom, all wearing safety glasses and hard hats. I nod to them and pass them by. Nobody challenges us.

'Maybe you still look like an engineer,' Jenny says.

We cross the road, back to the flat. As we climb the stairs, we realise we're still wearing the hard hats and vests.

Upstairs the front door is open. Murdo's shelves of notes have been ransacked. I check the cupboards and the attic, but whoever it was has gone.

'Burglars?'

'They've only messed with Murdo's papers,' I say. 'Anything of yours missing?'

'Take ages to check.'

'Archie?'

'He's got a key. Could come up any time.'

'Whoever it was must have been watching us. Maybe it's because Mary's flat's empty.'

The break-in's bad enough, but it bugs me even more if we're being watched. I find some of Murdo's tools and fix the lock as best I can. Then I fetch a big old bolt from the attic and screw it to the inside of the door as extra insurance when we're up top.

Later, we hear the loud muffled sound of a TV. 'Mary's back?' I say.

'You need to go down and see her.'

I put my tie back on, comb my hair, and go down.

'Hamish?'

'Thought I'd better let you know,' I say. 'I lost my Bristol flat.'

'I'm so sorry,' she says.

'Actually I'm upstairs. Archie had a key,' I lie.

'That's good. Someone needs to look after it until I decide what to do,' she says. She thinks it's her own flat?

I go back upstairs.

'Did you tell her I was up here too?' Jenny says.

'My secret.'

'What if she sees me?'

'Just kneel and pretend you're cleaning the stairs.'

***

Next morning, at breakfast, Jessica's there again to cheer me up. Her pink washing matches the underside of the white clouds, high above the rising sun.

Downstairs, on my way to get some rolls, I nearly bump into a well-dressed lady coming out the flats next door. Jessica! I recognise her hair and dress. I thought she was my age, but she's in her fifties. I try to catch her eye, but she looks straight through me and hurries on. I'm gutted, then chuffed, that someone so mature can look so fine. I feel better already.

After lunch, Jenny lifts my worn copy of Murdo's published book. She sits by the window, flicking through it. Then she stands up, brings it over to me, and points a pink nail at a date, underlined in red: 1668.

'You think Murdo highlighted it recently?' she says.

I kiss her on the forehead. 'Yes!' I grab my bag, tip out the four wee wooden numbers and stand them up on the table: one, six, six, eight. 'Year Port Glasgow was founded!' I tap an open page in my notebook. 'Billy was born around then too.'

She picks up the wee man from the mantelpiece. 'Can't have started the city if he was just born.'

I take the wee figure and tap Murdo's wee model of a ship's hull. 'A lot of his letters are to his brother David. Seems to have captained his ships.'

'Common thing in Bristol,' she says. 'Kept the business in the family.'

No. 118. Measure the River and Firth

The greatest threat to this town is its fragile connection to the sea. It cannot maintain a semblance of trade when it relies on a hundred lighters passing daily to and from the New Port.

You need look no further than Bristol to see that the solution is to make our river navigable. The Council have agreed my proposal to engage Watt, the surveyor, to measure the river and firth. He proposes to engage the Newport dirt boat to be brought up at spring tide and dredge the sandbanks at the Erskine ford to make it navigable to the Broomielaw at high tide. This town will never be a city unless we deepen its stubborn river.

***

'New Port?' she says.

'Old name for Port Glasgow. Sailing ships couldn't get any further up the Clyde until Billy deepened it.'

'Billy bollocks. We need to see Port Glasgow.'

***

Jenny doesn't believe in hanging about. Next morning, we head down the river walkway and over the Squinty Bridge.

'Walking there?' she says.

'Traditional route.'

A paddle steamer sits beneath the Science Centre tower, smoke wisping from its red and black funnels. 'The *Waverley*!' she says.

'Meant to be a surprise.'

'Comes to Bristol every summer.'

'Bristol?'

We join the short queue waiting to board. There's a cold wind, but we find a seat at the stern, behind the funnels, facing upriver. Once we move off, the wave generated by the ship washes along miles of deserted quays and shipyards.

'Guess big boats came right up here,' she says. 'Didn't realise Glasgow was so big.'

'Shipbuilder to the world.'

Jenny goes for a walk round the boat, to find the best spot to photograph the old docks and rusty cranes.

When she returns, I say, 'Murdo used to take me on this trip every year. Each time there were less and less remains of the shipyards.'

Most of the abandoned docks and quaysides are overgrown and sinking back into the mud. How long will it take for the river to return to its original state? I'd read about the Congo, where whole cities were abandoned, and reverted to jungle in a few decades.

I pass Jenny one of my latest letter transcripts, which mentions one of Billy's ships.

No. 119. A Bill of Lading

Dear Brother,

I enclose a Bill of Lading for 340 barrels Salted Herring, 260 barrels Salted Beef and 120 reams Calico Shirts in my warehouse, for the Mary at Port Glasgow.

I trust the 200 hogsheads of sugar are to your satisfaction.

***

‘The Mary?’ she says.

‘Captained by Billy’s brother, David. Had a warehouse at Port Glasgow to store their goods.’

‘But they were shipping out enough to feed and clothe thousands,’ she says.

‘All the workers.’

‘Workers?’ she says.

Then she goes down to see the engines. I pull out wee Billy. Two hundred hogsheads of sugar? I zip the sheet into my Pandora section.

Two hours later, we pass Dumbarton Rock, then Newark Castle. As we approach Greenock, a throng of passengers wait to board. We disembark and catch the train two stops back, to Port Glasgow. The main street’s mostly charity and pound shops. At the far end, a big red and black boat lies stranded on concrete paving behind railings, looking a bit the worse for wear. She reads out the vandalised sign beside it: ‘First steam-driven passenger boat in the world.’

‘I’ll get some sandwiches for lunch,’ I say, and head off alone. Back in city mode, I head down Scarlow Street.

No. 120. Port Glasgow

Walking through the town, I’m here and there. My body in the present but my head in the past.

I find Water Street, follow Fore Street. I look for Black Bull Close, Ropework Lane, but they’re gone. I stray into the kirkyard, note down the epitaphs:

George Hannah, Mariner, 1735.

John McDonald, Shipmaster, 1772.

William Sinclair, Cooper, 1773.

Robert Allason, Merchant, 1785.

Then I turn back up Custom House Lane. I want to climb up and steal the sign. But it’s too high.

***

I’m brought back to the present by a text from Jenny: *Where are you?*

We meet in a cafe in the converted town hall. Her bag’s stuffed with the usual mix of colourful clothes. She points up at a children’s mural on the wall, and a crudely drawn building with a big chimney.

'Brought your models?' she says.

I tip them out. 'The one with the chimney.' I stand it up on the table.

Jenny reads out the sign on the wall: 'Sugar houses, started the same year as Port Glasgow.'

I keep my head down, twiddling the wee model.

'You think maybe the sugar houses needed sugar?' she says.

'Back then, Scots were banned from the Empire.'

She jumps up, knocking over her chair. Heads turn. 'Can't you just take it at face value?' she says. 'If you find it doesn't work, fine. But don't bury your story to make it fit a string of jeelie pieces.'

I rap my own knuckles. 'End of lecture.'

She turns, eyes blazing, and goes through the back to the toilet.

Wow! She looks good when she's mad. But I don't want to wind her up too often, or she might never come back.

While I'm waiting, I study the old engravings of the town up on the wall. Dozens of sailing vessels are arriving at the harbour from the Americas. Then I go outside and wait for Jenny. When she returns, she's tied her hair back and cooled off.

Nowadays, despite the cry of the seagulls and the salty air, the Clyde's cut off from the town by a busy dual carriageway and a green wasteland. We cross the road at the traffic lights and head over rough grass towards the water.

'Where's the harbour?' she says.

'Under our feet. Popular story's all about industry and shipbuilding. But it started out as Glasgow's transatlantic port.'

We enter a windswept hinterland inhabited by dog walkers and empty Buckfast bottles. A rough path leads along the quayside into the wind, then peters out. To the side, big granite bollards lie half buried, tilting sadly. I run my fingers round the groove worn in the bollard's neck by countless ships' ropes. We reach a bit where the quayside turns inland.

'Entrance to the old harbour,' I say.

Down on the pebble beach, we look back up at the only bit of old quay that's survived. Just then, the sun comes out. The stones turn a myriad of warm reds, oranges and browns. I run my hand over the surface. Then I pull out my screwdriver and lever out a block at the bottom, where the mortar's been softened by the sea. It's the smallest bit I can see, but it's still too heavy for my backpack and I need both hands to carry it.

'This rock fetish is getting out of hand,' Jenny says.

I lay down my stone and sit on a bollard, head in hands. 'Ach, this is the equivalent of Bristol's old harbour. Another missing bit of the jigsaw.'

Further inland, the grass becomes a maze of humps and bumps, a green landfill, burying the old and new harbours. The source of Glasgow's fortune, buried and forgotten.

'We won't find Billy here,' says Jenny. 'It's even worse than Glasgow.'

Gutted, I lead her back to the station and we catch the next train back to Glasgow. As we pass Bishopton, I pull out a thick paperback, *The Prince and the Tobacco Lords*. I picked it up in a charity shop while waiting on Jenny. A tale of a Glasgow merchant family. One of the few Glasgow novels which goes right back to the Tobacco Lords. Jenny spots the woman in the long flowing dress on the cover.

'Chick lit?' she says.

The author's Margaret Thomson Davis. I admire Margaret. She made the effort to inject some life into the old tales.

She also sold more books than most historians.

***

Later, Jenny takes her laptop and goes off into a corner to do some work. She shows no sign of wanting to go home. I don't mind: she brightens up my life. But I can't fathom her set-up with the museum. She moans all the time that they take the loan of her, yet she's working on her laptop.

Why does she bother?

She's living next to me, hanging out with me, but I can't work out why. She's my cousin, sort of, like brother and sister, yet she edges on being over familiar. She comes home from work, has a shower, then plomps down on the sofa beside me, wrapped only in a big towel. If we watch TV together, and she lays her hand on my arm, it sends a buzz through me. She seems unaware she's leaking affection. At breakfast, she appears in her underwear, covered only by a baggy T-shirt.

On Saturday, she meets an old male friend in the street and hugs him. Friend or boyfriend? It bothers me for days. Another time, she's out early at the shops. When I meet her for lunch, she stands on tiptoes to kiss me on the cheek but stumbles, and our lips touch. It makes my day.

Maybe it's time to make the first move?

Later, we're both looking out the north window. I move behind her, put my hands on her hips, and brush her neck with my nose. She freezes, then pulls away.

'No, no, no!' She runs out onto the landing. When she comes back, she's fighting back tears. Without looking at me, she goes into her wee room and throws clothes into her bag.

I'm too embarrassed to speak. I go over to the table and pretend to read something on my phone. She comes out with her bag, crosses the big room, and leaves without a word. I look down from the window, watching her hurry up the street in her red coat towards the bus station. I go back into her room. It's still full of clothes, but mostly ones she's bought from charity shops.

A few minutes later, I spot her purse on the dining table. I grab my jacket, hurry downstairs and up Buchanan Street. I find her in the middle of the bus station, looking lost. She sees me and turns away.

I hand her the purse.

'It's my fault,' she says. 'Should have noticed what was happening.'

'Please.'

'There's a bus in half an hour.'

***

When I get back, I climb the spiral stair, duck through the low door and stand on Murdo's favourite side. My knees press against the parapet. Way down below, the bushes on the waste ground sway in the wind, making me dizzy. I might not last long myself, if I lived up here.

I prop the wee man up on the parapet, kneel and stare at him.

I've got two things keeping me sane: Jenny's friendship and your stupid quest.

A wee wagtail lands on the opposite side of the parapet and tilts his head. Has it come to save me?

The wee black and white bird's joined by its partner. I back off, take the wee man and go downstairs.

No. 121. Missing Evidence

You've come punting up the Clyde with your diaries and letters. Squinting through your telescope from the top of the steeple.

Your jigsaw's taking shape. Each new piece takes me further back. I've found the year you were born. But it's all too early. My mind's filled with cliches which are too late. Ships driven by steam, not wind. Building ships, not trading in them. Ships carrying tobacco, not sugar.

You lived too early. Your buildings are missing. Your harbour's filled in. All the evidence is gone. But because your story's written in thick hardbacks, and stored in important libraries, everyone believes it's true. But after your death you lost control, had no say where your story went. You entered a time machine, reformed with every new city book. Repeated, magnified for the tourists and transformed into legend.

Now it's getting dodgy. Jenny's getting closer to opening Pandora's Box. And when she does, we might both be flattened by the blast.

But now I've got more important things on my mind. She's gone and left me. What will I do without her?

***

I find a blank page in my folder and doodle in pencil:

I really like you.
I like being with you.
I want to spend more time with you.

Part Three
Bristol

Chapter 13

Jenny, Bristol

Too Many Men

On her way back to Bristol, Jenny called Kelly from the bus. 'Messed up. Fell out with Hamish.'

'Found out about Cato?'

There was silence, then Jenny said, 'Made a pass at me.'

'You overreacted?'

Jenny didn't answer.

'Since when did you become Miss Prim Goody Two Shoes?'

'I like him a lot, but we're always falling out.'

'Too many men in your life? Dave and Hamish and Cato and whatsisname, Billy, too.'

Kelly had to raise her voice to be heard over the whine of the bus cruising down the motorway.

'Just want to take it slow,' Jenny said.

'Isn't it slow already?'

'Complicated by all the quest shit.'

'Both too proud to admit what you're up to?'

Jenny cut the call.

A Stuffed Monkey

Jenny got back to her flat late and slept till mid-morning. To preserve her sanity, she went out to check the charity shops. In the Flea Market in

Corn Street, she spotted a stuffed monkey. He was in poor condition and missing one eye, but she couldn't resist him.

A Famous Writer

On her dad's pinboard, Jenny spotted a picture of another explorer, Walter Raleigh. What inspired her most about Raleigh was that, like her Roman scribe Cato, he'd been a famous writer, the founder of modern historical writing.

Above her desk she had a printout of Raleigh's motto: *To write a history of the world, but in the process, my own.*

Raleigh was a bit of a disappointment, though. She found a tatty copy of his *History of the World* in the library, but it was useless. Despite his ambition and fame, he'd only finished Volume One. It barely reached the year 100 BC.

However she did come across another Nevis connection online. On Raleigh's way home from his search for El Dorado, he'd anchored off the island for two weeks and had written home to his wife.

She tried to find Nevis on her childhood globe of the world, but most of the Caribbean islands were too small to name.

A Tiny Dot

After going into town, Jenny returned home with a big map of the Caribbean. She unfolded it and spread it out on the kitchen table. She found it hard to believe. Even on the big map, Nevis was still a tiny dot. Smaller than the Isle of Wight.

She needed to know more.

DNA

In recent years Jenny had chased some of her Dad's Bristol outsiders from Ireland, France and Portugal. More recently she'd taken a DNA test and it had got more interesting. The results confirmed that her African origins were via the Caribbean.

She knew tests by genealogy firms could be dubious, but it was hardly a surprise. In the centre of Dad's picture gallery was her grandfather, in trilby and heavy coat, newly arrived on one of the Windrush ships in 1951.

Servants or Slaves

Jenny had started chasing some African servants in Bristol. She had found quite a few press notices for people who had escaped from merchant's homes. Rewards were offered for their recapture.

The African who affected her most was in a painting she came across one day in the museum store. It showed a black girl kneeling at the bedside of Edward Colston. Could she be my ancestor? Jenny thought.

Lists of Slaves

Later, Jenny went round to her favourite archive and through the secret doors to Narnia. She climbed a stepladder and ran her finger down the spine of the next volume on the shelf. She always followed a logical pattern. Maybe she'd cover all the ledgers eventually. Maybe in about fifty years' time.

As she lifted down the next tome, a big spider ran along the shelf above her. She stumbled and nearly dropped the book. As the leaves fanned open, two sheets slipped out and wafted down onto the rough wooden floorboards. Carefully, she picked them up and laid them on the narrow shelf under the window. They were very old, and the writing was small: lists of slaves on a plantation, two years apart. She'd seen similar ones before. They were hardly unusual in Bristol. But originals were different. And they could be useful for one of her tours. To save time, she was tempted to fold them up and slip them inside her notebook, but she knew better.

She put them back inside the ledger and carried it back through the network of corridors to the public search room, before taking the sheets out to Jemima on the front desk.

'Can I photocopy these?' Jenny said.

'Where did you get them?' It was OK for readers to take index volumes to their desk, but not original documents.

'Fell out of a book,' Jenny said. She led Jemima back to her desk and showed her the index volume the sheets had come from. Jemima made notes in pencil on the corner of the sheets. Fortunately she was one of the nicer ones. She took the sheets back to her desk, pressed a silent buzzer, and John the technician appeared in his brown coat. He laid the sheets on his empty trolley and pushed it away out the door.

Half an hour later, John came back with his trolley and laid two photocopies on Jenny's desk, plus an invoice for ninety pence. Jenny smiled at John. Did she detect the faintest hint of a smile in return?

Nancy

At home, Jenny took out the photocopies of the slave lists she'd found in the archive. She scanned through the names. She spotted names Cato had mentioned. It was unlikely they were the same people, but one name stood out: *Nancy, aged fifteen, picker, Congo, value twenty pounds.* A line came back to her from Cato's last jotter: '*This mornin Niven beat & bucked young Nancy, age 15, by the side of the road & threw her in the ditch.*'

She added another name to her list: *Nancy, 15, picker, Congo.*

The Same Island

The other thing Jenny's DNA results had told her was which part of the Caribbean her family had come from. The Leeward Islands. Now she knew from her map that the Leewards included Nevis. The same island Cato had written about.

Jenny's head was buzzing with Cato and Africa and Nevis. Finally she had a connection she could relate to.

***

Jenny went to the library to find out all she could about Nevis. It turned out that in the early days, it was the source of most of Bristol's sugar. Cato's story was getting personal.

Jenny called Kelly. 'He came from the same island as me!'

'Cato?'

'From Nevis!'

'Isn't it time you published something?'

The Journal of Cato

DEPARTURE

Listen to me now. Luck, it is where you are born. My first voyage is a short one, from my home country to a small island off the coast. I am dragged up the beach & through the forest to a great stone fort.

Down to its vaults, where the smithy sends sparks billowin up to the roof. White-hot irons glow in the darkness.

Then pull, I am pulled aside by the overseer on the gate, chosen at random to be the lackey of the overseer. To be a counter, not the counted. Chained by one arm, not two, the other clutchin a stick of charcoal. Scratchin marks in the ledger, like the footprints of a crow. A mark in the great book for everyone who passes. Learnin slow. Learnin letters, numbers, words for names, readin, writin. Learnin the bones of Engly.

Then fortune, my good fortune runs out. The overseer chooses a new boy for his bed. Thrown, I am thrown in the queue with the counted. Fester & starve in the dark cellar for many days. Carried in small boats to the great ship. Squeezed below deck.

Great, so great is the pain of its memory, I will not speak of my ocean crossin.

Chapter 14

Hamish, Bristol and London

Next morning at breakfast, Jessica's there as usual. Blue washing. I watch her go back inside. I dread the day she won't appear. How will I get through the day?

I take my backpack and go downstairs for a walk. Round the corner, I bump into Archie.

'Where's your more attractive half?' he says. He takes one look at my face and says, 'Spiky girl. Needs handled with care.'

'What the hell do you know? Stay away from us.'

I wander the streets in a daze and stop at a cafe in the Merchant City. I try, in vain, to work on more of Billy's diaries and letters. I give up and go for a long ride on my bike, down the Clyde to Riverside, then up the Kelvin. I text Jenny several times through the day, but without a response.

Finally I work up the courage to call and leave a message: 'I've been avoiding dealing with my flat, need to come down and clear it. I've booked the bus.'

I've started packing to travel south when a text comes from Jenny: *What's the name of Billy's island?*

Need to leave for the bus, I say.

She phones me. 'It's important.'

'It's in my notes from the Glasgow books.'

No. 122. History of the Caribees

This morn I was in the library at Garthland with Father, bent over Grandfather's map of the West Indies stretched over the big oak table, weighed down at the corners with lead weights. I pushed my matchwood model of a sailing ship across the chart, re-enacting the second voyage of Columbus, in November 1493. It entered the Caribbean Sea, passing Guadeloupe, then turning north by Montserrat until it passed Nevis.

I had been asking Father to read me a story. Together we built and lit the fire. Father pulled down a big book from the shelves. We sat by the window overlooking the rain-swept fields and he read of blue seas and tropical islands. Later, when Father had gone, I sat by the fire and studied the book, The History of the Caribees. So far away, yet not unreachable.

Only last week Father sent a bale of cloth to his friend Colhoun on the George of Ayr for Nevis.

***

It's one of Murdo's quirks. If it's ever mentioned, he always has a standard response: 'Nevis? – Aye, the island, not the Ben.'

'You still there?' Jenny says.

I go over to the table and flick through my wee folder. The model!

There's so many Murdo models in the flat. With my phone jammed between my shoulder and ear, I cross to an alcove and lift the big island model onto the table.

'Years ago, Murdo made a model of a tropical island,' I say, 'cut from a single piece of wood.' I take a snap and send it to her.

'It's a giant version of the wee pyramid!' she says.

I tip out my bag of models. 'Must be important,' I say.

'Where did he get a chunk of wood big enough?'

'Emailing you a page from Murdo's Filofax. Got to go.' I hang up.

No. 44. Murdo and Big Tree Trunk

One day, I was walking on the Green with the boy. We passed a big oak which had come down the night before in a storm. I ignored the workmen cutting up the branches and pulled out two matches from my box in my pocket. I crouched down, gave the boy a match, and we used the tips of our matchsticks to count the rings on the newly cut stump. It took a while, but finally I tallied up the results.

'1668!' I said.

'When it was planted?'

'Aye.'

My exactness was dubious. When we got nearer the centre, the rings got thinner and closer together and became harder and harder to count.

The workmen were cutting the trunk into thick slices and hoisting them onto a lorry. I chose the thickest part, just above the stump, and paid the driver to deliver it to the pavement outside the close. It had to be lifted off with a crane, and was far too heavy to carry up five floors. So I went round to the Barras and hired a petrol-driven chainsaw. I attacked the stump in a frenzy of noise and flying woodchips, scattering passers-by, and shaped the outside into a rough cone. Then I hollowed out the inside, to cut down the weight, and staggered upstairs with it. I laid it on newspapers in the centre of the big dining table, rasping and sanding it smooth. For months you could smell the freshly worked oak in the big circular room.

In the end, it was a work of art. Polished and varnished. An oak mountain.

'A volcano?' said the boy.

It didn't look like the shape of any Scottish mountain. But I took some Lego trees, and together we stuck them around the cone on the summit. 'The rainforest,' I said.

***

Jenny texts back: *Can you bring the model down?*

The island's big and heavy, but I can't afford to upset Jenny again. Anyway, I need to start smuggling out Murdo's models before Mary chucks them out. The island model's a start.

I wrap it in bubble wrap and parcel tape, then put it in a big black bin bag. I find my backpack, stagger downstairs, and fetch my bike. I push the bike, holding the model steady on the rack. I make it to Greggs for breakfast, lay down the model and touch a stone outside for luck. An old man in a bunnet copies me, in slow motion.

At Buchanan Bus Station, I find the right stance for the early bus. The driver wants me to put the model in the luggage bay, along with the bike, but I'm afraid it'll get scratched, so I pay for a second seat. It'd be cheaper going by train.

I try to work on more of Billy's letters on the bus, but the motion soon makes me feel sick.

No. 123. A Young Gentleman Putting Out in the World

'Times change,' says Father. 'Your brothers follow the old ways, the army, the law and the Church. But I see a new career for you on the horizon.'

He pats a letter on his desk which arrived in the post this morning. From the writing, it's from Father's friend, Colhoun, on Nevis.

'I have a plan. A new road to fortune,' says Father. 'A young gentleman putting out in the world.'

***

Jenny meets me outside Temple Meads with a coffee in a cardboard cup. She holds the bike and stretches up to peck me on each cheek, then backs off. With a finger, she traces a big ring around my cheek and ear.

'Slept half the way resting on the volcano,' I say. 'Look, I'm sorry about—'

There's tears in her eyes. 'Let's not get into anything we might regret,' she says. She peels open the bin bag and the top of the bubble wrap. 'Murdo's model of Billy's island!'

'Like Tracy Island?'

'Without the puppets and rockets.'

'Made from one big tree stump.'

She runs her finger over the varnished surface. 'Love his stuff. The tree rings look like contours.' She scrolls through her phone and shows me her image of Nevis. It fits the profile.

'Why Nevis?' I say.

'Island where most of Bristol's sugar came from.'

'Bristol?'

'Think Billy was on Nevis?' she says.

I shrug.

'Lot of young Bristol men started out on islands like Nevis,' she says. 'As indentured servants.'

'Indentured?'

'Sort of apprenticeship. After three years, they got a plot of land.'

'Farmers?'

'A route to fortune. First time in history that ordinary young men could go out and become super rich. Some of the biggest merchants started out that way.'

I take a fresh sheet, then scribble down two words: *Nevis. Indenture.* Then I turn away and zip the sheet into my *Pandora* section. I get up and lay the model on the bike rack.

'You can store it at my place,' she says.

We wheel the bike and model round to her flat. As I struggle to lift it off the bike, I say, 'Murdo carved this when I was in my early teens.'

'So?'

'If it's Nevis, it means he's been chasing it for yonks.'

'Chasing Billy?'

I leave her and head back to my own flat. I can hardly open the door for the pile of mail. I know by the look of most of it that I don't want to read it. I spend some time packing boxes.

Later, I meet Jenny again, for a curry. She spends the whole evening talking about friends and distant family I haven't seen for years. Has she found something? If so, she's refusing to tell me about it until the morning, and I don't want to risk upsetting her. Right now, I'd rather stay friends than lose her altogether.

We part with a peck on the cheek.

***

Next morning I go back round to Jenny's. In the corner of her hall stands a stuffed animal. 'What's with the spooky meerkat thing?' I say.

'Saw him in a charity shop. Couldn't resist him.'

'Moved from clothes to stuffed animals?' I say.

'Ha ha.'

'Is he real?'

'Haven't seen him move yet.'

'Stuffed or a toy?'

'Why don't you ask him? He's an African green monkey.'

I peer closer. One eye's missing. I stroke his fur and sneeze twice. 'Looks brown to me.'

'Be nice to him,' she says. 'His name's Barry.'

Barry's dodgy eye follows us out the door.

Jenny shows me where I can store models in her attic: 'Sally's in Italy for a bit longer.'

Her attic's a big empty void. I could move the whole Glasgow Grid in here and rebuild it.

***

I pinch a Tesco trolley to transfer Murdo's grid from my Bristol attic to Jenny's flat. It takes several days. When Jenny isn't at work, she helps carry the models upstairs.

On the second day, she walks back to her flat with me. 'Why take such an odd route?' she says.

'Flattest way with the trolley.'

I don't tell her I'm avoiding my old office, midway between our flats.

***

I'm on my own, pushing the trolley full of models. Coming towards me is Trevor from Accounts, in his grey suit, purple shirt and tie. I look around for a doorway to hide in, but he raises a hand. When he reaches me, he looks down at the models and black bin bags in the trolley.

'How's things?' Trevor says.

'Enjoying the freedom.'

'Any luck on the job front?'

'Second interview tomorrow,' I lie.

'What you doing with yourself?'

'Bit of writing.'

'Writing?'

It's the first thing that comes to mind, but it does the trick.

'Well, good luck with the interview then,' Trevor says. He turns and crosses the road.

That got rid of him. Anyway, he isn't the type to share problems with over a coffee. But writing? It'll be all round the office in a flash that I've cracked.

Saw him pushing wooden toys in an old trolley.

Writing?

I couldn't have said anything worse.

No. 124. Lunch with Defoe

I met Defoe yesterday for lunch in the Tontine Tavern. Our citizens are too swayed by the praise of such great men.

I overheard Campbell again in the coffee-house this forenoon, repeating Defoe's exaggerations regarding Glasgow. I collared Campbell and said, 'Pray, have you never seen Bristol?'

Tis an easy route to free dinners, to heap praise on every city you visit, so that they in turn praise you as their benefactor.

***

I show it to Jenny.

'Your Billy was friendly with Defoe?' she says.

'Impressed?'

'Defoe was a chancer. Milked anybody he could for information. Gave a cheesy over-the-top description of every town in the country. Bet he gave a glowing one of Glasgow?'

I fumble with my wee notebook. '*The cleanest, most beautiful, and best built city in Britain.*'

'What about Bristol?' she says.

'*The greatest, the richest, and the best port of trade in Great Britain.*'

'Each city quotes his description, and thinks theirs is the best!'

I'm still not sure when she's winding me up. But most of the time, life with Jenny's good. She's mad, but in a fun way.

***

I finish clearing my flat. When I move into Sally's room, there's not much personal space.

I clear a space in Sally's desk and spend my time trying to unravel more of Billy's letters. There's still things bugging me about his career. Several correspondents refer to him as 'Colonel' Billy. I find the right bit in my notes.

No. 125. Commanded a Regiment

> *When he was eighteen, Billy enlisted in the army. He sailed the world. Rose to the rank of colonel and commanded a regiment. Advanced the empire. Battled against the French. Marched through the capital, victorious.*

***

Sailed the world? Could it solve the island issue? I pluck up the courage to show Jenny.

'Bugger me,' she says. 'What happened to the city's greatest merchant?'

I stand Billy up on the table and fit the wee sword to his right hand. 'Told you before. Maybe he started out as a soldier. Swapped to merchant in later life.' I tap the wee hat. 'Could be a soldier or merchant's hat?' I hold out my notebook. 'Says he served as a soldier, then he got his fortune through marriage to an heiress.'

'How long have you known?' she says.

'Seemed to complicate the story.'

'It's not about the history shit,' she says. 'It's about being honest.'

***

I go up to the big library in town and find the military section. I spend a couple of hours searching British Army records for Colonel Billy. When I get home, I show my notes to Jenny.

'Couldn't find him in the published records?' she says.

'Suppose lots of volunteers dropped through the net.'

'A colonel? He was responsible for hundreds of men!'

I sit looking out the window, then I get up. 'There's only one way to sort it.'

'Original records in London?'

I nod and look on the Trainline app, but it's too expensive. 'Guess it's the Megabus again.'

***

In the morning, Jenny sees me off before she goes to work. 'Good luck.' She stretches up, pecks me on the cheek and hands me a big bag of home-made sandwiches and two bottles of water. Just as well. The bus gets stuck in traffic and takes seven hours instead of three. I've booked a cheap B & B in Kensington, but it's too hot to sleep.

***

Next day, it takes half the morning to get to Kew, sort out a reader's ticket and get to grips with the ordering system. I need Jenny here, it's her speciality.

I find the right period for Billy, but still can't find him or his regiment. I speak to an assistant. Her badge says her name's Paula.

'There's not much more in the original documents than the published military records,' Paula says.

'Tried the big books before, but he's not there.'

'A colonel?' she says. 'It's impossible. If he's not there, he never enlisted in the army, let alone had a top rank.'

I go to the toilet and prop the wee man above a basin, in front of the mirror. Not a soldier?

The door opens. I slip the wee figure into my pocket, wash my face in cold water and head back to my seat. I sit in a daze, looking out the window at the river, trying to sort in my head what I've found.

***

At five o'clock, tired and with sore eyes, I step out of the public record office into the sun. Murdo's quest's the only worthwhile thing in my life, but it's falling apart.

Down by the river, the flowing water makes me dizzy, and I stumble and nearly fall down the bank. I sit down on the grass and try to stand the wee man beside me. What do I tell Jenny?

I find a cafe facing the Thames and order tea and croissants with jam. Before I can decide what to say, Jenny calls. I can hear traffic and footsteps in the background.

'Find him?' she says.

'No joy.'

'When you coming back?'

'Another sweaty night in the hotel. Catch an early bus tomorrow.'

No. 126. The Smell of Money

Great is my excitement today. Father is allowing me again to accompany him to Glasgow.

We disembark at the Watergait and stand waiting on our carriage, watching merchants board a lighter to return to the port.

When our carriage arrives, we reach the Cross. I sniff the air. Depending upon the direction of the wind, you can smell it anywhere in the town, the sickly smell of burning. It reminds me of Cook making jam from the apples in the orchard at Garthland.

'Aye, tis the Glasgow stink,' says Father. 'Burnt molasses from the great sugar-houses.' He points down Bell Street to a tall chimney. 'Your grandfather called it the smell of money.'

***

I catch the early bus back and sleep most of the way. Jenny meets me at a cafe opposite the station. Outside, a group passes in bright Caribbean colours.

'Ever done a slave trade tour?' I say.

'You think Billy was into—'

'Course not,' I say. 'Just curious.'

'You should come along on my kids' tour.'

'Sounds good.'

'You'd need clearance.'

'Last job was in an old nursery building. We all had to be vetted.'

'Cool.'

No. 127. Fell off the Edge of the World

You went travelling the seas at a young age, 'A young gentleman putting out in the world.' But which hat did you really wear?

You came strutting the planestanes with your coat and cane. You went sailing across the ocean in your soldier's hat, with your regiment of men. But I searched the capital for your records. You're missing from the books. I was right to be suspicious. A colonel in the army? Glasgow's greatest merchant? Something to do with sugar? Your story's going down the pan.

I don't know what's harder. Telling Jenny about you, or telling her how I feel.

Chapter 15

Jenny, Bristol

Lots of Catos

Later, round at her favourite archive, Jenny didn't have time to order anything out. So she went through the double doors to her secret room. She found a very old document with an alphabetical list of names: Census of Domestic Servants in 1725.

Carefully she turned the pages. Lots of ordinary Bristol names, but classical ones too: Apollo, Brutus, Caesar. There were also press cuttings: rewards for capturing escapees.

Under 'C', she found three Catos. Could any of them be her Cato? Each name had an address and owner. Lots of Bristol houses seemed to have kept Africans. Some had had more than one.

All the Catos lived in their masters' houses in Prince Street or Queen Square.

If only one was her Cato, she could write up his story. A Bristol story, not a Glasgow one.

Everywhere in the City

Jenny needed some Edward Colston background for her tour. Instead of googling him, she went round to one of the old libraries in town. She found a seat under the plaque on the wall, dedicated to Colston, the library's benefactor.

The assistant fetched a pile of thick old tomes. Jenny sat down and worked her way through. Pages and pages about Colston's bequests. Almshouses and hospitals for the poor. Celebrations by Victorian admirers. Colston was everywhere in the city, even in Jenny's old junior school. Every morning she'd had to stand and sing the school song, praising his benevolence.

The Same Interests

After a couple of hours, Jenny had gathered enough. She went and bought a sandwich and headed for the museum. Adult tours were fine. But she was getting cold feet about her children's tour. She threw half her sandwich in a bin. When she reached the museum, Hamish was standing at the door. Had she finally found a man with the same nerdish interests?

Jenny introduced Hamish to her colleague Jane and her boss Gertrude. Gertrude was prim and formally dressed, and looked older than she was.

Hamish is a bit conservative himself, thought Jenny. Maybe he and Gertrude would make a good couple. She hoped not.

Dodgy Subjects

Children trickled in the door, dropped off by parents.

'Remember, none of your flannelling – stick to the script,' Gertrude whispered to Jenny. 'We'll be in deep trouble if you upset the little dears. Their parents aren't too keen on them hearing about slavery in the first place.'

'Maybe kids are better at understanding dodgy subjects?' Jenny said.

'I'm warning you...'

As Gertrude turned away, Jenny made a face at Hamish. He smiled.

My Tour

Jenny went to the toilet, hid in a cubicle, and tried to work up the courage to face the kids. When she came back to join the others, she had a reprieve: it was raining.

'We can't have the little dears getting wet,' Gertrude said. She postponed the walk for an hour.

'It's only drizzle,' Jenny said. She wanted to get it over with.

A Wee Ship

The four adults were given three children each. Hamish got David, Sam and Lucy. Each took a big sheet of paper to make a colourful frieze expressing their personal view of their city. The adults helped them cut up paper shapes and plastic containers, which they painted in bright colours.

Hamish went over to his bag and slipped out Murdo's wee ship model. He helped Sally add drinking straw masts and paper sails. When Gertrude's back was turned, David pulled the milk bottle tops off Sam's artwork. Sam fetched more tinfoil to replace them. Then Sam drew a paintbrush across David's frieze. David seemed to think it was Lucy who'd spoiled his frieze, so he squeezed PVA glue onto the ends of her pigtails. Then he pulled the straw masts off Sally's sailing ship, and she burst into tears.

The session ended in a riot, with the girls sobbing, the boys separated to stop them fighting, and all their artwork spoiled.

A Bad Man

After a snack, Gertrude said, 'Time for our first tour.'

The children cheered, grabbed their coats and tumbled out into the street. After a safety talk, Jenny led them down the hill to the cathedral. She worked her way around the memorials and colourful windows, telling them her dad's tales of Bristol's most famous folk. She carried on through Orchard Street, to visit some merchants' houses, then on to St Augustine's Parade. Someone had erected an effigy of Edward Colston on his plinth. From a distance it looked like the real thing. But when they got closer, it was made of straw and wire. Someone had set fire to one of Colston's legs.

'Colston was a member of the Royal African Company,' Jenny said. 'Ran the slave trade.'

Sam moved right up to the figure and stroked the plinth. 'If he was a bad man, why's there a statue of him?'

Hamish caught Jenny's eye. Even Gertrude smiled.

Across the Ocean

Jenny carried on for a stop at the Corn Exchange, then back down via King Street to the harbour. She chose three volunteers and unrolled her big sketched map on the quayside. It showed Britain, the Atlantic Ocean, and the coasts of Africa and America in crude outline. The children gathered round. Jenny had asked Hamish to bring along his wee ship.

'Hundreds of ships left from here with Bristol captains and crews and sailed south' – she chose Lucy to sail the ship from Bristol down to the African coast – 'then they picked up folk and carried them across the ocean to America.' She tipped out a bundle of wee Lego figures. Men, women and children, all dark-skinned. 'See how many people you can get on the boat.'

The children descended on the bag and crammed as many figures as they could onto the little ship. Then Lucy sailed it across the Atlantic. It was overcrowded, and some fell over the side.

'The conditions were so bad that many died on the voyage,' Jenny said.

'Were there children on board?' Sam said.

Gertrude coughed and gave Jenny a warning look. But Jenny nodded. 'Yes, many were teenagers and children.'

Lucy started to cry. Another girl began sobbing.

'Told my dad we were doing the slave trade today,' Sam said. 'Told me lots died on the ships.'

Jenny nodded.

'How many died?' said David.

'Two out of every ten, on average.'

'And how many were on each ship.'

'Few hundred.'

''S a lot,' said Sam.

'Were they squashed to death?' said David.

Jane looked alarmed.

'We'll find out more in the second part,' said Jenny. She led them back up to the museum for lunch.

Stick to the Script

Gertrude came over to Jenny and held out her phone. 'Office meeting this afternoon. You'll need to do without me.'

During lunch, Sam came over to Jenny. 'What did the slaves do when they got off the slave ships?' he said.

Jenny thought then said, 'Maybe we can find out in part two.'

'You need to stick to the script,' whispered Jane. 'Tour's meant to be about the slave trade.'

'Script bollocks!'

Jane shrugged. 'I won't tell if you don't.'

Sugar Cubes

After lunch, Jenny gathered the children together and led them down to the oldest part of the harbour. They gathered round on a grassy bit beside the quay. Jenny opened her bag, rummaged about, and brought out Murdo's wee wooden barrel. She passed it to Sam, who opened it. She had packed it with mini sugar cubes. Sam passed them round and the children took one each and crunched them.

'There's two stories about Bristol and slavery,' Jenny said. 'This morning we saw the best-known one.'

'Slave trade?' said David.

Jenny nodded and turned to Sam. 'Can you repeat what you asked me at lunchtime?'

Everybody looked at Sam. He lowered his head and said, 'What happened to the slaves once they got off the ships?'

'Well done, Sam. The ones that survived the voyage were taken off the boat and scrubbed. They stood in the town square, naked.'

'Butt naked,' said David, with a giggle.

'Then they were sold and forced to grow sugar.' Jenny brought out her box of Lego characters again and passed them round. The children took one each, then Jenny also passed round a plastic yoghurt carton full of tiny spades and machetes. Without being told, the children knelt and began playing with the characters, pretending the grass was sugar cane.

'How much were the slaves paid?' said Lucy.

'They weren't paid.'

'I only wash the dishes for Mum if she pays me pocket money.'

'The overseer stood over them with a whip,' said Jenny. 'The children weeded the ground and planted.'

'There were children?' said Sam.

'How young?' said Lucy.

'Young as you.'

'Babies?

'The women weren't fed enough for them to be healthy and have babies.'

'That's sad,' said Lucy.

Jenny took out her two sheets from the archives, which she'd typed onto big sheets of paper. 'This is a list of Africans on the sugar plantation owned by a Bristol merchant.' She laid the sheets in the centre of the circle of children.

Lucy pointed to a name on the list. 'There's a Lucy!'

'And a Mary,' said another girl named Mary. 'And she's only a year older than me.'

The children ran their fingers over the lists, looking for their own names.

'Was Mary whipped?' said David, looking at Mary.

'They weren't treated well,' said Jenny.

'Was her back all cut and slit and bleeding?' said David. Some of the children started whimpering.

'David! We want to think of nice things,' said Jane.

'But it wasn't nice, was it?' said David. 'Did any of them die?'

Jenny brought out another sheet of paper. The same plantation, two years later. The children compared the two.

'Lucy's still there, but Mary's gone,' said Mary.

'Where did she go?' said Lucy.

'She died, didn't she?' said David. 'She was whipped too much.'

'She might have been sold to another planter.'

'But he might have been a paedo.'

'David!' said Jane. She lifted her hand, turned towards Jenny and made a slashing sign across her throat. 'Cut,' she whispered.

'How long did the slaves work for?' said Sam, twirling the wee barrel in his hand.

'Might last a few years, if they were tough.'

'They spent weeks on the slave ships, but years on the plantations?'

Jenny nodded.

'So,' Sam said slowly, 'why are we only told in school about the slave trade?'

'Telling you now,' said Jenny.

'But this isn't school, it's more fun,' said Sam.

The adults smiled.

They watched a replica sailing ship drift past, carrying tourists dressed in cardboard pirate hats, waving plastic swords.

Jenny pointed over at the old quay. 'This is where the sugar ships arrived.'

Sam stood up. 'How many slaves grew sugar?'

'Sugar was Bristol's biggest trade.'

'Bigger than the slave trade?'

Jane looked at her watch and cut him off. 'Time to go,' she said. 'Your mums and dads will be waiting.' She stood up, held out her arms and gathered all the children together. She tapped their heads and counted: 'Nine, ten, eleven?'

But Sam was over on the edge of the quay. Everyone turned and looked. The girls raised their hands to their mouths.

'Don't move!' called Jenny.

Sam ignored her, leaned right over the edge and touched the big stones. Jenny walked slowly towards him, her arms held wide, trying not to scare him.

'The sugar ships,' Sam said, 'it's like they kissed the quay.'

Jenny reached him, bent down and took his hand. His other hand was still rubbing the inside of one of the grooves worn in the stones by the old ships.

'Yes, Sam,' said Jenny, 'it's like the sugar ships kissed the quay.'

'Bristol kisses,' Sam said.

***

After the tour, Hamish waited in the cafe until Jenny had finished for the day.

'Next time I do a tour,' she said, 'we bring life jackets.'

They headed back round by the harbour. Jenny crouched down on the edge of the quay, and Hamish knelt beside her. He ran his hand inside a big groove worn into one of the stones. 'Bristol kisses,' he said. 'Brilliant.'

'Takes a child to notice.'

Hamish took his wee boat from his pocket and rubbed the wooden hull against the worn bits in the quay. Then he lay down on the rough stone and looked closer. As he rubbed, a shower of wee grains of sand trickled down into the water.

Jenny went back and sat on the bench and watched him. She opened a packet of nuts and raisins and started to eat the raisins. She picked out the nuts and threw them to a group of pigeons which had gathered.

'You don't need to wear away the whole quay,' Jenny shouted over.

He stretched down and collected some of the sand in his other hand. Then he stood up and slipped the sand into a paper hanky from his pocket, before joining Jenny again on the bench.

'Think many Bristol merchants owned slaves on plantations?' Hamish said.

Jenny shrugged.

'Don't think it's important?' he said.

She jumped to her feet, spilling the last of her raisins on the ground. 'Of course it's important. But the slave trade gets all the attention.'

'Jeelie piece?' he said.

She sat down again. But Hamish was serious. 'Maybe there's another story out there, a bigger story?' she said.

And whether they liked it or not, they were both trying to find it.

They sat watching boats in the harbour. Hamish broke the silence.

'Glasgow merchants… could they have owned Africans?'

'Not something you just decide. Need evidence.'

'Broomielaw kisses?' he said.

'Not that I've heard.'

'Phew.' He wiped his brow in mock relief.

'Bother you that much?' she said.

'Slavery?'

'Your city's image.'

'Long as it's better than Bristol's.'

The Way Home

Later, after tea, they went for a long walk along the river. Down on the shore, Jenny started picking up wee square-shaped stones. Finally, she kept one stone and threw the rest away. On the way home, they headed back round by the harbour. Jenny stopped, sat down on a bench and fumbled in her bag. Hamish sat beside her. She brought out the wee wooden barrel and laid it on his lap.

'Trying to sweeten me up?'

'Should have let Sam keep it.'

He took the barrel and shook it. But the sugar cubes were all gone. When he turned it upside down, out popped a wee rectangular block of stone she'd selected from the beach. 'A Bristol kiss!' he said, his voice breaking. It even had a wee flaw on one side, like it had been worn by a ship's prow.

Hamish put the stone back into the barrel.

'It's like paper, scissors, stone,' he said.

'Sugar barrel swallows stone?'

'Owning slaves was bigger than trading them.'

She smiled. 'Tours and books are fine, but you can't beat a model for truth.'

Chapter 16

Hamish, Bristol

Next morning, I walk Jenny up the hill to work, then cut down by the harbour. I bend down and rub my palm inside one of Sam's grooves. I want to lie for hours and scratch wee grains of sand from the stone. Watch them tumble into the water.

It's the only reason Bristol's lumbered with all the dodgy stuff. Because the ships nudged the quayside. Up and down with the tide. Back and forth with the wind. A million times, till they wore a groove in the stone.

A direct connection. One that can't be denied.

Murdo's right. Forget all the theory. There's more truth in a block of stone than a hundred books.

***

I meet Jenny after work. As we cross Queen Square, she does a wee twirl and holds her hands wide. 'Start of the merchant's city,' she says.

'Aye right.'

'No, really. Filled in the Marsh. Built the first city square in Britain. First sign of money and culture.'

'Think it's a coincidence both merchant cities kicked off at the same time?'

One of the terraced houses in the square is shrouded in scaffolding, but with no sign of work being done.

'One of the originals,' I say.

'No, this bit was rebuilt after the 1831 fire.'

'No, an original,' I say. 'Worked on it till recently.'

'Maybe you're worth getting to know after all!'

'Developer found it was original. Closed the site. Too expensive to renovate.'

She rattles the wire fence. 'Let me in!'

I grab her arm. 'Still got the code for the back door,' I say, 'but we might get arrested.'

'Come on.'

'Later. After dark.'

***

We come back at eleven. Jenny's wearing some kind of black leotard and headband. Apart from the coloured stripes round the wrists and ankles, she looks like a cat burglar. At the back, facing the quayside, is a high brick wall and a locked gate. 'Shit,' she says.

I kick a cast-iron door, low down in the wall. 'Coal hatch.'

She points at a CCTV camera on top of a lamp post. 'Help me,' she says.

Jenny drags a big industrial wheelie bin up against the wall. I fetch another, and cover the other side of the coal hatch. We stand together in the dark shadow between the bins. I can hear her breathing deeply from the effort of moving the bin. No one passes by. I kneel, prise a screwdriver under the rusty hatch and raise it up. 'You first,' I say.

She squeezes through the wee door, and I follow. We stand in the yard, looking up at the back of the tall building.

'Could get arrested for this,' I say.

'Not worth the effort unless there's risk.'

The back door's covered in a thick steel plate, with a heavy-duty combination lock. I slip out my phone, find the number and press the keys. The lock clicks and opens. I tug at the door handle. With a creak it swings open. We slip inside, close the door and switch on our torches.

'You'll need this.' I hand her a dust mask and take her hand. 'Watch your step,' I say. 'Some of the floor's rotten.'

With her other hand she caresses the balustrade on the main stair. 'You're right, it's original!'

'Half the houses were destroyed in the great fire,' I say, 'but this one was in the border zone. They assumed it was destroyed and rebuilt.'

Up on the first floor, we stop at holes cut in the front wall, around the window.

'Wall's extra thick,' I say. 'Seems to be an older wall behind a Victorian facade.'

Jenny puts her hand into the cavity and fumbles around. Then she stands on the windowsill, pokes her phone up into the cavity and flashes her camera repeatedly.

Sitting on the window ledge, we view the results. Jenny lets out a shriek and drops her phone in my lap. A wee face glares back at us from the bright screen. It might be overexposed and out of focus, but it's clear enough to show a wee gremlin poking out his tongue.

'A grot!' she says. 'Unseen for two hundred years.'

We work our way around the front of the building, feeling and snapping all the lintels we can reach. Each one has a different face. In the end we find seven. Jenny names them after their expressions: Cheeky, Dozy...

'Best thing I've seen in years,' she says. She gives me a hug.

'Best hug I've had for ages,' I say.

She freezes, then relaxes. 'Maybe you need to get out more.' Then she picks up a mason's hammer and chisel, stands on a windowsill and starts hacking at another window surround.

I grab her arm. 'Someone will hear us!'

'Got to see the other grots!'

'Not tonight.'

She throws down the tools and stomps upstairs in a huff, raising a cloud of dust.

I catch her up on the top landing, looking up at the ceiling.

'What's in the attic?' she says.

'Full of old papers. Client wanted them thrown in a skip. Probably all gone by now.'

A ladder lies propped against the wall, abandoned by the contractor. Jenny's halfway up before I can say more. At the top, she pushes up the hatch, and pokes her head through. 'Stuff's still here!' she says.

I follow her up. She reaches back and helps me through the hatch. The room has a coombed ceiling and two skylights. Our footsteps raise more dust, so we slip our masks back on. Trunks and piles of ledgers are stacked across the floor and on the shelves which line the walls.

Jenny touches a pile of papers. 'Dry! Must have looked after the roof.' She opens a book. Dust motes rise in the torchlight. 'Letter book. 1789. Should be in the archives.' She opens a trunk and lifts out another ledger. '1739. Back to when the house was built. It's priceless.'

'We could smuggle some out and sell them,' I say.

'Priceless historically, pillock!' She pulls a notebook from her pocket, tears out a page and writes a date. She places the note on top of the pile. She works her way around, putting dates on all the piles and trunks.

I copy her. 'Take weeks to sort them properly,' I say. 'It's like Murdo's models. Too much to deal with.'

After a while she says, 'Some Glasgow stuff over here.'

'Glasgow merchants in Bristol?'

'Think they were confined to their town walls?'

'Didn't think they got involved down here.'

'Involved in what?' she says.

I start working my way through the pile. Familiar names: Campbell, Bogle. Ships' names and lists of cargoes.

'Think there could be Billy stuff here?' she says.

'Billy bollocks,' I say, mimicking her Bristol accent.

Now and then Jenny finds names that interest her and places the papers near the hatch.

'Must be stuff here for every merchant in Bristol,' I say.

'Just the house owners. And their agents and partners.'

'You know who lived here?'

'One of the oldest merchant families in the city. Provosts and stuff.'

I find more Glasgow stuff in the corner. But what should I take? One ledger is less dirty, as it's inside a big trunk. The name rings a bell: ALEXANDER HOUSTON & Co. I wrap it in a black bin bag and slip it inside my bag. Then I push the others I've gathered to the side.

'Come back another night?' I say.

'Torches won't last much longer,' she says, stuffing wads of papers into her own rucksack. 'Can't carry any more.'

Before we leave, we peek into the other three attic rooms. Two are full of books and papers. 'I could stay up here for a few weeks, uncover its secrets,' I say.

'Enjoy being a hermit?' she says.

'Only if you hide up here with me.'

The last attic room's half empty, but the roof's leaked and most of the papers are ruined.

There's a bang.

She grabs my arm. Heavy footsteps echo from deep in the building.

'Shit, the owners!' I say.

We listen in silence. 'Nobody will look up here,' she whispers.

'The hatch is open!'

More loud noises come from downstairs.

'Should have locked the back door,' I say. Suddenly, Jenny crosses to the hatch, picks up a big piece of wood and thumps the floor, raising a cloud of dust. I try to grab it. 'What you doing?'

'Kids larking about.'

Footsteps recede, then nothing. We stand in silence for several minutes.

'They've gone,' she says. 'Just as scared as us.'

We pick up our bags, climb down the ladder and the four floors, and leave by the back door. The intruders have jammed an old screwdriver into the combination lock. It's impossible to lock it again, so I prop a brick against the door. We crawl through the coal hatch and head home, without meeting another soul.

***

In the morning, I wake first.

'You up yet?' I say.

'No, but I should be.'

'Not working today?'

'Later.'

I sit at the table with the big ledger propped up in front of me. She comes through, wearing a baggy T-shirt.

'Any luck?' she says.

'Cargoes. Loans. Bills of exchange.'

'Boring?'

She gets dressed and goes out. Once she's gone, I write furiously, copying out entries from the big book. I haven't told Jenny that dozens of the entries are for Billy's ships. Carrying sugar from the Caribbean. Biggest merchant house in the city, the books say. Founded by Billy.

Alexander Houston is Billy's nephew.

***

Later, I go for a walk along the riverside and hear sirens. When I reach the back of Queen Square, smoke's pouring from the upper windows of our building. A hole in the roof has exposed blackened rafters. Firemen on tall ladders pour water through the opening. I fumble for my phone and call Jenny.

'At Queen Square, our building's gutted by fire… Shouldn't have left the door open—'

'Woah! You stuck inside?'

'Out on the quay.'

'Back off. Just leaving work. Meet you in twenty minutes at the cafe on the corner.'

I wait in the cafe in a cold sweat until Jenny arrives.

'Passed it on the way,' she says. 'All the stuff in the attic will be ruined.'

'It's all my fault,' I say.

'Curse of old buildings. Only a matter of time before kids torched it.'

'There was a whole story up there.'

'Mostly business records. Only a fraction were any use. At least we retrieved something. It's more than we had before we went in.'

'I'm one of the few who knew the code. What if they find fingerprints or CCTV? I'll never work again.'

'Cool it. We wore gloves and balaclavas. It's exactly what the owner wanted. Now they can knock it down and build flats.'

'Trying to convince me or yourself?' I say.

Then she says, 'The grots! They'll all be lost.' She's suddenly on the verge of tears.

'At least we've got photos,' I say.

'But we can't tell anyone how or where we found them.'

'Too many secrets.'

I put out my hand and she takes it. I pass her a napkin to wipe her eyes, and she opens her mouth to tell me something but changes her mind. We sit facing each other, lost in our own thoughts.

Sometimes I'd like to crawl into the corner with her and whisper my deepest secrets.

***

Jenny goes home to change, but I head down by the harbour, along the river, then up the hill to the Clifton Bridge. But instead of crossing the bridge, I sit on a bench above the cliffs. I prop up the wee man on the arm of my seat.

If you were a soldier, how come you were shipping sugar? I say to him. Where did you get it? Did you grow it yourself?

I unzip my *Pandora* pocket and slip out my spare sheet. I add four new words:

Bristol

Colston

Sugar

Planter?

Then I add another word to the list, in pencil, so it can be removed if I'm wrong:

Slaves.

I clip the sheet into the back of the folder, beside my notes about Nevis, along with Eck's postcard of a tropical island.

No. 128. Full of Holes

I've come staggering down the streets with a bunch of clues.

A heap of old stones and a stuffed monkey.

An island model and a string of dodgy words.

A folder full of records for shipping sugar.

Your story's full of holes. Your ship's sprung a leak. When you crossed the ocean, you fell off the edge of the world. Disappeared for decades, came back a different person.

I need to move on. Find out what you were doing on the islands. Chase your story, not bury it.

***

Finally, sitting overlooking the Clifton Bridge, I know what to do. I might be running short of money, but I've got a savings account Murdo opened for me years ago that I haven't touched. I call Jenny.

'How do you fancy an exotic holiday in the Caribbean?'

'Thought you'd never ask.'

Part Four
The Caribbean

Chapter 17

The Journal of Cato

ARRIVAL

Finally, the ship halts. We are taken on deck & crammed into lighters. As we approach the shore, I am thrown into the sea. I pass underwater, but my feet touch solid ground. I stagger out of the surf, flanked by men with whips & clubs. They gather us in groups on the beach.

Along the shore lies a small town. Above its smoke, in each direction, stretch plantations of green sugar cane. Higher still is a forest of tall trees. Despite the early hour, the air is warm. As the light increases, the mountain clears, though the top is shrouded in white cloud, like the great mountain at home.

Fire, the first thing I smell is fire. Not the fire of cookin but of forgin. The ring of a blacksmith's hammer. The smell of burnt flesh. We lie on the beach in a group. I am held down. Hot, hot is the iron clamped around my leg. I try not to look at my ankle, to see why there is so much pain.

Many are the tongues here, but none have the words to express what we have come through.

TAKE AWAY MY NAME

Herd, we are herded towards the market square. Stripped, oiled & our heads shaved. Speak, I speak, but they do not understand.

Fingers are poked in every openin. We are naked, with no possessions. They have taken everythin, even our hair. We have reached the bottom. Tis not possible to sink lower.

The next day they take away my name. A black man with a hammer & four dies stamps the letters CATO on my manacle.

THE ROAD

Chain, I am chained together with a group of a dozen. A man with a whip drives us down the road. Run, he expects us to run, but we are still unsteady from the motion of the ship. The road is dry & contorted from hard use. Wheel ruts are twisted into mounds & braids thicker than a man's thigh, like a writhin carpet of ropes. Set as hard as iron in the heat.

We jog along in loose formation, tryin not to trip. Tryin to keep in step, to ease the pain on our shackled ankles. Behind us a large mulatto with a whip & stick drives us forwards with curses. The younger Scalags in front, whether men or women, are naked. Even the youngest have the scars of old welts on their backs, from their driver's whip. As we cross the ghut, a young girl stumbles & falls. Halt, we must halt, lest we drag her along. Instead of helpin, the overseer sets upon her with a stick.

The ghuts are crossed by crude stone bridges, but most of these are ruined, washed away by a recent storm. At each ghut, we must descend into the deep gully, then up the other side. There is insufficient water in the ghuts to flow, but green pools lie at the bottom, covered in clouds of flies & mosquitoes which stick to our mouths & eyes.

CROWS STRUNG FROM A FENCE

As we cross one of the ghuts, I see a blackened shape hangin from a large Carrion-tree. From afar, like a hog, over-cooked & ready to eat. As we approach, I notice that tis a man, trussed up by the feet & badly burnt. As we pass close by, his charred body is also mutilated. Along the road I see other similar shapes, like great crows strung from a fence to scare off other birds. What monsters come out at night here to do such things?

Learn, the first thing I learn on this island is to look away.

The track is close-set with vegetation, which provides welcome shade from the afternoon sun. Every so often gaps appear. The dense growth is only a boundary strip, like a thick hedge, but composed of trees & bushes of every variety. This strip bounds the cane pieces in each plantation. It seems that each planter wishes to enclose his estate & keep his business to himself. Through the strip I hear the sounds of hoes diggin in the fields. Sometimes I see right up tracks to big plantation houses surrounded by verandahs.

A SCARECROW

After a mile or more, we turn up one of the tracks. The wind is comin towards us & I can smell it before I see it. The fragrance of wood-smoke, cookin & animals. All mixed with the sweetness of burnt sugar. The sound of an axe splittin wood, the clatter of cookin pots, children's voices & a dog barkin. Above it all, the vanes of a windmill sweep across the grey mountain in the background.

Smoke drifts among the trees & the orange light cuts through it in rays. In the centre of the bustle stands the plantation house. A pair of young boys drag a heavy bundle of firewood across the yard, leavin a trail in the dirt. In a shady corner of the yard, I see what I first think is a scarecrow. As my eyes grow accustomed to the shade, I see tis a black man, trussed forwards against a tree. The low sun picks out the suppuratin weals on his back.

We are allowed to sit. A girl comes out with a ladle & a bucket of water, which we pass round & drink. When I raise my eyes, the mountain looks down, a hazy pink in the dyin light of the sun.

THE WEEDIN GANG

The first few days I am put to weedin with the children & old folk. Work, the work is not hard, but the sun is too hot & the food too small. At night we sleep on the hard ground, but I am too tired to care.

Then I am selected & purchased by Colonel Smith.

'Twas the very next day I was collected by yourself,' I say to Maria. 'Thanks to you, I escaped the cane gang, for a while.'

Hard, hard is the work in the cane gang.

THE CANE GANG

Lucky, lucky am I to spend a few months assistin Maria. Then my good fortune runs out. The planter next door takes a dislike to me, beats me & tells tales.

'Boy's old enough now to do some proper work,' says Smith. He takes me by the ear & throws me in the third cane gang.

See, I only ever see Maria again in the distance. Never again do I feel her kindness.

Howsoever she has taught me well. Thenceforth I resolve to store my diary in my head.

THE HIGH PIECE

'Fast-fast!'

Weeks, my first weeks in the cane gang pass in a daze. At day cut, we line up for the roll-call. The heat of the sun burns my back, the wind parches my lips. Before I begin, I am already weary. Aim, my only aim is to reach the end of the day. There is no other purpose. If the sun hides behind a cloud, it will call a truce & we will have one enemy less.

'Fast-fast!'

Apollo cracks his whip & drives us up the rough path from the village to the High Piece. Our line of thirty men & women stumbles & trips. We disturb a pair of egrets, risin pure & white & free into the dawn sky. The sun is already hot. The view from our furrow is a few acres of dark earth. One brown square in a patchwork of canefields, each hemmed in by strips of bush. Behind us, the mountain rises beyond the trees, topped by its ring of cloud. I dream of escape to its top. But this island prison is too small, just the slopes of this single fire mountain. Too small to escape.

THE THINGS I LACK

Diggin, hoein, plantin – all I do is shift earth to plant sugar cane for the Buckra. The only Engly words I need are for the things I lack.

Food, water, sleep. The second are for dirt. Brown dirt, red dirt, black dirt. Dirt between my toes, in my hair, my eyes, grittin between my teeth. Dirt soured by ashes from the boiling work, by shit from the cattle, soilin our cuts & grazes.

'Fast-fast!'

Apollo's deep voice booms across the cane piece, his great black hand wipin away sweat from his brow with the handle of his whip. Over in the corner, the bony cow strains against its frayed rope. Through each workin day she circles the stake, followin the shade of a tall Palmetto-tree. As she circles the tree, she is my sundial, her motion markin each passin hour.

I THANK QUASHEE

Most times I work hard. If the boy or girl next to me works harder, I try to copy them. If I work too hard, before the end of the day I fall over. But fallin over is much worse than bein whipped. Because if you fall over & cannot get up you may never rise again. The gang will work around you till dusk, when two will be selected to drag you away. If they cannot revive you, they will dig a shallow hole by the Hookee-tree & bury you.

Today I wear the shirt of my friend Quashee, age seventeen, who was struck down yesterday. Bury, we bury him at day cut. His shirt protects my back from the sun.

Quiet, I say a quiet thank you to Quashee.

HIS NAME IS BILLEE

'Change-change!' shouts Apollo.

Move, we move to the next furrow. The cow's shadow points to noon. The morn is almost finished. No one thinks of the afternoon. We stop for rations & water.

While we rest, Colonel Smith comes up the track from the great house with a new overseer & leaves him sittin in the cool shade of the bush. Hear, I hear the new overseer's name is Billee. I watch him from under my brow. New, he is new to the island, whiter than any other white. White as the whites of your eyes, only sicker. Blue is his coat, with many brass buttons. His hair is a strange colour of red. Tall, he is so tall & lanky that he stoops even when he sits. He sweats on the edge of the field, watchin us, writin in his wee book.

They say this Billee is the Scot brought out by Colhoun to train as an overseer. Scot? The word turns into a grey whisper. It blows through a crack in the wall, down the slope of the mountain & out to the ships anchored in the roads.

SOMETHIN NOTABLE

Ask, I ask again, 'What is Scot?' Maybe somethin notable enough to stand out. Maybe to mock. Sambo says Billee has the look of a man whose tribe forget him. Maybe a little like myself. Young. New to the island. Learnin fast.

I do not tell the others that I know a wee bit Engly from the Fort, that I did some writin for Maria.

The afternoon passes in a blur.

As the last bell sounds, I can barely stand. The cow is now in the shade. I look up towards the mountain, its cloudy cap turnin a bright pink. We stagger back down to the village.

WRITIN IN MY HEAD

When I started I had a smatterin of Engly, from my time in the fort. My own tongue fades, among countless others. In the canefields I have no writin tools save a sharp stick, so I write in my head. Put into words the smell of the soil, the heat on my head, the sting of the whip on my back. Choose, I choose the words carefully, as if I am puttin them down on the page. Store them deep, pull them out now & then, polish them. Buildin a wish to survive. Hopin one day I will write them down on paper.

Chapter 18

Hamish, St Kitts

'Needle in a haystack.'

'How did Columbus ever find them?' says Jenny.

Something small pokes out of the sea.

'Which comes first?'

'Nevis?'

'Can see St Kitts behind.'

'St Christopher?'

'Modern name's St Kitts.'

'Is this the way Raleigh came, from the south?'

'Still look very small.'

Our plane circles Nevis, topped by its ring of white cloud. Brightly coloured buildings take shape on the coast. So small, surely not the capital? A church. Higher up, terraces of green. Higher still, dense rain-forest. The plane banks and drops towards its bigger neighbour, St Kitts, a mile or two further on. Bigger? It's maybe fifteen miles long, but with Munro-sized mountains down its backbone. Way down below, a bus circles the island on the coast road. At the south end, a branch climbs steeply, then falls away to a peninsula.

'Reminds me of Arran in the Clyde,' I say.

'Bit more lush.'

As the plane taxis to the terminal, ruined towers poke above the vegetation.

'Sugar mills,' says Jenny.

'Welcome to St Kitts,' says the captain.

The plane door opens and we're hit by a hot breeze. A customs official pats me down, then taps my pocket. I pull out my wee wooden figure and hand him over. The man lifts the wee figure to his ear and shakes him. He gives me an odd look, then hands him back.

In the taxi, we glimpse more of the circular stone towers, up overgrown tracks. Like medieval castles, out of place on this farming island.

When we reach town, we grab our bags from the boot and find a seat in the shade. Jenny goes off to buy a drink from the shop across the road. An unfamiliar bush gives welcome shade from the hot sun. Globules of translucent resin stain the far end of the bench. One golden globe has trapped a dead insect. When I try to pick it off the seat, it leaves the tips of my fingers sticky.

When Jenny comes back, I say, 'Mind if I go for a walk?' I leave her with her drink, pull out a map, and head off on a whistle-stop tour of the capital. My hand brushes a Victorian cast-iron railing. I stop and grab a photo of the wee logo: McDowall Steven & Co. Ltd., Glasgow.

No. 129. Searching for a Townhouse

Walking through the capital, I'm here and there. My body on St Kitts but my head in Glasgow. I pass through The Circus, up Fort Street. Along Cayon Street, down Market Street and back by Bay Road.

Looking for a story, three hundred years too late. Picking up fragments, uncovering tracks. Fact and fiction. Myth and history.

Searching for a townhouse. Best in the town. Rented out to the Governor. You're a top man here too.

Aye right.

***

Soon I'm sweating in the direct sun. Should have left my backpack with Jenny.

On a street corner, a boy hawks wooden models of the circular towers, carved from some kind of giant gourd. Big versions of Murdo's wee model. The joints in the stonework are deeply scored, like they're built from thousands of wee bricks. 'Windmills, mon,' the boy says.

I choose the biggest and bring out my wallet. We'd been told to bring two types of dollars, US and Eastern Caribbean. But when I pull out my ECs, the boy's face falls. 'US?' I say.

The boy smiles. I pay an extra five dollars for the shopping trolley, and the boy empties his wares onto the pavement. I load my backpack inside, plonk the model on top and head down the road. Around the corner, dozens of the same trolleys sit, free of charge, outside a supermarket.

On another corner I buy a wooden African mask from a lady with her wares spread on a rug on the pavement. I've always wanted one. It's expensive, but she assures me it's genuine.

In the square is a big English-style church, out of place on this exotic island. A tour group are leaving by a side door. I look at my watch, hide my trolley in a bush and slip inside. I find the tower steps and climb to the top. A flag flies from a white pole, the Caribbean mix of red, green and yellow. A happy flag. The view's amazing, but it's the hottest spot in town.

All around stretches a rectangular grid of streets. If Murdo lived here, he'd have modelled all the buildings in the grid. But, like in Glasgow, all the older buildings have gone. I rest my hands on the parapet, then jump back. The stone's burning hot.

I jump again as my watch buzzes. 'Where are you?' Jenny says.

'Up the church tower,' I say. 'Can you see me?'

She waves, a tiny figure down below.

Out in the bay, a big cruise ship approaches.

What was it like, arriving here three hundred years ago?

No. 130. I Arrived Here Safely

My Dearest Father,

I arrived here safely the 12th inst., after a satisfactory voyage south to the Canaries, then we caught the trade winds west. The climate is very warm but is tempered on the higher slopes by the breeze. I sit here watching a green monkey on the verandah consume a mango. I have a mind to catch one and train it as a pet.

I trust you received my letter from Tenerife. Your letter of 3rd Feby was here on my arrival.

Our ship entered the Caribbean Sea a few days ago, passing Guadeloupe and many other small but mountainous islands. Finally we came in sight of the Leewards, curving gently to the north. The island loomed through the morning mist, a perfect cone rising out of the sea.

During the long weeks of my voyage, I learned to read the motion of the ship, the creaking timbers, and slap of the swell against the hull. That day I sensed that we had stopped. A great bustle was soon afoot. I packed my small bundle of possessions, wrapped my precious books in cloth. I donned my best coat in blue wool with gold buttons, but resisted wearing my wig, as the day was already hot. On deck was a great commotion to unload the cargo onto the small boats and carry it ashore. Three other ocean-going vessels lay in Charlestown roads and the quickest to offload would achieve the best price. Several boats came out from the shore, touting for business, and I soon negotiated the short passage.

As I crossed in a small boat, a brief but heavy down-pouring diluted and evaporated the mist. The vista opened like a curtain in a theatre set, solely for my own benefit. The recent rains made the whole face of the mountain verdant and welcoming. The capital lay stretched out along the shore. Above it, for several miles in each direction, were plantations of sugar cane of the most verdurous green. Higher up still was a forest of innumerable tall trees. Despite the early hour, the air was already warm. As the light increased, the summit of the mountain cleared, though the top was still partly shrouded in white cloud, like a cap of snow.

The short wooden quay was too busy, so I stepped off the boat into the surf. I knew not if it was the strength of the waves, or the shock of my feet upon solid ground, but I fell over. When I staggered back to my feet, I was soaked to the skin. A fitting baptism to my new life.

It is with the greatest pleasure I hear all my dear family and friends at Garthland are well to whom pray make my compliments.

Your dearest and most obedient son, Billy.

***

It's too hot. On the way back down, I bump into a well-dressed lady. She's pleased at my interest in her church, but assumes I'm American. When I correct her, she says, 'Why would a Scot come to our little island?'

I thank her for her invitation to a Sunday service and recover my trolley. On a street corner, I kneel in my wee ritual and run my fingers over a piece of stone. Ouch! I haven't learned my lesson. A large lady in a bright red dress gives me a wide berth, but doesn't throw me a coin.

The top halves of the buildings are timber, painted in bright colours. But the bottoms are solid stone: small, square blocks, like the Romans used on Hadrian's Wall. The stone bases look older than the wooden tops, like they're trying to tell me something. But how old are they? I might be a structural engineer, but here my X-ray eyes are out of focus. Everything's so different it makes me dizzy.

I buy a bag of mangoes from a stall across the road. They're incredibly cheap. I love mangoes when they're ripe and juicy. I keep coming across windfalls in the street, squashed underfoot. Then, on a waste plot, I spot another cast-iron railing: GEORGE SMITH & CO., GLASGOW.

There was no mention of connections with my home city, yet the clues are all around, like a secret history. The railing's rusty and falling down. I look around, pick up a brick and hit the top rail. The cast iron shatters. I break bits off at either end, until all that's left is the word 'Glasgow'. I slip it into my backpack and carry on. I don't know anyone here, but most of them are coming towards me.

I'm still going against the flow.

I sit on a hot wall. A lizard runs out and gives me a fright. Everything's colourful and different. Over in the park, I kneel and pick at the white bark of a tree. The grass is coarse and hurts my knees. The pavements are surfaced with white ceramic tiles. I run my fingertips over the smoothness. I want to blend in, suck in the culture, but I stand out like a tourist.

On a street corner, an old man wearing a straw hat smiles. 'Shopping?' the man says. His name's Jimmy and he offers me a tour.

I shake my head.

'You from Glasgow, mon?'

'Is it the shorts and white legs,' I say, 'or the old Celtic T-shirt?' I'm not a football fan, but it matches my green army shorts.

'Recognise the accent,' Jimmy says. 'My cousin lives in Aberdeen. Been there twice. Nice place, but cold wind.'

'Aye right,' I say, with the tourist's suspicion of a rip-off. But Jimmy describes Union Street and a pub I know. We have a chat about the Granite City.

'Here,' says Jimmy. He takes off his straw hat and holds it out.

'No,' I say. But Jimmy takes pity on my sweaty brow and plops the hat on my head. Then he picks the wooden African mask from my trolley, turns it over and taps a wee logo on the back: MADE IN CHINA.

I say goodbye to Jimmy and move on. The streets are busy with locals. Passers-by smile at my trolley. Sympathy for a tourist, or do they know I've been ripped off?

At the bottom of the street, I reach the shore. A group of pelicans tussle in the surf. At the top of the beach is a vertical bank. The sand's grey, but near the bottom is a darker layer. I pick out wee bits of red tile. Start of the town? I might be four thousand miles from home, but nothing's changed.

At the far end of the beach is a stretch of driftwood. I gather some to fill the gaps in my trolley. Maybe we can have a barbecue later.

Finally I reach the location of Billy's townhouse. I'd hoped to get a picture of something grand, fitting his rank. Maybe put it on the cover of the book? But it's just a modern building.

I look closer. The top part might be new, but it has a more solid stone basement than the others. I need to reach over and touch it, crawl inside and explore. Find something sharp and dig out a sample. But there's a kennel in the corner of the yard. I'm not desperate enough to risk my life. Not yet.

I head back along the shore road, to where Jenny's reading her thick paperback. She looks up. 'Shit, it's Robinson Crusoe!'

I spot my reflection in a shop window, wearing an old straw hat, pushing a trolley full of firewood and my worldly possessions.

'Made a new friend?' she says, knocking off my hat. 'How are you going to get all that stuff to our hotel?'

'Hotel?'

She puts her book away and heaves her backpack on top of my trolley. We head along the street, Jenny snapping the brightly coloured buildings. I kneel again and run my hand over the stone blocks in a basement storey. Jenny copies me. 'Volcanic?' she says.

'*Skirt and blouse*, stone below and brightly coloured timber above,' I say, showing off my local knowledge. 'Bottom half's a hurricane shelter. Top half gets blown away.'

'So the bottom half's much older,' she says.

For once she's on my wavelength.

Further on, she catches me glancing at the logo on a railing. She puts on her glasses and reads it out: 'Walter Macfarlane, Glasgow. Knicker labels!'

I look baffled.

'Like when you kick off your undies,' she says, 'and you spot on the label where they're made.'

We turn down beneath a white colonial building, towards the pier. I reach up and touch the soffit of the arch. Jenny tries to copy me but can't reach. I lift her by the waist and she stretches up and copies my wee ritual.

Arches? I've been here before. A portal to something earlier. They also give good protection against the sun.

'We need a taxi,' I say.

'While you were on your travels, a cute driver named Leroy gave me his card.'

She's found a new boyfriend?

'Offered to give us a quick tour before we find our hotel.'

Jenny calls Leroy. He draws up with a small wicker picnic basket on the front seat. He points at me. 'Dude comin too?'

'He's my cousin,' she says. 'He doesn't bite.'

I abandon my trolley and driftwood. We climb in the back. The taxi speeds off with a squeal of tyres, then jumps to a halt at a crossing. The basket falls onto the floor with the sound of breaking glass. Leroy raises a hand. 'Sorry.' But the sun's setting. The tour will need to wait for another day.

Leroy doesn't take long to reach our accommodation. He stops at a group of chalets with wide verandas, on a tiered slope. We have the disorientated feeling of tourists arriving in a strange place after dark. It's off season and the place looks deserted. We find number five and pick up the keys from under the mat. Inside, it's warm and musty. I open a window, but a cloud of insects hangs outside, so I close it again. I click the switch marked: Air Con and two wobbly ceiling fans kick noisily to life. Over in the corner, the fridge rumbles. The place is clean, but basic.

Jenny goes back into the bedroom to unpack her bag. Something scuttles along the skirting and she runs back out of the room.

'Hotel?' she says. 'There's no way I'm staying.'

'The beach clubs are extortionate,' I say.

'I'm not going in there.'

'We only paid a small deposit,' I say. 'We can look for something else tomorrow.'

We're too tired to argue. Jenny bunks down on the sofa and falls asleep.

***

Next morning, we call Leroy and he picks us up at nine. We've had nothing to eat since the day before. Leroy stops at a cafe.

'Why you come here, mon?' he says. 'Island's quiet in summer.'

'Thought the weather was the same all year round?' I say.

'Yanks only come here at Christmas, when it's cold at home. Tell me, mon, where can I find my island's history?'

Everyone we meet's interested in their past.

'Looking for somewhere to crash,' Jenny says.

'I have just what you need,' Leroy says. 'My cousin's villa.'

We look at each other, but he spots us in the mirror. 'Very good villa. On the beach.' He drives beyond the capital, parks at a clapboard house by the side of the road and jumps out. We shake hands with his cousin Anthony, who leads us down a narrow, overgrown track towards the sea.

Villa? It's a shack on the beach. The toilet and shower are up on the edge of the bush. I frown, but Jenny smiles. It's got a certain charm, and sits on its own, unspoiled beach. I notice it's only got one bedroom, with a double bed. Jenny doesn't comment.

'How much?' Jenny says.

'Try it for a day or two,' Anthony says, 'then we make a deal?'

Jenny steps forward and shakes hands. 'Perfect,' she says.

Back at the taxi, we fetch our bags. Anthony's wife comes down with fresh linen and towels, and a few provisions. She switches on the fridge and puts the milk and butter inside.

'My sister wants to go to England,' she says. 'Has many forms to fill in. Perhaps you can help?'

Apart from the living room and double bedroom, there's a wee box room at the back. I take my stuff through. We unpack then sit in the kitchen, and Jenny makes tea. My wee folder lies on the table, loose sheets of paper poking out the side. Jenny pulls out my list of Glasgow railings from the capital.

'More knicker labels?'

I shrug. 'Haven't seen any Bristol ones.'

'Maybe now we're here we can dump the city rivalry?'

No. 131. This is Different

You've come dancing across the ocean with your regiment of men. Sailing the seas with your rank and finery. Writing letters home to your brother and your parents.

I've come following in your footsteps. Walking the streets of the capital. Looking for evidence.

Some things I'm sure of. The name of the island. The picture on the travel brochure. The turquoise sea, backed by tall mountains. Sun, sea and sand. It's not a regular holiday island, but it's all I can fit it into.

But this is different. Something from my childhood. Far away in my Second City of Empire.

I'm all mixed up. I've come all this way. To a distant island.

And all I can find is Glasgow connections.

Chapter 19

Jenny, St Kitts

The Two Cs

Next morning at dawn, Jenny watched a pair of birds sail above the sea on black-tipped wings, their yellow heads outstretched. One dived and the other hit the water with a long white splash. She called Kelly.

'Where are you?' Kelly said.

'Caribbean.'

'Ha ha.'

'Really.'

There was a long silence, then Kelly said, 'Island?'

'St Kitts.'

'Chasing the two Cs?'

'Sun and sea?'

'Cato and Coz?'

A Sea of Green

After breakfast, Jenny's first priority was the archives. Hamish followed her up the path.

At the top of the track, she turned and headed along the road towards town.

'Shouldn't we wait for a bus?' Hamish said.

The sun was extra hot. It wasn't long before their clothes were damp with sweat. Cars stopped, not just taxis but locals, offering a lift: 'You crazy, mon? Nobody walks in this heat.'

All along the road, they were hemmed in by a sea of tall, green grass. The only let-up was the odd stone windmill tower or brick chimney, poking above the green.

Sun or Rain?

Houses were strung along the road which circled the edge of the island, like they'd been pushed down the hill by something more important.

'Garden sheds?' Hamish said.

'Give them a break. All you need's a chalet in this climate.'

Ahead, a church bell began to toll. Well-dressed children tumbled from doorways, followed by their parents. Their brightly coloured Sunday best belied their humble dwellings. As the locals passed, each raised their umbrellas, greeting Hamish and Jenny with big smiles. The locals filed inside the church.

'Umbrellas for the sun or the rain?' said Jenny, screwing up her eyes at the sky.

'That a rain cloud?'

'It's not very big.'

A moment later they were engulfed. They'd been warned about tropical showers and had packed lightweight ponchos at the bottom of their bags. But, by the time they found them, they were soaked to the skin. So were the contents of their backpacks, which had spilled out to release the ponchos.

The shower passed as quickly as it had come. Jenny's hair was bedraggled by the rain. Her purple eyeshadow had run down her cheeks. Her bra showed through her wet blouse. Colour from her bag had bled into her skirt.

An Exotic Holiday

Jenny pointed to a big hoarding by the roadside advertising a beach resort. Smiling white couples lounged by the pool, sipping colourful cocktails, picking at expensive food. 'You promised an exotic holiday,' she said.

They continued walking, their clothes drying in the heat but their feet still wet and squidgy. Drivers still smiled and waved, but they no longer stopped to offer a lift. Jenny and Hamish bought bottled water from a kiosk and turned up a side road to sit in the shade. Hamish took off his trainers and laid out his socks to dry.

Finally they surrendered to a friendly boy in his late teens, in an old pickup truck half full of bales of straw. He dropped them in the central square and refused a tip.

Fit In

They found a cafe on a corner, on the first floor, under a pergola decked with flowers. The tables overlooked the street. Jenny noticed the logo on the cast-iron railing on the balcony, in little letters: LION FOUNDRY, KIRKINTILLOCH. Hamish sat down and covered the logo with his bag.

Jenny leaned back in a chair and fanned herself with her hat. 'It's perfect!'

'You can order,' he said.

'Why me?'

He smiled. 'Ach, you fit in.'

She grabbed her bag and knocked over her chair. As she stormed down the stairs, she bumped into the waitress.

When Hamish caught up with her, she was in tears. He put his hand on her shoulder, but she shook him off.

'You bastard. You think I fit in here because of the colour of my skin?'

St Kitts Archives

Jenny went off on her own. At the shops, she bought a pencil, notebook and a bag of boiled sweets.

The two islands were united as one country, but St Kitts was bigger and had the main archive. She joined a queue at the big white government building, in full research mode. As she waited, she opened the sweets, but they'd stuck together in the heat. A couple of uniformed men, with guns in their belts, searched her bag. There was no system for checking in or getting a reader's ticket. She longed for the familiar rituals.

Despite the informality, the archivist, Viki, was more than helpful. Jenny found a desk in the corner, took her pencil out of its case and laid it in its slot. She opened her new notebook, took a deep breath and opened the first tome. She worked her way through several volumes.

From her experience, she was sure she'd find something about Cato. But she found nothing.

'A worker?' Viki said. 'Sorry, there's very little.'

Workers? No matter how hard Jenny looked, everything she found was about the planters.

Their Richest Possession

Jenny took Viki's advice and went round to the Heritage Society, where she spoke to a helpful lady called Hazel. Hazel told Jenny how she'd been chasing the African origins of folk on her island. Strewn across the table were copies of faded lists.

'I'm looking for names of workers,' Jenny said.

'They were their richest possession,' Hazel said. 'Wrote them all down.'

'Can I look?'

'You need to meet Anna. She's been collecting lists for years.'

'Do you have her number?'

'I'll need to ask her permission first,' Hazel said.

Jenny called Hamish. They met up and got a taxi home.

Anna

The next day, Jenny was in town checking out the clothes market. Her phone rang. 'My name's Anna. Hazel gave me your name. I believe you're into lists of workers?'

An hour later, Jenny met Anna in a cafe. She was a tall local lady, with long grey hair plaited with coloured beads. She wore a bright T-shirt and denim skirt. Jenny bought cold drinks.

'I'm interested in workers on a plantation,' Jenny said.

'Makes a change. Most folk are looking for planters. Even the apologetic ones.' Anna brought out a folder full of typed sheets with an alphabetical index to plantations. She tapped her folder. 'Two hundred to one,' she said.

Jenny nodded and tried to look intelligent.

'They'll tell you it's ten Africans to one white,' Anna said, 'but that includes the planter's family and the overseers and all his lackeys. But it's two hundred to one. One planter owning two hundred Africans. That's the rule on this island. Two-hundred-acre plantations. One worker per acre. That's the rule.'

Jenny nodded again.

'They all have lists,' Anna said. 'No matter how little survives for their estate. The Africans were their most valuable asset, so they recorded them, tallied them, named them.'

They chatted about the island, then Jenny said, 'It's not just the history. My family came from here.'

'I know,' Anna said. 'We all came from Africa, but you can tell which part by the shape of your face. Your profile, your stance.'

As they sat by the window, Anna picked out passers-by and tried to guess which part of Africa their ancestors came from.

'You collect the lists?' Jenny said.

'Full of details. Names, ages, occupations.'

'Countries of origin?'

'That's the ultimate goal. Not some terrible story about captivity. Just to know where we came from.' Anna brought out a typical list. Jenny ran her finger down the list slowly, reading names, while Anna watched. 'That's the difference between you and most of the folk who come looking,' Anna said. 'You read the names, but they only count the numbers. That's all they're interested in, big numbers.'

'White folk?' Jenny said.

'Who's your planter?' Anna said.

'Name's Colonel Billy.'

Anna changed her tone. 'Nothing for that name,' she said, too quickly.

'Don't you need to check?' Jenny said.

Anna looked at her watch and stood up. 'Sorry, I've got another appointment. Need to go.'

'Please!' Jenny said.

Anna sat back down. She paused, then seemed to make a decision. 'You're Hamish's cousin?'

'You've met him?' Jenny said.

Anna shook her head. 'Promise to keep a secret?'

Jenny crossed herself.

'Murdo's here,' Anna said.

'He's alive!'

'But you can't tell Hamish.'

'You're shacked up with him!'

Anna stood up again. 'You think that if a white man befriends a black girl, he's got to be shagging her?'

Jenny held up her hands. 'Didn't mean it that way. Just thought you were close.'

'Close to Murdo! I thought you knew him?' Anna explained how she'd met Murdo. How she'd been a mature student in Glasgow, and how they had a common interest. How he was desperate to visit the island, though his health was in decline.

'Can I meet him?' Jenny said.

'Told you too much already.'

'Just to ask some questions.'

'He won't allow it.'

'I don't understand,' Jenny said, 'how he controls everyone.'

Anna sighed. 'You, me...'

'Hamish,' Jenny said.

'His mate Eck.'

'Maybe it's time we broke the cycle?' Jenny said.

'I can't guarantee anything, but you can come up and see the lists for Colonel Billy.'

Jenny nodded. It was a start.

Smiling Back

Once they parted, Jenny walked the streets of the capital to clear her head. She sat in a park and watched folk of all shapes and sizes pass by. She nodded politely, and everyone smiled back. She looked into their faces, trying to see a family resemblance. If she could take their DNA, would they be her distant cousins?

It was odd. Hamish was here chasing a white planter. But all the faces smiling back were black. Everything was back to front.

Let a Good One Go

Jenny's phone rang. It was Kelly. 'How's progress with Coz?' she said. 'Still living like brother and sister?'

'He's too trad Scottish male to open up.'

'Too dependable for your restless nature?'

'Dunno.'

'Jesus, Jen, you've found the perfect guy, but you're scared he'll dumb you down? Prefer someone less reliable?'

'Don't just want a holiday fling.'

'What's more important, getting on with Coz, or the history shit? This holiday's your big chance. You want to let a good one go?'

Can I ever get close to him when we're hiding so much? Jenny thought.

Restless Spark

Jenny headed out on the path beyond the edge of town, until she came to a sort of shanty village. She sat in the shade and watched a farmer digging. How long did it take to dig a whole field with only a spade? She took her notebook and tried to describe the scene, like Cato might have done.

Then she stopped on a corner and watched a woman fill a stone vat from a wonky tap. The woman scrubbed her clothes with a big block of soap. Across the yard, a boy played with a stick in the dust. Further along, a young girl tended goats in a corner of a dirt yard.

Jenny heard an animated voice. Round the next corner, a local man sat under a tree, tapping on his laptop, shouting into his phone. Power came from a frayed overhead wire from a solar panel in the roof of what looked like a pig shed. When she passed the open doors of the shed, a shiny new Mercedes sat inside.

Jenny smiled to herself. Nobody conforms to a stereotype, she thought. Maybe, buried deep inside, I've got the restless spark of the folk here.

Civilised

Jenny bought some fresh croissants for lunch from a baker's stall. On a whim, she caught a bus up to Cayon Church. She spent time wandering around the graveyard. But all the early graves she could find were for planters and their families. The workers were still invisible, even in death.

What if she couldn't solve it with records? Records were a kind of surrender to a civilised manner. But nothing that happened here was civilised. It was like John in his brown coat in the archive back home. It was all too slow, and she needed fast.

But that was the paradox, she thought. Even if you're a revolutionary, you need to do the donkey work first. Otherwise your protest is just hot air.

The Journal of Cato

CHOSEN

Today, chosen, I am chosen with another boy from our field gang to go with Massa Billee to the top of the ghut. We climb the beaten path towards the highest cane piece, our shackles chaffin our ankles.

We reach the top corner of the plantation beside the ghut, where Khus-khus grass grows tall. Massa Billee takes out his pencil, sharpens it with his pocket knife & draws in his notebook. I watch him make the line thicker or thinner with a little tilt of the point. I notice the strange freckles on his white skin, like a sprinkle of mosquito bites.

Massa Billee says, with loudness in his voice, 'We dig channel from burn to here.'

Later I learn that burn is Scotch for river. Most of the year, burn is dry. Massa Billee moves his hands, mimin where he wants us to dig. Speakin words he does not expect us to understand.

I CANNOT ANSWER

Hear me now. This is my chance. I know I am crazy. I know the whites are out to riddle you, rhyme you, strip you down & buck you. Why not run away, kill Colonel Smith, buck his woman & his pretty daughters. Strike him down with a hoe, crush his skull with a rock & run to the mountain. Why do I not escape?

I cannot answer. The curse of this small island robs us of the desire to be free. Now is never the time. Always manyana, as Pedro the cook say. Maybe one day, if I am desperate enough? There is nothin to stop us but fear & the mountain.

INJUSTICE

The Buckra live on solid ground, sippin tea on their verandahs. The worst thing in my life is not the whippin but the injustice. No matter how hard I work, how much I obey, the whip cuts my back as often as the lazy boy beside me.

Look, I look up into Billee's deep blue eyes. 'Massa, you wan dig, carry water across?'

His eyes screw up in the sunlight. 'You impertinent Nigger. You speak English?'

I scratch 'YES' in the dirt with my finger. Tis unthinkable for us to look a whitey in the eye. Brothers are whipped, cut, killed for less. Maybe tis only because Billee is new that he excuse me.

'A Nigger who speaks & writes. I may have use for you.'

The boy beside me looks at me, not understandin, but knowin I have crossed a line. That by talkin to Billee I have begun to distance myself from him, from all my brothers & sisters.

TEACH HIM GOOD WRITING

Week, a week later I am on my last legs. I will not survive another day in the fields. Billee comes up the path at dinner bell, whispers to Apollo, takes me out of the cane gang. Prods me down the path ahead of him with his stick. Takes me to the shady spot where One-arm John sits.

Without lookin at me he says to One-arm, 'I have a need of a new clerk. Teach him good writing.'

THE OFFICE

Remember, I remember, the first day I set eyes upon this office hut. Overgrown with tall weeds & creepers. Billee reaches up & pulls down a vine & bunches it in his white hand. 'Fetch a machete from the store,' he says. When we come back, he pulls at the weeds. 'Clear the growth from the office.'

One-arm John tells me that since he stopped writin the books have been neglected & the hut has been disused & overgrown. Drop a seed in the soil of this island & a few weeks later tis a tall plant with shiny green leaves. Another few weeks & you will be pickin its fruit. Left alone, the bush will march down the hillside & bury you.

But sugar cane is more stubborn, needs more care.

BILLEE'S PLANS

Later, inside the office, as I sweep round the high desk & stool with a broom, Billee speaks aloud of his plans: 'You cannot run a plantation without good book-keeping.'

Though I am his only companion, Billee looks through me. Speaks to the walls, the ceilin, not to myself.

Tis dry inside & the back walls hold shelves of big old ledgers, their covers every shade of brown.

'Bring my letters here from the house. From now on, you are my scribe. Every letter & instruction that I write you shall copy into a ledger, so that I keep a record of all that I write.'

NEAT ROWS OF WORDS

One-arm can read Engly, but has not wrote since they cut off his arm for eatin windfall mangoes in the high field. But teach, he teach me all he knows. How to collect egret feathers. How to cut the nib at the right angle. How to take the big brass ruler & draw a straight line. How to dip my pen in the ink & copy Billee's letters before he sends them down to the ships anchored in Basseterre Roads.

'But write, I can only write a few words,' I say.

'Soon you will learn. Anyhow, neatness come before rightness. The Buckra never read letter books, only glance at neat rows of words.'

NAMES I KNOW

The first thing I copy out is a list of goods & chattels. I pick out those whose names I know from the canefields.

I know Cudjo.

I know Congo.

Jacko & I worked side by side on the high piece & Caesar loaded the cart.

Arran handed out the hoes at day cut & collected them at dusk.

Edinburgh was Billee's favourite for a time, until he chose Coffee.

Sally & Nelly I know from the fields.

A few weeks later, Jacko & Sally are missin from the list. Jacko was nineteen, but was struck too hard by Apollo & did not rise to his feet again. Sally was fifteen. She was beat n bucked by Peterson & his factor after they drank too much brandy on Tuesday forenoon. She was found by the side of the road. Billee had me carry a note to Peterson requestin £20 compensation for Sally & a shillin for her burial. Peterson paid only £15, for Sally was blind in one eye from a lick o' the whip.

GLASGOW

One day Billee dictates a letter, orderin four thousand brick & a cast-iron door from Scotland.

When they arrive, he engages the mason to build a brick extension to the rear of my hut. Separated from the front by a heavy iron door. In the centre of the door are cast three words: EAGLE FOUNDRY, GLASGOW. Tis the first time I have read the word 'Glasgow' & know not what it means.

Many shelves are built in the brick room, to store the plantation ledgers.

'Every night,' Billee says, 'ledgers must be kept in the brick store, with the door locked.' Many times Billee chastises me for leavin the door open. Many times he berates me for havin too many ledgers out front. 'If the books are in the brick store, they are safe from fire,' he says.

MY OWN PLANTATION

Massa Billee works hard for planter Smith. Makes a good profit. Receives offers from three other planters to work for them, but he takes the letters to Smith. Smith increases Billee's allowance by ten pounds a year.

Billee has a special book where he has me tally what he has saved. 'One day I will have my own plantation,' he says to his friend Jamie.

Talk, Billee talks with assurance in his voice. Believe, his friend Jamie almost believes him.

SHADOW

Sit, I sit here at my high desk, finishin copyin Massa Billee's letters. Spend, I spend my life in his shadow, thus my fortunes are mixed with those of Massa Billee. So I ask again, which story do I tell? My own or Massa Billee's?

When Billee dictates his letters, he pauses, testin words to find the one with the most power. Like spells, his words make things happen.

He writes home about his life here. But who will write of us? Of those who toil far away from our home, unseen, our lives passin like autumn leaves?

GOODS & CHATTELS

At the back of the office, on the top shelf above the ledgers, are three printed books. A Bible, a book of navigation charts & *Burton's Sugar Cultivation.*

I bring down a big ledger. Open it at the page for the day I landed here. I run my finger along the line. See my name wrote, 'Cato'. So many names.

List of Goods & Chattels, says the headin. Even the cattle are named & valued.

Where did we come from? Most of my fellow Scalags are brought from Guinea; those from the Gold Coast raise the highest price in the market. A boy or girl like myself, above 16 years of age on arrival, is worth £30 sterling.

We are kept in line by the letter of the law. The penalty for stealin sugar is the loss of ears, for a second offence, death. Sentence is administered by Justices of the Peace, who inflict what penalty they please.

Since I arrived, Davee & Paisley, both sixteen, ran off from our plantation. Howsoever, there is nowhere to run on this small island other than the mountain top. Caught, they were caught in two days by the dogs & trussed up by the feet in the sun. Then, at dusk, they were cut down & stretched upon the wheel, their arms, thighs & leg bones broke all to shivers with an iron crow, then flung into a large & fierce fire to be burnt alive.

This was carried out in front of us all.

Look, we could not look away.

MOTHBALLS & BREECHES

One day I watch Billee rub the ears of the oxen turnin his cane mill. More care has he for his beasts than for myself. Nevertheless, it true, it. No matter how much I am ignored, I only survive as long as Billee needs me.

Now that One-arm is gone, only Billee & I frequent the office. Come, he comes up most days after sundown. He peruses the books, then he has me kneel & serve him.

When he is quite gone, only the smell from his breeches & powder from his wig still linger.

Only then, when he is out of ear-shot, do I spit, his taste lingerin in my mouth.

Jenny's Family Album

Jenny opened her notebook at her list. She added *Sally, 15, blind in one eye, £15.*

Chapter 20
Hamish, St Kitts

No. 132. A Trainee Sugar Planter

Dear Brother,

You ask about a position here for yourself. I suspect that you are of too tender a disposition to train as an overseer on a sugar plantation. I recommend that you continue to attend navigation school in Glasgow, and pursue your ambition of venturing to sea. Good ships' masters are scarce here.

You enquire more about my life here. My duties are to tally plantation accounts, imports and exports. To entice the workers to make good sugar. I have great ambitions to please Smith, the owner. My friend Jamie warns that my ambitions are too great, that if I work them too hard they will drop, if I cut the rations some will die. Howsoever, if a man does not take a chance, and follow his instincts, he will not succeed. There are many openings for an ambitious overseer, even a Scot, to rise through the system and become a planter.

***

I clip my latest letter transcript into the wee Filofax. Not a soldier, now an overseer?

Just then a gust of wind moves the blind and knocks wee Billy off the window ledge. I poke my head out the window. The wee man's embedded head first in the sand, like an ostrich.

Is this what I'm reduced to? Burying all that I find? What am I scared of?

I leave the wee man outside.

Jenny arrives back from town and throws me the remains of her bag of croissants.

'Where you been?' I say.

'Island archives.'

'Anything for Billy?'

'Billy bollocks.'

***

Later, I sit outside on my own on an old, faded deckchair. It's too bright in the sun to read my tablet, so I go back into the verandah. We face each other across the old table, both typing. I look up. 'What you doing?'

Jenny snaps her laptop shut, grabs her sun hat from a hook at the door and heads down the beach. She spends half her time poring over her laptop, working on her museum stuff. I still don't know what it is, and she's too touchy to risk asking.

No. 133. I Was Shocked

Dear Brother,

Further to my last, I have been advised by Colhoun to be more careful in my homeward correspondence. I ask you not to share my frankness regarding the mutilation and demise of the escapees Cudjo and Johnee with Mother and Father. There are a great many Negroes here, and any losses are easily replenished by hundreds more brought daily to market, off the Guinea sloops.

I must admit I was shocked at the first appearance of human flesh exposed to sale. But surely God ordained them for the use and benefit of us all. You may say that such ideas are very despotic, but if you consider that we have near two hundred blacks to one white, you must own them to be quite necessary.

I have yours of the 5th inst. and I am very glad to hear of your welfare and all your family and friends in that part of the world. Will Colhoun sends his regards to father.

I have not else, but am with my service to all friends, your most affectionate kinsman and humble brother, Billy.

***

I slip out my sheet of dodgy words from the compartment at the back of my wee folder. I only write one letter: 'N'. I fold the sheet in two and zip it back into my Pandora section. There isn't much space left. What will I do then?

I make a decision and slip the wee folder into my backpack. I climb the track to the road, hitch a lift into town, and pluck up the courage to find the library. Am I turning into Jenny?

The island section has a row of thickly bound books. I open the first one. Lots of facts about sugar planters. It's also a British Government publication: I could have seen it in any big library at home.

I run my finger along the dates embossed in gold on the spines. In the index are lots of Scottish names: Colhoun, the friend of Billy's dad. I copy out the information. Colhoun was a sugar planter. Sent his sugar back to Glasgow.

The records go back as far as Murdo's magic date, 1668. My wee wooden numbers stand on the mantelpiece back in the shack. It's hardly a coincidence that Scots came here the same year as Glasgow's first sugar house was built. But I soon get bored and go back to the counter.

'Interested in a Scot,' I say. 'At home it says he was a soldier, but I think he was a planter.'

'You need the militia,' says the girl. Her name's Linda. I write down 'militia'. Linda leads me through to a small open courtyard and leaves me with more books.

In 1705 he was elected to the island council. Appointed a lieutenant, then a colonel. In the *militia*, not the British army. Appointed by his cronies. There's so many entries for Billy that my hand hurts making notes.

When Linda comes back through, I say, 'Militia?'

'Dad's Army of the Caribbean,' she says. 'Cobbled together to keep the French at bay until the British navy arrived.'

'A colonel in Dad's Army?'

'Same with most of the planters,' she says. 'Gave them status when they went home to Britain. Allowed them to mix with the landed gentry. Pretended they were officers, not planters.'

Pretended? What do I tell Jenny?

***

Next morning I'm up first. We haven't spoken since the day before, but I make a decision. I need to bottom out the soldier stuff.

I call Leroy, who comes for us in less than an hour. 'Can you take us to Brimstone Hill?' I say.

Because I've mentioned the fort, Leroy starts the military tour. Battles with the French. He seems to think, because we speak English, that the French are our worst enemies.

Leroy stops at a place called Bloody Point. 'Where the whities wiped out our ancestors,' Leroy says, making eye contact with Jenny but ignoring me.

'Africans?' she says.

'No, mon, the natives. Some of us is part Carib.'

We carry on, very fast, along the narrow main road. A big hill looms ahead, towering above the low land beside the sea.

'Brimstone Hill,' says Leroy. He drives up the winding road to the summit at breakneck speed. When we stop, Jenny hands him some US dollars.

'Come back in a couple of hours?' she says. Leroy nods and speeds off.

The fort's unlike anything else on the island. The summit's fortified on several levels. Everything's built of thick stone. A symbol of colonial power. We have the place to ourselves, and it's hot up top, but there's a nice breeze. We explore the battlements, then have a snack in the shade of a tree.

Jenny takes off her shoes and moves lightly around the grassy plateau in her long, light dress, poking at cannons and stonework. Her little twirls are an expression of freedom. She may not be a great dancer, but there's a grace to her movements. I could sit and watch her all day. I'm on holiday with the perfect girl, but all we do is argue.

Then we split up to explore. I stick to the shade, in a cool building with thick stone walls. The museum. I read the plaques fixed to the stone walls. There's plenty of dates and battles, but little about those involved.

Back out in the sun, I find a concealed corner. Just as I'm digging a piece of old stone from the wall, Jenny appears, giving me a fright. 'So Billy led battles here against the French?' she says.

I dislodge the chunk of stone and put it in my backpack. 'Why would the British army build such a massive fort to defend a backwater?' I say.

Together, we cross to the edge of the summit and look out over the island. The slopes are covered in a sea of green, broken only by the tops of stone windmill towers poking up through the vegetation.

I need to be honest with Jenny. I take her arm and turn to face her. 'Went to the library yesterday,' I say. 'Wasn't a soldier.'

'Bit of a coincidence, just before we came up here!'

I sit down on the grass and hold out my phone with my notes, but the sun's too bright.

'What's harder?' she says. 'Admitting what Billy's up to, or being nice to me?'

I turn away.

'We're missing something.' She pulls out her phone and makes a call. Leroy appears right away. He's been waiting round the corner.

***

At bedtime, I go through to my wee room. I don't have a bed, just a mattress on the floor, but it's fine. The lower you get, the cooler the air. I fetch my wee wooden man from outside in the sand, and stand him up on the bedside table.

'You've to be on your best behaviour,' I tell him. 'You owe it to Murdo to help me finish his story. And I don't want any more dodgy stuff.'

'What?' Jenny calls from the other room.

'Talking to myself.'

'You mean talking to your wee toy,' she says.

I prop the wee man on the arm of my seat. 'You were only sixteen. What did you do on a sugar plantation for eleven years?'

I fetch my folder and a pencil.

No. 134. Looking for You

I've come touring your island. Climbing to the summit of your fort.

I've copied Jenny. Gone looking for you in the library. Chased your story.

Now I've got too many questions.

Tobacco or sugar?

Soldier or planter?

Jekyll or Hyde?

Chapter 21

Jenny, St Kitts

Anna's House

The next day, Jenny made an excuse and went back into town. She followed Anna's directions to her house, on the edge of Basseterre, on steeply sloping ground. When Jenny arrived, Anna was sitting on the front verandah, reading. She beckoned her to come up.

Inside, the walls were lined with shelves stacked with papers, and the folder was already lying on the table. Jenny sat down and Anna slid it in front of her.

'Canada Hills,' Anna said. 'Colonel Billy. There's an Upper Canada Plantation too.'

Jenny worked her way through the names. Anna went through and made tea. As she came back through, Jenny called out, 'Oh shit.' She nearly knocked over the tea tray.

Anna looked over Jenny's shoulder at the name she'd stopped at: *Jenny McNight, 29, field slave*. 'You?' Anna said.

'Same age, too.'

'I'm sorry. Could she be a relation?'

'Closest I'll ever get.' Jenny sat back. 'That's the difference between Hamish and me.'

'For you it's personal?'

'Is it OK if I copy out the lists?'

Anna nodded and went back out front to read.

An Elderly Man

As soon as Anna left the room, Jenny got up to explore. Out in the back garden, rising up the terraced slope, she'd never seen so many colours of bougainvillea. She took a photo, then climbed the snaking wooden steps. Halfway up was a pink flamboyant tree in full bloom. At the top was a small wooden building. In the shade of an awning, an elderly man with long white hair and a beard, wearing a large straw hat, sat at a table.

'Murdo!'

Murdo was sorting a tray of grotty artefacts, like Hamish's treasures dug from the ground. He stood up slowly. Jenny stepped forward to embrace him, but he turned and sat back down. He's no better at emotions than his grandson, she thought.

She put a hand on his bony shoulder. 'How are you?'

He didn't answer.

Jenny sat down at the table, facing him. He was a lot thinner than when she'd last seen him. His eyes were hidden under the shade of the wide brim of his hat. 'You need to talk to Hamish,' she said. 'Thinks you're dead.'

Murdo patted his chest. 'Still breathing, I think.' He sounded just like Hamish, but hoarser.

'You set us up with all the Billy shit.'

'Would you have got so far if I'd asked nicely?' he rasped, then broke into a coughing fit.

'If you're here, why don't you chase it yourself?' Jenny said.

Jenny heard footsteps behind her, and Anna appeared. Jenny grabbed a piece of pottery from the tray and held it in Murdo's face. 'Still believe in all your layer shit?'

'Until we dug up another story, which buggered it up.'

Anna interrupted. 'He needs to rest!'

'Seems fit to me,' Jenny said.

'Today's a good day.'

'I'm fine,' Murdo said.

'You expect us to keep chasing Billy-boy, despite what he was up to?' Jenny said.

'Thought you were more interested in his sidekick,' he said.

'What do you know?' she said. Then she jumped to her feet. 'You've seen my transcripts?' Jenny looked at Murdo, then Anna. 'Eck? The little bastard!'

Murdo sat back and the brim of his hat lifted. For the first time Jenny saw his piercing blue eyes. He might have been frail, but inside he was sharp as a tack. 'Hamish seen them?' he said.

She didn't answer.

His lined face creased even more, into a smug smile. 'Thought you'd hide them.'

Jenny stood up. 'You know nothing about me, you old bastard! You set us up!'

'It was the only way. I'm running out of time!' He raised a hand to his mouth, coughing.

Or was he laughing?

Anna went into the summer house and brought back a glass of water. Murdo took a sip, then held up a hand. 'Look,' he whispered, 'I'm sorry. I've been working on this for a long time.'

'He always wanted to come here,' Anna said. 'Sort it all out. Now he's made it, he's not fit.'

Murdo looked at Anna and said, 'Taken years to unearth the truth, sort it out, write it down. Then Sod's Law. At the last minute Cato comes along and turns it upside down.'

'Archie's trying to stop us,' Jenny said.

Murdo grabbed the table and tried to stand up, but failed.

'Thought he was your best mate?' Jenny said.

'Too many want to bury it,' Murdo said.

'Glasgow?'

He shook his head. 'Would you be here if it was just about Glasgow?'

'Cato was in Bristol?' she said.

Anna moved between them. 'He needs to rest.'

'I'm going,' Jenny said.

'Wait,' Murdo said. He got up slowly, shuffled into the summer house and came back with a folded piece of paper, which he held out.

Jenny took it and turned to go down the steps, then said, 'I can't hide it from Hamish that you're here.'

Alive

Once she was out of sight of the house, Jenny stopped in the shade and took a few deep breaths. Then she laughed out loud.

What am I doing here, chasing a story for an old man I barely know, she thought. What does Hamish see in him? Does he know he's being used? The difference between her and Hamish was that Hamish wouldn't mind. But that didn't mean that if he met Murdo, they'd embrace.

She called Kelly. 'Found Murdo!' Jenny said.

'Thought he was dead?'

'Old bugger's alive. And he's not the good old grandpa from the fairy tales.'

'He's on the island?'

'He's an old bastard. And he's working us like puppets: me and Hamish. Bristol and Glasgow. Cato and Billy.'

'You need to tell Hamish, or you'll lose him.'

'I don't know why we're chasing his stupid quest.'

'*His* quest? Thought you were doing it for yourself?'

Jenny cut the call.

Entice the Negroes

Jenny unfolded the piece of paper Murdo had given her. It was a photocopy of an old document. Some sort of contract.

> *I, the undersigned, swear to serve an indenture as a trainee overseer on the Sugar Plantation belonging to Daniel Smith, lying in Figtree Parish, Nevis, between Figtree Pond and Long Point, for an 11-year term from 1st July 1694.*
>
> *I swear that I am aged sixteen or above and in good health. My salary will be a cask of butter, a box of candles, 50lb. of soap, a hogshead of wine and 50 pounds sterling money per anny. My task is to entice the Negroes to make good sugar for my master.*

The signature at the bottom was crude. He was only sixteen, but Jenny had no doubt that it was Billy. She searched Google Earth for Figtree Pond and Long Point.

Then she called Hamish. 'Need to go to Nevis.'

The Journal of Cato

MY WRITIN FIX ME

Slow, slow, the light swells, till all the clapboard planks in the walls stand clear. Though writin fix me to this desk, restlessness a-ride my soul. Since old One-arm John was beat again & died, this office has become my home, my work, my life. I lean back on the chair's hind legs & count the knots on the boards. I make it fifty-six. If a visitor looks in at my high desk & chair, maybe he thinks tis dragged at random to this place. Angled to the walls of this office, drawn back from the window. Or maybe tis carefully chosen.

My world I view through the frame of this office window. Most times I see the red dust yard & the Palmetto-tree & the Prickle-pear fence, & beyond them, over the great house, the chequerboard of cane pieces that stretch to the western slope. If I raise my head from the ledger in front of me & look away right through the window, I see the sea sparklin with day cut. Ahead of me, though the hour is early, a great clankin of hoes is startin up on earth & stone.

As I cannot see the hard work, my mind banishes it & my eyes rise to the green tree tops & the bright coloured birds. To the left, topside, is the mountain, its peak appearin through the grey cloud of dawn.

Howsoever, a new wind blows down from the mountain, touchin only high places as it comes. Wide is my window & many is the time I imagine it opens onto some other place. If I screw up my eyes I follow the bush strip, my mind's escape, my salvation.

This day my mind starts wanderin, followin imaginary tracks up the bush strips boundin the cane pieces. Up, up to the mountain. My eyes, my nose, my ears start openin again. I scent many things in the breeze which pass & are gone. Some I know & some I am learnin.

Remember, I remember only those places which stand high on the road I am travellin. Between each plantation runs a boundary strip a few yards wide. A thick hedge, made of a jungle of trees & bushes of every variety. A steep overgrown ghut connects my hut with the boundary strip, between us & Mountain Plantation.

A SECRET ROUTE

One evenin at dusk, climb, I climb through the window, crouch low under the bush & thorns & creep down the ghut. At the end, I stumble upon an animal path which passes along the centre of the boundary strip. Great is my excitement at my discovery. A secret route up to the mountain, or down towards the sea. High trees lock hands over my head. Dusk falls & I must return to my hut, lest my absence be discovered.

Every night in my bed in the rafters, I dream of walkin further up my secret path. Outside the office I walk only in the shadow of my master. Countin supplies, ship landings, wanderin the market, makin notes beside him as the cane gangs work in the heat. It true, it, never have I walked out myself, beyond the red dirt path to & from the kitchen.

A NEW WIND BLOWS

Most days, an hour before Massa arrives after breakfast, an hour after he goes down for dinner, I have time for thinkin & readin. That evenin, before day goes into night, I begin my journey. I lock the door from the inside, set my foot on the sill & climb out the window. I slip down into the ghut & push through the bush into the animal track down the middle. Hidden by the trees & bushes either side, I head uphill. I will not venture far this first night, with only an hour before darkness to cover my return. Every so often I have to climb over a great pile of rock stones raised up from the fields.

Most nights I turn back, well before the cane lands rise into the forest & the mountain top.

Weeks I wait for the day when I am alone from sun up to evenin star.

A SCOTCH VOICE

This is the day that I have a few hours to myself.

Leave, I leave early, climb up, up through the edge of other plantations, skirtin great houses, restin behind the stone towers of windmills.

Pass, I pass the back of Figtree church, where the Buckra go up on Sundays in their fine clothes. Many is the time I sit outside waitin on Massa Billee. Listenin to Buckra-speak drift through the window from the pulpit in a Scotch voice. Plenty-plenty stories about noble livin.

Howsoever, when they come back out, they beat n buck Negroes the other six days of the week.

MY PATH

As I climb, breath does not come easy. Heat falls from the sky & rises from the ground & then from inside of me. My heart comes up to my mouth & there is no breath left inside my chest. I stop & listen. Quiet it is here. A green monkey creeps in, looks on & is gone.

Hear me now. I cling to my path as a stone foundation, a trail to the heart of the island, to my own heart. I walk between trees as familiar to me as ribs. I touch their bark. The rough beaten path is my skin. The leaf canopy high above is a roof over my head, rustlin in the trade wind. My path winds its way down the mountain into the distance. Longer, it takes me longer than I planned to return. On my way back down, I walk through the dark. Night-clouds cover the moonshine.

Fear comes upon me until I see the silhouette of my hut against the sky. I cross the yard, fight my way through the bush to the window. But the ground is low here. I can barely reach the sill with my fingertips. I am too tired to climb up. Rest, I rest. I waken at day cut, the sun flashin through the trees. I find a branch & lay it against my hut wall & at last I am able to climb inside.

Yesterday was a hard day & the long today is only hours away, but look, I look forward to my next outin.

HERMIT

This day, topside cane lands, is a narrow strip of tilled ground where mulattos grow provisions, keep a few chickens & pigs. In the distance, I see a brown-skinned man. Restin in a sugar-bag hammock, under a shelter weaved from a skeleton of Dogwood branches, with a sugar hogshead for his table, wearin a necklace of jumbie beads. As I approach, his eyes are bloodshot, his speech slurred from home-made rum brewed from molasses skimmed from gash sugar. Offer, he offers me a dirty glass, but I refuse.

'You join me for supper?'

Name, his name is Hermit.

Great is my fear that Hermit will report me for walkin out, but he waves me to his side. His shelter overlooks more growin crops than I have ever seen, crammed together in a long plot. Such a howl comes from the hunger ridin in my belly. He reaches over & plops four big sweet potatoes & a pinch of salt into a battered copper pan of hot water.

'Who your Massa?' Hermit says.

'Massa Billee.'

'Billee the Scot? Word is, he is a tough Nigger.'

Crazy, crazy is Hermit, callin Buckra Niggers, callin myself 'Sir'.

'What be a Scot?' I say.

Hermit has answers for everythin. 'Scots be a tough sort of white Nigger. Engly send Scots chasin after runaways. Last week Jamie the Scot chased a runaway from Mountain Plantation, caught him, staked him out, whipped him, left him in the sun for two days, then poured boiling water on him.'

Hermit tells me his father was once Governor of the island, that his mother was an African princess. Know, I know not what to believe. All I know is, because Hermit's skin is a shade lighter, he has more chance than most of us. Like bein half a man.

As Hermit's vegetable patch stretches along the top of the next plantation, stand, like our friend Irish, he stands often in front of Judge Mills, tryin to prove his ownership.

Hermit knows all that happens on the island. He says, 'Yesterday, I hear planter Hamilton took a young girl by the side of road near Bath Springs, beat n bucked her.'

'It true, it,' I say. 'Worst thing is not the beatin & killin – but the buckin of our sisters.'

'Maybe, maybe, but does it not also prove, deep down, that the Buckra do not hate us. They may beat us, cut us, treat us worse than animals, but they take our women more times than they take their own pretty white wives.' Hermit reaches over for a dirty woman's corset hangin on a stick by the fire. He drapes it over his head, like the wig of Judge Mills, raises a finger & says, 'Imagine you is lord of a small island – everybody else is young women, all Buckra daughters – half naked, chained to the roots of trees. Would you be good man, not lie with them?'

Later, in my cot in the eaves, I weep, knowin I am no better than the Buckra.

A BUCKRA DIGGIN

Some days I explore different trails, cut down instead of up to visit Hermit. Bottomside our plantation, the secret path opens onto a sandy field, smaller than a cane piece, with many different crops a-growin.

One day I see a Buckra diggin. First time on this island I seen a whitey turn a furrow. This buckra dress like a Scalag, in osnaburg shift & trash hat. His fork bites deep into the soft bottom then turns it over. Then he sits down among the roots of a big Ackee-tree & smokes a tobacco pipe. I stay in the shade of the bush, but he looks towards my place & calls, 'Come here.'

Digger's name is Irish. Mostly he grows tobacco, with a few provisions on the side. Seen, I have seen him at the market. He knows I am Billee's boy. Irish sits down, whittlin at a stick with a big knife. His house is a cabin with shingle roof & a verandah to the south. As we sit talkin, through a gap in the trees, the morn comes up out of the sea & looks on us awhile.

Some nights, after dusk, I lock my door, climb out my window & go down the path to his plot. Teach, Irish teach me to play poker. 'Maybe a boy earn a few provisions, writin letters for me,' he says.

Irish tells how he is tryin to hold onto his land, but slow, slow, the big planters are drivin him into the sea. I write for him, to the Island Council, the Governor, the Lords of Trade & Plantations. Sometimes if tis too dark, if there is no moon, I sleep under his hut & return to my office before day cut.

LORD OF THIS PIECE

Irish is a man of few words, but over many months he tells his story. I sit with ears a-listenin.

‘I be lord of this piece. Last small farmer on this island. My grandfather arrive with the first English settlers. Took a wife from the Caribs.’

Irish has only one hand. Tell, he tells many stories, how he lost the other. Fightin pirates. Rescuin Scalags. Attacked by a shark. Tells so many tales I know not which to believe.

One day, copyin Billee’s letters, I write: *Send me 50 barrels of Irish beef from Cork.*

Later ask, I ask Irish what his name means. I know nothin of countries, of Irish, of Scotch.

‘A few years ago,’ he said, ‘Scalags here was white. Scotch & Irish. Maybe not true Scalags but treated much the same. Came out on promise of an acre or two of land after three years workin for a farmer-settler.’

The more I hear of this island’s stories, the more confused am I.

***

Jenny’s Family Album

Jenny McNight, 28, fieldworker, value £35.

Chapter 22

Hamish, Nevis

The following morning, we join the queue for the Nevis ferry. Folk gather, clutching belongings and bags. An elderly lady is pulling a goat along with a rope. The goat nibbles at other people's bags.

Once the ferry moves off, the sea breeze is cool and refreshing. As we round the tip of St Kitts, Nevis comes into view, its central volcano capped by a ring of cloud. Jenny grips my arm. 'King Kong's island.'

'The Lost World,' I say. 'You're hurting my arm.'

The capital we'd seen from the plane looms closer. Brightly coloured buildings nestle in a sea of green.

The engine's thrown into reverse, and the ferry glides towards the quay. Bubbles of blue-green water rise to the surface around the propellers. The ticket collector opens the rail. Jenny takes her wallet from the inside pocket of her short blue dress and fumbles for the tickets. On the pier, a local lady holds up a piece of cardboard with my surname scrawled in big, crude letters. The lady approaches and says to Jenny, 'Mrs Hamilton.'

'No,' Jenny says, pointing at me. 'He's Hamilton. I'm his cousin, sort of.'

'Mrs Hamilton,' she repeats, and taps her ample chest.

'No.' Jenny tries to avoid the tourist cliche that locals are a bit simple. Then she says, 'You're a Hamilton too?'

The lady gives a big smile.

As we head for the van, Jenny pokes me in the ribs and whispers, 'A nice black lady sharing your Scottish surname? Who fits in now?'

***

Mrs Hamilton drives us round the tiny capital in her minibus, past the government building, the ruins of the Bath Hotel, the slave market. Then we head up the road circling the island. We visit a sugar plantation which has become a small luxury hotel. Each part of the sugar works has been turned into a piece of art, among landscaped gardens. 'Trying to disguise its purpose?' Jenny whispers.

Later, over lunch in the great house, I pluck up the courage to ask, 'Your surname's Hamilton too?'

'Yes, yes. Back at abolition, the workers had no surnames. Took the names of their Scottish masters.'

I choke on my salad. 'Scottish?'

'Take a look at the phone book,' Mrs Hamilton says. 'Lots of the islanders have Scottish surnames.' She smiles. 'And there ain't many of them is whities neither!' Mrs Hamilton has an infectious laugh. Jenny revels in an open fit of laughter.

Out in the hall, while the ladies go and freshen up, I peruse some old plantation documents, framed on the wall. Nearest our table is a faded invoice — *sixty hogsheads of sugar, shipped to the South Sugar House... in Glasgow.* I take a snap with my phone.

Once outside, I sit in the van with the door open, trying to mellow the heat of the interior. The ladies come out, Mrs Hamilton turns the ignition, and we head off again.

Next is a fancy entrance with a big sign: HAMILTON BEACH RESORT. 'Used to be Hamilton Plantation,' says Mrs Hamilton.

A strange gurgling noise comes from the back seat. I've never seen Jenny in such a good mood. She clears her throat and shouts, 'Stop!' She insists on photographing the two Hamiltons on a bench, beside the big HAMILTON PLANTATION sign. Large ornamental palms sit in enormous rusty iron pans. 'Sugar boiling vessels, what do you call them, coppers,' she says.

Then Mrs Hamilton offers to take us to some sites of battles.

'Nelson?' Jenny says.

'Our island's most famous resident!'

'Er, no thanks,' Jenny says. 'I think we've seen enough military stuff.'

Mrs Hamilton drops us at the pier. We thank her, and Jenny gives her a generous tip. We climb out, but stop short of the ferry and look at each other.

'Stay a bit longer?' I say.

We buy some clean clothes and toothbrushes from the market and find a room with two single beds in a small hotel. We spend the rest of the day relaxing by the pool. It's too hot to sunbathe, so Jenny lies in the shadow of a tree in her underwear.

The girl on the desk assures us that the room has air conditioning, but it only has ceiling fans, which rattle and keep us awake half the night.

Chapter 23

Jenny, Nevis

Out of Place

Next morning, Jenny bought a cheap umbrella to keep off the sun. Hamish mocked her for its garish colours, but soon joined her under it. They headed along the beach, past a row of holidaymakers in white hotel T-shirts, exercising to music. Jenny took off her shoes and paddled in the surf. She photographed the turquoise sea and picked up unusual shells. Young couples, glistening with oil, lay sprawled on white plastic sun-beds. Jenny could almost hear their skin sizzling. A local boy sat in the shade of a palm tree, selling windmill models at twice the price Hamish had paid in Basseterre. They sat down in the shade of an umbrella. The boy approached with a wad of tickets. They got up again and carried on.

'Ever feel out of place?' Hamish said.

'Beach holiday bollocks,' Jenny said. 'Time to head for the bush.'

Birds and Plants

Jenny took Hamish by the arm. She drew him up onto the rough track which bordered the shore. They headed along the dusty path, stopping for breaks in the shade. Luckily, the breeze was stronger today, and the heat of the sun was reduced by high cloud. She stopped under a pink flamboyant tree and spread her big map on the dusty ground.

'Where are we going?' he said.

They turned left up an old track between thick bushes. The path kept going, climbing slightly. Trees bearing strange fruits loomed over them. 'Wish I knew the names of the birds and plants,' Jenny said.

They stopped for a rest in the shade of a big mango tree. Hamish reached up and pulled down a branch. He picked two fruit and handed one to Jenny. With his penknife, he showed her how to split and slice the fruit, leaving the big stone in the centre.

She pointed up a narrower track. 'Let's try that one.'

'My legs are scratched enough,' he said. 'What if there's snakes?'

A monkey jumped through the trees and startled them. The path narrowed, as if it was about to peter out, but they stumbled into a clearing. Before them was a series of overgrown ruins. Arched doorways, built of squared volcanic blocks, on rising terraces.

'Inca temple?' Jenny said.

They sat on a log in the shade for a rest. 'OK,' Hamish said, 'what's the story?'

'Plantation where Billy started out.'

'Something from your archive visit?' he said.

She tapped the side of her nose.

Billy's Plantation

After they'd shared a bottle of water and some biscuits, Jenny pulled out her camera and went to explore the nearest structure. Hamish joined her under a series of vaults on a massive stone base. Slightly higher up was a big rectangular building, its pitched roof a skeleton of timbers. A piece of corrugated iron rattled in the breeze. At the top of the slope was a ruined circular wall.

As they reached the main building, the sugar-crushing rollers came into view through a ragged window opening, rusty but intact. Hamish stepped through a doorway. Above him, the spoked flywheel of a steam engine curved up into the rafters.

Jenny climbed through the opening and circled the big machine with her camera, stepping over rubble and broken shingles. 'Hey!' she called.

Hamish followed her round the back of the big engine. Cast along the base in huge letters was: A. & W. SMITH, GLASGOW 1889. 'Two centuries too late,' he said.

'But part of Billy's legacy.'

'Or just a coincidence.'

She pointed at the logo on the cast-iron tanks in the corner: Duncan Stewart & Co., Glasgow 1866.

He held up his hands. 'OK, more than a coincidence.' Apart from the vegetation and the brilliant sunlight, it was a scene of industrial decline from home. Out of place on this tropical island, but trying to tell them something. 'Lucky we're not here for a beach holiday or we'd never have found this.'

'Speak for yourself,' she said.

Round the side was a ruined stone structure, some sort of dormitory? Spaced along the wall were rusty iron chains. Jenny turned away.

'Cattle?' he said.

'Aye right.'

'Copying me now?'

Back at the engine house he said, 'It's amazing.'

She turned on him. 'Amazing for who? The folk who did all the work, or the planters who raked in the profits?'

Cato's Shack

Jenny circled the fringes of the clearing. On the edge of the bush was the shell of a narrow shack, above a steep slope. She pulled aside the vines and stepped onto the cracked stone-flagged floor. To the front was a rotting timber frame, on the point of collapse. The rear half was built of red brick, roofless but intact. At the back were remains of shelves. In the corner, under a fragment of roof, stood a few books. She touched one and it crumbled to dust. She stepped back, pushed aside more branches to take photos and stood on something metallic.

She bent down and brushed aside a covering of leaves. It was a rusty iron door, studded with rivets. She kicked aside more leaves: Eagle Foundry, Glasgow.

A shiver ran down her spine. She looked up towards the mountain, framed by the rotting rectangle of the window. She took out her phone, opened the file of her Cato transcripts and found the right place: *My world I view through the frame of this office window.../my mind starts wanderin, followin imaginary tracks up the bush strips boundin the cane pieces. Up, up to the mountain.*

Cato's shack? It meant far more to her than the remains of the sugar works. She wanted to clean up the old door, hire a truck and take it home.

Shit, she thought. I'm turning into Hamish.

Nathaniel

Jenny crossed back to where Hamish sat. She wanted to show him the door, tell him about the shack, about Cato. But footsteps approached. An old man appeared, heading along the narrow path, carrying a white cane. He stopped and stood still, facing towards them.

'Good afternoon,' Jenny said.

The old man's face creased in a smile. 'Call me Nathan,' he said. He sat down and started to talk. 'Worked here in the sugar works till seventy-nine.'

'How did it all work?' Jenny said.

Nathan stood up and held out his hand. Jenny took it and he led her up to a circular foundation. The bush had grown over half the works. Jenny helped Nathan pick his way through the rubble. 'Harvest time was just crazy, mon,' he said. 'Cane spoils after cuttin, so needs crushin quick, quick.'

Hamish squatted and ran his hands over more iron rollers. Their frame was embossed with the logo of another Glasgow firm.

'Was it dangerous?' Hamish said.

'My best friend caught his fingers in the rollers, would have been drawn right through if the foreman hadn't cut off his arm. Once he got better, boss sacked him 'cause he could only do half the work.'

Hamish avoided Jenny's gaze.

Then Nathan led them round the back of the circular foundation and poked around the loose stones with his feet. 'Stand here, missy.' Nathan put his hands on Jenny's waist and patted her bottom. 'You follow behind.' The old man gestured to Hamish.

They shuffled along, one behind the other, in a wee row, like some silly hen night dance routine. They followed the narrow channel from the mill to the boiling works while Nathan explained, in sequence, how it all worked.

When he finished, Nathan said, 'Just keep climbing and you'll reach the main road.'

Jenny kept scratching her legs. They were covered in wee red bites. 'So much for jungle walks,' she said.

'Sandflies,' Hamish said, 'from the beach.'

A Descendant

They followed Nathan's directions uphill. After a bit, they stopped in the shade for a rest. A figure appeared in the distance, coming down the track towards them, carrying something long in each hand. As the big man got closer, Jenny could see he was wearing a torn T-shirt, ripped denim shorts and carrying two machetes.

'Let's move,' Hamish said.

'Relax,' Jenny said, patting his knee. As the man got closer, his arms were thick and muscular, and his machetes glinted in the sun. Hamish jumped up, but Jenny grabbed his belt and he stumbled back. 'What's up?' she said.

As the man reached them, he raised one of his machetes in greeting and smiled a big friendly smile. Then he disappeared around the corner.

'I was just thinking…' Jenny said.

'Yeah?'

'If I lived here, growing a few crops to support my family, then I came down this quiet lane and spotted a descendant of the white bosses, I would take my sharpest machete, cut off your balls, and leave you for dead in the ditch.'

'Thanks very much.'

Friends

They climbed for another half hour, then sat under the shade of a big tree and waited nearly two hours for a bus back to town. They were too late to catch the last ferry, and had to spend a second night on Nevis. They asked for a cooler room, but the ceiling fans were even noisier. The fan above Jenny's bed hung from a loose screw in the ceiling. She lay awake all night, watching it wobble, hoping it wouldn't drop and slice her to pieces.

She reached out and touched Hamish, but he was asleep.

Could they survive here as friends?

Could they be real friends if she kept Cato hidden?

If it ended badly, would she be to blame?

READ LIKE A SCOTCHMAN

Thenceforth, every time Billee is away, I climb up the secret path to visit Hermit. Hermit tells many tales & I try to think of my own stories in return.

Tell, Hermit is the only person I tell about my journal. Sometimes I read to Hermit. Today he say, 'You read like a Scotchman. All your Engly you have learned livin in Billee's shadow. Someday soon I will turn around & you will stand there in your three-cornered hat, your wig & your staff & your long nose & you will have turned into Billee.'

'No!' I jump up & run off down the path. I stay away from Hermit's plot for a week. But back, I come back, for I know Hermit speaks the truth.

MEANNESS

Say, I say to Hermit, 'Succeed, how does Billee succeed? How does he make more profit than most other planters?'

Once again Hermit dons his wig. Puts on his serious Buckra voice & says, 'It true, it. Spend, you spend much of your time in Billee's shadow, so your story is not your own but the story of Massa Billee.'

Again I feel like walkin off, but I bury my anger with soft answer. 'Perhaps you speak the truth.'

'True, true, it,' he says, 'that Scots is the meanest Niggers on the island. Meaner than any other overseers.' Hermit puts on a Scotch voice. 'Aye, aye, the road to higher profits is less imports.'

'& suffer, tis we who suffer from their meanness,' I say. 'Small is the food in our hands & thin is the soup, but Billee makes it weaker.'

'Kill, they say Billee killed twelve Scalags in his first year.'

'Aye, but twas by his instruction, not by his own hand.'

'But how many more has he killed by his meanness?' says Hermit.

From my book-keepin I know the cost of food & from whence it comes. Salted herrings from the Clyde. Oats from Ayrshire. Salted beef from Galloway. Osnaburg shifts from Paisley. Wherever in the wide world do such places lie? Do their farmers, their workers, their weavers know how they profit from our misfortune?

GREAT IS THE DANGER OF WALKIN OUT

This evenin I come back down to my hut at dusk & the door lies open. A key is in the lock on the outside. My heart enters my mouth. Billee has been about lookin for me! Quick as I can, I run down the long path towards the kitchen. Great is the danger of walkin out after curfew. Guards patrol the paths. Ahead, around a corner, I hear voices. Billee & Apollo!

I turn into the bush & slip around the monkey path, past them. Tis near dark & I fear that they will hear me & call for the dogs. But gradually beyond, I am beyond them. Then I return to the path around the next bend.

Face, my only solution is to face them. Turn, I turn back up the path to meet them. They look up when they see me a-comin.

Without liftin my head, I say, 'Sorry Massa, Cook sent me on an errand.'

Apollo raises his stick to beat me, but Billee waves him off & turns to me. 'Go back to the office & do not run errands for others again without my permission.'

WHETHER TO LIE OR DIE

'Where you come from?' Hermit says.

'The Buckra say we are all Africans, but what is Africa? The place called Africa is too large, a Buckra word, not known by those who live there.'

Hermit dons his wig & his serious voice & says, 'So, Cato, the question is, whether you have deserted your brothers & sisters by workin for Billee?' He holds my wrist, lest he has offended me & I try to run off.

'I was chosen to work for him, I did not advance it myself.'

'You do not answer my question. Is it better to lie in Billee's bed, or die with the rest in the canefields?'

'I have no choice what I do. Tis every Scalag for himself. We are all alone on this island. If the worker beside you falls down, & you extend a helpin hand, you too will be struck down.'

'So the rule of the island is, do not make friends?'

'The well-behaved Scalag is no better than the rebel. He carries out all the orders he receives, eats only the rations, observes the rules. But violence strikes him as often as the lazy worker beside him. When the blow comes, he will be maimed & fester for a while, or if the blow is too hard, he will die on the spot.'

'How then to survive with so many troubles around you?'

'Because great may be the troubles, but until the day I am struck too hard, they do not add up to a whole. At any time, we only cope with the worst, & the rest must wait behind. As the pain from the last blow comes to an end, another one lies ahead, a whole queue of others. Thus we cope with one thing at a time. Tis only if we lose the will to live that they are tallied up & rise to overwhelm us.'

Tell, I tell Hermit that yesterday I saw a planter's son take another young girl & buck n beat her by the side of the road. 'Write, I write it all down,' I say, 'to show how evil the Buckra are.'

Hermit raises his finger, sits back & says, 'So, Cato. The Buckra sugar planters. Be they devils or be they ordinary men like us, whose fine dark skin fade to white in the sun?'

Think, I think about this for a while, then I answer, 'You ask if the planters are real men, black men whose skin has turned white. Same, I am not the same as the planters, but as you once say, I am a wee bit like Massa Billee, a wee bit like the Scotch, because they are outcasts like myself, outcast even from my own people because I write for Billee.'

'Why do the Engly planters hate the Scotch so?' he says.

'They do not hate the Scotch like they hate us. Nor do they hate them as much as they hate the Dutch or the French. They do not even say out loud that they hate them. But hate, they hate the Scotch behind their backs.'

'It true, it. Many times I have heard it. Maybe bein a Scot on this island is a bit like bein a Scalag.'

'Aye, they may not beat the Scotch. They may not cut them, starve them, whip them, buck them, make them eat shit. But the Scotch are still outcasts.'

'They hate the Scotch, but say, they say the Scotch are the best managers, best catchers of runaways, toughest overseers,' says Hermit.

'Tougher than their Engly sons, who come out all dressed up, drinkin Madeira all day, complainin about the heat.'

'But the Engly do not understand. Once they allow the Scotch onto the lowest rung on the ladder, knowin they are tough & have a good schoolin, should they be surprised if the Scotch rise to be their equals?'

'Everythin the Scotch do, they must try harder, because the Engly hope to see them fail, & because the Scotch try harder, they do better,' I say.

Hermit pours himself another cloudy measure of rum. 'Deep down, do the Engly really hate the Scotch?'

'Once the Scotch rise to the top, they buck n marry the pretty daughters of the Engly planters.'

'Any place you find Engly, you find Scotch. Not just on these islands, but Irish say there are also many on Antigua & Barbados, on all the islands.'

'It true, it. A Scot captured me, taught me Engly in the fort in Africa. Scots crewed the ships, many are the Scots on this island, & Billee the Scot is my Massa.'

Finally, Hermit sits back, takes another cloudy sip of rum & dons his wig. He leans forward & strikes the hollow log with his wee hammer in judgement. 'Niggers, they may call us Niggers on this island. But Scotch, the Scotch is the Nigger of the world.'

KITCHEN LUCY

I first meet Lucy when she brings my rations every day from the kitchen. Although she is only fifteen, Lucy is pretty & already a favourite. The Buckra take her in the bushes, around the house, by the side of the road, anywhere they fancy.

One day Lucy says, 'Where you come from?'

'Same place as you, other side of the great ocean.'

'You speak good Engly, where you learn?' Lucy says.

'Before I was brought here, I spend a year at the fort on Sao Tome, countin Scalags, writin down their names.'

BROTHER & SISTER

Sometimes Lucy cries, & if no-one is about I hold her in my arms. Firm are her breasts & warm is her heart.

Some nights she sleeps beside me in my rafter cot. I hold her, but I do not touch her below. The Buckra wear her, tear her, buck her, force her every way, till she is no use to any man.

For a while I am sad that our love is only like brother & sister, not man & woman. But one night, as the rain beats the roof above our heads, the wind tears the leaves from the trees, we hold each other like never before. So tight, the biggest hurycane on earth will not separate us.

ALL AFFECTION LEAD TO PAIN

Next day, after the storm, I tell my friend Hermit about Lucy.

Look, Hermit looks me in the eye. 'Friend,' he says, 'all affection lead to pain. On this island, death is around every corner. Only rule of survival is every man for himself. Make a friend, take a lover, soon the Buckra will beat her, maim her, kill her. Then they come back & haunt the one they love the most. Better if they kill you first.'

SADNESS & BITTERNESS

Some days Lucy comes up late, with more bruises on her face & breasts. Great is my sadness & bitterness walks with me.

Then, one day, when tis time to get up & greet the day, Lucy does not come up at all. I ask Cook where she has gone, but Cook looks away. In the dark space between my head & the rafters I cannot find her.

Two weeks later I find that Smith sold Lucy to McKendrick in St Thomas Lowland Parish, who has a weakness for young girls.

Kill, I long to kill every Buckra on this island.

A GREAT PLANTER

Eleven years Billee serves as overseer. Eleven years I copy his letters, tally his books. Eleven years Billee save.

In the final year of his contract, once a month, I sail with Billee across to St. Christopher. He inspects pieces of cane land which are for sale. Befriends the planters, tallies & measures. Talks to his friend Jamie of great plans to build up a plantation of his own.

THE FRENCH FLEET ARRIVES

When the French fleet arrives in '06, everyone flees to the mountain.

Fortunate am I that I am not in the canefields & have time to run. Many of my brothers & sisters are cut down or sold by the French. For many days, down below, the French cut & burn, cut & burn.

Lost, my first two journals are lost. Great is my pain. Once again store, I must store my story in my head.

Tis many weeks before the British fleet is sighted & drives out the French. Howsoever, by then all the plantations are ruined.

Nevertheless Billee falls on his feet. Finish, he has finished his trainin. St. Christopher is on the rise. He has already acquired 30 acres there. The first Scalag he purchases is myself.

Once again sail, Billee sails the short passage from Nevis to St. Christopher, this time with all his worldly goods. Sit, I sit in the stern of the boat.

Billee makes plans to be a great planter.

FLORA

To work his first wee plot of land purchase, Billee purchases thirteen Scalags. He instructs me to write down their names. The eldest is nineteen years old. The youngest is Flora, age thirteen.

The next few years are lean years. But fortunate am I. Billee grows little cane, but writes many letters. He sells his land & purchases a better cane piece. Improvin, always improvin. Measurin, always measurin.

Rarely do I have the privacy to write my journal. Move, we move many times. Tis impossible to hide my journal.

Store, once again I store my story in my head, to write down another day.

Jenny's Family Album

Jenny added two names to her list:

Flora, 13.

Lucy, 15, kitchen worker, St Thomas Lowland Parish.

Chapter 24

Hamish, St Kitts

No. 135. From Nevis to St. Christopher

Dear Brother,

The mail has been stopped these four years since the French invasion. I have written to you regularly but am unsure what you have received, thus I will sum up our situation.

The French poured up the beach and drove us up the mountain. Horatio, my green monkey, was killed in the invasion, which caused great sadness. Ninety-seven Negroes also perished on our plantation, but more may be purchased at a good price, as the market is now very low. Replacing a monkey is more troubling.

Twas the final year of my training. It took two months for the fleet to arrive with our soldiers and drive off the French. Most of the cane was burnt and the sugar-works torn down. Only three windmills were left standing. They say Nevis will never again be the jewel in the crown of the Empire.

Howsoever, I made the short crossing from Nevis to the larger isle, St. Christopher, which has suffered less damage. I brought nothing with me but my scribe Cato, who I purchased from Col. Smith for £35.

During my training I was able to save a wee bit. I have also raised a loan and have begun to build up a few acres of cane land and ingratiate myself with the planters here.

I long to hear from you and remain your most obliged kinsman and humble servant, Billy.

***

In the morning, after breakfast in a cafe, I say, 'What time's the ferry?'

'Check out the archive first?'

We find it in a small colonial building.

'Looking for records from before 1700,' Jenny says.

The female assistant opens a cupboard. On the floor is a huge pile of shredded paper. 'All that survives,' she says.

'Hurricanes?' I say.

'Insects, earthquakes, wars, volcanoes. Hurricanes especially.'

No. 136. Hopes of Acquiring Two Hundred Acres

Dear Brother,

As the French have been driven out from their half of the island, we are in high hopes of Westminster sharing out the French plantations between the best of us here. They say we are each to be granted no more than 200 acres, but I have an eye on 400, with the prospect of long credit to pay back the purchase price. Despite the setback on Nevis, my dream of being a planter may come to pass sooner rather than later.

The island Council have also elected me Lieutenant in the militia here. We drill in the square with wooden rifles, with much show but little spunk.

***

To the side, covering one wall, is a big old map of both islands. Each plantation's marked by a wee windmill symbol and the owner's name.

'Here!' says Jenny. She points to a mile or so north of the capital. 'Billy's plantation!' His name's written twice, beside two wee windmill symbols and a name, Canada Hills.

We take photos of the map and go for lunch, then catch the ferry back to St Kitts. When we land in Basseterre, I say, 'Canada Hills?'

Jenny calls Leroy. But he's busy. We take another taxi to the nearest point on the road to where Billy's plantation's marked on the old map. Jenny's reluctant to be left in the middle of nowhere.

'Come on,' I say. We let the taxi go and cross the road into the waist-high scrub, then head uphill. I shield my eyes from the sun. 'That a chimney up top?'

It's not long before our arms and legs are cut and scratched by the bushes. Something rustles in the undergrowth, the wind starts to get up, and we're soaked by a heavy shower. 'I've had enough bushwhacking,' Jenny says.

Back in Britain we'd have carried on, but the weather and vegetation have beaten us. Down on the road, we're lucky to catch a taxi home. By the time we get back to the cabin, it's difficult to stand up in the gale. The wind howls through the open windows, from one side of the shack to the other. We're sure it'll blow the flimsy building away.

We grab a few notes and valuables and stagger across to the wee toilet, clinging to each other against the gale. The toilet doesn't look much stronger than the shack, but it's built against a big old tree. Behind is a wee store. We jump inside and slam and bolt the door. There's barely space to sit on the sandy floor. Despite the racket from the wind, it's cosy and secure and we're both worn out from our Nevis adventure.

We fall asleep, leaning against each other like orphans lost in a storm.

***

In the morning, Jenny stirs first. It's quiet outside. She unbolts the door and we tumble onto the sand, stiff from our cramped positions. Our shack is still standing, none the worse for wear. The wind's gone and the sun's shining. Anthony comes down the path to check we're OK.

'Hurricane?' I say.

'No, mon, just a little storm. Hurricane's a hundred times worse.'

Leroy had told us about his experience. 'Worst thing was when we came back out of our shelter,' he said. 'Wasn't a leaf left on a tree on the island.'

I'd read about the worst on record, when there was hardly a *tree* left standing on the island.

'Ever since the hurricane,' Leroy said, 'started goin' back to church.'

***

After breakfast, we find lots more shells than usual, washed up by the storm. Jenny collects unusual ones.

We stop in the shade and study our photos of the old map. 'Must be a track leading uphill,' I say. 'We need to hire a driver. Go back and try again.' I search the Web and find Earl. 'Advertises rugged tours.' I call him. 'He'll pick us up in an hour!'

Earl's a big local man, with a friendly smile and a silver Land Cruiser. The interior's plush and air conditioned. I sit back and relax.

'Canada Hills,' I say. 'In Cayon.' I hand Earl my phone with the map.

Earl strokes his chin. 'Knew it as a kid. Big quarry might have taken it away.'

'We'd like to try,' Jenny says.

Earl jumps out at garages, farms and shacks, seeking directions. He seems to know everyone on the island. We head up rugged lanes, between fields of goats. At one point we end up back where we started.

'He's taking us on a wild goose chase,' I whisper. 'Ripping us off.'

'Leave him be.'

Then we turn into an open area surrounded by ruins. We're still down at road level, but I know where we are. 'Lower Canada! Billy's lower plantation.'

To one side are the remains of the plantation house. Skirt and blouse: a two-storey rotten timber frame on top of a solid stone basement. Across the yard are the massive arched remains of two boiling works, one a complete ruin.

'Goes back to the days of the French,' says Earl.

The other one has a door built over one arch, used as a store. I poke a wee piece of volcanic stone from each structure and put them in my bag. Several huge boiling coppers lie scattered around, used as drinking troughs for goats. Higher up, on a bare yard, is a big circular arc of stone.

'Billy's windmill?' Jenny says.

'Someone's knocked it down and pinched all the stone.'

'Too near the road,' Earl says. 'Whole place has been scavenged. More chance of finding things higher up.'

From the works, a track heads up into the bush.

'Jump in,' says Earl.

It soon gets steep and rough, two stony wheel ruts with long grass in the middle. The vehicle can tackle it easily, but the bush narrows on each side, scratching the paintwork. Earl stops.

'Need to come back tomorrow, with my jeep,' he says.

***

Next day, Earl can't come till lunchtime, so we go into town. I buy Jenny a cool drink from a kiosk, and we sit in silence in the centre of town, in the shade of a big clock tower. We take in the bright colours, the bustle, the strange sounds and smells. Then Jenny turns and runs a finger down my spine. 'What's that?'

I shiver and turn around. A bold logo's cast on the base of the green clock tower. I stand up, pull out my phone for a picture, then change my mind and fumble in my bag. I unfold some sheets of paper and a thick pencil. 'Can you hold it flat?'

Jenny smooths a sheet over the first few letters. I rub the surface with the pencil, bringing out the logo. It takes three sheets to cover the whole inscription: SUN FOU NDRY, G LASGOW.

'Bit of a coincidence,' I say.

She jumps to her feet. 'A hulking great Glasgow monument in the heart of the capital? Isn't it trying to tell you something?'

'Everything's different,' I say, 'but I feel at home.'

'*You* feel at home?' she snaps. She plomps down again, turns away, and pulls out her book.

I go off again and come back with ice lollies. But they melt in our hands and drip onto our trainers. Jenny throws hers in the bin.

'Find some better shade?' I say. We get up and turn a corner into a grassy square dotted with bright red flamboyant trees. In the centre is a fountain.

Jenny points to the logo on the base. 'Another Glasgow monument?'

'There's a sign over there.'

She reads it out: 'Marketplace of the Negroes.' Her shoulders drop. Then she says, 'Should have done this before. Need to introduce you to someone.'

Jenny takes my arm and leads me through side streets to someone's house. Sitting on the veranda is an older woman, who Jenny introduces me to as Anna.

'Is it OK to come up?' Jenny says.

Anna shrugs and we climb the wooden stairs. In her study, the walls are stacked with rows of bulging folders. The shelves are built from bleached driftwood, supported by old bricks stamped: Hurlet and Airdrie.

'Scottish bricks!' I say.

Anna turns away and goes into the kitchen.

'What's her problem?' I whisper to Jenny. On the desk over by the window is an old manual typewriter. An Olivetti. On the shelf above is a row of wee wooden models of local houses. I pick one up and sniff it. I turn on Jenny. 'Murdo?'

'Should have told you,' she says.

'He's here?!'

'*Was* here.'

I go round, peering into every room. I find Anna in the kitchen. 'Where is he?' I say.

'I'm not his keeper,' Anna says.

'You're hiding him.'

'We need to go,' Jenny says.

As we leave the room, I spot Anna slipping Jenny an envelope. Anna shuts the front door and we head down the street.

'He's been here?' I say.

'Been and gone, according to Anna.'

'Where to?'

***

We catch a taxi back to our shack, in silence. I sit on the verandah looking out to sea. Jenny comes out.

'He's come all the way here and I didn't know?' I say.

'You're doing enough for him, chasing Billy.'

'He's not well. I need to see him.'

'He's not the most emotional person.'

I stand up. 'You've met him!'

She holds up her hands. 'Should have told you.'

'When?'

'First time I was at Anna's.'

'Why didn't you tell me!'

'Anna was helping me. I didn't know what to do.'

I press against the old table, arms rigid, trying to control myself. 'Shit, Jen, it's the only reason we're here, chasing his stupid quest.'

'He's an old bastard.'

I turn and she runs indoors. She comes back out and throws a folded piece of paper on the table.

'Gave me this,' she says. She leaves me with Billy's indenture. Just as I finish reading it, she comes back again, clutching her phone. 'Earl's up on the road,' she says.

I leave the piece of paper on the table under a book, grab a few things and follow her up the track. At the top, Earl sits revving the engine of a clapped-out red Toyota four-wheel drive jeep. It's got big chunky tyres and wooden benches on the back. We climb aboard and Earl speeds off. Up in the open, it's too windy to talk. As we slow at the suburbs, I say, 'Still hiding stuff?'

'*Me* hiding stuff?!' She stands up and thumps the roof of the cab with her palms. Earl screeches to a halt. Jenny grabs her bag, jumps off the back and disappears round a corner.

Stuff it, I need to do this myself. I climb down and get in the front, beside Earl. We drive off, leaving Jenny on her own. Earl heads back to Lower Canada, then up the track. Two thirds of the way up, a big boulder blocks our way.

'Sorry, mon,' Earl says. 'On foot from here.'

'It's OK, I'll go on myself.'

'Sure? Call me when you're finished and I'll pick you up.' Earl smiles and adds, 'Down at the bottom.' He reverses noisily down the steep track.

I continue climbing on foot, in the full sun, resting every so often in the shade. I wish I'd brought more to drink.

Finally, hot and sweating, I reach a plateau on the summit. Across the clearing stands a great conical tower, tapering slightly towards the top. Billy's windmill!

I circle the stone structure, taking lots of photos, then sit in the shade of the arch. I pull off my shirt and lay it out to dry in the sun. I close my eyes and rest my palm on the warm stone, and a weight falls from my shoulders.

Billy's plantation. The source of his fortune. Finally I've reached my goal.

I circle the windmill again, looking for footholds, but it's too well built. Way up top, I see vegetation growing around the lip. Some stones might be loose. At the back I grab a thick vine and climb to the top. Across the south of the island, above the vegetation, I pick out the tops of sugar mills. I balance my backpack on the cope, pull out the wee book and find the page I transcribed last night.

No. 137. A Tough Constitution

Dear James,

I thank you for the plan you sent me for laying out my sugar-works at my new high plantation at Upper Canada, which I am satisfied will serve extremely well. I agree that a great copper of 200 gallons will suffice, decreasing to one of 50 gallons, and a fire below, on a stone base, with four arches.

And a new windmill, built of stone, at the highest point. I propose keeping a separate gang of Negro houses, entirely distinct from my lower plantation, under the chief direction of a new overseer. You propose the new lad just landed from Bristol, however he must be of a tough constitution, preferably a Scot.

***

I send Jenny photos of the windmill and the view, but it's too hot in the full sun to stay up for long. I manage to dislodge a few stones and throw them down. It's a bigger problem getting myself down. I hold on to the vine, and start to climb down, but the roots pull off the wall. I hit the ground like the giant in Jack and the Beanstalk. I lie still as the adrenaline recedes, waiting for the pain. My ankle hurts. I get up and hobble around.

From the stones I threw down, I select the best, and put them in my backpack. The windmill's close to the edge of the quarry. I lie on the edge and peer over the thousand-foot drop. A few more years and it'll all be gone. I look around for the rest of the sugar works, but all I can see is the ruined top of a brick chimney, poking above a dense thicket of bush. I should come back with a machete.

I limp across, slip off my backpack and crawl into the bush. After a short distance, my knee hits one of the sugar-crushing rollers, come loose from its frame. The ultimate sample! I try to lift it, but it's solid iron. I'm in my childhood comfort zone. Undergrowth. Industrial ruins. From the rollers, the remains of a paved channel slopes gently downwards.

Hemmed in, I squeeze through bushes, following the sugar channel, until I crawl onto the top of a massive stone structure. The boiling works? It's completely overgrown. I push through the vegetation on my stomach, no longer caring about scratched arms and legs. I slide across a row of big rusty cast-iron boiling coppers on top, three, four, five… Shit. I dip my foot in something warm and wet. Each copper has a pool of stagnant green water at the bottom. Instead of copper number six, I tumble head first over the edge, my fall broken by bushes. At the bottom, I face a big arched opening. I switch on my phone torch and crouch inside. There's a strong smell of animal urine. I turn right into a central passage. The walls are so black and crusty with soot from the old fires, it's hard to see anything, even with the torch.

At the far end, I come out through another arch into the green shadow of the vegetation. Something rustles in the bush above, then jumps down, startling me. I break through into a small clearing and a monkey sits watching. Slowly, I pull out my phone and get a photo before it turns and jumps away into the bush.

A green monkey?

In the dim light, I've entered an imaginary land. I face a brick wall, with a wee cast-iron door built into the side. The door has an elaborate handle and an arched top, like the entrance to a hobbit house. I tug it open, but it's full of ash. The steam engine boiler? I pull myself up the slope at the side and reach a flat area.

There's a square hole in the ground, with a metal cover lying to the side. It's too tempting. I climb inside and hang by my fingertips, but my feet don't touch the bottom. It's a risk, but I need to let go. I fall a short drop into cool water, up to my knees. Underground tanks? If they'd been full, I could have drowned. I switch on my phone torch again. I'm among a labyrinth of brick piers supporting a vaulted roof. Something touches my leg. I shiver. Eels? In panic, I dance up and down, keeping my legs alternately clear of the water, trying to ignore the pain in my ankle.

The bright hole in the roof is just out of reach. Nearby, a heap of bricks, fallen from the roof, poke above the water. Still marking time in the water, to keep the imaginary creatures at bay, I build a brick platform, until I can stand above the surface.

Finally, I pull myself up and crawl out of the bush into the warm sun. I recover my backpack and lie on the hard ground, shaking and exhausted. I've come all this way and I can't get any pictures of the sugar works? I'd need to spend hours clearing vegetation to get decent photos.

Then my phone buzzes. An email from Linda at the library in town. I find a shady spot, out of the direct sun, where I can read the screen.

No. 138. Flora

1706 St Kitts census: Billy has thirty acres of cane land. He owns thirteen Africans: four men, six women, two boys and one girl.

The list includes their names and ages.

The list ends with Flora, age 13, fieldworker.

***

I lean back against a tree, my eyes blurring with tears, and pull out the wee man.

I knew you were an overseer. But owning's different.

Thirteen people.

A wee lassie named Flora. Flora was thirteen. You overworked her in your fields. Underfed her. What else did you do to her?

Jenny's words come back: *What did they do to become devils?*

***

Something moves on the edge of my vision, spooking me. My water bottle's almost dry. As I turn, I stumble. At the side of the sugar works is a vertical bank. I kneel in the shade. Lower down it's just reddish soil. But halfway up is a dark strip. Above the layer is ash and bits of charcoal from the boiler. I use the wee man to poke at the layer and dislodge a bit of stick. Or is it a bone? It's the first time I've dug up signs of something living from my layers.

I get up and limp across the open ground behind the sugar works. The surface is mounded into regular humps. I trip over another stick poking from the ground. It scratches my shin, drawing blood.

It's another bone. Sharp and broken and bleached by the sun. A goat? Too big.

More bones poke through the surface, disturbed by animals. A human hip?

Then a smaller one. A child?

I drop to my knees and retch. Then I jump up and kick dry soil over the bones, but I expose a human jaw. I hobble away, across to the cliff edge, behind the windmill.

Worn out, tears staining my dirty face, I lean back against the stone wall. I hold up wee Billy and look him in his squinty eye.

'It's either you or me.'

I step forward and lift my arm. As hard as I can, I chuck the wee wooden man out over the thousand-foot cliff.

'That's for Flora.'

I collapse on the ground and roll back against the rough stonework of the windmill. In the distance, blurred by my tears, is the cone of Nevis, capped by its ring of white cloud.

It's time to go.

I struggle to my feet. Take a last swig of water. Pour the dregs over my head.

I'm knackered. Dizzy. My clothes are filthy. My ankle's sore. My arms and legs are scratched.

Crossing to the edge of the plateau, I stagger down the steep track. After a bit, I rest on a big rock. I hear a tinkling noise, and a ghostly figure climbs towards me. An old shepherd. His possessions hang from thick strings around his neck and jangle as he walks. He looks me up and down. 'You OK, mon?' From one of his strings hangs a plastic bottle. He offers a drink. It's cloudy and warm, but I accept it gladly. Then the old man heads on, up the slope. It brings more tears to my eyes.

Shit, the people here are so nice. I don't deserve their kindness.

Finally, when the track starts to flatten out, I lie in the shade and call Earl. His boy appears in half an hour and drives me home. I get back, hot, dirty and exhausted. Jenny isn't back. I go down the beach and bathe in the sea to clear my head, and clean my cuts and grazes.

Then I have a long drink of water and fall asleep on the sofa.

No. 139. The Final Time

You've come driving me to the end of my tether. Lying one time too many.

I've found your plantation. Tripped over the bones.

This is the last of my quirky notes to you. I've chucked you away for the final time.

I thought your plantation was my destination. But my journey's only half done. I need to finish this detective trail. Uncover the rest of your story. Expose what you were up to.

Then I've got to write it down and take it back to my city.

Chapter 25

Jenny, St Kitts

Mount Misery

After she jumped off Earl's jeep in town, Jenny wandered the streets. Should have told Hamish I met Murdo, she thought.

She reached a bus stop, but the next bus wasn't for an hour. She called Leroy. He appeared in ten minutes. 'Mount Misery,' she said. The name fitted her mood.

Leroy looked behind her. 'Just you, or all the family?'

'Family bollocks.'

The Summit

Leroy drove Jenny as high as the road would allow. He offered to be her guide, but she was in no mood for company. He sketched a map of the route to the summit on a pad of paper, and left her. 'Just keep climbing.'

It was hard going. Once she reached the shade of the rainforest, she was out of the sun, yet it got hotter and more humid. She entered another world where everything was different: the light, the vegetation, the colours, the bird calls. The path wasn't easy to follow, and was crossed by huge, writhing tree roots. The small roots tripped her up, but others were so big she had to clamber over them.

Something rustled high in the trees and followed her in the green gloom. She should have taken Leroy's offer of company. As she climbed higher, her phone pinged with a text from Hamish: *Where are you?* He kept sending texts, but she ignored them.

Finally Jenny came out into the sun. Hot and tired, she struggled up onto a big rock on the summit. Way below her lay the crater. The view might be spectacular, but it wasn't a good place to be when you were fragile. The backbone of St Kitts stretched away to the south, with a string of jagged peaks for vertebrae. Today the air was so clear she could see right to the end of the island. Beyond it was Nevis, its profile familiar, like it had always existed in her head. Far away in the other direction was the blue serrated edge of St Eustatius.

Perched on the rock on the summit, Jenny opened a mango she'd picked on the way. She took out her knife and tried to copy Hamish's way of opening it, but ended up with a mess of stone and skin. She watched as a line of tiny black ants appeared from a crack in the rock. They crossed to the remains of her fruit, swarmed over it, then joined a second line, which staggered back to the crack with pieces bigger than their bodies.

Why am I still hiding everything? thought Jenny. She checked her phone for a signal, and called Kelly.

'What now?' Kelly said.

'Fell out again.'

'You can't keep hiding stuff. It'll drive you mad.'

'I'm all mixed up.'

'He's just as confused as you. He needs time,' Kelly said.

'Time?!'

'How long's it been known about in Bristol?' Kelly said.

'History buffs have always known.'

'But how long did it take to get down to street level?'

'About two hundred years.'

'Maybe Hamish needs a few more days?'

As Jenny sat on the highest point of the island, taking in the view, she was only half-listening to Kelly's rant. She was thinking about Anna and Murdo, how they'd worked together. She agreed with one thing: Hamish was just as mixed up as her.

It was time to be honest.

Jenny stood up and took a long drink from her water bottle. She brought out her camera and took pictures of the panorama. Then, rejuvenated, she descended the mountain, leaping over tree roots, until she reached the bottom in a fraction of the time it had taken to climb up.

Truce

When Jenny got back to the shack, Hamish was asleep on the sofa. She was shocked by his appearance. His face and arms were scratched, and he looked ill. She poked him and persuaded him to have a shower, but he still looked terrible. 'Truce,' she said.

In silence, they put together a picnic supper. Jenny took a full bottle of Martini from the fridge and slipped it into Hamish's backpack, along with two plastic cups. As the sun set, they headed along the beach, each collecting an armful of driftwood.

Out at the point, they built a fire and cooked potatoes in foil. Neither of them were drinkers, but while they waited for the potatoes to cook, they sipped their way through the bottle.

After they'd eaten, Jenny got up and walked beyond the fire and sat facing the sea. The reflection of the moon was blurred by her tears. Somewhere in the distance a dog barked.

Hamish appeared out of the dark, giving her a fright. He rested a hand on her shoulder and sat down.

The Truth

They sat in silence watching the phosphorescence of the waves in the moonlight.

Sitting side by side, Hamish's story came out in a whisper:

Canada Hills.

The windmill.

The undergrowth.

The eels.

The bones.

'Owned a wee lassie. Name of Flora.'

He held out his phone and showed Jenny the message from Linda. 'Thirteen altogether.'

'Looks like paradise here,' she said, 'but the truth's still buried.'

'What can we do?'

'It's too much to take in. Maybe we need to do what everyone's done to date. Bury the bad stuff. Stick to the old stories.'

Hamish turned and faced her in the moonlight. 'Shit, Jen, I've had enough of hiding things. It's not about bad and good, it's about the truth. Not for Murdo or Archie or anyone else, but for us.' He gave a big sigh and lay back full length on the sand.

'We need to work together,' she said.

He nodded, his voice cracking. 'Working together would be the best thing ever.'

She climbed on top of him, her knees straddling his chest. For an instant he was buried in her flowing skirts. Jenny pulled her dress back from his face, leaned forward and kissed him. Then she sat up and drew her skirt back and forth across him. 'Maybe when all this is over...' she said.

They got up and walked back along the beach, arm in arm.

The Journal of Cato

A MAN NEEDS A MAID

Jamie the Scot, Billee's best friend, finishes his apprenticeship five years before Billee. Die, Jamie's boss Tovey dies of fever. A month later, Jamie says to Billee, 'I have my eye on Tovey's widow.'

Jamie weds her within the year. Arrange, he arranges for her daughter Mary to walk out with Billee. Everyone knows that Billee prefers a boy in his bed.

'But a man needs a maid,' Jamie says. 'Like it or not, a spouse is the route to social success.'

PLAYS AT SOLDIERS

Billee sells his skills as measurer & map-maker. Buries his Scotch accent. Befriends the wealthiest planters. Is elected to the island Council. On Saturdays he dresses up again & plays at soldiers on the beach.

The planters promote each other, call themselves Major & Colonel. The richer the planter, the higher the rank. They call themselves militia. They line up the poor whities, march them through the town with sticks for rifles.

Soldier? At every rumour of the French fleet on the horizon, Billee & his cronies flee like scared children & hide in the mountains.

A PLANTATION

Stand, I stand in Billee's shadow & hear everythin. News comes that the sugar plantations on the French half of St. Christopher are finally to be split among the British. Billee is in high hopes of success. He has his eye on a former French plantation named Canada Hills.

He succeeds. As Jamie says, Billee always succeeds, whatever he does.

Howsoever, Billee is not content with Lower Canada. He sets about buildin a second plantation on his high ground.

'You are not satisfied with one plantation, you wish to have two?' says Jamie.

'Unless a man build & improve, he stagnates,' says Billee. 'There is nothin more dangerous for a planter markin time. Markin time is too close to walkin backwards.'

THE WINDMILL

One day, Massa Billee selects eight from his best field gang & hands out picks & shovels. Follow, I follow them up to the highest corner of the plantation. We dig & dig until we form a great flat plateau on the slope. Then Billee gives me a long wooden post & hammer & he scratches in the dirt. Everyone stands & watches as I drive the post into the centre of the level area. Then, with a long string, Billee scratches a circle in the red dirt. Young Glasgow cries out in Creole that tis sorcery, but gang-master Apollo silences him with his stick.

Carts arrive from the quarry & I sit & tally the square blocks of stone as they are off-loaded. Six Scalags dig the foundations, then the masons start buildin the curvin walls, up, up.

Months ago, Billee dictated a letter to order special stone from Scotland as ballast on two ships. The ships are delayed by contrary winds off Antigua. Work stops for a week while we wait. Two masons arrive with the stone. I recognise from their voices that they are Scotch. They complain of the heat & say 'Aye' like Billee. Build, they build the great arched entrance to the mill.

Say, they say tis the largest windmill on the island. Many other planters ride up to watch. They say that the mill will not be finished by next harvest. That it will not withstand a hurycane. They say Billee will run out of money.

But Billee knows he is buildin it when the Scalags are least employed in the fields.

BLANK

An enormous thing is Billee's windmill. Swallowed the labour of a hundred men. Each cube of stone quarried & cut & shaped. Thrown up into a great circular tower.

Each stone a memory of one of us. But the face of the stone is blank. Nothin is scored in its surface to speak our names.

BLOOD THE MILL

When the wall is risen to its full height & the copes are fitted, I climb up the wooden scaffold. From the top see, I can see back across to Nevis.

The millwright has already been workin on the machinery. The iron gears & rollers have arrived from Scotland. In the back of the wall is a wee arch. We lay a fireclay channel from it down to the boilin coppers.

The mill is finished in time for harvest. Massa Billee appears on his horse, carryin an armful of freshly cut cane.

'Tis bad luck,' says Jamie. 'First we need to blood the mill.'

Two big Scalags come up the hill, draggin Avon from the mid field gang. His back is cut with stripes from the whip.

The sails are unfurled, the great vanes creak & start to turn & the mill is sett a-goin. From where I stand I hear a cry & see them feed Avon's fingers between the iron rollers of the mill. Hope, there is no hope for Avon. The mill cannot be reversed. His hand & arm are drawn in, the bones crackin. The screamin stops as he faints. I turn away as he is drawn beyond the shoulder.

A great crack, like the burstin of a coconut, disturbs the birds in the trees.

Later clean, I begin to clean the remains of Avon from the channel behind the mill, to make way for the sugar juice.

'No!' says Billee. 'Tis bad luck.'

Wonder, I wonder. Far away in the place called Scotland, before they put the sugar to their tongues, will they notice tis stained pink? Will they taste the tang of sweat of my brothers & sisters? The essence of Avon, the young fieldworker?

LEAVE WITHOUT ME

Great is Billee's success. Great too is his turmoil that he cannot achieve full ownership of his cane land.

He visits the Governor of the Leewards. Writes to a place called Westminster. Talks of sailin to London to petition the King.

Great is my fear that Billee will leave without me. That he will sell me. That I will descend once again into the canefields. Strength, I no longer have the strength.

I would not last a week.

Great too is my fear of another ocean crossin.

Billy's Law

At the end of the latest jotter, Jenny found a copy of a printed legal document: *Act for the More Effectual Prevention of Negroes Running Away (1722)*:

> *It has been found by experience that the laws now in force for punishing runaway Negroes, including burning and amputation, have proved too mild and gentle to curb and restrain them.*
>
> *It is notorious that Christopher, belonging to Colonel Billy, Johnny Congo, belonging to Lieutenant Matthew, and Antego Quamina, belonging to Major Bachelor, have, for a long while past, aided and abetted bands of fugitive Negroes in this island.*
>
> *It is henceforth declared lawful to apprehend and suffer such Negroes the pains of death, without fear of legal penalty. And any*

white person who shall apprehend them and deliver their bodies, alive or dead, in whole or in part, shall receive a reward of £30.

Jenny's Family Album

Jenny opened her full list:

Cato, 17, scribe, Cameroon, £35.
Bella, kitchen maid.
Peggy, 15, house servant, Scotland.
Nala, sister, Cameroon.
Nancy, 15, picker, Congo.
Quashee, 17, fieldworker.
Sally, 15, blind in one eye, £15.
Jenny McNight, 28, fieldworker, £35.
Flora, 13.
Lucy, 15, kitchen worker.

Chapter 26

Hamish, St Kitts

Next morning, after breakfast, Jenny goes out for her usual walk.

I open her folder. Inside is the envelope that Anna gave her as we left her house. I open it, slide out four sheets and unfold them. The top two are titled 'Upper Canada' and 'Lower Canada': Lists of men, women and children, with ages, occupations and values in pounds sterling.

At the table out on the verandah I tally up the names. Then I take an empty cornflakes box from the kitchen down to the shore and gather tiny shells along the surf. Once I've collected enough, I take them back, kneel down in front of the shack and lay them down in rows of ten:

Upper Canada: 197.

Lower Canada: 213.

Then I fetch the wee windmill model, and poke it into the sand beside the shells.

When Jenny comes back along the beach, I say, 'Yesterday thirteen was bad, but now it's four hundred.'

She rests a hand on my shoulder and sits down beside me on the sand.

'Why's nobody found this before?' I say.

'Same story in Bristol,' she says, 'nasty stuff always sinks to the bottom.' She picks the best shells from the hundreds I've collected.

'Time to go home?' I say.

'Still haven't had my holiday.'

She's spent half her time on the beach, but I'm not going to spoil the mood by arguing. She goes inside, brings some tea onto the verandah. Then she picks up the other two sheets from Anna's envelope: deeds for plantations on other islands.

'Billy owned more?' I say, 'St Vincent, Grenada, St Lucia…'

'Always wanted to see St Lucia,' she says.

'Billy's grandson retired to their plantation there.'

'Bit of a distant connection?' she says.

'Provost of Glasgow.'

'OK.' She sits thinking.

'What?' I say.

'Murdo mentioned Grenada.'

'Think he's gone there?'

'Is he fit enough?'

I find a map on my phone. 'Grenada's only a few hundred miles south.'

Jenny makes a call. 'Anna says the British Airways flights make a detour to Grenada after Antigua, half empty. We can upgrade our tickets to take in a few days on Grenada on the way home.'

'Did you ask her if that's where Murdo's gone?' I say.

'Would she tell us if he had?'

***

Because Jenny's helped Anthony with his sister's papers, he won't accept any rental for the shack. We leave an envelope on the table with all the US dollars left.

Before we leave St Kitts, we head down under the arch of the big colonial building. I reach up and touch the stone, one last time. Then Jenny calls Leroy and he takes us down to the wooden pier at the end of the island. We stand together and watch as the setting sun turns Nevis's ring of cloud a deep pink. Jenny rests her head against me.

'Thanks for bringing me here,' she says.

Chapter 27

Jenny, Grenada

Grenada

They caught the British Airways plane south to Grenada. When Anna heard they were going, she said to Jenny, 'My sister manages a vacation complex in Fort George. It's off season. She'll fix you up for next to nothing.'

Sure enough, Anna's sister got them a chalet, within walking distance of the capital. As it was quiet, the girl on reception also served at the bar, cleaned the pool and made the beds.

'Think Murdo's here?' Hamish said.

'He wasn't fit to go into town, let alone fly here.' As far as Jenny could see, all the other properties were empty.

Hamish said to the pool girl, 'Seen an old British guy with white hair?' The girl shook her head.

A Real Holiday

They sat on white plastic chairs on their verandah. Jenny unfolded a map she'd bought at the airport and laid it on the table. 'Don't see Billy's plantation,' she said.

'Need to find Murdo.'

Jenny went down the slope to the pool. She had it all to herself. Hamish sat in the shade with his papers and rang a bell. The same girl donned an apron and came to serve at the bar. They bought cold drinks.

Hamish picked up Jenny's towel and shouted to her, and she climbed out of the pool and joined him. She sat back and sipped her drink. 'Finally, a real holiday,' she said.

Their chalet had real air conditioning, but it sounded like a tractor revving outside the window. An hour before bedtime, they cranked it right up, then switched it off overnight and put up with the heat.

Time to Go Walkabout

Next morning after breakfast Jenny spread out her island map again and turned it over. On the back was a street map of the capital. She drew a line to the archive, the library, then through a tunnel to the supermarket. 'Time to go walkabout,' she said.

Although it was early, it was already hot. The road to the capital was lined on both sides with waterlogged ditches. Beneath the surface, something moved. Jenny grabbed Hamish's arm. 'Lizards?'

'They don't like water.'

When they came to a junction and stood still, big slow-moving creatures swarmed out of the ditches. 'Land crabs,' Hamish said.

The creatures crawled slowly towards them. Jenny waved her arms and shouted at them, and they slowed down. 'Gross!' she said.

They were saved by a brightly coloured van which tooted its horn and stopped. A boy jumped out and offered them a ride. Another van stopped across the street, and another boy vied for their custom, going the opposite way. The jazzed-up vans were the island's buses. Fancy paint jobs, tinted windows, double chrome exhausts. Each one had a driver, and a young boy riding shotgun to drum up customers.

They accepted a lift from the bus heading for town. The fare was incredibly cheap. They shared it with a wizened, toothless man and a large woman carrying a crate of green and red mangoes.

Fort George was set in a steep semicircular bay overlooked by colonial forts. As they circled the bay, the brightly coloured tin roofs stood out, replaced after the last hurricane. They left the bus in the centre.

The Scots Kirk

On the spur linking the fort to the central peninsula, they passed a big church, still roofless from the last big storm. Jenny pulled out her camera and took a photo of the sign: THE SCOTS KIRK. Further along, she tapped an iron railing: Saracen Foundry, Glasgow. 'Not alone here either?' she said.

Hamish spotted more 'knicker labels' on street furniture and balconies overhanging the street. Despite the Glasgow logos, the cast-iron balconies had a French feel.

Jenny tapped her guidebook. 'Island was French until the British moved in, mostly Scots.' She frowned. 'Says the Scots treated the French as bad as the Africans, 'cause they were Catholic?'

'Long story,' he said.

They climbed up some steps to the main colonial fort on the peninsula. Cannons pointed in all directions from ragged stone battlements. A friendly American couple insisted on telling them about their country's invasion of the island in the 1980s. The large woman pointed out bullet marks in the wall. It took Hamish and Jenny nearly an hour to shake them off.

'There's another three forts,' Hamish said.

'Fort bollocks,' Jenny said.

Archive Mode

Jenny brought out her street map and led him down to the government archives. Young lawyers' clerks, male and female, smartly and colourfully dressed, thumbed through big old ledgers of property deeds. Hamish smiled.

'What's so funny?' Jenny said.

'It's you in archive mode. Doing something boring but trying to look cool.'

She poked him in the ribs. One young man had folded his ledger so far back on itself that the spine had split. Loose pages dropped between his legs and joined a crumpled pile on the floor. In most of the ledgers, a chunk of pages was missing at the start. 'It would give an archivist at home a heart attack!' she said.

The ordering process was a remnant of colonial farce. First they had to queue at a glass window and purchase a stamp, then go to another window, hand in the stamp and use it to order out their ledgers.

Despite the missing pages, it didn't take them long to find lots of references. 'Billy?' she said.

'Billy the second. Mentions several of his places, including Belmont.'

'He's got more than one?'

'Murdo could be somewhere here in town,' Hamish said.

'If we find Billy's plantation, maybe we'll find Murdo.'

The Chocolate Museum

On the way out, they stopped at a big map on the wall. As usual, the sugar plantations were marked by wee windmill sketches. Most were on the flatter ground around the top of the island. Hamish pointed with his finger. 'Belmont!' he said. He took some shots of the map with his phone.

Jenny pulled out a tourist leaflet. 'Two reasons to visit Belmont,' she said. 'It's now the chocolate museum!' She brought out a bar in a brightly coloured wrapper she'd bought in the airport. 'Made here, on the island.'

Brother and Sister

'We need some provisions,' Jenny said. They found a supermarket through a spooky rock tunnel under the peninsula. At the door, a tall guard in uniform insisted that Hamish leave his backpack in a side room. Hamish was about to argue, then Jenny pointed out that everyone was doing the same thing.

When they came back out, Hamish collected his backpack and turned up the street with the supermarket trolley. The same guard shouted across to him, 'Hey, mon, you can't take the cart home.' Hamish was ready for an argument, but the guard disarmed the situation with a big smile. His name was Anthony. He helped them fit the shopping in Hamish's backpack. 'Why you come to our small island?' said Anthony.

In the evening they sat at the table, facing each other as usual, doing their own thing. They might be on holiday together on a tropical island, but they were still living like brother and sister, sleeping in the same room in single beds.

A Bus Down There?

Next morning, Jenny was up at dawn to get ready for a trip. They didn't have much cash left, only local currency, but it was more than enough for the bus.

The small van filled up with folk in the suburbs. Just when they thought it couldn't take any more passengers, an old man climbed aboard, clutching a lamb. Then they started to climb the mountain range. The young driver drove as fast as he could, with no regard for bends. It was only because they were packed like sardines that they weren't thrown onto the floor. But nobody said a word. They reached the top of the central volcano, then it got much worse. They hurtled back down the far side on the narrow, twisting road, with an unguarded precipice on one side. Jenny pointed out rusty wrecks, way down below. 'That a bus down there?' she said.

They reached Grenville and staggered out.

Jenny was pale-faced and sick. 'There's no way we're going back that way,' she said. Then she spotted a brightly coloured market.

'I'll leave you to recover,' Hamish said. He left her at the stalls, hired a bike from a shop and carried on a bit further to check out some windmill ruins.

Belmont

Two hours later, they met up again. Hamish took one of Jenny's bags, and they stopped at a stall to buy some sandwiches for lunch. Then they found an old, battered taxi which took them on the short trip.

With Michael at the wheel, they reached Belmont in ten minutes. The chocolate tour was just starting. A young girl demonstrated how the cocoa beans were dried and processed. The beans looked like grey, slimy lumps of saturated fat.

After the tour, Jenny said, 'Don't think I'll ever eat chocolate again.'

As Powerful as a Million

While Hamish went to the toilet, Jenny found a spot for a picnic on a patch of grass in the shade of a fig tree. A fireclay gutter ran under the tree, clogged with squashed and broken figs. Overhead ran an aqueduct, which had once carried water to a big rusty water wheel across the yard. Scattered around were lots of big boiling coppers.

Hamish joined her. They ate their sandwiches in the shade of the arch of the sugar-boiling works.

'Guess what was grown here before cocoa?' she said. She pulled out a second-hand paperback from her bag and held it out. 'A present.'

It was a bit faded and tattered: *The Diary of Anne Frank.* He turned on her. 'You think it's as bad as the Holoc—'

'Shit, it's not that,' she said. 'It's just a hint...'

He took the book.

'...that maybe one story's as powerful as a million.'

A Third Sheet

On the way out, in the big wooden museum shed, they spotted a timeline for the plantation, mounted in a cracked picture frame.

'First planter to take it from the French was John Aitcheson, from Airdrie, near Glasgow,' Hamish said.

'Had two hundred and seven fieldworkers, including forty-five wenches,' Jenny read.

'In 1767 it passed to another Scot, Alexander Campbell, who had the right to own any children born to the workers on the estate.'

Jenny ran her finger along the next line. 'Then it was Alexander Houston,' she said. 'Governor of the island in 1796. Billy's nephew.'

'Don't you see?' he said. 'It's not just St Kitts and Nevis, it's massive.' Hamish brought out the envelope Anna had given to Jenny and tipped out the four sheets. Then he looked inside the envelope. There was another sheet stuck to the side. He pulled it out. It was a photocopy of an old deed. 'You and your chocolate tour,' he said. 'There's another Grenada plantation! We're at the wrong one!' Hamish scrolled through his phone for the pictures he'd taken of the map at the library. 'Mount Alexander!' he said. 'It's only a few miles north! Murdo's bound to have gone there.'

Their battered taxi appeared and dropped off an American couple. 'Free?' Jenny said.

Michael took them the short trip to Sauteurs, a village on the north coast with brightly painted houses and verandahs. 'Thanks, we can walk from here,' Hamish said to him.

The road was narrow, flanked by dense bush, and Hamish had misjudged the distance. Every so often the road forked, and they were unsure which branch to take. After their long day, they were worn out in the heat, but Hamish was determined to find the plantation.

'Lost?' Jenny said.

'Map's not accurate. And it's hard to follow the road on Google Earth, for all the trees.'

Mount Alexander

Just as they were about to give up, they reached a driveway flanked by stone gateposts. MOUNT ALEXANDER. Hamish stopped and leaned against one of the pillars.

'Tired?' said Jenny.

'Not sure I can cope with more bones.'

Jenny started heading up the steep drive, so Hamish followed. They reached a huge sugar copper, overgrown and half-full of rainwater, big enough to bathe inside. Above was the boiling works, massive ruined stone structures rising up the tiered slope, buried in ivy. The entire hillside had been formed into stone terraces.

Hamish stopped and pointed. Away to the left, in the distance, two big dogs were running uphill.

'Haven't seen us,' Jenny said.

As quickly as they could, they headed back down to the road and sat sweating by the entrance.

They waited for a few minutes. Then Hamish stood up. 'I'm shit-scared of dogs, especially big ones, but we've come all this way. I'm going to have to risk the rabies.'

Jenny followed a few paces behind. They headed back up again, photographing everything they saw. Then the dogs rushed down towards them.

'Here boy.' Jenny held out biscuits meant for their snack. The dogs cornered her, wolfed the biscuits and ran off.

Then they came up over the crest of the hill. On a raised mound stood the biggest windmill they'd seen on any of the islands. They circled it, speechless. Across the plateau was a big modern house. A local girl came out, flanked by the dogs.

'Sorry for the intrusion,' Hamish said.

'You like our windmill?' the girl said. She was the housekeeper. The owners were away.

'You haven't had another visitor? An old Scottish guy with white hair?'

The girl shook her head. They sat in the shade of one of the windmill arches and she brought them cold drinks and more biscuits, which they shared with the dogs.

Hamish touched the rough stone. 'Billy's windmill.'

Jenny pointed to a date stone above the main arch: 1763. 'His son's.'

Once the girl went back to the house, Hamish took out his screwdriver and levered out a piece of stone.

'Can't resist trashing the place,' she said.

'A wee memento.' They sat in silence, then Hamish said, 'Murdo would be over the moon to see this.'

She put his hand on top of his. 'Murdo bollocks. This is our moment.'

Shortcut

They found a shortcut back to Sauteurs and took the bus back by the flatter route, round the west coast. On the way, the small van had to pull over to let a big tourist coach pass. Further down, they met another big modern bus, parked at a viewpoint. Overweight tourists stood in a row, all snapping the sunset.

In the seat in front of them, a girl clutched a cage of live chickens. 'I'd rather see it this way,' Jenny said, leaning against Hamish.

How Many

The next day, over lunch by the pool, Jenny held out her tablet.

'Mount Alexander?' he said.

'Anna emailed it.'

'How many?'

'Big plantation.'

'How many?'

'Three hundred and fifteen.'

He sighed and sat back.

'What?' she said.

'Proves it's not just Billy's generation. It's massive. It's Billy, his son, all their mates…'

'It's too much. Just stick to Billy.'

'What now?' he said. 'Anna says Murdo's definitely not here.'

'He's still controlling us,' Hamish said. 'Probably brought us here to check it out for him.' Then he said, 'Where is he?'

'Bristol.'

'Time to go home.'

Part Five
Back to Britain

Chapter 28

The Journal of Cato

TOMORROW WE REACH A NEW LAND

Eh, but I am restless tonight. I light the lamp, hang the hammock in the corner of the hold. No sleep came to me last night. Tomorrow we reach a new land. Another island, Cook says. From the back, under the sackcloth cover, I find my journal, write a few lines, but the light is too poor. Memories arise, bringin wetness to my eyes. But men must not cry. Cryin is the end of purpose. But forget, I cannot forget my memories.

Eh, but I am restless. Through the half-opened port-hole I hear the shouts of the pilot-boat arrive to lead us up-river to the town they call Bris-tol. Cold winds blow in. Many scents & sounds come under the door. Tar & timber & the dampness of stored sail-cloth. Rum & food & laughter from the captain's cabin, where Massa Billee rests & seeks to overcome his ocean sickness & eat dinner.

THE CITY

Sail, we sail up-river on this October evenin when the days grow short & candles burn in the windows by the quay. The tide & the pilot-boat lead us up the narrow channel. Walls of rock tower over us. As we turn a bend, the city opens out before us. Never have I seen such a thing.

As the ship is tied to the dock, I stand behind Massa Billee, clutchin the bag of letters ready for the post. Letters dictated to myself when he was lyin gaggin in his bunk, too overcome by sickness to move.

We tie up among a forest of other ships, masts & sails. Ships so close-set we must cross a sea of decks to reach dry land.

THE SIGN OF SUGAR MONEY

Move, I move my feet to find firmness on the stone quay after the long voyage. Never have I seen so many ships in one place. Strange are the smells. Wood-smoke mixed with horse shit. Candles & rottin vegetables. But most of all the sweet sickly smell of burnt sugar. Above everythin, the fug from the sugar-houses hangs over the city like a cloud. Everywhere I see stone houses with the shape they call pediments above the door, the sign of sugar money.

Dark, the dark falls early. The city begins to light up, window by window, street by street, each room with its glowin fireplace.

Told, I am told to make my way to the house of Billee's cousin, John Day, to make arrangements for a carriage. Howsoever, Day already awaits our arrival on the quay. A fine carriage has he, tho tis barely needed, for his mansion backs onto the harbour.

Day doffs his hat & greets Billee. 'I am sorry that your wife was unable to accompany you on the homeward voyage.'

'My son Billy is yet too young to cross the ocean,' says Billee, 'but I am in hopes they will follow soon.'

'Your house on the bridge is not yet ready. I have arranged for you to lodge with us in the Marsh.'

Load, I load the luggage onto the coach & we pass a short distance from the docks through a lane into the square. A black servant shows me to the garret which I am to share with five others.

Later, Day returns. 'We dine tonight with Yate at the Red Lodge,' he says.

Many are the Bristol connections between Massa Billee & his wife Mary. The Days & Yates, two of the city's sugar families, are her kin.

STONE WALLS

In Bristol everyone is hurry-hurry. See, I see a great deal of open land around the city, but the people live one upon the other & throw their rubbish from their windows. Narrow are the streets & sharp is the wind from the west, which brings rain.

Walk, I walk in shelter under the piazzas. Push, people push me all about & I must jump to escape gutter-water. Strange, strange are the buildings. Stone worked from the earth, stacked up & cemented. Houses of stone which will endure storms. Yet I am told no hurycanes blow in this cold, wet land. No earthquakes shake their foundations.

All surrounded by stone walls, which show what belongs to each. In my home country no place belonged to one man. No fences which said: *This is mine.*

From my rear garret I look out on the ships in the river. I dream of stealin aboard one & returnin to my home. But where is the captain who could tell me from whence I came?

A SUIT OF GREEN VELVET

We settle into life in the city. By the time the sun comes back, Massa Billee dictates letters to myself. Lunch & dinner he spends socialisin. He uses the title Colonel, bestowed upon him by his planter friends, as if he has spent a career in the military. On Friday he meets a Major who questions him regardin his regiment. For a while, no talk comes from Billee. Then he says, 'Ah, but my rank was in the militia, leadin the defence against the French in '06.' Lucky, lucky it is that this Major knows not that the militia were of less use in battle than a pack of monkeys tossin mangoes.

Sent, I am sent to a tailor who fits me out in a suit of green velvet & a three-cornered hat. Tis the fashion here for servants to trail their master everywhere. Once again, spend, I spend my days in Billee's shadow. Watchin everythin, sayin nothin. Only after dark does he seek solace in some secret tavern & I have time to write my journal.

THE MARSH & THE RED LODGE

Durin these weeks in Bristol, Massa Billee's life moves between the Marsh & the Red Lodge. Then we move into Mary's house on the Bridge. Billee sails to London by Plymouth on plantation business, but leaves me behind. Fear, tis always my fear that he will find another servant, a younger scribe to replace me.

Alone, I am alone for the first time in many years. Spend, I spend my time in the small library, perusin books. Writin in my journal. I don a coat & hood & walk the streets of the city. Run, I am free to run. But where does a black man hide in a city of whites?

Chapter 29

Hamish, Bristol

We arrive back at Gatwick early in the morning, knackered after the long flight, and catch a bus into the centre.

'Don't want to go on a long flight ever again,' Jenny says.

'Suppose it beats a sailing ship.'

I tap my tablet. 'Billy's ships. Want to check the records in the capital on our way home.'

'We've only just landed!' Jenny says.

'Can't miss the chance while we're here.'

'I'm starving,' she says.

All we can find open is a McDonald's.

'Need to slum it for once,' I say.

'I'm ready to eat anything.'

The coffee revives us. I pinch a trolley from a supermarket and throw in our bags. We arrive at the big library as the doors open. The newspaper section's on the top floor. We start checking shipping arrivals.

'Nothing worse than microfilm readers for wearing you out,' I say, then, 'Look at this.' I write a new heading and start copying out entries for the year Billy arrived back in Britain. 'There's lots,' I say. But Jenny's dozed off, her head on her arm.

No. 140. Billy's Ships

– Thursday Jan 5: The Mary, sighted off Dover, from St. Christophers.
– Saturday Jun 27: The Mary and the Hope, arrived at Gravesend with sugar from St. Christophers.
– Thursday Jul 4: The Hope, for St. Christophers, is still detain'd at Dartmouth by contrary winds.
– Saturday Dec 11: The Mary and the Industry were sighted off Deal, arrived from St. Christophers...

***

When Jenny wakes, she looks at my notes. 'Owned all these? Must have been important.'

'But he wasn't using the Clyde?'

'Maybe 'cause London was the main market?'

***

On the bus back to Bristol, we doze most of the way. Jenny's flat smells musty, so we open all the windows. From the trail of clothes it looks like her sister's been back but gone again.

I check the attic. 'Thought Sally might have thrown out all my models.'

'Sally won't toss out her own junk, let alone anyone else's.'

Jenny works her way through a pile of mail.

'Any work?' I say.

'Museum's offering me the usual three half days, basic.'

'Better than nothing.'

'What about you?'

'Need some sleep.'

I clear a space in Sally's room, and Jenny fetches fresh sheets.

***

Next morning, I wake early. Jenny isn't up, so I go to her room and throw back the curtains. The sun's shining. I turn on her radio and say, 'Walk?'

We head up the hill to the park. At the top, the city's bathed in early-morning light.

'Nothing's changed,' she says.

I shiver. Despite the sun, it's chilly compared to the Caribbean. 'It might be boring and familiar,' I say, 'but we need to keep up the momentum.'

'Need a few days rest.'

'Need to find Murdo.'

I call Aunt Aggie, but she says she hasn't seen him. Jenny tries Eck, but he doesn't answer, so she leaves a message.

We keep walking and have breakfast in a cafe. Then Jenny goes into an old-fashioned stationery shop and buys a packet of HB pencils, a rubber and two packets of expensive lined paper for my wee Filofax. Then she leads me round to her favourite archive. I look up at the sign.

'No!'

'What if Billy spent time in Bristol?' she says. 'We need to check.'

'Bristol?'

Inside, she shows me how to register and order out papers. She even lets me take her favourite seat. She finds a desk herself at the window, and keeps an eye on me. She's ordered me out some Bristol merchant's papers to check. They're brought by a man in a brown coat. I shuffle the papers. Twiddle my pencil. Study the people around me. Stare at the clock on the wall. I endure it for an hour, then I get up. 'I'm sorry,' I whisper. I brush past her desk and leave.

Back at Jenny's flat, I unlock my bike, inflate the soft front tyre and oil the chain. I screech to a halt under a low vault, stand up on the pedals and touch the old bricks.

Still needed this. A portal to something earlier.

Objects mean most to me. They're real. I can stub my toe on them. Stuff the archives, I need solid evidence.

If Murdo's here in Bristol, where will he go? What's left to chase?

There's posters all over the place about the Slave Trade tour. An exhibition at the museum about the merchants and captains involved. It's everywhere in the city: The Middle Passage. Bristol ships. Bristol merchants. Carried folk across the ocean in their millions.

But what about the next stage? The ones who survived? What they were forced to do on the islands? All I've got is numbers. Where's their owners?

Across the quay is one of Jenny's Bristol kisses. I kneel and rub my palm inside the groove in the stone. It's good, but it isn't real until you've crossed the ocean and seen it for yourself. Further downriver, I fill my panniers with driftwood for the stove. Then I squeak along Orchard Street to the row of Georgian houses. The grots still poke their tongues back in defiance.

Did your owners have plantations? I ask them. *Did they own lots of Africans? Is that where all the money came from?*

Too many questions.

I can't resist the tang of coffee which seeps from a pavement cafe, and take a seat outside. The waitress eyes my rusty bike and driftwood with suspicion, and serves everyone else first. I give up and leave.

I need to sort it. Show Jenny I can do it my way.

I follow Jenny's lead and search the upper storeys of buildings for sculptures and logos. There must be something.

There's lots of allusions to empire. But the ships up on the spires are too high to photograph. A frieze on a bank shows the story of minting money, but no hint of what was sold. Lower down, the bases of statues are easier to see, but more subtle. Neptune, Triton and mermaids, even dolphins on the stump of Colston's plinth. On a big building, cherubs carry around suspicious-looking containers. If it's sugar, where are those who grew it?

Lots of Billy's planter friends seem to have come from Bristol. They might have left records on paper, but I need to find them in the streets.

Murdo knows more than he's let on, but does anyone understand? Not just here, but there. It all depends on those who went away. But why do the city's stories only tell of here?

Further along, I lock the bike and go into a supermarket to buy a drink. I pass the home baking section and stacks of sugar. I pick up a heavy blue and white bag and peer at the label. My hands are gritty. Why do sugar bags always leak?

I lift out another, then another. They feel solid in my hands. More honest than books. But where did the sugar come from? They all have a wee Union Jack on the side, but it's too cold here to grow sugar. I have half a dozen bags at my feet. A security man, dreadlocks piled under his cap, comes over and asks if he can help. His name's Steve.

'Trying to work out where the sugar comes from,' I say.

'Sugar beet,' Steve says, as if he's asked the question every day.

I nod.

'Used to come from the Caribbean, but they decided farmers could grow it here. Put my dad out of a job. Never worked since.'

'St Kitts?' I say.

Steve smiles. We have a long conversation, then shake hands. I help him put the bags of sugar back on the shelf. Stuff the archives, I've found the answer in Tesco!

Next I go round to Waterstones and check the 'local' section. There's plenty of books about the Middle Passage, but not about sugar plantations.

Outside again, I unlock my bike, fly back down Park Street in the slipstream of a van and stop at one of the bookstalls by the dock. The girl on the stall has long blonde hair and wears fingerless woollen gloves.

I browse the rickety tables. Then I strike gold in the antique section: Sproak's *Bristol Sugar Houses*. It's in good condition. I push my bike over to the girl, who's rolling a fag. 'How much?' I say.

'Sixty quid.'

'I'm not a collector,' I say. 'Just want to read it.'

'Strange thing to do with a book.' Then she smiles a crooked smile, lights her cigarette and takes a deep draw.

I pull out my phone, cross to the window of a cafe on the quay and tap into their Wi-Fi. I check the price on eBay. There's two second-hand copies of Sproak available, but they're even more expensive. I'll never understand how you can get almost any novel on eBay for a pound or two but history books are extortionate. Are history geeks more gullible?

Cigarette Girl catches my eye and beckons me back. She squints through the smoke from the fag dangling from the corner of her mouth. 'Might have a copy that's falling apart,' she says. She burrows in a box under one of the trestle tables and pulls out a book with no spine, in three separate parts. She thumbs through, checking it's all there, then hands it to me. Her fingers are long and slim and her gloves are fluffy and multicoloured. Beneath the hard exterior, she's got piercing blue eyes and is quite pretty.

'How much?'

'Swap it for the firewood?' she says.

'Deal.' I unload the driftwood into a big cardboard box.

'If you ever fancy a cuppa, or have some spare kindling to trade, I'm the third barge from the bridge.'

'It's good to know that if I end up on the street I still have options.'

Round the corner, I find another cafe. I lock my bike and sit inside, near the window. I pull out three things: the bits of my newly acquired book, my worn city map and Murdo's wee sugar house model. A young man in a bright red jumper comes over.

'Stay as long as you like,' he says in a strong West Country accent.

I frown, but the man points up at the sign over the counter: Book Cafe. I smile and order a latte, then splash out on a huge piece of home-made carrot cake.

That's three new folk I've spoken to today. These days, it doesn't take much to keep me happy.

At the front of the book is a list of dozens of sugar houses, all over the city. It's like some kind of secret discovery!

My worn city map has split down the middle. I place the bits together like a jigsaw, find a thick marker in my bag and start putting big crosses at the locations of the sugar houses, with names and dates.

'Another coffee?' Red Jumper asks. He looks at what I'm doing. 'Good book?'

I show him the faded cover: *Bristol Sugar Houses*. 'Know anything about them?' I say.

'Guess Bristol was a big sugar port.'

'Earlier?' I say.

'You mean the Middle Passage?'

'No,' I say, too quickly.

'Most folk are cool with it nowadays.'

When I leave, I cut back round to the flat, lock up the bike and go upstairs. Jenny's back, working on her laptop.

'I'm sorry,' I say. 'Archives aren't my thing.'

She turns away and ignores me.

***

After dinner, I sit at the table, shuffling my plantation tallies. Each list has a number on top: 197, 213, 315. 'And it's not just Billy,' I say. 'There's lots of Scottish planters on the island. And lots of islands.'

She shakes her head. 'It's a recipe for madness. Best to stick to Billy.'

I go back to working on another Billy letter. Jenny sits opposite. I lean over and say, 'Can I ask you something?'

'Sounds dangerous.'

'Just history stuff.'

'Worst of all.'

I reach across the table and give her a gentle push with my fingers. 'Some of the sugar planters on the islands were Bristol men, but I can't find anything about them here.'

'Doing a Murdo again?'

I shrug.

'Asking me about Bristol when you really mean Glasgow?'

***

Later, I try my aunts again to see if they've heard from Murdo, but neither has.

Although I'm tired, I can't sleep for thinking about Murdo. It's hard to explain to Jenny. He might not be the easiest person to get on with. But we've got a common purpose. More than anything, I need his advice on his book.

What shall I do? Publish all the dodgy stuff?

Or do what they've done for centuries. Bury it.

Chapter 30

Jenny, Bristol

Gusto

Hamish had sent Jenny pictures of birds, unicorns and rams' heads on buildings. Copying her hobby? They should be doing it together.

Then she remembered something. She went round to Clare Street. High up, the stone face of a black man poked from the side of a building above Caffe Gusto. She took a photo for her family album. The man needed a name. She could have gone into the cafe and asked, but she decided to call him Gusto.

Jenny said hello to Gusto, but he looked a bit worn. She sent the photo to Hamish. Then she added Gusto to the names inside her notebook.

As she passed her aunt's flat, she rang the doorbell. Aggie invited her in.

'Any sign of Murdo?' Jenny said.

'Who's asking, you or Hamish?'

'He's been here?'

'Couple of nights. Then he went north. But he's on his last legs. Had to help him round to the station. Won't listen to sense.'

Murdo's back in Glasgow? Should I tell Hamish? she thought.

As she was leaving, Aggie slipped Jenny an envelope with her name on it.

Billy's Bristol Houses

Jenny didn't need to sniff the envelope to know it was more clues from Murdo. Folded inside were several sheets of paper, with a sketch of a Georgian house on the front. On one page was a photocopy of an old document, written in flowing script: *The last testament of Billy's wife Mary.* Mary had died young, just after Billy brought her home. Her family had been from Bristol.

The document contained several pages of household goods, and names of properties where they were kept: the Red Lodge on Bristol Bridge, even her favourite place, Queen Square. The same houses Cato had mentioned.

Yes!

Jenny got up and hurried round to the archive. Tweed Suit was still there. For once, she didn't kick his desk. She felt a bit sorry for him. With her bright clothes and irreverence, she thought she was different from the others.

But was she really? Was this her fate, to be an archive spinster? Wandering the dusty corridors, looking for an elusive document?

It didn't take her long. She knew exactly where to look for city property deeds.

Billy hadn't just passed through Bristol. He'd owned a house, right in the heart of the city! Billy bollocks, she thought. It means Cato stayed here too! Means I can publish Cato's story as a Bristol story!

Jenny kicked off her boots, lifted her skirts and climbed up onto her seat. She stepped onto her desk, held out her arms and shouted, 'Yes!'

Every head in the room turned. The archivist at the front desk stood up and nodded to John in the corner, but John looked the other way. He gave Jenny time to climb back down, slip on her boots and carry on with her notes as if nothing had happened.

Later, as Jenny passed John to go home, she popped a mini Fudge bar into the top pocket of his brown coat.

The Closest

As soon as Jenny got outside, she called Kelly. 'Billy had Bristol connections, stayed here, owned a house!'

'Slow down,' Kelly said. 'Copying Hamish now? Chasing buildings?'

'Shit, Kel, Cato doesn't have shelves of records like Billy and his buddies. All I've got is his words and the places he lived. But if he stayed in Bristol, it solves everything!'

'What'll Hamish say if you steal Billy from Glasgow?'

'Glasgow bollocks. It's my big Mary, Queen of Scots moment!'

'Didn't think you were into the epic stuff.'

There was silence, then Jenny spoke up, her voice breaking. 'Shit, Kel, it's the opposite of epic. Cato's story's my story too. My family. Where we came from.'

Jenny sent Kelly a photo of the house sketched on the front of the papers. It was a terraced townhouse, not a country mansion.

'The Georgian House,' Kelly said.

'Museum in town?'

'Spent three days there last summer doing the guide thing.'

'Seen enough slave trade stuff.'

'Owners were sugar planters, not slave traders.'

A Better Way

Jenny headed back round to the flat. She needed to reach out to Hamish.

She might not admit it, but he'd changed the way she looked at the past. Layers and stones, buildings and places. It was even more nerdish than her history hobby. But maybe it was a better way of doing it.

The Journal of Cato

THE AFFAIR OF THE PLANTATIONS

Fear, my fear of bein replaced by a younger scribe is unfounded. Massa Billee returns to Bristol from London in ten days, in good spirits. The affair of the plantations is to be settled. He is to receive full ownership of Canada Hills.

Billee spends days dictatin letters to his planter friends. He complains of the weather. Howsoever, tis worse for myself, who has never, ever felt such cold & damp. Billee talks often of returnin to the island, but others try to dissuade him. He dictates a letter to his wife.

On Friday, John Day has arranged for Massa Billee to meet Defoe.

DANIEL DEFOE

On Tuesday, Massa Billee dons his best red coat & hat & we cross the square with Day to meet Daniel Defoe in the Llandoger Trow.

As ever stand, I stand behind, in the shadows. Defoe is well versed in matters of trade & manufacture. Billee purchases a bottle of Madeira & orders lunch.

'What is the news from the Leewards?' says Defoe.

'The planters fear drought & a poor harvest,' says Billee.

'The harvest would needs be very poor indeed for a sugar planter not to make a profit.'

THE PLACE WITH A FUTURE

After they have dined, Billee speaks of his plans for settlin on a country estate within a day's ride of London or Bristol.

'But Glasgow is the place with a future,' says Defoe. 'You must settle there. Not because you are Scotch, but because it has the most ambitious merchants & the finest buildings. They say your friend Campbell's mansion is the best in the country. Tis a good time to buy a share in a sugar-house there.'

'I have friends in Glasgow, but the sugar market is low,' Billee replies.

'Then you must revive it,' says he.

That night, Massa Billee dictates a letter to his brother in Edinburgh, to keep an eye open for a country estate in North Brittain.

Chapter 31

Hamish, Bristol

The next morning, during breakfast, I pull out the pieces of my sugar house map. I find some Sellotape in a drawer and stick them together. I lay out the new pencils and rubber Jenny bought me, then use one of the pencils to plot a route on the map. We've barely spoken since the day before, but Jenny's curiosity seems to have overcome her mood. When I put on my jacket, she follows me down to the street.

'Sugar House tour,' I say.

'Bristol expert now?'

I lead her round to the corner of Guinea Street, to the site of a sugar house. But she points the other way, up the street.

'Seen the grots?' she says. 'Best in Bristol.' She hijacks my tour and leads me to two very old, white-painted houses, one with a Dutch gable. Above all the windows and doors are wee grots.

'Birds!' I say.

'Dolphins!'

'A parrot!'

'Devils!'

'OK, they're more interesting than sugar houses,' I say, 'but I still need to understand the sugar connection.'

She shrugs and follows me along Redcliff Street, by the banks of the Avon.

I tap my map. 'Three sugar houses beside the river from the 1680s.' I struggle over the fence.

'Be careful,' she says. For once, she doesn't follow me.

The tide's out, and it's a long drop into the muddy river channel. I climb down into an inlet and stand on a big stone, to avoid sinking into the mud. Jenny watches from the fence.

Like a scholar in a library, the muddy bank in front of me is my bookshelf. I reach out and run my fingers over the gritty bank. Instead of picking a book, I pull out a piece of broken red brick. I try to push it into my pocket, but it's too big.

I climb back over the fence and hand Jenny the dirty brick. She traces her finger along a wiggly line on it that looks like a letter *S*. 'S for sugar house!' she says.

I grab it from her, wrap it in a supermarket bag and put it in my backpack. 'What you smiling at?' I say.

'Come here.'

I move closer.

'Your mouth's dirty,' she says. She takes a hanky from her pocket and wipes my mouth. The hanky smells of roses. We stand in a wee trance, looking at each other.

'We should develop a joint sugar tour,' I say.

'You'd be too bossy,' she says.

We reach Bristol Bridge. I look at my map. 'East Tucker Street sugar house.'

She stops and holds out her arms.

'What now?' I say.

'Don't baffle folk with dates and stuff. Average punter doesn't know the difference between 1680 and 1880.'

I've got all the sugar houses marked on the map: Counterslip, Duck Lane and Hallier's Lane. I keep going, she follows. We reach the only survivor, Lewin's Mead.

'Ach, it doesn't look like a sugar house anyway,' I say, and move on.

Jenny takes the lead and bypasses the site of two more, then we come to the site of St Augustine's. 'Bristol's second,' she says. 'Set up to refine sugar from Nevis and St Kitts.'

I flop back against a wall. 'If only it was still here, it might make all the island stuff real.'

'We missed the most important one,' she says, and leads me back round by Castle Park. 'St Peter's,' she says. 'Bristol's first.'

'You knew about them before,' I say, 'and you didn't make the jump to plantations?'

'Not a big issue here with the public.'

'Shit, it's complicated,' I say.

'Wasn't great for African folk either.' She turns to face me. 'Look,' she says, 'I know what you're trying to do.'

'I'm trying to finish Billy's story, find what he was up to at home. Show how big it was.'

'You're trying to sort out Bristol, Glasgow, the whole fucking country.'

'But owning people was much bigger than trading them.'

'It's not about bigger. It's just different.'

'Ach, it's like the old city stories – impossible to change.'

We've reached an odd state. We spend most of our spare time together. If we go to a cafe, she sits beside me, not opposite. When we walk, she takes my arm. Anyone watching might think we're partners, even if our minds are worlds apart.

She takes my arm.

'More sugar houses?' I say.

'Sugar house bollocks. Should have thought of this before we went to the islands.' She leads the way up Park Street, then left, along a terrace of Georgian tenements. She pulls open a big door bearing a City Museums logo. The first thing I notice is a faded engraving of a tropical island on the corridor wall. I recognise its profile immediately.

'Nevis!' I take out my phone for a photo, but she pulls me on.

'Later,' she says.

At the end of the corridor, a small group have gathered, about to start a tour. Jenny introduces me to the curator, Jill, a museums colleague. Jill's small and timid and looks too young to be leading a tour. She starts taking us round.

'Pinney, the owner of the house, went out to a Caribbean island called Nevis as a teenager... he became a sugar planter and had a sugar-importing business here in Bristol...'

Then we're given twenty minutes to roam on our own. I take photos of everything: pictures, text, lists of workers on Pinney's estate. There's a story on the wall about an African named Pero who stayed in the house.

I notice a family tree. Most of the story's about a Pinney who went out a century too late. But the first Pinney went out to Nevis the same time as Billy. In the corner is a framed census of Nevis. I run my finger down the list, until I reach Billy's name.

'Haven't seen you smile so much since you stroked an old piece of stone,' Jenny says.

'Glasgow could open a museum like this, in Billy's house!'

'If it had survived.'

We go back and join Jill for the second half of her tour.

'This is a diagram of a sugar plantation. First the freshly cut cane was crushed in the windmill... At this time Pinney owned more than two hundred Africans on his plantation.'

It's all so familiar, I could stay all day. But then, to my surprise, Jill switches from sugar planting.

'Sugar merchants like Pinney made a fortune buying and selling people... carried them across the ocean—'

'Can I ask a question?' I say. My voice echoes in the hallway. Jill stops in mid flow.

'Ask away,' Jill says.

The audience glare at me.

'You said Pinney made his money from trading Africans?' I say.

'Absolutely,' says Jill.

'But I thought he was a sugar planter.'

'Yes?'

'So was he a planter or a people trader?' I say.

Jill looks cornered. The front row of the tour look daggers at me.

'Er, it's all part of the sugar triangle...' Jill says.

Jenny elbows me.

A tall guy at the front with a Bristol accent speaks up, 'At least we were advancing the empire, unlike you Scots, who weren't even there.'

I ignore him. 'I'm not trying to catch you out,' I say to Jill. 'Actually, I've been to Nevis.'

'OK, smart-arse. You want to lead the tour?' says Tall Guy.

'Leave her alone,' whispers Jenny, tugging at my sleeve.

I say no more. At the end, before we leave the museum, we pass Jill. 'Sorry,' I say. 'It wasn't personal.' Jill gives a sheepish smile.

Outside, we cross the road into the park. We climb to the top of Brandon Hill and sit beneath the Cabot Tower.

'Need to go back and read all the stuff properly,' I say.

'Wednesday,' Jenny says. 'Jill's day off.'

'Ha ha.'

She pulls a book from her bag and hands it to me. *The Pinneys of Bristol and Nevis.* 'A present.'

'It's just what I need. I could scan the text and paste Billy in!'

We get up, head down to the harbour and cross Pero's Bridge. 'One of Pinney's slaves,' she says.

'Named the bridge after the slave, not the merchant?'

I have the spark of an idea, but it disappears as quickly as it came.

Chapter 32

Jenny, Bristol

Just One More Thing

The following day, at breakfast, Jenny sat at the kitchen table. Through the window, between a gap in two tall buildings, she could see a wee bit of the river. Bits of boat passed by in the sunshine. When Hamish came through, she said, 'Just one more thing.'

'I've had it with tours,' he said.

Jenny ignored him and got ready, appearing a few minutes later in a colourful dress. She took his arm and walked him to the front door.

The Red Lodge

Jenny halted in front of the Red Lodge.

'City's oldest house,' she said. She pushed open the big wooden door and they entered the panelled hall. The curator was another of Jenny's workmates. 'Don't upset her,' Jenny said. The place was spooky: wooden floors and panelling. Jenny's friend gave them a brief personal tour. Near the end, they stopped on the main stair. Jenny nodded up at a series of portraits. 'Billy's cousins,' she said.

Hamish peered at the captions. 'Yates? They're in his letters. Visited them when he came back from St Kitts!' He took some photos, then he sat down on the worn treads and touched the wooden banister. 'Billy climbed this stair?'

'Impressive?'

'But it's Elizabethan. Far too early.'

'Makes a change from too late,' she said, and stomped down the stairs into a side room to speak to her friend.

Hamish appeared a few minutes later, tail between his legs. 'It's great. Really.'

An Hour's Ride from Bristol

They crossed to a cafe on the other side of the road. Hamish took off his jacket and bought Jenny a coffee and a big slice of her favourite chocolate cake. There was only one pastry fork, but she cut it into pieces, moved closer and fed every second piece to Hamish. When they finished, she said, 'Come here.'

He leaned forward and she took a corner of the napkin and wiped a piece of chocolate from his mouth. Then she kissed him on the lips. Hamish flushed and fumbled with his wee Filofax. He opened it at another of Billy's letters.

Dear John,

I have spent these past weeks touring the country visiting my friends and relations in this part of the country. My intention is to seek a country estate within an hour's ride of Bristol and bring home my wife and son and settle down with my wee family. I also have a mind to acquire a share in a sugar-house here.

My brother's ship is expected any day with your shipment of sugar and molasses.

Your most affectionate kinsman, Billy.

***

'He planned to settle in Bristol?' Hamish said.

She nodded. 'Now you can dump all the dark stuff down here.'

But Jenny reached out and put her hand on top of his. 'Shelve the city rivalry?' she said. She slid a sheet across the table, covered in her small, neat writing. 'Transcript of Billy's wife's will,' she said. 'Found it yesterday, in the archive.'

Hamish started to read it, but she snatched it back. He frowned, but she smiled.

'Later. After the highlights.'

Bristol Bridge

Jenny led him down to the river. They stopped, facing Bristol Bridge. The information board had the familiar engraving of the tall, timber-framed houses crammed together across the bridge.

'Billy's was near the middle,' Jenny said.

'You're joking!'

'Inherited it from his wife's family.'

Hamish walked further downstream, turned back and took lots of photos. 'Pity the old bridge is gone,' he shouted back at her.

'Still there,' she said. She pointed down at the water. 'Original arches underneath.'

Hamish couldn't hear her properly for the traffic. They crossed the bridge and descended a stone stair to a lower walkway. He climbed over the railing and stretched out over the water but couldn't reach the first arch. Jenny took one hand and he stretched further and ran his fingertips over the big rough stones. 'Foundations of Billy's house!' he said.

'If you had the chance you'd be chipping off a sample.'

'Need to hire a boat,' he said. 'And a grinder.'

'Sad bastard,' she said.

'Only problem, it's in Bristol, not Glasgow.'

Jenny ignored him, held on to his hand and gave a smug smile.

'There's more?' he said.

She took his arm and led him further down the harbour and over a swing bridge. The sun picked out a multicoloured terrace and a rainbow sheen on the oily water.

Can I love someone I'm fighting with? Jenny thought. Being with Hamish was like navigating rough seas on a raft. They were heading for the crest of another wave. How long would it be before they tumbled down the other side?

They headed along the quay, then up Grove Avenue into Queen Square, and averted their gaze from the burnt-out shell across the square. They took in the Georgian pediments, the Palladian windows, the mix of painted facades and warm Bath stone.

'OK,' she said, 'which is your favourite?'

'In the whole square?'

She nodded.

'That's easy.' Hamish pointed to the original, over in the corner, backing onto the river. Of all the houses in the square, it was the best kept. They crossed to the front. The brass sign said it was now the headquarters of English Heritage. Wee faces peered through the railings from the lintels. 'More grots!' he said.

'What if I told you Billy stayed here, wrote letters here? That the original owner was his partner, his wife's cousin?'

Hamish climbed up on the gate. 'It's amazing!' He jumped back down and gave Jenny a big hug. Then he struggled up onto the wall and over the railing. He stretched up and touched one of the grots above a window.

Jenny pointed up at a CCTV camera on the eaves. Hamish climbed back over the gate. 'I wonder which room Billy stayed in, way back in the 1720s?' he said.

'So far back, the square was still called the Marsh.'

'So early, it's almost Queen Anne, not Georgian.'

They peered across the small garden, into the window, and tried to see beyond the lace curtains. No doubt it was stuffed full of foostie furniture, trying in vain to recapture a lost era. Hamish stuck out his tongue at a grimacing grot above the window. The lace curtain twitched and a posh-looking lady peered out. He was about to turn away when the lady screwed up her face, stuck out her tongue back at him, then closed the curtain.

Jenny laughed.

'Maybe it's common for visitors to grimace at the grots?' he said.

'Yes, children, not thirty-year-old engineers.'

'There's more?'

They were right up on the crest of the wave. There was only one way to go.

'Billy's cousin who stayed here,' she said, 'along with those we met earlier, ramped up Bristol's trade with the Caribbean.'

'They owned people too?'

The wave swamped them. Jenny sat down on the wall, looking at the ground. It had been such a good day, but there was always a catch.

'Suppose you can't avoid that sort of stuff down here,' he said.

Jenny turned away and walked off alone.

The Journal of Cato

NORTH BRITTAIN

On the 26th sail, we sail from Gravesend to Leith in North Brittain, to lodge with Billee's relations near Edinburgh. More & more he speaks of settlin in Glasgow. Of acquirin the three signs of success: a town-house, a country estate & a sugar-works.

We ride east for two days towards Glasgow. For many miles we see the spire of the High Kirk. We enter the town from the east, along the Gallowgate, through the cross. We reside a few days at an Inn in Argyle Street.

A FINE HOUSE

Three days after we arrive, I follow Massa Billee round from our tavern to view a town-house. Tis a fine house from a distance, with large gates & many windows, & was built in recent years for his friend Campbell. The front is topped by the great three-sided symbol they call the pediment. I believe that Campbell must also be a sugar merchant.

Howsoever, though from the outside tis the finest house in the town, the inside is a shell. The joiner speaks of riots & destruction. We tour many rooms, kitchens & a garret. In the library, the books have been scattered from their shelves. From the windows at the rear, a great orchyard & garden stretch as far as Back Cow Loan, enclosed by a high wall. To the west are fields & the Dumbarton Road beyond the West Port. But already parts of the ground on the west side are staked out & portioned for buildin.

In the parlour at the front, a fire has been lit to fend off the cold. But sit, Billee cannot sit. All the furniture is broken or has been carried off.

Yet Billee is in good spirits. He sees the opportunity of a bargain.

A BLACKAMORE

Arrive, when I first arrive in the city, crowds watch my every move. A blackamore, a novelty. I shadow Massa Billee around the city streets in my bright coat & brass buttons & silver collar. I cannot hide in a sea of white. Campbell already has two of us. Bogle another.

Like peacock feather hats, the height of fashion. Many more serve indoors, unseen below stairs.

Apart from myself, Massa Billee has brought twenty-seven. Five have already died. Lucinda, Davee & Paisley died from the pox. Peggy was beat too hard with the stick & Flora died last week givin birth to another of Massa's bastard childs. Hermit was correct. Say, they say we are inferior. Yet Massa Billee lies more with the servants below stairs than with his well-bred pale-faced wife.

THE WEIGHT OF THOUSANDS

This morn, I look across the road & see my friend Hero followin Buchanan from the coffee house. Down the street a coach passes with two more ridin on the back. Dressed from head to foot in green footman's livery. Visible yet invisible. Those of us in the streets are the sole trace of our brothers & sisters on the islands.

'Each of us carries the weight of thousands,' I say to my friend the bookseller, 'out in the sugar islands.'

'A man can only carry his own weight. That is sufficient.'

'How many folk here know?'

'Know?'

'Know of the toil in the islands which builds a city.'

BUILT FROM SUGAR

Glasgow is a place of narrow alleys & many beggars. But a few steps west, the merchants walk their gardens & orchyards behind high stone walls. This city holds a secret, the secret of how tis growin from a town.

Walk, I walk the Trongate. The crest high on a wall tells a tale of a saint, a bell, a fish. But all cities are built from legend. Search, I search the lanes & wynds for truth. A man on a street corner shouts that the city is built to please Mammon.

But I know in my heart this new city is built from sugar.

Chapter 33

Hamish, Cardiff to Glasgow

'Risk?' I spot the game poking out from a pile of jigsaw boxes on top of a cupboard, and I find a step-stool and lift down the box. The game's so old the wee counters are made of wood, not plastic. The red ones have lost most of their colour, where a child's sucked them. 'Haven't played since I was a kid!' I say.

'Not in the mood for games.'

'It's the counters I want. Don't the beanies count as ten?'

I start laying out Billy's slave tally in red counters. One hundred, two… but I soon run out of red ones and need to add the other colours. I reach seven hundred. 'It's a lot,' I say.

'But it's not the full tally.'

'More plantations?'

Jenny passes over her tablet. Some sort of contract?

No. 141. A Success

To Madm Penelope Mead,

Dear Madam,

I have the honour of yours of the 6th August. The lease I hold so successfully of your lands on St. Christopher draws so near a close that I am pleased to offer to take your plantation into my own hands for a further five years on the same terms. I flatter myself that my management to date has been a success. Now is the time, in my opinion, that it will require greatest care to plant canes and keep the Negroes in line. I have always been so fortunate, ever since first being known to you, to have your favour and esteem that we shall upon this occasion remain in the most friendly terms.

I am with all gratitude and respect good madam, Your most faithful and most obliged humble servant.

***

'Who's Lady Penelope?' says Jenny.

The reference at the end is for Glamorgan Archives, Cardiff. I search through my wee folder. 'Mother-in-law of the planter Billy trained with on Nevis,' I say.

'What's he offering to do with her plantation?'

'Act as her attorney.'

'A soldier, then a merchant, now a lawyer?'

'More slaves?'

'Dad always told me a good lead's like the tip of an iceberg,' she says. 'You start with no more than a hint, but you end up drowning in information.'

'Think we're at the drowning stage?'

'We need to check all the icebergs,' she says.

'Need to get back to Glasgow. Find Murdo.'

She tapped his notebook. 'Cardiff's only an hour by train.'

'Never been.'

'Lots of charity shops.'

'Knew there was a snag.'

I tip all the wee beanies and cubes back into the Risk box. Once again, I start looking at train timetables.

***

Later, I say, 'The Cardiff deed. Where did it come from?'

'Anna sent it,' Jenny says.

'Murdo still leading us up the garden path?'

She leaves the room.

I'm still confused. We keep falling out, but has she softened? She's even kissed me. But we're too tied to the ups and downs of Billy's story.

***

The next day, we catch an early train to Cardiff. Jenny leads me down to the pier. I spot streets and buildings with Scottish names: Rothesay House, Bute Street, Mount Stuart Square.

'More knicker labels?' I say.

'Lord Bute,' Jenny says, 'owned half the Welsh coalfield.'

'Another dodgy Scot?'

Leaving Jenny at the shops, I head up the High Street, my body in Wales but my head in Glasgow. Ach, I love exploring new cities, but right now I don't have time.

I reach the record office. I'd emailed what I wanted the day before, so it's waiting for me. Maybe I'm getting the hang of this archive lark?

It doesn't take long. I'm out before lunch. I'm tempted to go walkabout and explore the city, but I text Jenny and we meet in the museum cafe.

'Hardly started the charity shops,' she says.

'You've had two hours!'

'Thought I had all day. Any luck?'

'Billy was attorney for two other plantations at the same time as running his own.'

'He really *was* a lawyer?'

'Attorneys were planters who looked after other estates if the owner went back to Britain.'

'Must have been popular.'

'Or a tough nut.'

'Not someone you'd want to work under.'

'Another four hundred,' I say.

No. 142. One Thousand, One Hundred and Twenty-Six

2 Canadas: 197 + 213 = 410

Grenada = 315

Cardiff Mead = 401

Total = 1,126

***

'You're going to run out of beanies,' says Jenny.

I push the photocopies from the archive across the table. 'There's another Flora, an Agnes, another Jenny... all in their teens.'

Three teenage girls sit at a table in the corner, talking loudly. Two are dark-skinned.

'Nobody's been bothered about it for three hundred years,' Jenny says.

***

We tour the art gallery for a while, then catch the train back to Bristol. As we head into the Severn Tunnel, half asleep, Jenny snuggles up and lays her head on my shoulder.

Later, back in Bristol, I say, 'Mary called back. Hasn't seen Murdo, but reckons he's been back up in his den without her knowing.'

'Time to go north?'

'Via Manchester.' She shows me the second of Anna's papers from Murdo. Billy was attorney for another plantation, and the records are held at the city's John Rylands library.

***

Next morning, we catch an early train north. We get off at Deansgate and head through the streets, towards the Science and Industry Museum.

'Remind you of Glasgow?' she says.

'Apart from all the red brick.'

We have a quick lunch in the museum cafe. I'd rather explore the museum with Jenny, but I need to keep up the momentum. I leave for the John Rylands Library, and find the list of Stapleton papers. There's lots. After a couple of hours, I get a serious dose of archive fever and leave. I meet Jenny at Pizza Express.

'That was quick,' she says.

'Billy was attorney for the Stapleton plantations.'

'Another jumped-up planter family?'

'Stapleton was governor of the islands. Another two hundred and sixty-four under Billy's control.'

No. 143. One Thousand, Three Hundred and Ninety

2 Canadas: 197 + 213 = 410

Grenada = 315

Cardiff Mead = 401

Manchester Stapleton = 264

Total = 1,390

***

I lay my head on my hands.

'There's also depreciation,' Jenny says.

'Deaths and replacements?'

'Adds up to thousands over the decades.'

'Times all the Glasgow sugar planters,' I say. 'It's like totting up sugar hogsheads, not people.'

'It's too much to take in,' she says. 'It's why Bristol's taken so long to accept it. Folk can't relate to millions. Just write a story.'

'A novel, not facts and figures?'

She nodded. 'About people, not numbers.'

'My turn to go off in a huff?' I say.

'Time to stick together,' she says. 'No matter which way this goes, we need to stay friends.'

Friends?

We sit in silence, waiting for our food to be served. We've booked a Premier Inn at Salford Quays. To save money, we share a twin room. We each face the wall, lost in our thoughts.

***

In the morning, we catch a yellow tram to Piccadilly. I've never understood why Manchester isn't on the main London to Glasgow line. And it's a Sunday. We need to make two changes. Then it gets worse. Northern Rail are on strike. And there are engineering works on the West Coast Main Line. Nobody warned us when we bought the tickets.

By 4 p.m., the train has only made it to Lancaster, where we're stuck for the night. We find a B & B in the centre, facing the castle, and dump our bags.

After tea, we do a lightning tour of the town. The evening sun warms the tops of the pillars and pediments. 'It's like a dream,' I say. 'Georgian buildings everywhere.'

Jenny's in a better mood too, taking photos of everything.

We head down a steep cobbled lane to Market Street. Then round by Penny Street and Dalton Square. The sun's still out, so we take a long loop up the tree-lined river path, across the big aqueduct and down the north bank. Back over the Millennium Bridge, we end at the tall warehouses on St George's Quay, warped and twisted like one of Murdo's models.

'Never seen so many survivors,' I say. 'It's even better than Bristol.'

She smiles, then she stops and holds out her arms.

'I know that stance,' I say.

'It'd be brilliant, if we had time, but aren't we going over old ground?'

I point at the water. 'City on a river.'

'Hardly a city,' she says.

'Once upon a time, when cities were small and dense, and grew thanks to trade.'

'Long way from the sea?' she says.

'Deepened the Lune. Ships came right up.'

'Same old story?'

'Same old story.'

'Think there's a link between Georgian money and slavery?'

Further along, I point up at the street sign on an old brick warehouse: SUGAR HOUSE ALLEY.

We continue in silence and come to a small, paved area, lit by street-lights, overlooking the river. Wee metal figures stand on some sort of modern memorial.

Jenny reads the text. 'A hundred slave ships sailed from here. Two hundred, if you count the ones that went via Liverpool. Tens of thousands of people.'

'Bit far north?' I say.

'You mean getting closer to Glasgow?'

We've become mesmerised by the buildings. We stand together, looking out over the reflections of lights in the river. Then we go for a pizza, but it's tasteless and the crust is too hard and I go to bed early.

***

Next day, our train isn't till later, but Jenny's revived. 'We need a long walk,' she says. She buys some sandwiches and drinks, lets me pay, and loads them into my backpack. She takes my hand and leads me off in the opposite direction from the city, down under the big railway viaduct, past industrial ruins, until the countryside flattens out along the Lune. The closer we get to the sea, the stronger the wind. Eventually we reach a tiny hamlet, half-drowned by the tide. We pass between walls and hedges and find a sheltered spot, but struggle to eat our picnic lunch in the wind. I help Jenny unfold her map. We get up, turn a corner and scramble over a wall. At the end of a small field is a solitary grave, surrounded by hundreds of wee mementoes: pebbles, cheap jewellery, plastic toys, messages painted on wee stones.

Here lies
Poor Sambo
a faithfull Negro
Who
(Attending his Master from the West Indies)
DIED on his Arrival at Sunderland.

Above the plaque, another one affixed, asking visitors to: RESPECT THIS LONELY GRAVE.

With her back to the gale, Jenny slips out her phone. I watch her add the name to a list: *Sambo.*

The name disturbs me. I'm not sure why. 'You planned this?' I say.

'Read about it last night.'

I lay my hand on the gravestone and take a wee shell that's been in the bottom of my pocket since Nevis. I lay it on top of the stone. We stand together in silence, gazing out to sea. On the shore, the wind's even stronger. Far away, Blackpool Tower pokes like a needle above the grey horizon.

'It's not much,' I say. 'One man, compared to a whole city.'

'Easier to cope with than thousands?'

'Maybe it doesn't need big numbers,' I say, 'to write the story.' I lift the end of her scarf and wipe a tear from her eye. She takes the other end and wipes my eyes too. 'Must be the wind,' I say.

We stand for a while, watching the waves. Clinging to each other against the gale from the sea, as if it'll tear us from the earth.

'Thanks for showing me Sambo,' I say.

As she leans against me, a spark flashes between us. For a brief moment, we're on the same page. We come to a decision, even if we don't fully understand what it is. But we both know, deep inside, that there's no going back from the lonely grave at Sunderland Point.

Chapter 34

Hamish, Glasgow

We get back too late after our long walk to catch our train, and spend another night in Lancaster. Next morning, after breakfast, we catch the early train. Fortunately, Lancaster's on the main line to Glasgow.

At lunchtime the train rolls over the Clyde into Central Station. The sandstone of the buildings sparkles in the sun. If I look closely, I can see it has a granular texture, as if it's less solid than I thought. Made of crystals, like sugar.

We head for Murdo's flat, hoping to avoid Aunt Mary. The storm doors are firmly shut. Mary's away again.

It's a bit spooky. A used coffee cup lies on the draining board, and a pipe in the big ashtray by the window. A small wheelie suitcase stands in the corner, unopened.

'It's like he'll appear back any minute,' Jenny says, climbing the spiral stair, 'but the bed's not been slept in.'

'He can't have gone away again without his stuff,' I say.

'Where else could he have gone?'

We climb the spiral stair to the wee eyrie. I press my knees against the parapet. Only the low wall separates me from a six-storey drop.

'Could he have fallen?' Jenny says.

I work my way round, looking down. 'The dome's too big. He'd have caught the slates, then the gutter on the way down.' I stop on the south side and point. 'Gutter's broken, and a few slates are missing.'

'So where's the body?' she says.

I lean further forward and peer down to the big skip in the back yard. 'Builder's working across the lane. Every time the skip's full, it's taken away and replaced with an empty one.' I shiver. 'If Murdo fell into the skip, he'd have gone straight to landfill.'

Jenny turns and embraces me. 'I'm sure he's fine. He's always been one step ahead of us. All the more important to finish it.'

'What's left to find?'

***

Jenny sits down on the big sofa and makes a list:

Murdo.
Billy's mansion.
His country estate.

I pass her an envelope which came in the post.

'More clues?' she says.

'Job offer. Start in a fortnight.'

'Glasgow?'

'Anywhere. Working from home.'

'Two weeks to finish the quest?'

I'm even more spooked about sleeping in the flat, in case Murdo comes back, but Jenny persuades me to stay. I find an address book and phone round Murdo's mates, but nobody's seen him. Archie's the only one who doesn't answer.

***

Next morning at breakfast, Jenny's standing at the window. Then she moves to the side. 'Sorry,' she says. 'I'm blocking your view of the woman between the chimneys.' I turn away, cheeks red.

I'm trying to finish Billy's letters, and struggling to split the story into chapters. I unclip my notes and lay them out in wee piles on the table, Murdo's models acting as paperweights.

No. 144. A Very Good Town-house

Dear Brother,

Since my last, I have now finished an agreement with Mr. Campbell for his great house, gardens and orchyard at Glasgow. The house is a very good house, but much out of repair from the mob, but I am told for £500 I can get it in good order, so that it will be sufficient for my wee family, being a large house, and the best of any in the town, even in the whole country.

I have this day engaged a blacksmith to erect a new railing, six feet tall, atop the front wall. And also a joiner to build a new pair of gates of solid oak, thickly dotted with iron studs. Wilson the mason has already widened the opening sufficient to admit my carriage and four. He is now engaged in building two lofty stone portals, equal in height to the points of the railing. Rowan the sculptor, recently arrived from London, has already inspected and taken order of monumental pieces from Cowcaddens Quarry, of sufficient size to fashion pieces of sculpture, representing clusters of human heads and busts, for the parapet. And for the gateposts, great sphinxes facing each other, all in accordance with Gibbs's latest architectural designs.

***

On top of one of my piles of papers is the wee house model. After breakfast, Jenny finds a big magnifying glass in a drawer and peers at an engraving of the mansion. She hands me the glass. 'On the wall by the gate…'

'Sphinxes?'

All around the room, Murdo's sphinxes peer out from nooks and crannies. I jump up and flick through my notes. I pull out a blue sticky note and read it out:

'The mansion may have been demolished more than two hundred years ago, but an early history says the sphinxes were saved.'

'Think we can find them?' she says.

***

For the next two days I work on finishing the letters, while Jenny goes for walks alone with her camera.

'Found anything interesting?' I say.

'I've got a dragon, griffins, caryatids, a phoenix, seahorses, angels, and umpteen lions, unicorns and cherubs, but no sphinxes. There's something suspicious up a Greek Thomson church tower. But I'd need binoculars to be sure.'

***

Later, Jenny's out again. She calls. 'Found them! The sphinxes. From Billy's gateposts.'

'Aye right.'

'Honest,' she says.

'Where?'

'Museum store.'

'What they like?'

'Same as the brass pair on Murdo's mantelpiece. Could be exact replicas.'

'Can I come and see?'

I hear her speaking to someone called Tony in the background. 'Meet you at the bridge under the canal at three,' she says.

***

She's been doing it on the sly. Emailing the museum curators. She's found them in an old red-brick factory building used as a museum store, behind the canal at Maryhill. They're mounted on wooden trolleys, like something from Tutankhamun's tomb. Lions' bodies, eagles' wings and women's heads. The heads have been broken off and are lying to the side, and the labels tied to them with pink ribbon look like blindfolds. I reach out to the nearest one.

'Sorry, you can't touch,' says Tony.

When his back's turned, I rest a palm on one of their haunches. It's cold and rough. 'Photos?' I say.

Jenny gives Tony a sheepish smile.

'Maybe a couple,' he says.

I flash off as many as I can before he holds up a hand.

***

Afterwards, we head under the canal to Maryhill Road, for the bus back.

'You're still grinning like the Cheshire cat,' Jenny says.

'Can't believe they've survived. Need to come back after dark and steal them,' I say.

'You might be the chief suspect.'

At Kelvinbridge, we catch the Subway back to the city centre, then round to the site of Billy's house.

'Sphinxes in Argyle Street in 1724?' I say. 'It's pretty cool. He was definitely ahead of his time.'

'It's pathetic,' she says. 'Two lumps of stone and you're back into epic mode.' I give her a side look. I'm still not sure when she's serious. But she turns and gives one of her big smiles which melts my heart. She looks up at Billy's derelict east wing. 'Think we could get inside?'

At the corner, we wait until a couple pass by, then squeeze through the fence into a wee back court. The windows are barricaded, but the plywood in the smallest window's been forced to the side. 'Up for it?' I say.

Inside, we follow the main corridor, then head up a grand stairway. The interior's been trashed. On the top floor, we enter a big bright room. I open a door in the corner, and a wee spiral stair rises higher. We climb up to a wee turret, with hardly enough space to stand. Over Jenny's shoulder, I can see down the length of Argyle Street. We're nearly as high as Murdo's flat.

'I could stay up here for hours,' she says.

We head back down through the building. Jenny talks loudly, and I keep trying to hush her, listening for sounds of other visitors. Torn sleeping bags are strewn around, and the remains of cooking. From the ground floor, we find a stair down to the basement. I point to one side. 'Must have been a link to the main house, through the basement,' I say.

'There'll be nothing left. The road above's been dug up too much.'

We reach a vaulted stone corridor. Traffic rumbles overhead. 'We're under Glassford Street!' I say.

Halfway along is a big studded oak door. 'Looks a lot older than the Victorian building,' she says.

I take the big screwdriver from my backpack and prise at the door's hinges. The wood at the bottom's soft and damp. Suddenly, with a loud crack, the whole door tips towards us. We jump to the side as it crashes to the floor. We cover our mouths and noses from the cloud of dust. Then a much bigger rumble shakes the floor.

'Oh shit,' says Jenny, and turns to leave.

I grab her arm. 'Train in the Argyle Street tunnel. Help me with this.' Using my screwdriver, I try to part the boards in the door.

'What you doing?'

'Original piece of timber,' I say.

I prise off a thick board, then angle it against the wall and jump on it, breaking off the rotten part at the bottom. Jenny points her torch into the gloom behind the old door. As the dust settles, we duck into a small, vaulted chamber. The whitewash on the bare walls has turned a damp brown. Something rustles among debris in the corner. Jenny's still on the point of running off. One wall is bare earth. I point at a dark strip near the bottom.

'You need to get a life,' she says. 'You can't tell your story through layers of soil. You need to write it down, write about people.'

Poking from the ceiling is a row of big brass hooks. On the floor is a chain, but when I touch it, it's just a rusty pattern in the earth. At the end is a brass ring, dull and green but still intact. A manacle? I pick it up. Jenny wipes it with a tissue and slips her hand inside.

'Kept folk down in the basement?' Jenny says. She goes back out into the corridor and inspects the side wall. 'Original basement of the mansion?'

'Need a piece of stone too.' I spot one that's cracked. 'Lime mortar. It's soft.' I prise out a piece, the size of a brick.

'Sad bastard,' she says. But she touches the stone too.

'Maybe a wee bit of magic might rub off?' I say.

The ground rumbles again. I stuff the stone and piece of wood into my rucksack and we climb back upstairs and out the back window, without meeting anyone. Then we head back to the flat and get a Chinese carry-out on the way.

***

Archie's left several voicemails, but I've been ignoring them.

'He'll want to know what we found on the island,' Jenny says. 'Surprised he hasn't called me.'

'Aye, you'd tell him everything.'

My phone buzzes again. I give up, go out the door and answer Archie's call.

When I come back, I say to Jenny, 'Wants me to meet one of his friends for coffee.'

***

I meet them outside Princess Square. We shake hands, and a narrow escalator takes us up to a posh cafe. Archie's friend's called Bert. When Bert takes off his coat, he's wearing a heavy gold chain around his neck, decked with all kinds of symbols. He's the master of some trade association or other. Does he need to express it in public?

'Any news of Murdo?' I say.

Archie doesn't answer.

We make small talk and order coffee and cake. Then Bert says, 'You're a historian?'

'Engineer.'

Bert looks at Archie. 'An amateur,' Archie explains.

'Aye, aye,' Bert says, speaking louder, stroking his gold chain. 'We've got a great city. Second City of the Empire. Workshop of the world. European City of Culture. Host of the Commonwealth Games.'

The waitress interrupts with our coffee and cake.

Bert points away out the window at the sailing ship weathervane, on the top of the Merchants Steeple, glinting gold in the sun. 'Shipbuilder to the world and I'm proud of it,' he says. 'Ma faither was in the yeards in the sixties.'

Aye, the 1960s, but the sailing ship's from the 1660s. I know, I've been up there and touched it.

'Archie tells me you're writin' a book,' Bert says.

'Finishing something for my grandpa.'

Archie butts in. 'Aye, aye. Always rockin the boat, Murdo.'

Bert ignores me. 'Not many boats left in Glasgow these days.'

'If we release the money for the book, we need to know it's kosher,' Archie says.

'Aye, right,' I say.

Bert looks at Archie again. 'Let's get to the point,' he says. 'You don't wanna be writin' anythin' which damages the city.'

'Maybe the city can stand up for itself?'

'If our merchants were into something dodgy, I think we'd know by now.'

'You think Glasgow's immune?'

Archie raises a hand to try to calm things.

'With Facebook an' that it can work both ways,' Bert says. 'You tarnish my city, it might come back and bite yer arse.'

'That a threat?'

'You don't want a pretty wee black lassie pourin' poison in your ear.'

I jump up, knocking over my coffee, and head for the door.

Archie hobbles after me and grabs me by the arm. 'Sorry,' he says. 'That was out of order.'

I shake him off, hurry downstairs and head home. When I get back to the flat, Jenny says, 'How'd it go?' She takes one look at my face and says no more.

Chapter 35

Jenny, Glasgow

Jenny's List

Jenny slipped out her list of African names. When she'd started out, she'd had only three: Cato, Bella, a kitchen maid, and Peggy, a servant. Now she had a dozen, with ages, occupations, value, for some even their origins. Not to mention her namesake, Jenny McNight, and all the others on Billy's lists for Canada Hills. For Gusto, she even had a photo.

It was just like her dad's collection of city characters. Hadn't she moved on?

The Merchant City Festival

Jenny hadn't sent Eck any of her Cato transcripts since meeting Murdo. But thanks to Hamish's call, Eck knew they were back, and was keen to meet up.

On the way, she bought a Big Issue. As she waited for Eck, she spotted an advert for tour guides for the Merchant City Festival the following week. Me doing Glasgow tours? she thought. But she needed the money. She sent off an email, quoting her experience of leading tours in Bristol.

A lady called her back later for a chat. 'Nobody here knows anything about slavery.'

Later, Jenny was startled by her phone ringing. The Merchant City Festival lady. She'd got the job.

What would Hamish think?

The Journal of Cato

A HOUSE IN THE COUNTRY

Billee tells the joiner that we are to seek a house in the country, until his town-house is sorted. He has me write to his brother in Edinburgh, to seek a country estate within a day's ride of Glasgow.

He considers Scotstoun, which is on the market, but the premium on its coal reserves is too high. Then he finds an estate a day's ride west of Glasgow, home of the Barons Semple, with its great tower & loch.

MY NEW COUNTRY SEAT

After we have been in Glasgow town but a few weeks, Billee says, 'Now we go to my new country seat.' We leave the town & take quiet roads where people work on either side in the furrows. Many stunted crops grow in the Scotch fields, & when they do grow, they grow slow. We pass through villages & cross rivers on stone bridges. Then we turn from the road into the drive beside a loch, until a bend in the drive reveals the house.

A castle, Billee calls it: a great tower, six storeys high, stands with its damp feet in the edge of the loch. Tis the biggest & tallest house I have ever seen. Built of stone, followin the fashion of the Buckra, but worn & blackened with age. With arches & alcoves & narrow stairs which twist & turn. In one corner is a higher tower with thicker walls & smaller rooms.

HIS CASTLE

We turn through a big gate into a courtyard & spend the rest of the day unloadin carts. Billee tours the lower floors, with myself in his wake, & chooses his chamber.

'Have a fire built here & bring up my bags.'

Talk, Massa Billy talks of showin off his castle to his friends. But soon he is restless. Inside is colder than out. The windows are too small, 'built for conflict, not comfort', he says. The timbers in the upper tower are spoiled by water – the lead has been stolen from part of the roof.

After a few days, Billee accepts the offer of lodgings from his neighbour, the Laird of Johnstone, until tis all dried out.

THIS STUBBORN LAND

Talk, Billee talks of buildin a mansion. He summons Watt, the measurer. 'I have spent my life in the Indies, in the heat of the sun,' says Billee. 'My new house must face south.'

'Facing the loch, sir?' says Watt.

'The loch plays no part in my decision. My plans are well advanced to measure & drain it, creating above 500 acres of new farmland. I have not gott where I am today by accepting compromise. It is essential that this stubborn land is measured & moulded to my most exact requirements. No expense should be spared to impress my friends who will visit from the south.'

LONDON

Restless, restless is Billee to travel again & bring his sugar trade from the Thames to the Clyde.

After a week, he leaves for New Port Glasgow, Bristol & London. For once, he leaves without me, takin the boy, Coffee, instead. Coffee is 15 & has Massa's nose & brusque manner & is learnin readin n writin. Great is my delight to have time to myself, but greater still is my turmoil that Coffee will replace me.

MY JOURNAL

Fear, my fear in sailin here was that I would lose my journal. Howsoever all I needed do was place it among the plantation ledgers. So precious are they that Massa Billy kept them under his bunk on the ship. Little was the danger that he would find my journal & read it, for I am keeper of the records & Massa does not read them himself but instructs me to locate entries & read them aloud.

When we first arrive, Billee left myself & an old couple from the village to look after the castle. The couple rarely venture above the kitchens. I am lord of the upper floors. I choose a small room at the top of the tower, with a thick door which seals against draughts & has a pane of glass in the small window. I spend two days carryin firewood up for the tiny fire. Apart from the pain in my leg, tis the best time of my life.

Spend, I spend fine days in the south corner of the roof, sittin in the sun, with a view of the whole parish. The library has been ransacked but not robbed. I light the fire & spend my days sortin the books. When I find one of interest, I open it & dry it by the fire.

I secrete my journal in a slot in the corridor wall for the night. Perhaps this is where I should leave it for posterity, to be rediscovered far in the future. In a few weeks I may be cast from Billee's side, replaced by another, no longer able to write freely.

THE COLONEL'S CREDIT

'Can you go to the village & secure some vegetables?' says the old woman. Tis the first time that I have been asked, not told, to fetch anythin.

'Where am I to find money?'

'The Colonel's credit should be good in the village. After all, he owns it & everyone in it.'

'Owns it?'

The villagers ask many questions. Shock, tis a shock for myself for whites to speak to me as a man, not a lackey. Great is their curiosity & many are their questions.

'Does Billee have a son?'

'Who is his mistress?'

'Will his brother be the parish minister?'

'Is he a fair man or a scoundrel?'

I know not how to answer.

A NEW HOUSE ERECTED

One day from my rooftop lair see, I see two figures in the distance, on the rise of Court Hill. A man in a three-cornered hat & a boy, fussin with a three-legged device. A few days later I spy them once more, in a small boat on the loch, droppin a knotted rope over the side, like sailors soundin a reef. Later that day, Watt the surveyor & his assistant come a-knockin at the kitchen door.

'Cato?' says Watt – tis a statement not a question. 'I have come to measure the stone in the castle.'

'Measure stone?'

'It is to be taken down within the month & a new house erected.'

I look up at the slot where my journal is hidden. 'The whole castle? What is your task?'

'I am a surveyor. I measure things for your master.'

'Plantations?'

'I make maps.'

'Of Africa?'

'Of rivers, fields, estates.'

'You are familiar with the map of Africa?'

'A wee bit.'

'Half way down the coast is a great mountain.'

'Aye, I can picture a wee sketch, a fire mountain.'

'Born, I was born on its slopes, but I cannot name the mountain or country.'

'Every man deserves to know his place of birth,' says Watt.

Tis the first time in thirty years I have been called a man.

TORN DOWN

Next day, I overhear Billee. 'The old castle of the Semples must be torn down,' says he. 'There is no place in my plans for draughty towers, no matter how old or important they may be.'

Billee dictates a specification for his new mansion:

'I desire a low & long house of ashlar-work with four pavilions, forming a panorama, with the coach-houses on the east & the stables on the west.

'The house should be no more than two storeys high – plus basement – with rustic corners & a large cupola in the middle, crowned with three globes, very elegant & well furnished, as merits the latest fashion, following Gibbs & Palladio.

'If we require a distant view, then I must have a temple on the hill, like my friend Cunningham has on his Buckinghamshire seat, & the house must have water to the north: falls, cascades & trout ponds. If there is no burn at that spot, then I am well-versed at diverting one.

'To the west should be laid out a bowling-green, pleasure-ground & walled garden to raise flowers & vegetables of every kind, with a hot-wall & large hot-house, ninety feet long: inferior to none in Scotland.'

DRAININ THE LOCH

Massa Billee engages thirty men to dig for six months to widen & deepen the river at the outlet of the loch, to drain it dry. They dig a canal the length of the loch, with branches to the mansion & pleasure grounds.

Each day I go down to tally the progress of the works. I count the men drainin the loch, up to their knees in mud, diggin the canal. I watch the gang workin at the quarry & buildin the dikes across the estate.

Great is the dismay of Billee's tenants at his new stone dikes. 'His walls block our roads to market,' they say. 'His draining prevents our cattle reaching water.'

One fine day, Billee decides to tour his lands & meet his tenants. The families live in narrow stone cottages with a straw roof, & their livestock reside in the eastern end.

Billee tells McNair the factor to knock at the door. McNair wades through a brown pool of cow shit & knocks twice.

After three hovels, rage & bitterness walk with Billee's voice. 'Such is the temper of the creatures here that they choose to live upon potatoes & oatmeal on their own dunghills. How can they pay their rents when they cannot keep the shit from their doors? We need new tenants who care about their charge.'

SOMETHIN EXTRAORDINARY

Billy engaged a ship's carpenter from Rotherhithe to build himself a wherry, light & neatly contrived. It holds six sitters & goes with oars or sail. On the stern is Billy's coat of arms & a flag-staff.

In fair weather he sails with his visitors upon his canals & picnics on Peel Isle, & tis somethin extraordinary.

A Problem

Jenny added Coffee, age 15, trainee scribe to her list. But she had a problem. She'd finished what she thought was Cato's last chapter. But, according to his handwritten index back at the start, there was another chapter.

How could she write Cato's story if his final chapter's lost?

Chapter 36

Hamish, Castle Semple

No. 145. My Head Has Turned

You will most certainly conclude my head has turned, when I tell you that I have bought Lord Semple's country estate with his mansion house, being one of the best estates in Scotland. What you and my friends on the islands will think of it, I know not, but I can tell you it is extremely well liked by all my friends here.

***

'Need to visit Castle Semple,' I say.

'How far?'

'Twenty minutes on the Ayr train.'

Jenny stands up. 'Let's go.' She's wearing a short red dress, black tights and flat shoes.

'It's very rural,' I say.

'I'm fine.'

***

We catch the Ardrossan train from Central and get off at Howwood. Across an old stone bridge, we follow a country road, to the site of the east gates of the estate. Way up on the summit is a circular tower.

'Why do I find windmills sinister?' I say.

I scramble over the estate wall. The hillside's dotted with cattle.

'Bullocks,' she says. 'I'm not going in there.'

I climb back onto the road. 'Glad I'm not wearing red,' I say.

We carry on until we're just out of sight of the cattle. I help her over the wall, take her hand, and we climb the steep hill. Our path's blocked by a deep, hidden ditch.

'Edge of the deer park,' I say.

'Bit posh for this part of the country.'

'Think they're only found in Surrey?'

After a bit of scrambling, we reach the ridge. Clumps of rock peep out of the grass. At the west end, the tower rises out of the bedrock: an octagonal folly, not a windmill. Jenny starts counting the square ashlar stones in the wall of the folly.

'What you doing?' I say.

'Must have owned an African for every stone.'

Away down the loch is the remains of Billy's mansion.

'He bought all of this, laid it all out?' she says.

'Improved it, drained the loch.'

I show her an entry from Billy's diary.

No. 146. Rode Round the Loch

Monday 26th: A dry day. Mr. Boucher came from Edinburgh to lay out my gardens. Rode round the loch with the Lairds of Craigends and Houston, and dined with the minister of Kilbarchan.

***

'All this to show off to his friends?' she says.

'Thought you'd be impressed.'

Thunder appears in her eyes. 'Can't you see what you're doing?' she says. 'You might think you're cool now, trying to expose him. But you're still telling *his* story. One story instead of thousands.'

'But I've got all the numbers.'

'It's about people, not numbers. Billy gets all the fame, but the ones who did all his work stay invisible.'

She stomps off downhill. I catch up with her, and we descend past a ruined bridge over a burn, then along the edge of the loch. Between two ancient trees, we face the site of Billy's mansion.

'Big medieval castle stood right here,' I say. I show her a sketch on my phone. 'Billy knocked it all down and built his mansion.'

The four surviving pavilions stretch out as far as we can see on either side, but the mansion's missing from the middle, demolished down to its basement.

Jenny points to a hole in the basement wall. A window's been blocked up, but the bricks have come loose.

'No,' I say.

Each of the four pavilions has been converted into a private house, but nobody's about. I follow Jenny over. She kneels and crawls through the window opening. We switch on our phone torches. We're inside a finely built, vaulted basement, with rubble scattered across the floor. Steps lead down to an oval tunnel, with water running along the bottom. We step into water up to our shins.

'It's freezing!' I say.

We wade along the tunnel, towards light at the end. I keep stopping to take photos. Finally, we come out into a shallow pond, lined with crumbling rubble. Water pours into it from cascades.

'No shortage of samples here,' she says.

I look her up and down. 'Like the punk look.'

Jenny's feet are soaked, her jacket's muddy, and her face is dirty. 'Help me up,' she says. I take her hand and we climb up onto an old railway embankment, now a cycle path. Then higher up to the remains of the walled garden.

I fumble with my notebook. 'Said Billy grew the best oranges and lemons in Scotland, after the Duke of Argyll.'

'How long did his family own this?' she says.

'Down to his son and grandson, all named Billy.'

'Then what?'

'Sold it to the Harvey family.'

'Locals?'

'Biggest sugar planters on Grenada.'

'Should have checked out their plantations,' she says.

'Remember you went to the market?' I pull out my phone and scroll through more windmill photos.

'Still hiding stuff?' Jenny says.

'The Harveys had four plantations, four windmills. All I could find in the time.'

She waves her arms in the air and kicks the earth. 'So everything here's down to sugar money?'

I lead on, along the cycle path. We turn off to an old, roofless church, with a square tower. 'Collegiate Church,' I say. 'Goes back to the fifteenth century.' From the outside it's a plain rubble building with a square tower. But inside is a special place. A medieval knight lies in a recess in the wall, carved from grey sandstone.

'Did he bring any Africans back?' she says.

'Twenty-nine when he returned from St Kitts.'

Her voice is breaking. 'Any trace of their graves?'

I show her a sketch of an old gravestone with Billy's name on it, and kick the gravel. 'He's buried here somewhere.'

She makes an odd sound and drops to her knees. She picks up a piece of slate and tears at the gravel. 'Bastard!'

I bend down and prise the slate from her hand. 'You can't do that. It's a scheduled ancient monument.'

'Scheduled bollocks.' She throws herself face down. I put a hand on her shoulder. After a minute or two, she rolls over and sits up, shaking, with her head down. I help her up. We're both even wetter than after the tunnel. Her tights are torn by the gravel and her mascara's streaked down her cheeks.

We head back, in silence, round the loch to Lochwinnoch station, like survivors of a disaster. On the train, she lies, silent, with her head on my lap, all the way back to Glasgow.

***

Back at the flat, Jenny is still saying nothing. I can't think straight, so I try to work up the enthusiasm to start clearing up Murdo's den. The big noticeboard, made of dozens of cork tiles, takes up half the wall. In the centre are my A4 sheets, each printed in big letters with Billy's epitaphs. Jenny comes over and starts reading out a crude rubbing, right at the top of the board:

He was one of the Most
Virtuous and Wise
sons of the City
What He did in Secret
is believed to be not inferior
to what He did in Publick

'How could anyone know what he did in secret?' she says.

'It's not Billy,' I say, 'it's your rubbing from Colston's statue in Bristol.'

'Colston?' she says. 'He's finished, chucked in the harbour.'

I tap the one below. 'This one's Billy. Or is it his grandson?'

Erected as a memorial of esteem
for his private virtues,
he was of fine character,
gallant romantic,
singularly endowed with talents,
and every good and praise-worthy disposition,
zeal for the public good,
and promoted the prosperity of Scotland

'Private virtues?' she says. 'That's the most annoying thing of all – the claim that he was a good person.'

'Nobody's perfect,' I say.

'It's not about right and wrong, it's how they claim to be good, even in their secret thoughts.'

'End of lecture?'

Jenny ignores me and continues.

He held the regard of everyone, as he stepped
with his tall gold-headed cane along the causeway…
His coming had opened up new prospects of wealth for the city…
He was the most notable figure in town
the 'darling of the city'
who did much to shape its social and human qualities.

She reaches up and starts pulling down the sheets, tearing them into small pieces and throwing them in the bin. I don't have the energy to stop her. I sit back at the big table. Then she turns on me. 'Finished Billy's letters yet?'

'I'm trying to expose him, not celebrate him.'

'But aren't you still promoting the white man? You think you're bringing this big, new story back to your city. It's the same in Bristol. Even if they're being exposed, all we hear about are the merchants. The workers stay hidden. Where's their stories?'

I slide over my tally of Billy's slave numbers. 'I've got thousands!'

'You need individuals.' She fumbles with her pile of papers on the other side of the table, pushes across her copies of Anna's slave lists for Canada Hills. She pokes them so hard with her finger she makes a hole in the page. 'Invisible? That's the biggest lie of all. They're all here! Names, ages, occupations.' She grabs Billy's list of Castle Semple tenants, crumpling it. 'And we've got exactly the same information for his tenants here in Scotland! The only reason the Africans are invisible is because they worked further away!' She stands up, grabs her coat from the door, and runs downstairs.

***

Jenny returns two hours later, with her hair cut.

'Like the hair,' I say.

'Too straight.'

'Funny how those with straight hair want it curly, and the curly ones want it straight,' I say.

'You mean black people.'

'Black—'

'Want their curly hair straight, like the whites.'

'Just admiring your hair. Don't think of you as black or white.'

'I'm proud to be black.'

She gets up and heads again for the door. I cross the room and grab her arm. She turns, looks up with her big brown eyes and dissolves into my arms. It all comes out. Her dad. The faces in the street. The names on the lists. Jenny McNight.

'Don't you see?' she says. 'It's about my family. They came from the islands.'

***

Later, fetching shopping from Tesco, we meet an old friend, Jim, who insists on taking us for coffee. Jim talks like a Glaswegian, but he was born in Nigeria. We're not in the mood for talking, but we tell him a bit about our island adventure.

As we leave, he says, 'Need to show you something.' He leads us round via London Road, past a very old house. 'Long ago,' Jim says, 'the owner kept an African in the basement. The African's name was Negro John. It wasn't his real name, it was a given name.'

One African in Glasgow? It isn't much. But we agree that it's a start.

***

Before Jenny goes to bed, she comes through. 'By the way, got a job next week, doing tours.'

'Sculpture and stuff?' I say.

'Merchant City Festival.'

'Expert now on Glasgow?'

She slams her bedroom door so hard she knocks one of Murdo's sphinxes off its shelf.

I climb up top and look down again at the broken gutter.

Where are you?

Is this what you planned all along?

Chapter 37

Jenny, First Glasgow Tour

An English Story

On the morning of her first tour, Jenny woke and checked her tablet for press reviews of her trial run the day before. She clanked up the spiral stair and threw her tablet on Hamish's bed.

'The Glasgow Slave Trade Tour, by Jenny McNight

'To Glasgow, Ms McNight brings an English story of guilt and the slave trade. She tells of Scots in the early English Empire, when we've known since school that they were banned. She tells of Glasgow merchants making fortunes from dodgy Caribbean sugar, when we all know it was finest Virginia tobacco. She tells a politically correct tale, which has no place in Glasgow. Aye, Glasgow, where we can be thankful that its fine merchants were a class above the English slave traders.

'PS Am I allowed to mention that she is young, pretty, English and black? Aye, she's more than welcome here, but she needs a few lessons in Scottish history.'

***

'Slave trade?' Hamish said.

'Press title, not mine.' She turned and climbed back down the stairs, sobbing.

Hamish followed her downstairs. She was putting the kettle on. He touched Jenny's arm, but she shrugged him off. 'Can I help with the tour?' he said.

'Just come along and jeer.'

Hamish went out alone for a ride.

Time to Show

Jenny came to a conclusion: It was time to show him Cato's jotters.

She hurried down to the copy shop on the corner and printed out her transcripts. When she got back, Hamish was still out. She left the pile of sheets on the table with a note on top, held down by the wee model of Billy's mansion.

My Name's Jenny McNight

Jenny's tour group met in Royal Exchange Square. She passed round her handouts.

Just before the start, Hamish appeared at the back. Jenny was too busy welcoming folk to acknowledge him. 'My name's Jenny McNight,' she shouted above the traffic.

She went round everyone and let them introduce themselves. About half were locals, the rest tourists: Australian, Polish, Japanese.

The Story

Jenny led them along Argyle Street to the corner of M&S, and pointed at the middle of the road. 'Today we're going to hear the story of Glasgow's greatest merchant, by visiting some of his haunts.'

Hamish raised a hand at the back and tried to catch her eye.

'The mansion which stood here was the earliest and most prestigious townhouse in Glasgow, maybe in the whole of Britain. It was owned by the city's leading merchant, who we'll call "Colonel Billy". We can imagine the building standing here…' She unrolled an old engraving of the mansion and held it up. 'Billy's story's covered in all the old books, but reality tells a different story—'

'Think the city books are wrong?' said a local man in a red baseball cap.

'You can be the judges,' she said.

'But they've stood the test of time,' said his partner, in a yellow T-shirt.

Overseer of What?

Jenny led on down the Stockwell and stopped by the Clyde.

'From the 1640s, small boats went up and down from here to Port Glasgow. The goods were transferred to bigger ships, which sailed out to the Caribbean. Some folk settled out on the islands. One was named Colhoun. By the 1660s he was a sugar planter on an island called St Christopher. When Billy was sixteen his father arranged an apprenticeship through Colhoun.'

'Says he was a colonel in the army?' said Red Baseball Cap, holding up the tour leaflet.

'Instead of becoming a soldier, Billy went out in his teens and spent eleven years training as an overseer,' Jenny said.

'Overseer of what?' said a man in a blue Rangers top.

'Work it out yourself,' said an English voice from the back.

'Thought he was a city hero?' said Red Baseball Cap.

'What about the soldier?' said Yellow T-shirt.

'His rank was in the militia. Dad's Army of the Caribbean,' Jenny said.

'Where d'you get this stuff?' said Red Baseball Cap.

'From Billy's own letters,' Jenny said.

Good Churchgoing Scots

They moved on. The next stop was halfway up the Stockwell.

'This was the site of the South Sugar House. Glasgow had four sugar houses by 1700. In his late forties, Billy came back to Bristol a very rich man.'

'Thought this was about Glasgow,' said Rangers Top.

A small local lady wearing a green shell suit, who held hands under a big umbrella with her tall friend, interrupted. 'Aye right, but good churchgoing Scots couldn't have been involved?'

Her tall friend nodded. 'How could Scots be involved when they started the Enlightenment?'

'Adam Smith spoke against it,' said Wee.

'Rabbie Burns refused to go out,' said Tall.

'Scots abolished it,' said Wee.

'The English did it all,' said a male voice at the back.

'Liverpool and Bristol,' said another.

'And Tony Blair apologised for it,' said Tall.

'End of story,' said Wee, and the pair walked off.

The City's Past

Jenny was still avoiding eye contact with Hamish. She carried on.

'When Billy finished his apprenticeship, he started to buy land to build up his own sugar plantation. He also bought some Africans to grow sugar cane.'

There was a general moan from the remaining Glasgow side of the audience.

'How can you claim this changes the city's past?' said Rangers Top.

'I'm not claiming anything.'

'It's hardly typical. How many did this Billy guy own?' said Rangers Top.

'Guess.'

'Ten?'

Jenny raised a finger.

'Twenty? Thirty?'

'Two hundred and four, at the beginning, then one thousand three hundred and two,' she said.

There was an intake of breath.

'Any evidence?' said Rangers Top.

Jenny took off her backpack and slipped out a few crumpled photocopies. 'What's your name?' she said.

'Why?' said Rangers Top.

'Your first name.'

'Frank.'

She put on her glasses and looked down the second sheet, 'African number fifty-six: Frank, fieldworker, value £30. There's also a cow named Frank on the last page,' she said, and handed the sheets to him.

The audience laughed. Rangers Top scanned the sheets and stuffed them into the hands of the girl next to him. 'Why can't you leave it alone?' he said.

'Leave it?'

'Why dig it up after all this time and try to brainwash us?' he said.

'She is not brainwashing anybody,' said a Polish girl at the front. 'We have all come along freely.'

'It's all just political correctness.'

Jenny was trying to gauge where he was coming from, then Frank said, 'Aye, keep the ethnics happy.'

Several folk started to shout at him, but Frank took his girlfriend by the hand and they walked off.

The rest carried on.

Started with Sugar

Jenny turned along Osborne Street, then right, through the deserted underpass and out into Argyle Street. Across the road, they faced up Virginia Street.

'Much later, Glasgow had strong tobacco connections with Virginia. But it all started with sugar plantations in the Caribbean.'

'Make this up yersel?' said Tartan Shirt. 'This is more like the Edinburgh Fringe than a history tour.'

'Aye, very good, but shouldn't the Africans be grateful?' said Tweed Cap. 'Thankful they ended up in civilised countries like America, not darkest Africa.'

'And, by the way, my family wasn't involved,' said Tartan Shirt, and walked off.

As the group headed off again, two more couples abandoned it, leaving only one of the locals.

Life Was Hard

At the end of the tour, Hamish went home alone. Jenny joined the remainder of the tourists in an old-fashioned tearoom in the square.

'Didn't Scots abolish slavery?' said the young man with the Liverpool accent.

'Why make such a fuss about Africans, if most slaves were white?' said Tweed Cap. 'What d'you cry them, dentured servants?'

Jenny held the door open. 'Indentured.'

'Sort of cancels it out,' he said.

They all sat down at a big table.

'Aye, and it was Africans who originally sold Africans,' he said.

'And life was hard for everybody back then,' Jenny said.

'Specially the women,' said Morwenna at the front, and with a sigh went to order the teas.

Once they parted, without a word to Hamish, Jenny caught a bus to stay the night with Kelly.

Chapter 38

Hamish, Glasgow

On the way back after the tour, I text Jenny: *It was great, just ignore them.* When I get up to the flat, the first thing I spot is Jenny's pile of A4 printouts lying on the big table. I lift off the wee windmill model. On top is a note in Jenny's writing: *Should have shown you these ages ago. Better late than never. Luv Jen xx.*

My finger lingers over *luv*. Then I make a cup of tea and sit down at the table. I slide the pile of papers in front of me and read the title: THE JOURNAL OF CATO.

I switch on the desk lamp and start to read. Cato's voice slips into my head and I lose myself in his words. Billy's there too, in the background, not in the black and white of the old books but in Technicolor.

***

Much later, I wake with my head resting on the final sheet. I rub my eyes. It's dark, and Jenny still isn't back. Where is she? I check my phone.

Staying the night at Kelly's. See you tomorrow.

I get up and crawl into bed.

***

At dawn I make a cup of tea. It's too early for Jessica, but the day's going to be fine. I go for a walk by the river. When I get back, after breakfast, I take *The Journal of Cato* up to the wee eyrie and read the whole thing again.

So this is what she's been up to? There's so much about Billy. Why hasn't she shown it to me? It would have saved lots of time.

Ach, I'm just as bad. I've hidden Billy's story too.

I need to talk to Jenny.

No. 147. Two Lives

We've been living two lives, me and Jenny.
Glasgow and Bristol.
Scotland and Nevis.
With a different version of truth for each.
But now I've found a third life.
One who stood in the background and took the notes.
He was silent, but he saw the truth.
He was the one who felt all the pain.

Chapter 39

Jenny, Second Glasgow Tour

Tell Cato's Story?

When Jenny got to Kelly's, they went out for a meal. She told Kelly about the tour, how most of the locals had walked off.

'You've got three more days of tours,' Kelly said. 'What you going to do?'

'Got a bigger problem. Left Cato's jotters for Hamish to see.'

'At last!'

'He won't speak to me ever again!'

Kelly was silent for a bit. Then she said, 'What if you tweak your tour? Tell Cato's story, not Billy's.'

'They'd have even less time for an African.'

'Hamish coming along again?'

Jenny shrugged.

'Maybe it's the way to break it to him.'

What to Say?

Kelly's words bugged Jenny.

Tell Cato's story? She had nothing to lose.

She lay awake all night, working out what to say.

He's Read Them?

In the morning, Jenny had breakfast with Kelly, then caught a bus back to the flat. Hamish was out, and Cato's transcripts had been moved. Had he read them?

She changed and had a shower. Before she left for her tour, she put another sheet of paper on the table, under the wee model.

Two Stories

On the second day of the tour, there was a similar mix of attendees. Two Canadians turned up without booking, but Jenny let them tag along. Hamish appeared again at the back of the group.

She started off by leading them a different way from the first day. Instead of the front of M&S, she went round the back, to Garth Street.

After the usual introduction, she said, 'I'm going to tell you two parallel stories. Two lives which came together three hundred years ago, at random. Their names are Billy and Cato. Billy owned all the land here. In later life he was a successful merchant, a multimillionaire by today's standards. A leading player in turning Glasgow into a city. Billy's mansion faced Argyle Street and his garden stretched back five hundred yards, through where we're standing, to Ingram Street.' She tapped a red-painted kerb with her toe, where the street had recently been patched up. 'A few months ago, workmen dug up the skeleton of an elderly man here. He was identified as of African origin. His name was Cato.'

'He was buried here?' said a tall girl in a yellow jacket. She bent down and touched the kerb.

Jenny nodded. 'Beside Cato, in a sealed glass jar, inside a brass trunk, were his writings. Today we're going to cover his story in his own words.'

'Thought this was about a Glasgow merchant,' said a girl in a pink top.

'We know the merchant's story through the writings of his servant,' Jenny said.

'A black man who could write?' said Pink Top. A moan rose from the rest of the group.

'Yeah,' Jenny said. 'Had a tough time at school myself. All these bright white kids—'

'Didn't mean it like that,' said Pink Top. 'Just seems unlikely back then.'

Jenny turned away and led on, round to Jamaica Street.

'Why's it called Jamaica?' said a guy wearing a green scarf.

'Use your heid, big man,' said a local man in a brown jacket.

'Billy was born into a wealthy family in Galloway. Aged seventeen, he went out, not to Jamaica, but to a smaller Caribbean island called Nevis.

He started an apprenticeship as an overseer. Cato was born in Cameroon on the slopes of the tallest mountain in West Africa. He was captured aged fifteen, and never saw his parents or sister alive again. He was carried to a slave fort on an island off the coast. He spent nearly a year there, and was picked out at random to tally fellow slaves. In doing so, he learned the rudiments of English. Then he was carried across the ocean, along with three hundred and seven other men, women and children. Forty-nine died on the crossing.'

She waited for a comment, but the group were silent.

'Like Billy, Cato arrived on Nevis. He was washed and oiled and displayed naked in the slave market. Fingers were poked in his mouth and his private parts. Then he was purchased by a sugar planter. By chance, it was the same plantation where our Glasgow man, Billy, was training.'

'Bit of a coincidence? Make this up yersel?'

Jenny slipped out a few photocopies and passed them round. 'Copies of some of Cato's jotters,' she said.

Scribe

Jenny led on, then stopped again.

'When Billy discovered that Cato knew a little English, he took him out of the field gang, and under his wing as his scribe. Cato would remain in this role for nearly fifty years. Billy finished his apprenticeship and moved across to the adjacent island of St Kitts. He began buying up land and built up his own plantation. He also bought thirteen Africans to grow his sugar cane. One was a wee girl called Flora.'

A strange noise came from the back of the group. 'He owned children?' said a small lady holding her granddaughter's hand.

'Within a few years Billy owned two large plantations, each worked by two hundred Africans. He was regarded as a tough manager, good at making a profit. He also ran plantations for friends who had gone home, controlling more than a thousand Africans at one time. Any questions?' she said.

The audience were silent.

Twenty-Nine

As they moved off, Jenny brushed past Hamish. He gave her a thumbs up.

She led them down Glassford Street and stopped in Argyle Street. 'By 1724, Billy was a very rich man and decided to come home and settle in Glasgow. He brought with him a retinue of twenty-nine African men, women and children, including Cato. By this time both Billy and Cato were in their late forties. Within a few years, lots of Glasgow merchants brought home African servants. If you were around back then, you would see them passing, dressed in bright livery, riding on the back of coaches.'

'Servants?'

She shrugged. 'Call them what you want.' She pointed to the centre of the street. 'Just here stood Billy's Shawfield mansion. He purchased it on his return from the Caribbean. Cato resided here for the next twenty-five years. Perhaps we can picture him, looking out the skylight from his wee room in the attic.'

Sensible Questions

Jenny led the group further down the Stockwell and stopped again. 'When Billy came home, Glasgow already had at least four sugar houses.'

'Thought it was tobacco,' said Brown Jacket.

'Much later,' she said. She pointed across the road. 'South Sugar House stood here. The sugar was brought up the Clyde from Port Glasgow in small boats to the Broomielaw. Then it was carried here in carts to be processed and crystallised. Billy bought a share, then the whole business. He also had a shop where he sold his sugar. At the same time, Billy also bought a country estate, where he built a mansion. To mix with the landed gentry, he pretended he'd spent his career as a colonel in the British army.'

'A cover-up?' said Yellow T-shirt.

'Maybe to enhance his status,' she said. 'When Billy died, he was celebrated as the most important man in the city. Cato was forgotten until his story was dug up.'

'Cato never saw his family again?' said the Canadian girl.

'His sister was raped and killed when he was captured. His parents didn't fare any better.' She waited for sarky comments, but there were none. They asked sensible questions. No one walked off.

The End

Once Jenny had finished, some of the tour group stood chatting for half an hour. Then an Eastern European couple invited Jenny for a coffee. Hamish went off alone.

Afterwards, Jenny headed back to the flat. On the way, she passed the end of Garth Street. Someone had laid flowers on Cato's resting place.

Chapter 40

Hamish, Glasgow

When I get back up to the flat alone, Cato's papers have been moved to the side and replaced with a single sheet of paper.

I lift off the wee windmill model. More of Cato's writings? But from the pencil date in the top corner, Jenny transcribed it a while ago. Why keep it separate?

It's more composed than the rest, more poetic, as if Cato spent a long time polishing it. I pick it up and read it slowly.

The Journal of Cato

THE MOST PEACEFUL PLACE IN TOWN

Sent, sometimes I am sent on an errand across the stone bridge to Gorbals, to Allason the bakers. On my return, if the hour is early, the tide is high & nobody is about, I climb the great oak on the southern bank. I am not as young as I was, but my tree has many branches, like a ladder, & I rest high in its branches. Peace, tis the most peaceful place in all of this growin city.

TWO CITIES

Calm, calm is the water & high is the tide & still is the wind. If I look north, I see not one but two cities, one upon the other. But, as with my own image in the lookin glass in Massa's parlour, nothin I see in the two cities is equal. In the top city, men & women & horses tramp the streets, free to do as they wish. Howsoever in the bottom, if I look carefully among the shadows & ripples of the river, there is a great mass of dark & naked bodies who writhe & toil. Every smile & couplin of lovers in the upper city is reflected by a cry & a buckin in the lower. Yet there is no one there to hear.

For the breadth of the ocean washes away the truth.

THOSE WHO HAVE CROSSED THE OCEAN

This new city has been so carefully constructed that whosoever lives in the upper city knows not what is happenin in the lower. Yet the upper depends entirely on the lower for its foundation, & though they sit one upon the other, nothin so close together has ever been so far apart. Cross, only those of us who have crossed the ocean & returned know the secret of the reflected city.

For the breadth of the ocean washes away the truth.

THE WEALTH OF GREAT MEN

The upper city knows only departures, not returns. Those who depart from hence, cross the ocean & come back changed, possessin untold wealth. But tis a known fact, even in this land, that the wealth of great men comes from the labour of many small men. The say each merchant sucks the life from a hundred, nay a thousand others, for the riches they bring to this city from the islands.

For the breadth of the ocean washes away the truth.

A CITY BUILT ON JUST FOUNDATIONS

Burrow, the inhabitants have burrowed another city underground. A city of tunnels & catacombs. All their white corpses are carried down to be judged not by a Christian God but by a voice of reason. A god of the earth who seeks a city built on just foundations. The job of judgin the dead is assigned to a group of hooded & winged sisters, & close, if you are close enough to look carefully under their cowls, you will see the brown eyes of the just, of dark-skinned angels. But if the day has come for you to descend there, tis too late to repent.

For the breadth of the ocean washes away the truth.

THE BREADTH OF THE OCEAN

Hope, is there any hope for the merchant who lays his hopes on his treasures on earth? They say that each one who goes below finds less & less room as the charnel house fills with the bones of those who profit from the sweet desire. Thus the city of the livin above is propped up more & more by the brittle bones below.

For the breadth of the ocean washes away the truth.

A GRINDIN OF BONES

On winter nights, I go down to the kitchen in the basement to warm myself by the range. Rest, I rest my ear to a dark layer in the wall. If I listen carefully, I sometimes hear a wailin & grindin, as if of bones.

For the breadth of the ocean washes away the truth.

***

When I finish reading, I slide the page aside, get up and lift my jacket from the hook by the door. I stick my phone in my pocket and step into my trainers. I descend the six floors to the street in a daze. I turn towards the river, cross Victoria Bridge and look back at the old city.

Was it the Greeks or the Romans who had to cross a river? Something to do with dying?

The tide's the lowest I've seen. The skeleton of the old boat sticks right out of the mud. Two policewomen stand smoking behind the Sheriff Court, with their backs to me. I climb over the railing. The path from the hole in the fence makes a dark tunnel through willow trees to the riverbank. Under a tree is a den, built from old wooden pallets. Every time I come, there's more signs of rough sleepers.

I climb down the manhole and along the brick tunnel to the beach. Across the river, traffic roars along Clyde Street. Up on the bridge, buses sit idling at the lights. Nobody looks down. City's turned its back on its river.

I pick up a big stone and step out, one foot at a time, along my wee causeway, towards the wreck. I try to put as little weight on the stones as possible. It reminds me of a recurring dream from my childhood: if I walk as slowly and carefully as possible, I might rise off the ground and hover.

As the stones thin out, I add my big rock, but it makes no difference. I take another step, and my trainer starts to sink in. Then I lunge forward and my left leg sinks up to the knee. I'm stuck. As I try to push on, my leg sinks further.

A couple of metres ahead, near the boat, is a big tree, washed down by the river. If I fall forward, maybe I can reach it. Or I might sink face first into the mud and drown. Without another thought, I lunge forward. I fall flat in the mud, but my fingers grab a branch of the tree.

I pull myself out of the hole with a big sucking sound, leaving my trainers behind and pulling my trousers down to my ankles. I drag myself along the tree and roll into the skeleton of the boat, pulling up my filthy trousers. I'm covered from head to toe in stinking, oily, grey mud. I lie back against one of the boat's ribs and try to clean off the clods.

At one end of the wreck is a pool of water left by the receding tide. The water splashes on my face. It tastes of salt. Upriver, under the arches of two bridges, I see white water at the tidal weir.

I pull at a piece of the boat. It's still rock-hard. Each rib has a wee Roman numeral carved into it by the boatbuilder. Finest quality hardwood – I like that. A century or two in the river, and still legible. I wonder what part of the Empire the timber came from before it was dragged up this godforsaken river to build a boat.

High above, a jet crosses a blue gap between the clouds. I shake my fist at it. You set me up. Knew I'd fall for it. Knew I'd chase the proud city hero shit. But even if I try to expose you, you'll remain famous. All your chattels will stay invisible.

But they're not invisible any more. I've read one of their stories.

I fumble in my pocket for my phone, but it's gone. Five hundred quid lost in the mud. I've come full circle, across the ocean and back to this muddy, salty river.

As I lie back, the sun comes out from behind a cloud. Then, finally, tired and wet and shivering, I see it. Jenny's been trying to tell me for ages.

I need to tell a new story, not repeat an old one.

The story of someone who crossed the ocean.

Cato's story, not Billy's.

A warm, contented feeling spreads through me. My clothes might just dry in the sun. A smile cracks the mud on my face. Stranded in this hulk in the middle of the Clyde, I'm the luckiest guy in Glasgow.

A chancer.

A prophet.

St Mungo in his wee fuckin' coracle.

***

After a bit, water starts to lap at the muddy heels of my socks. The only way back, apart from shouting to bring out Ben whatsisname in his wee rescue boat, is to wait. Wait until the tide rises enough to swim for the bank. At least it's late summer. The water temperature's risen from Arctic to Baltic. Hypothermia's still possible, but not definite. As the cold water reaches my bum, I squeeze between the wooden ribs and launch myself towards the bank on my back.

Halfway to the shore, I touch the bottom and crawl up the beach. I wash myself as well as I can in pools of grey, salty water before I scramble up the wall.

I pad across the bridge in my stocking soles, ignoring the looks of passers-by. When I reach the door, it's open. But it isn't Jenny. I can smell cigarettes.

'Archie!' He's looking through the papers on the desk. 'Lost something?' I say.

He jumps and turns to face me. 'Look what the Clyde dredged up,' he says.

I ignore him and strip naked in front of him, leaving a filthy wet pile at my feet. He looks me up and down, turns away, and struggles up the stairs and out the wee door for a fag. I take a quick shower, put on jeans and a T-shirt, then join him up top. He's lighting another fag from the stub of his last.

'Jenny's transcribed Murdo's Dead Sea Scrolls,' I say.

'They're colonial claptrap, fabricated to mess up the city.'

'Murdo thought the city could stand up for itself,' I say.

'Why can't you leave it alone? You're no better than him. Prefer the scribblings of a darkie to the city's greatest merchant.'

Archie grabs my shoulder and I nearly lose my balance. As he spits out the offensive word, his cigarette shoots from his mouth. It bounces down the slates in a shower of wee sparks, then disappears over the edge.

I see it in a flash. 'You pushed Murdo!'

'It was an accident!' Archie says. 'We were arguing over a roll of papers. He was on his last legs, but he was determined to get up here. Had to help him. He lost his balance. Luckily for me, he went straight into the skip.'

I take a step back, stumble and grab the parapet, blinded by tears.

'You don't think I regret it?' he says.

'That's it. I don't want any money from you or your bigoted mates. Just get out of my flat.'

'*Your* flat?'

Archie gives up trying to light another fag, ducks, and disappears through the wee door. I give him a minute, then go down to the front door and bolt it. I climb back up to the mezzanine and lie on the bed, tears welling up.

***

After a bit, I hear knocking at the door. I go down and hear Jenny's voice.

'What's happened?' she says.

'Murdo's dead.'

She grabs me and holds on until I calm down.

'I was right. He fell and went straight into a skip and off to landfill,' I say.

We sit at the table, facing each other. She takes a wad of hankies from the box and hands me them. 'He jumped?'

'They were arguing. It was an accident.'

'He was dying.' She stands up.

I wave a hand and change the subject. 'Thought the second tour was great, by the way, especially as you've hidden it from me for so long.'

Jenny spins round and slaps me across the cheek. As I dodge the blow, she catches my nostril with her nail. I reel away, nose bleeding.

'Sorry,' she says.

I grab another wad of paper hankies from the box on the table and press them to my face. 'Ach, I deserve it,' I say.

We cross the room and collapse, side by side, on the sofa. 'I'm sorry,' she says again.

'Me too.'

'Stop fucking apologising.'

'We're equally at fault.'

'I was worse. I was doing it for my career,' she says.

We sit in silence.

Jenny goes to make a cup of tea. I take it and we climb up to the eyrie. The sun's setting down the river.

Murdo fell from here. From his favourite spot.

I turn away, hiding more tears.

***

The cold wind drives us back downstairs.

'Meant to say, when Murdo fell, Archie says they were arguing over a roll of papers.'

'Cato's final chapter!' she says.

'Must have gone to the skip.'

'Or Archie's got it.'

'Can't publish without the last chapter.'

Jenny puts on a jacket and goes back upstairs alone. Five minutes later she comes back down, smiling. 'Called Anna, she's got a copy. She's going to scan and email it.'

'Murdo wasn't daft,' I say. 'It's too valuable not to have copied it!'

'What now,' she says, 'finish the story and get it published?'

'What about Archie's money?' I say.

'We can publish online for next to nothing.'

***

In the end, Jenny finishes her tours using Cato's story, not Billy's, and gets good reviews. Together, up on Murdo's big table, we lay out a copy of Cato's final chapter. Then we sit, side by side, each with a lined sheet of paper in front of us. Jenny, the expert, has the first go. Then I try to unravel the trickier words. Soon we get into a rhythm.

***

Two days before I start my new job, we finish transcribing Cato's final chapter and decide to get out for a bit. Walking up the Stockwell, I grab Jenny's arm. 'Look!' I say. An American tourist, in pink shirt and blue-and-orange checked shorts, holds up a big iPad and snaps the Bonnie Prince plaque. I shake my fist at him, in Murdo's memory.

In the Trongate, in front of the site of Billy's mansion, a deep hole's been dug in the pavement, enclosed by red and white plastic cones. I step between the cones and jump down.

'Be careful,' Jenny says, then, 'What the hell?'

I take her hand and help her climb down beside me. She crouches down, picks at the dark layer in the side of the trench and pulls out part of a broken mug. She wipes it clean and smiles. On the side of the jug is a wee blue figure, wearing a cocked hat.

'One you planted earlier?' she says. I give her a wee shove. 'So where did it come from?' she says.

'Not just here, but there?'

'Aye, Murdo knew all along.'

I help her back out, a bit muddy. She stops at a stall and buys a bunch of red roses. We cross Glassford Street and head through what was Billy's back garden into Garth Street, and stop at the painted kerb. Jenny lays the flowers on Cato's resting place. We stand in silence.

Suddenly, there's a howl like a banshee wailing, and a freak gust of wind blows a bunch of newpapers round the corner from Virginia Street.

'Think I've let Murdo down?' I say. 'For failing to write Billy's story?'

'Didn't he want you to chase Cato from the start?'

It makes sense. The house model. All the clues. Cato's jotters.

'Why didn't you say?'

'Would you have listened?'

We take a shortcut through Virginia Lane and over to George Square. Then we turn west into St Vincent Street, for the long walk over the hill to the big library. It starts to drizzle, but we don't care. We've survived tropical storms.

Upstairs in the Mitchell Library, the old newspapers are held on microfilm. Jenny runs her finger down the list and finds the reference number for 1749. We cross to a wall of wee metal drawers and find the correct cardboard box. She opens it, pulls out the plastic reel, and unravels the string holding the film tight. Together we fumble to thread the film through the rollers.

Jenny switches on the big old machine. The screen lights up and a fan rumbles to life. A dull image appears on the screen, back to front. I pull the film out, turn it over and rethread it. Now it's upside down. Jenny turns a big knob and it spins round.

I scroll through until I find the month, then the day. Jenny climbs up on her chair, but I stop her before she steps onto the desk. 'Yes!' she cries. Heads turn in the big room.

I help her down. There's a big ladder in her green tights.

No. 148. A Negro Man

Run away
from Castle Semple
a Negro Man, named CATO:
he is old, pretty tall, ill-legs,
with squat or broad feet.
A sufficient reward will be paid for him.

***

I reach up and touch the screen with my fingertips, as if I'm touching the original page of the newspaper. I copy it carefully into my wee folder. Then I look around to check nobody's looking. I slip out my phone and take a few photos of the dim screen, hoping one will be in focus.

Jenny's smiling and crying at the same time. 'He's real!' she whispers.

***

Back outside, Jenny takes my arm and we head all the way east to the Cross, then up the High Street.

‘Wait,’ I say. I lead her across the queue of traffic to Provand’s Lordship, round to the stone heads in the back. ‘Last time we were here, you asked a question,’ I say.

She looks up at the contorted faces and nods. ‘What did they do to become devils?’

The rain’s gone off and the sun comes out. We cross the road again, over the Bridge of Sighs and up the rocky hill. We follow the path to the edge of the slope and sit, in silence, on the roof of a mausoleum, to eat our picnic. Away in the distance, the Clyde winds its way like a silver ribbon towards the ocean. On the four corners of the roof are wee stone sphinxes. I reach out and run my hand over one. ‘It’s good that we found one,’ I say.

‘A sphinx?’

‘One African in Glasgow.’

‘One’s a start.’

‘Now I need to publish,’ I say.

‘The story of Cato?’

‘The spanking striptease story.’

She jumps down and I chase her along the path. When I catch her, I hold her arms and she turns, rises onto her tiptoes and kisses me, a long lingering kiss on the lips.

Jenny points to a shady spot of grass between two tombs. Then she raises her flowing skirts and says, ‘Lie down.’

Chapter 41

The Journal of Cato

MY FINAL CHAPTER

In my seventieth year, nothin but loneliness inhabits my days & nights. Howsoever, a traitor am I. Many times should I have died. As my friend Hermit once said, why does it fall to some to endure & some to wither?

I stand up. My legs are stiff. I look out the library window, at the long snow-covered garden. Cold, the day is cold & white. Now & then a blackbird flies across the deep blue sky. Here I stand, familiar now with the birds on a third continent. As if knowin the names & habits of birds is all that matters.

MY OWN TALE

Inside the garden tis quiet, but over the high stone wall rises the smoke & bustle of the streets.

High, I sit at my high desk, finishin copyin the letter. I dab the ink with the blotter & push the big ledger to the side. From under the desk, I slide out my note-book containin my own tale & run my fingers over the rough paper. All is written here, crammed in tiny script in this thin book & in the others hidden under the floor-boards of my garret. Like my own life, only a few blank pages remain.

The house is quiet. Massa Billee lies in his sick bed & the servants are in the basement. I shiver & throw a few more coals on the fire. I sharpen the nib of my quill, dip it into the ink & write for the last time: THE JOURNAL OF CATO.

A simple tale, of a nameless people, told by an old man in an ordinary town on the cusp of bein a city.

LAST TESTAMENT

My Massa lies downstairs with his lawyer, redraftin his last testament. I descend the stair to the library. The fire has reduced to a dull glow in the grate. I shiver & cross to the window. In the distance, the Tolbooth clock strikes five. Close, I close the curtains, shuttin out the winter gloom.

TIME TO GO

The next day, we move back to his country house in his best coach. Finally, tis time for me to go. I have no possessions but my journal.

Next morn I wrap it in my coat. I steal some bread & some fruit from the orangery & place it in my bag. I tell Cook I am goin on an errand to Paisley. I walk to the village, where I have arranged to catch a ride on the baker's cart. At Paisley harbour, I trade some fruit for the short sail on a lighter, by the Cart & Clyde, to the Broomielaw. I keep my hood up, my face in shadow.

At dusk, I follow the lanes to the side gate of Massa's garden. I lift the big brass key on the string around my neck, open the gate & peer inside. Nobody is about. Down the garden, no smoke rises from the chimneys of the great house. Howsoever keep, I keep out of sight behind a hedge. I make my way to the summer-house, up in the back corner of the great walled garden.

I climb down the six stone steps & enter the basement by the low door, then climb the ladder through the hatch. I shut the thick curtains in the French windows & build a fire in the wee grate, relyin on the growin darkness to hide the smoke. I eat the last of my bread & drink water from a bottle, then arrange some sacks on the floor. I lie down & fall quickly asleep.

Finally, after all those years, I have escaped. Great was my fear that each winter would be my last. Or worse, Massa Billee's last, then his lady would throw me out.

SPIRITS ASCENDIN SKYWARDS

Open, I open one eye. My left cheek rests on the rough floor-boards. On the grey wall above the fire, a narrow vertical streak begins to appear on the faded timber wall. A ray of daylight from a gap in the curtains behind. I take a deep breath & roll over, rise stiffly to my knees. I throw back the curtains. Blinded by the light, I gasp out loud. Scottish weather. Dazzlin sunlight, yet thick frost.

I let the sun's warmth enfold me through the panelled doors. The front of this pavilion has more glass than the windows of a merchant's house. I look out over the big garden. Eight acres, enough to sustain a family, yet private behind its great wall. On the edge of a city yet anonymous.

This winter's morn, everythin glistens white. The hedges, maze, bare trees, fountains & ornaments. All distorted through the waverin glass. The life-size sculptures in the garden vibrate in the sunlight & unsettle me. As I watch silently, steam rises from their silhouettes. Spirits ascendin skywards as the early-mornin sun melts their frosty coat.

MY SHELTER

The sun edges higher. Through the walls of this summer-house, I can feel the carts rumblin on the cobbles behind the great wall. The early-morn bustle of Back Cow Loan. The smell of bakin, of brewin, of horses.

The sun silhouettes the great mansion at the far end of the garden. I feel safe from its eyes, its pryin rear windows. My shelter pokes above the maze of hedges, bushes, trellises, elevated on its stone basement. But the branches of a row of fruit trees, though leafless, align to conceal me. With my Massa lyin sick in his country house twenty miles away, his town-house is empty, its rhythm frozen by his illness. Still, I must take care.

I open the curtains fully, let the sun pour in, grateful for its warmth. I cannot light the fire again till dusk lest its smoke reveal me. I lift the hatch in the wooden floor & force my agein legs to descend the ladder again into the cold stone basement. Hidden behind the garden tools & dry firewood, in ceramic jars, is my food store, gathered over previous months. I remove a stopper, scoop out a handful of oats. Mix them in a copper bowl with a little water from a glass bottle. Climb back up the ladder & place the bowl in the ashes of last night's fire, to warm a little. I drink from the water bottle. Hope the ice down in the garden pond is not so thick that I cannot collect more.

MY THIRD DAY OF FREEDOM

I stagger slightly as I open the side door of the garden. Shuffle through a pend, up the Trongate. Tis my third day of freedom. The hunger & cold make it hard to separate thoughts from reality. My old scars hurt. In the Glasgow streets I stand out, mostly due to the colour of my skin. I draw together the front of my coat against the winter chill, pull up my hood & raise my scarf to conceal my face. As dusk is fallin, my fears of discovery are less.

I turn into Gibson Street, then left again. I enter a narrow pend, more alley than street, more gutter than alley. The top storeys of the buildings tilt inwards, a narrow line of dark sky between them. A faded sign over the small shop says: JAMES CROSS, PRINTER & BOOKSELLER. As I open the door, a bell rings. I hope that Cross has no customers at this late hour. I pass through to the backshop, then up a narrow flight of stairs.

'Ah, Cato! I found your quote. Tis from Defoe!' cries Cross the bookseller.

THE RICHEST IN THE LAND

Cross holds between two fingers a part-devoured apple. Shuffle, he shuffles across to a wall covered from floor to ceiling with books. The floor creaks under his weight. The room is warm. A generous fire glows in the grate.

'Tis at the part where the great novelist informs us of some lesser-known facts about *Robinson Crusoe*. I have a first edition somewhere.'

The bookseller carefully wipes apple juice from his fingers with a blue handkerchief. He pulls out a small well-thumbed leather-bound volume from the shelves, returns to his desk & takes another bite from his apple.

'Tis before his famous shipwreck on the desert island. He writes how Crusoe spent eight years in the Atlantic trade.' The bookseller opens the book at a place marked with a strip of red silk. He adjusts the spectacles on his nose, lifts the book high & reads Defoe's words aloud: '*I acquainted myself with the manner of planting and making sugar, and seeing how well the planters lived, and how they got rich so suddenly, I resolved I would turn planter among them.*' He finishes his apple & wipes his hands with a cloth. 'There it is. The part which is omitted from the children's editions. Tis your master's life in a nutshell,' he says, '& the essence of new wealth in this city!'

'Aye sir, but with a different end,' I say. 'Instead of a castaway on a desert island, Massa Billee became one of the richest men in the land.'

THE STORY OF MY LIFE

'Where have you been these past weeks?' says Cross.

'Massa has been ill & I have been waitin upon him.'

'Tell him I am asking after him.'

'Easy, tis not so easy. I am no longer in his service. Of my own choice, if you follow my meanin?'

'Ah!' says Cross, & asks no more. He is one of the few in the city I can trust. He changes the subject. 'Have you brought your manuscript, then, for me to read?'

Promise, he has promised to publish the story of my life. I open my coat, pull out my journal & unwrap the cover. I hand it to the bookseller. If I had handed him a bottle of the finest brandy he could not have looked more excited. 'I still have a page or two to add. I will hand it in soon,' I say.

'I shall read & treasure this, Cato. Come back in a week & we shall discuss it further. Can I offer you a meal, a bed for the night?'

'A crust of bread & some gruel would be welcome, but I have a refuge.'

MY SECRET GARDEN

Out, I need to venture out into the city more often. Purchase some bread. Through the secret side door, down the lane into the back streets. But I raise too much attention. My dress, my limp, the colour of my skin. Most of the shop-keepers around the Cross know me. By the middle of the week, I doubt not, there will be an advert in the *Journal* offerin a reward for my whereabouts. Posted by the Lady Isabella. I will no longer be free to leave these walls.

But who will think of lookin for me here, in my Massa's garden? As winter approaches, all six gardeners are laid off, so I have it to myself. My own secret hidin place. My food will last several weeks. I can light a fire under cover of darkness. Sunshine to keep me warm durin the day is a bonus. After that, who knows? Will my sick Massa live another week? Will his jealous mistress seek me out? Do I care? For the first time in my life, my time is truly my own.

My mind is drawn back twenty years to family parties here. Relatives & friends sittin around the table, spillin out onto the terrace of this pavilion. The French doors thrown open, lettin in the summer heat. Children runnin around the paths, scolded if they became too boisterous. Billee's second wife in her flowin dresses, charmin everybody.

A RAGGED BOY

Frost, the frost lies for several days. A group of sparrows gather, their feathers puffed up against the cold. I watch their ragged hoppin over the stones. A noise above my head startles me. A scratchin on the lead roof. Only a bird. A pair of magpies flap down, explore the garden.

Then a larger movement. A dog? No, it stands up. A thin, ragged boy. Poorly dressed against the cold, he stands by the east wall.

Where the drain from the pond passes beneath, in a pipe. Barely crawlin space for a cat, but the boy is so thin he has squeezed through.

I step back behind the curtains lest he sees me. He disappears behind a hedge, follows the path to the vegetable plot. Little remains at this time of the year. He struggles to pull up an old turnip from the frozen soil, then a leek, & wraps them in a dirty cloth. I think of knockin on the window, offerin him some food, but he is as wary as a fox. He would simply scurry back to his hole.

MY WEE GARRET

Like the tales of the elephants that my father told, I have returned near the end of my days to a familiar place. My secret lair.

I have planned hidin here for so long. Yet now that Massa Billee is dyin, why should I stay in this outbuilding when I have a key for his mansion? I leave by the basement door. Walk the length of the garden to the back of the house. Take the keys from around my neck & unlock the kitchen door.

In recent years, twas my task to run this town-house. Until the Massa was too ill, he spent most of the week here. John still comes twice a week, on Mondays & Fridays, lets in two women from the town to clean. But that has dwindled since Massa Billee has been unwell. I am wary of lightin a fire to heat food in the kitchen, so I fetch some dried biscuits. I take them up to my wee garret. But the skylight window is too small to gain much heat from the sun.

THE RUN OF THE HOUSE

Then I laugh aloud. I have the run of this great house, yet I still hide away in the attic!

As the sun sets I build a fire in the library & light the paper. The flames spread & soon I have a roarin fire. I unwrap my old journals. I fetch a new blank notebook from the shelves, still thin, but thick enough to take my last chapter. Hermit was correct. Learn, I learn most of my English from Massa Billee. Now I even write like him. But change, I will not change my style in my final days.

Write, this may be the last time I write this out. Once I am finished, I will carry it to Cross the bookseller. But will he ever publish it? Cross is a fair man, but who in Glasgow will read the story of a Scalag?

I have a mind to place my diaries here on the shelves among Billee's old plantation journals from when he first arrived on the island. Perhaps in the future someone will find them. If you read them now, many years hence, was my hidin place a success?

THE DARLING OF THE CITY

Six days & nights have I remained here undiscovered. Sleepin by day in my little garret, wrapped in several coats. Eatin & writin here in the library all night by a roarin fire. John has been twice durin the day, I heard him below. I keep the kitchen tidy & no one suspects I am here. One night I light the fire in the blue room & sit in Massa Billee's chair. But tis not the place for me.

The newspapers are still delivered twice a week to the front door & yesterday I read a notice:

> *On Thursday morning last, Colonel Billy was seized with fainting fits, at his seat of Castle Semple, of which he died about three in the afternoon. He was a gentleman who, with a fine character, acquired one of the largest estates in this country. Inhabiting the finest residence in Glasgow, he was the most notable figure in town, owner of a noble mansion in the country and a rich estate in the Indies. With ships on the seas and cargoes of sugar and rum constantly coming home, he had the social prestige of his army rank. His coming opened up new prospects of wealth for our city.*
>
> *He was the darling of the city, and did much to shape its social and human qualities.*

FINISH MY STORY

Sigh, I let out a great sigh, tear the page from the newspaper & place the sheet between the leaves at the end of my journal.

I know not how long I can remain here undiscovered. The cold troubles my leg durin the day. The old stripes on my back from the lash are sore when I lie down. Sometimes I have pain in my chest.

Time, tis time to finish my story & hide it for the last time.

A REWARD

A notice has appeared in the press offerin a reward for my capture. Tis not safe to take my manuscript round to Cross the bookseller.

Massa Billee's funeral party left from the house for the High Kirk, but I hid in the attic. Now they are gone, I pass the nights in the library, readin by the fire.

DISCOVERED

Add, I add another week. I was discovered today in the kitchen by the care-taker. She is a stern woman. I know not whether she will tell the mistress. Howsoever, Billee's son intends movin in, thus I must go.

I lay out my accoutrements on the kitchen table: a wee brass trunk from the store; a long glass jar from the kitchen; some thin pieces of lead torn from the corner of the summer-house roof; a big cork from a kitchen jar; a length of wire & an old cloth.

Take, I take my roll of papers, slide them inside the jar & trunk & bury the trunk. Then I will vacate this mansion & spend my last days in the basement of the summer-house.

Read, if you read this, dear Friend, my writin has not been in vain.

Ask, I will ask you three questions. Only three.

Did Glasgow truly become a city?

Did the black man ever become his own Massa on the sugar islands?

Did Glasgow acknowledge his labour?

***

The End

Acknowledgements

This book owes a debt to many folk, but three stand out who have helped my writing expand well beyond engineering reports and factual history. For more than 30 years Tom Welsh has encouraged me to combine sources (history) with the landscape (archaeology). Secondly, the late Prof. Charles McKean motivated me to expand my research well beyond conventional bounds. Finally, Alan Steel, historian and professional storyteller, challenged me to write history in a more adventurous manner.

I am grateful to Renfrewshire Local History Forum for allowing me to edit their Journal for 20 years. Similarly, to the editorial board of Scottish Local History. For the research behind the novel, I have been indebted over the years to the archives and libraries listed in the published books and articles on my website. I acknowledge the Creative Writing Tutors at the Universities of Glasgow and Strathclyde, including Cathy McSporran. I am particularly grateful for the assistance of Helen Sedgwick, who helped knock this novel into shape, and for the editing skills of Sarah Terry. Also thanks to Indie Authors World for helping put the book together.

Writing has spanned at least three generations of my family. My late father, Douglas Nisbet, published several local history books. My niece, Christine Coltman, beat me to writing my first novel by several years with *Isabel Hope*. Most of all, I acknowledge my friend, partner and travelling companion, Sheila, and our three children, Douglas, Neal and Nicola.

This book is built on the foundation of many other books and authors, and I can only mention the most influential. Penelope Lively's 'City of the Mind' was an early influence, and we both share a debt to Italo Calvino. I was inspired to write less conventionally by the vision of Caribbean author and fellow engineer Wilson Harris. Mary Kingsley's 'Travels in West Africa', assisted my understanding of the landscape of Cameroon. For Cato's voice, I was helped by meeting locals on St. Kitts, Nevis and Grenada, and by V.S. Reid's 'New Day'. Like anyone trying to make sense of a dark subject, I was influenced by Primo Levi.

Paragraph No.79 in the novel, The City Books, is based on Charles McKean's paper 'Architecture and Glasgows of the Imagination' (1990). Public comments on Jenny's Glasgow tours are based on personal experience, including giving numerous talks and guided walks, from Kelvingrove Museum to Glasgow's Merchant City Festival. Finally, the 1749 press notice offering a reward for Cato's escape can be found in the *Glasgow Journal*.

Author's Bio

Stuart Nisbet is an engineer by occupation and a historian by inclination. Although his first degree was in engineering, he completed a PhD in 18th century Scottish history, as a mature student. He has published widely on mills, merchants and slavery and held honorary fellowships at three Scottish universities. In his retirement, he has been employed as a history tutor and tour guide. This is his first novel.

The author has been chasing this story for more than thirty years, since first discovering adverts for runaway Africans in the Glasgow press. That humble beginning raised a curiosity and an ambition to chase one particular runaway, named Cato. This trail led from Glasgow to Lancaster, Manchester, Bristol, Cardiff, London, Nevis, St Kitts and Grenada.

Although this book bears a resemblance to a historical story, all events are fictitious. Anyone interested can find more about similar characters in real life in the author's published books and articles. But that's history, not a novel.

Printed in Great Britain
by Amazon